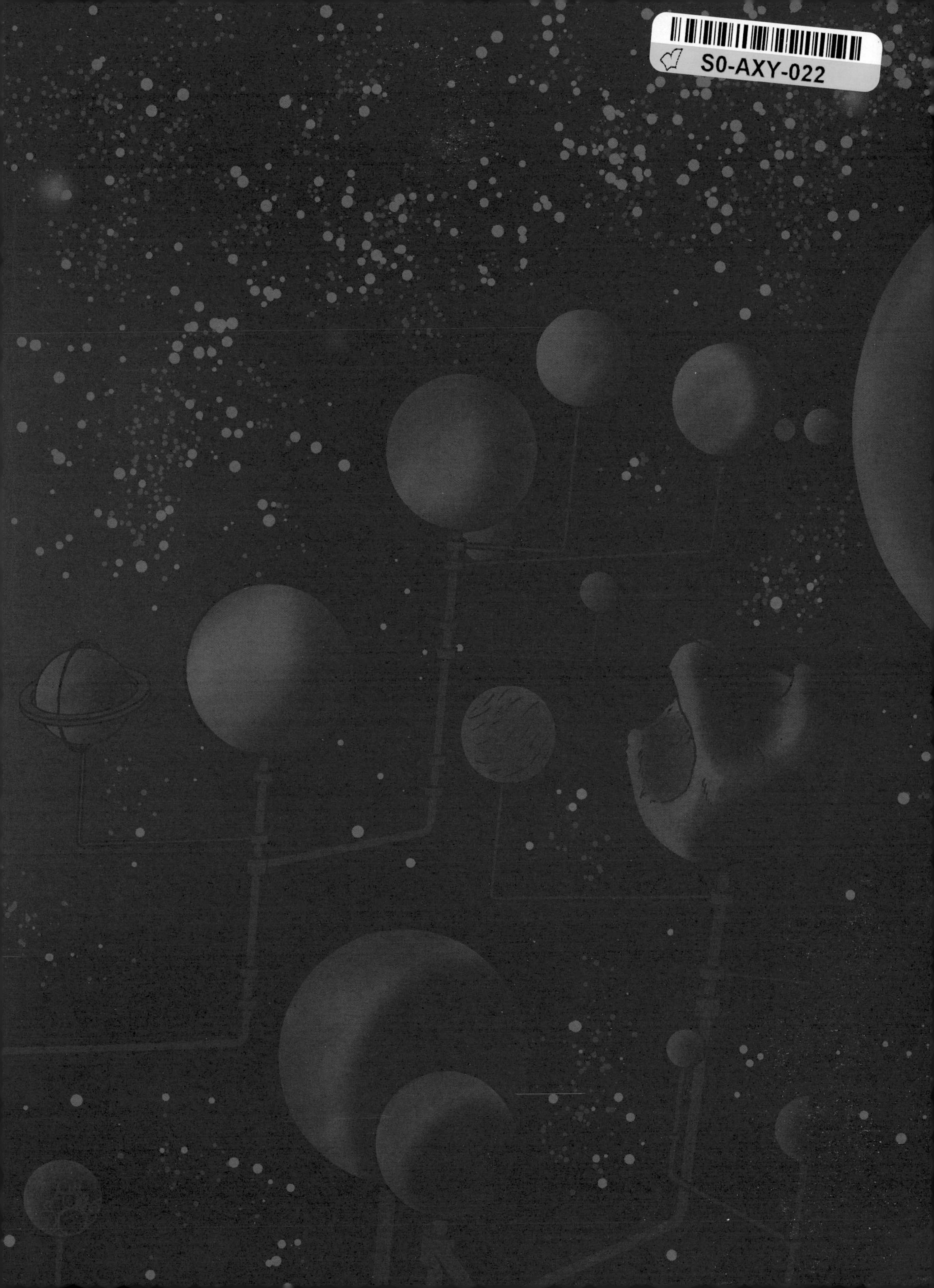

IAN EDGINTON
Writer

I.N.J. CULBARD
Artist

REBELLION®

Creative Director and CEO: Jason Kingsley
Chief Technical Officer: Chris Kingsley
2000 AD Editor in Chief: Matt Smith
Graphic Novels Editor: Keith Richardson
Graphic Design: Simon Parr & Sam Gretton
PR: Michael Molcher
Publishing Manager: Ben Smith
Reprographics: Kathryn Symes
Original Commissioning Editor: Matt Smith

Originally serialised in *2000 AD* Progs 1800-1811, 1850-1861 & 1888-1899. Copyright © 2012, 2013, 2014 Rebellion A/S. *Brass sun* ™ Rebellion A/S, © Rebellion A/S, all rights reserved. No portion of this book may be reproduced without the express permission of the publisher. Names, character, places and incidents featured in the publication are either the product of the author's imagination or used fictitiously. Any resemblance to actual persons, living or dead (except for satirical purposes) is entirely coincidental.

Published by Rebellion, Riverside House, Osney Mead, Oxford, OX2 0ES, UK.
www.rebellion.co.uk

UK ISBN: 978-1-78108-269-0 • US ISBN: 978-1-78108-284-3
Printed in Malta by Gutenberg Press.
Manufactured in the EU by LPPS Ltd., Wellingborough, NN8 3PJ, UK.
First published: December 2014
10 9 8 7 6 5 4 3 2 1

Printed on FSC Accredited Paper.

A CIP catalogue record for this book is available from the British Library.

For information on other *2000 AD* graphic novels, or if you have any comments on this book, please email books@2000ADonline.com

To find out more about *2000 AD*, visit www.2000ADonline.com

BRASS SUN

THE WHEEL OF WORLDS

BRASS SUN CREATED BY IAN EDGINTON & I.N.J. CULBARD

Clockwork Cuckoo
Or How Brass Sun Came to be!

The book that you're now holding should not actually exist. It was meant to be a different tale entirely, but as sometimes happens with stories, it took on a life of it's own and demanded to be noticed. Let me wind the clock back a few years and explain. I was putting together an outline for another series when I decided that I need some reference for an Orrery – a mechanical model of the solar system, that illustrates the positions and motions of the planets.

Having found a few astonishingly intricate versions, that classic question reared it's head. 'What if?'. What if it was real? What if there was an actual clockwork solar system? How and why soon followed and that did it. This new idea kicked the old one from the nest and screamed for attention.

One of the reasons I enjoy doing what I do is that I love world building. It appeals to the megalomaniac in me and probably keeps me from trying to take over the world or something. Anyway, the next few days were a perfect storm of ideas at the end of which, I had 95% of the entire story, the planets, their peoples and histories all worked out and especially those of my protagonist, Wren and her compatriots. And the title of course - *Brass Sun*.

Likewise, there was only one home for such a long form, clockpunk science fiction series and that was legendary UK comic weekly, *2000 AD*. The same goes for artist Ian Culbard. We'd previously worked together adapting the canon of Sherlock Holmes novels into graphic novels and he'd also guest starred on a *Stickleback* Christmas yarn. We were now looking for something more substantial to work together on and *Brass Sun* fitted the bill perfectly.

There are times when putting a project like this together can be painful and laborious, like having teeth pulled. But once in a blue Moon, when the fates are smiling, everything falls smoothly into place and runs, well, like clockwork!

Ian Edginton, September 2014

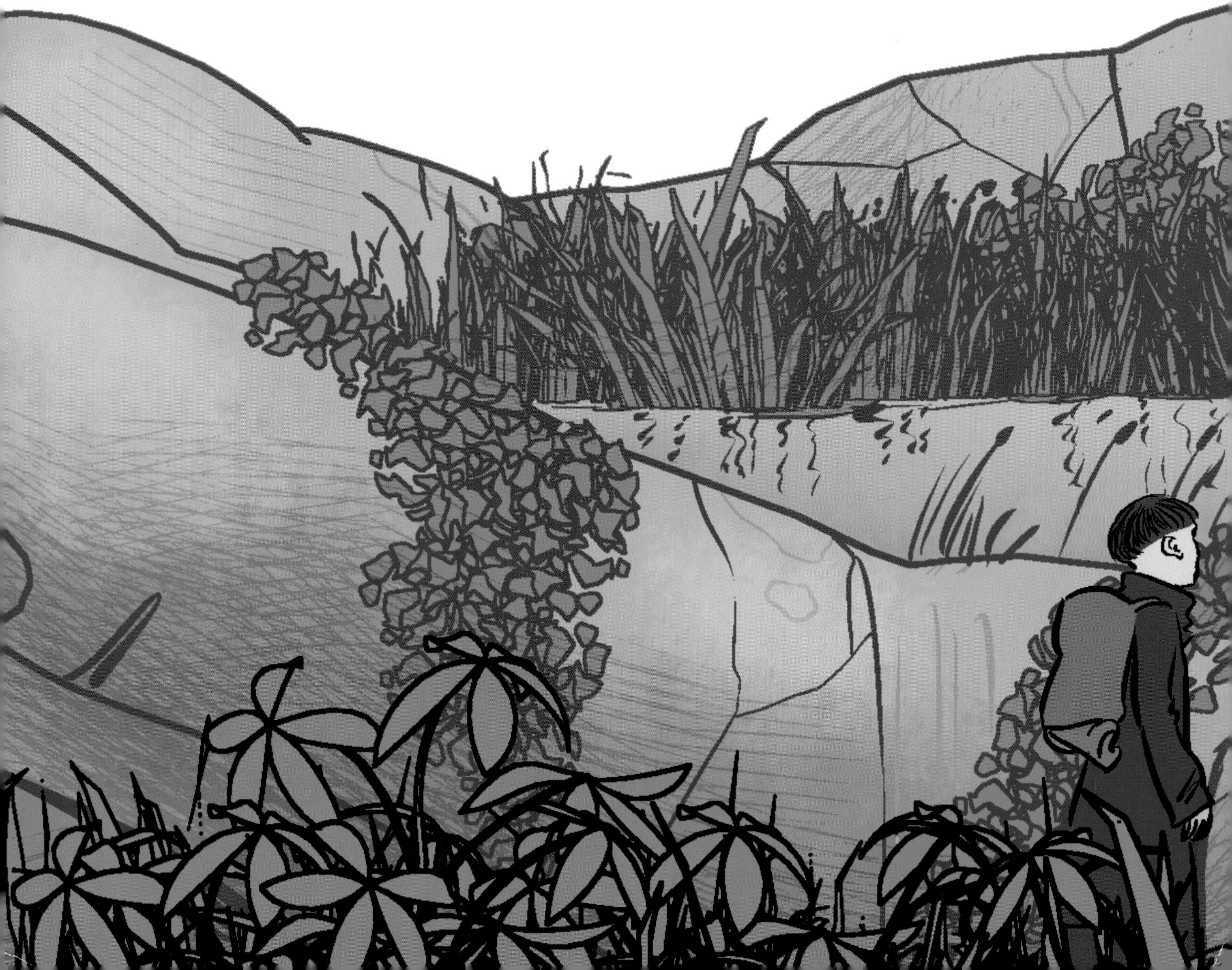

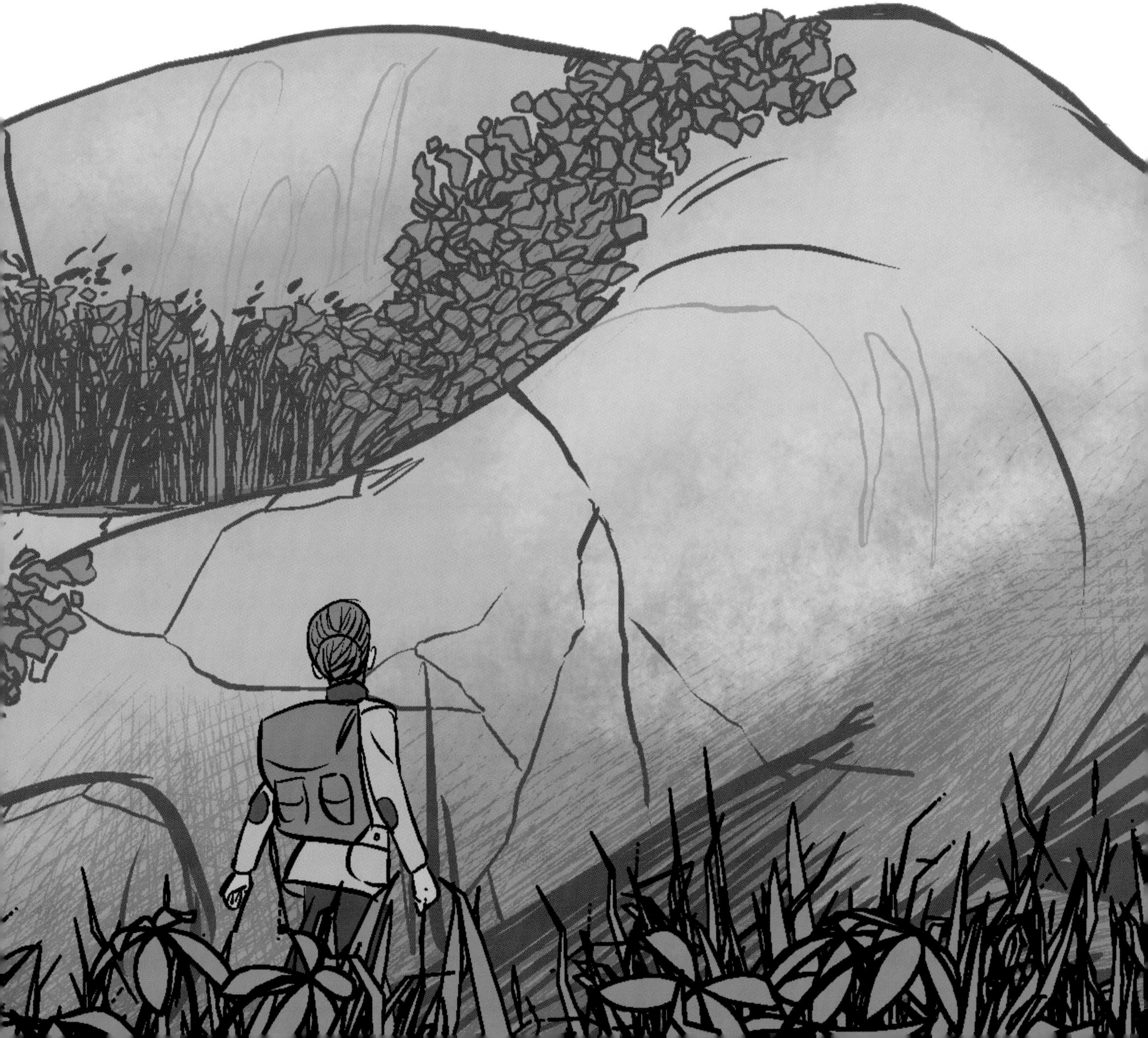

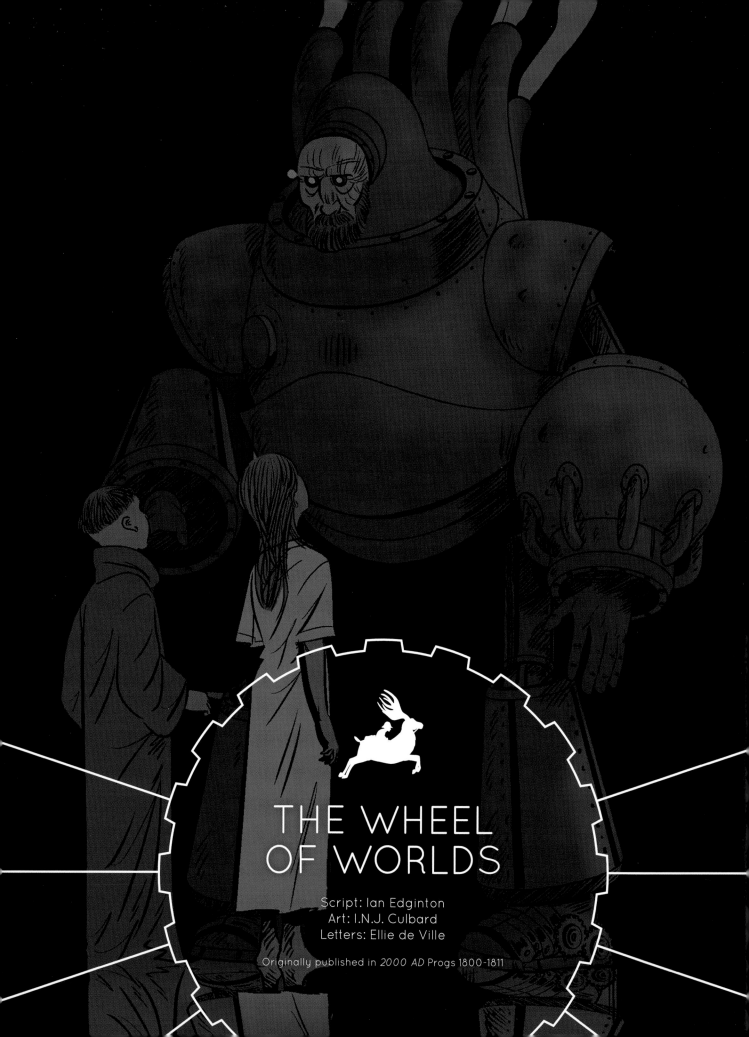

THE WHEEL OF WORLDS

Script: Ian Edginton
Art: I.N.J. Culbard
Letters: Ellie de Ville

Originally published in *2000 AD* Progs 1800-1811

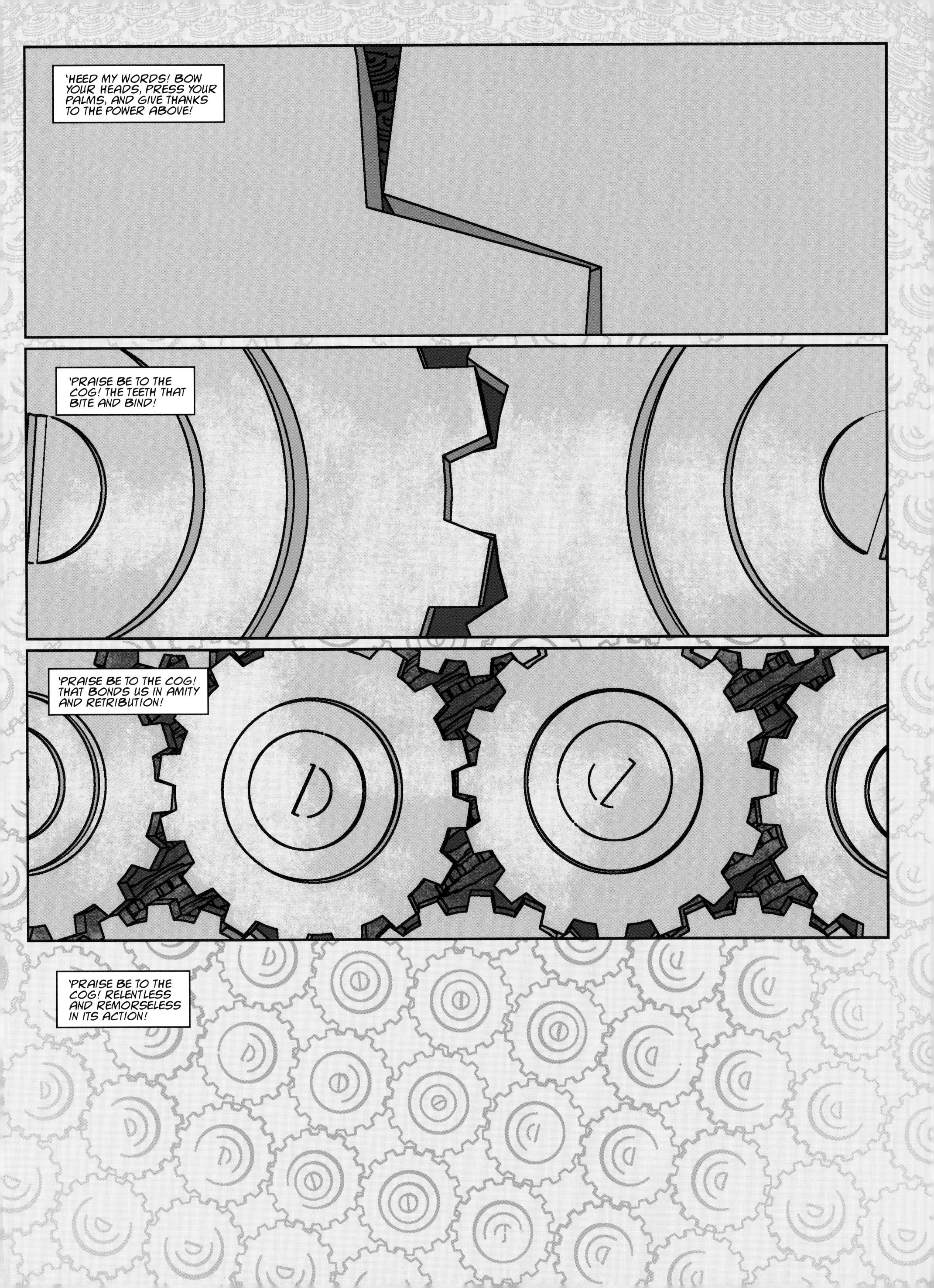
'HEED MY WORDS! BOW YOUR HEADS, PRESS YOUR PALMS, AND GIVE THANKS TO THE POWER ABOVE!
'PRAISE BE TO THE COG! THE TEETH THAT BITE AND BIND!
'PRAISE BE TO THE COG! THAT BONDS US IN AMITY AND RETRIBUTION!
'PRAISE BE TO THE COG! RELENTLESS AND REMORSELESS IN ITS ACTION!

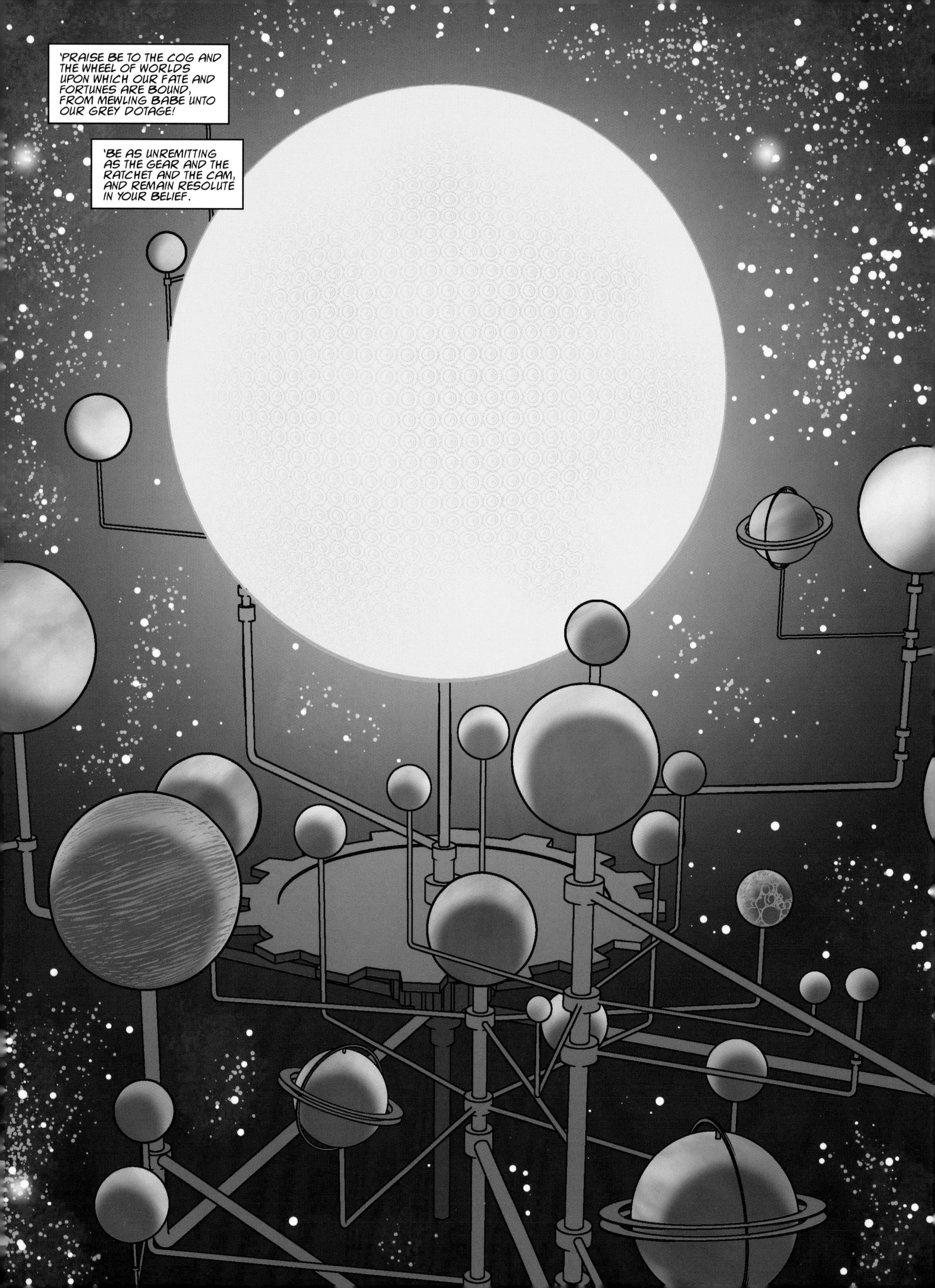
'PRAISE BE TO THE COG AND THE WHEEL OF WORLDS UPON WHICH OUR FATE AND FORTUNES ARE BOUND, FROM MEWLING BABE UNTO OUR GREY DOTAGE!
'BE AS UNREMITTING AS THE GEAR AND THE RATCHET AND THE CAM, AND REMAIN RESOLUTE IN YOUR BELIEF.

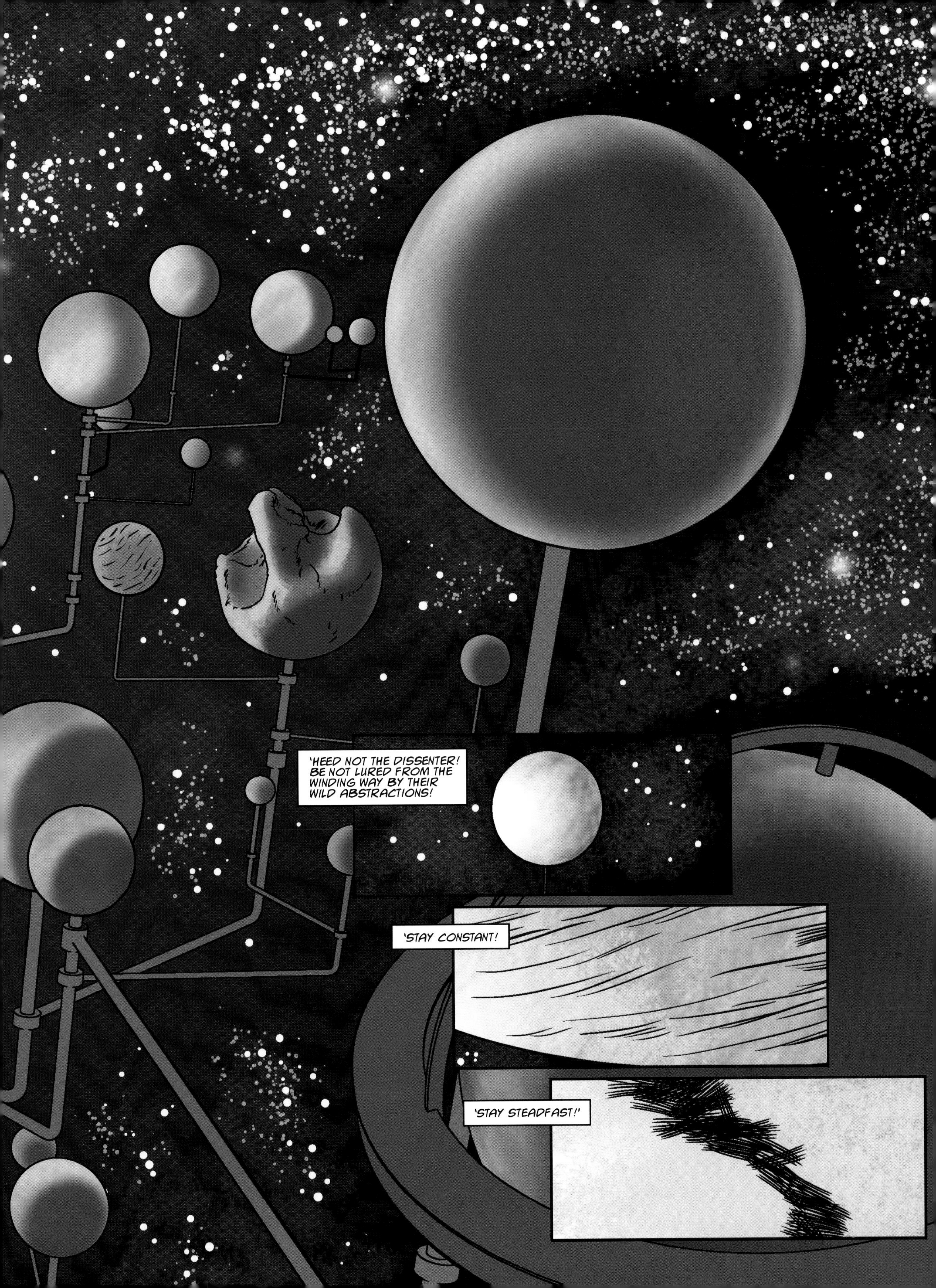
'HEED NOT THE DISSENTER! BE NOT LURED FROM THE WINDING WAY BY THEIR WILD ABSTRACTIONS!
'STAY CONSTANT!
'STAY STEADFAST!'

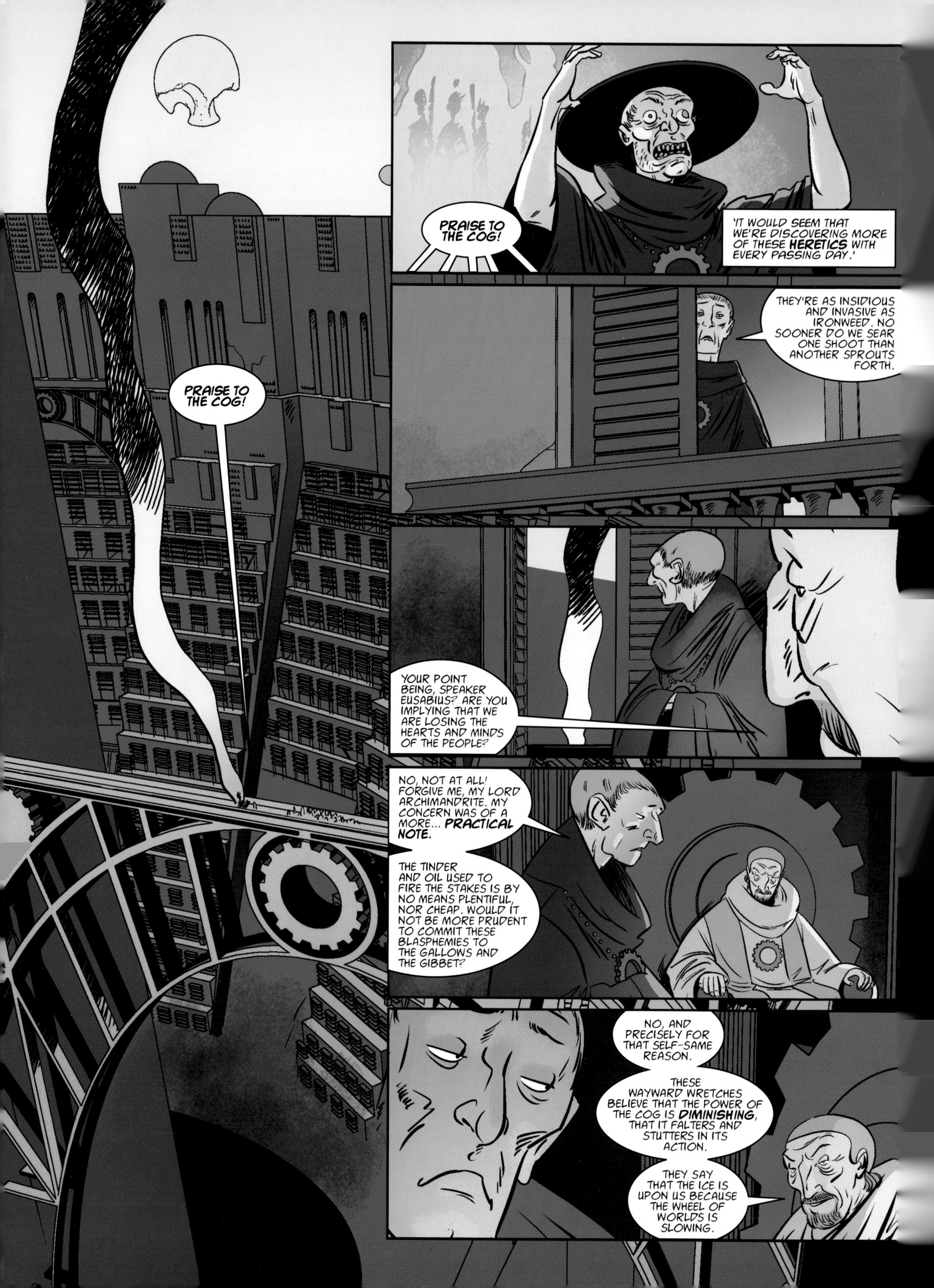
PRAISE TO THE COG!
PRAISE TO THE COG!
'IT WOULD SEEM THAT WE'RE DISCOVERING MORE OF THESE HERETICS WITH EVERY PASSING DAY.'
THEY'RE AS INSIDIOUS AND INVASIVE AS IRONWEED. NO SOONER DO WE SEAR ONE SHOOT THAN ANOTHER SPROUTS FORTH.
YOUR POINT BEING, SPEAKER EUSABIUS? ARE YOU IMPLYING THAT WE ARE LOSING THE HEARTS AND MINDS OF THE PEOPLE?
NO, NOT AT ALL! FORGIVE ME, MY LORD ARCHIMANDRITE. MY CONCERN WAS OF A MORE... PRACTICAL NOTE.
THE TINDER AND OIL USED TO FIRE THE STAKES IS BY NO MEANS PLENTIFUL, NOR CHEAP. WOULD IT NOT BE MORE PRUDENT TO COMMIT THESE BLASPHEMIES TO THE GALLOWS AND THE GIBBET?
NO, AND PRECISELY FOR THAT SELF-SAME REASON.
THESE WAYWARD WRETCHES BELIEVE THAT THE POWER OF THE COG IS DIMINISHING, THAT IT FALTERS AND STUTTERS IN ITS ACTION.
THEY SAY THAT THE ICE IS UPON US BECAUSE THE WHEEL OF WORLDS IS SLOWING.

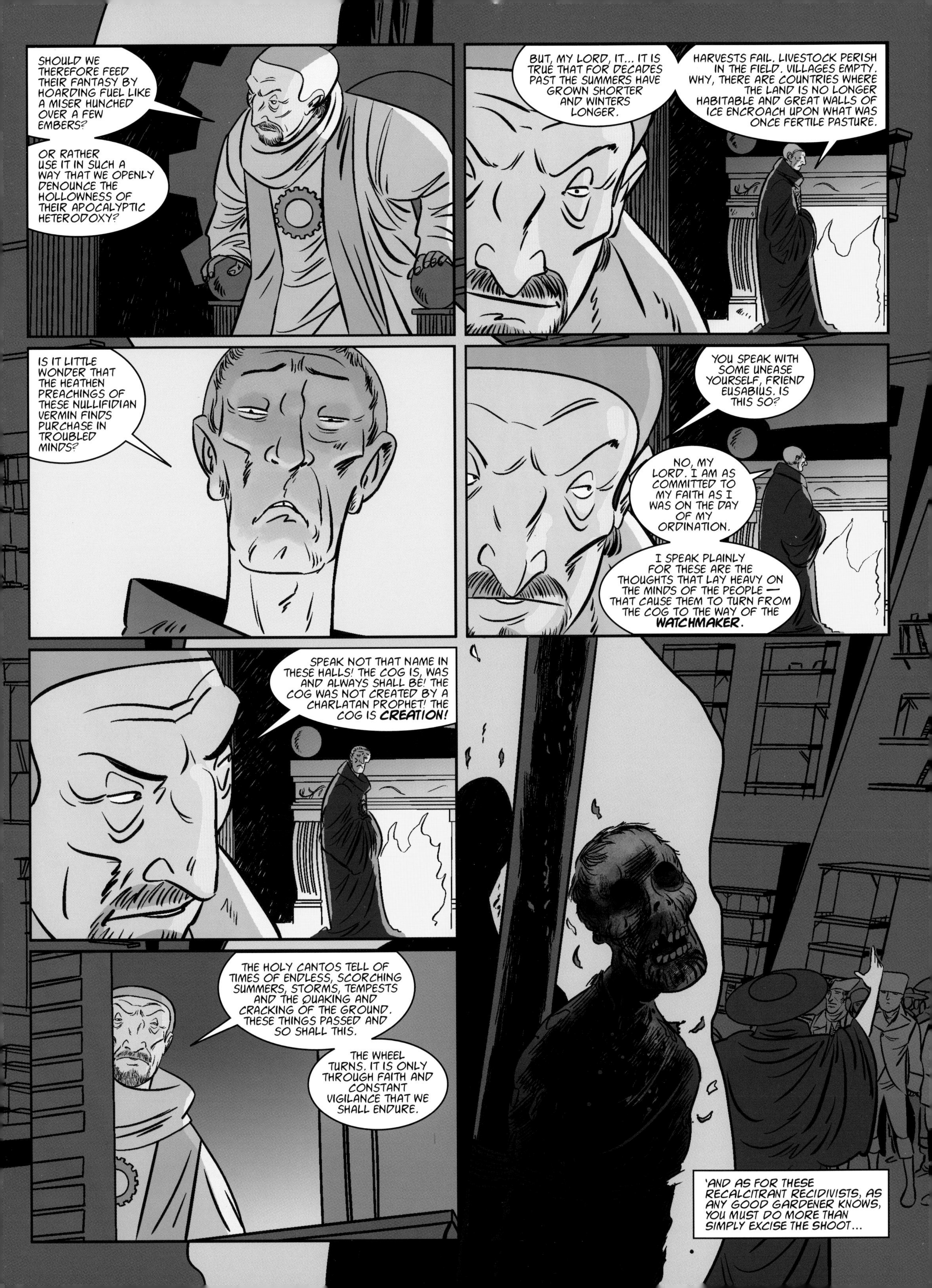

SHOULD WE THEREFORE FEED THEIR FANTASY BY HOARDING FUEL LIKE A MISER HUNCHED OVER A FEW EMBERS?
OR RATHER USE IT IN SUCH A WAY THAT WE OPENLY DENOUNCE THE HOLLOWNESS OF THEIR APOCALYPTIC HETERODOXY?
BUT, MY LORD, IT... IT IS TRUE THAT FOR DECADES PAST THE SUMMERS HAVE GROWN SHORTER AND WINTERS LONGER.
HARVESTS FAIL. LIVESTOCK PERISH IN THE FIELD. VILLAGES EMPTY. WHY, THERE ARE COUNTRIES WHERE THE LAND IS NO LONGER HABITABLE AND GREAT WALLS OF ICE ENCROACH UPON WHAT WAS ONCE FERTILE PASTURE.
IS IT LITTLE WONDER THAT THE HEATHEN PREACHINGS OF THESE NULLIFIDIAN VERMIN FINDS PURCHASE IN TROUBLED MINDS?
YOU SPEAK WITH SOME UNEASE YOURSELF, FRIEND EUSABIUS. IS THIS SO?
NO, MY LORD. I AM AS COMMITTED TO MY FAITH AS I WAS ON THE DAY OF MY ORDINATION.
I SPEAK PLAINLY FOR THESE ARE THE THOUGHTS THAT LAY HEAVY ON THE MINDS OF THE PEOPLE — THAT CAUSE THEM TO TURN FROM THE COG TO THE WAY OF THE WATCHMAKER.
SPEAK NOT THAT NAME IN THESE HALLS! THE COG IS, WAS AND ALWAYS SHALL BE! THE COG WAS NOT CREATED BY A CHARLATAN PROPHET! THE COG IS CREATION!
THE HOLY CANTOS TELL OF TIMES OF ENDLESS, SCORCHING SUMMERS, STORMS, TEMPESTS AND THE QUAKING AND CRACKING OF THE GROUND. THESE THINGS PASSED AND SO SHALL THIS.
THE WHEEL TURNS. IT IS ONLY THROUGH FAITH AND CONSTANT VIGILANCE THAT WE SHALL ENDURE.
'AND AS FOR THESE RECALCITRANT RECIDIVISTS, AS ANY GOOD GARDENER KNOWS, YOU MUST DO MORE THAN SIMPLY EXCISE THE SHOOT...

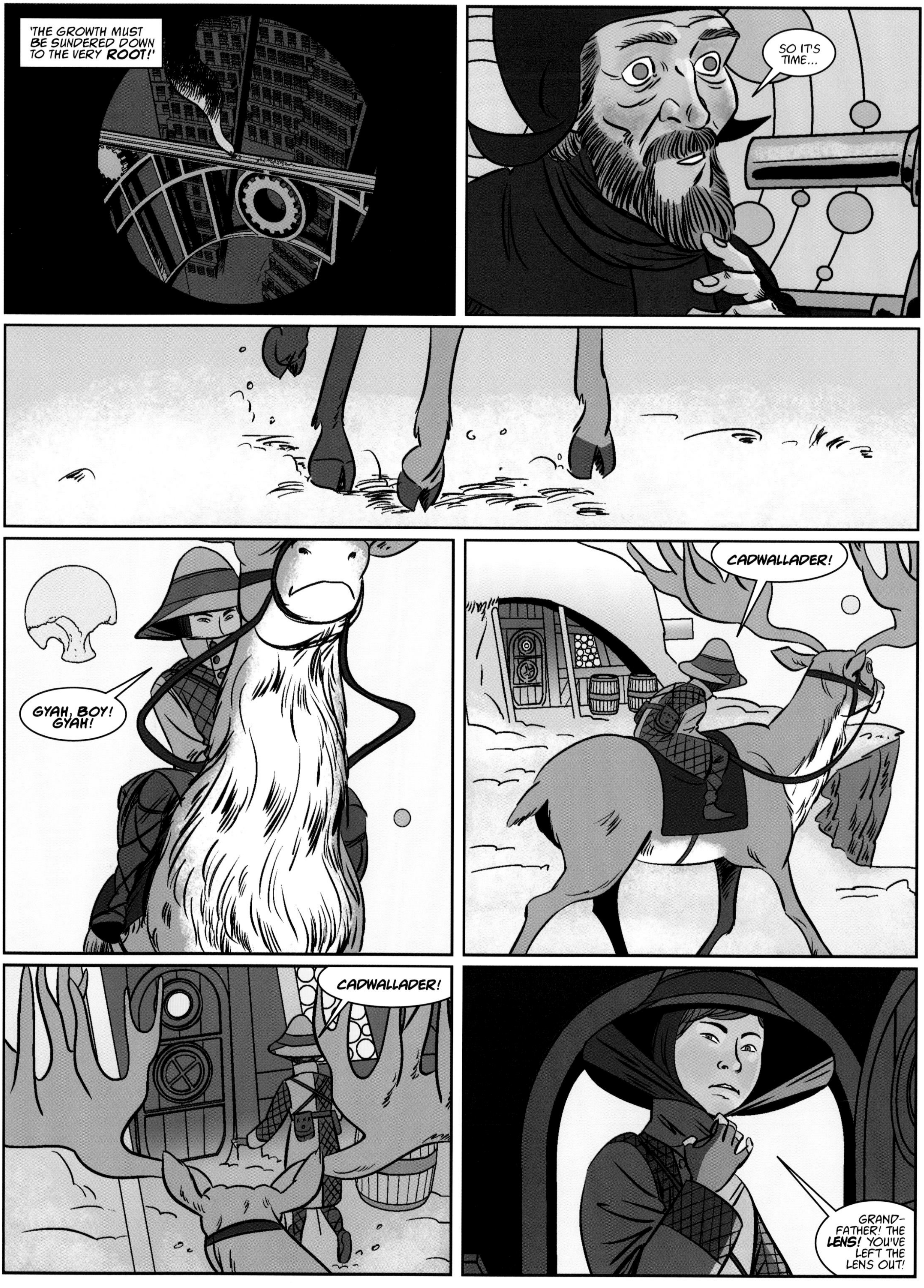
'THE GROWTH MUST BE SUNDERED DOWN TO THE VERY ROOT!'
SO IT'S TIME...
GYAH, BOY! GYAH!
CADWALLADER!
CADWALLADER!
GRAND-FATHER! THE LENS! YOU'VE LEFT THE LENS OUT!

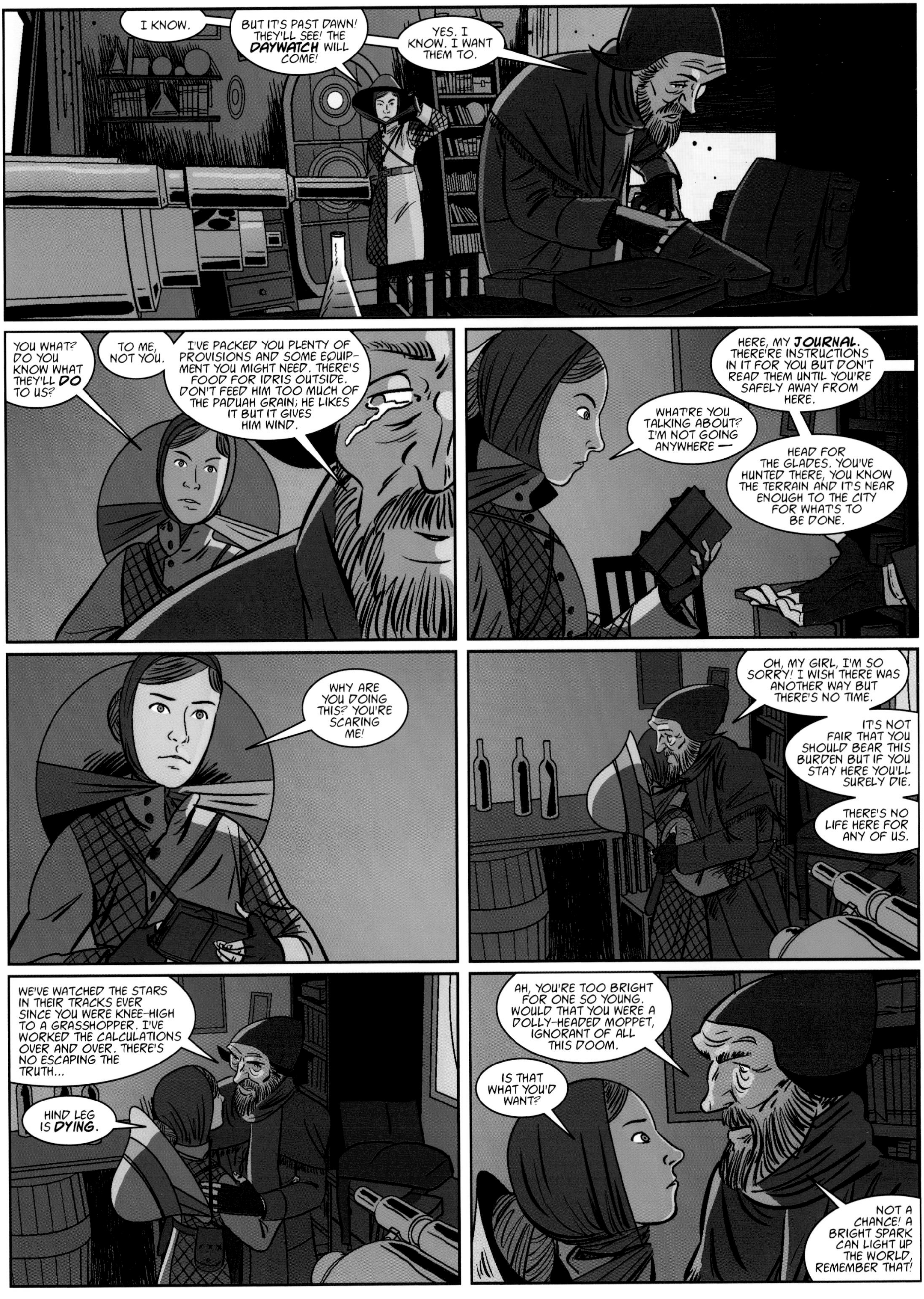
I KNOW.
BUT IT'S PAST DAWN! THEY'LL SEE! THE DAYWATCH WILL COME!
YES. I KNOW. I WANT THEM TO.
YOU WHAT? DO YOU KNOW WHAT THEY'LL DO TO US?
TO ME, NOT YOU.
I'VE PACKED YOU PLENTY OF PROVISIONS AND SOME EQUIPMENT YOU MIGHT NEED. THERE'S FOOD FOR IDRIS OUTSIDE. DON'T FEED HIM TOO MUCH OF THE PADUAH GRAIN; HE LIKES IT BUT IT GIVES HIM WIND.
HERE, MY JOURNAL. THERE'RE INSTRUCTIONS IN IT FOR YOU BUT DON'T READ THEM UNTIL YOU'RE SAFELY AWAY FROM HERE.
WHAT'RE YOU TALKING ABOUT? I'M NOT GOING ANYWHERE —
HEAD FOR THE GLADES. YOU'VE HUNTED THERE, YOU KNOW THE TERRAIN AND IT'S NEAR ENOUGH TO THE CITY FOR WHAT'S TO BE DONE.
WHY ARE YOU DOING THIS? YOU'RE SCARING ME!
OH, MY GIRL, I'M SO SORRY! I WISH THERE WAS ANOTHER WAY BUT THERE'S NO TIME.
IT'S NOT FAIR THAT YOU SHOULD BEAR THIS BURDEN BUT IF YOU STAY HERE YOU'LL SURELY DIE.
THERE'S NO LIFE HERE FOR ANY OF US.
WE'VE WATCHED THE STARS IN THEIR TRACKS EVER SINCE YOU WERE KNEE-HIGH TO A GRASSHOPPER. I'VE WORKED THE CALCULATIONS OVER AND OVER. THERE'S NO ESCAPING THE TRUTH...
HIND LEG IS DYING.
AH, YOU'RE TOO BRIGHT FOR ONE SO YOUNG. WOULD THAT YOU WERE A DOLLY-HEADED MOPPET, IGNORANT OF ALL THIS DOOM.
IS THAT WHAT YOU'D WANT?
NOT A CHANCE! A BRIGHT SPARK CAN LIGHT UP THE WORLD, REMEMBER THAT!

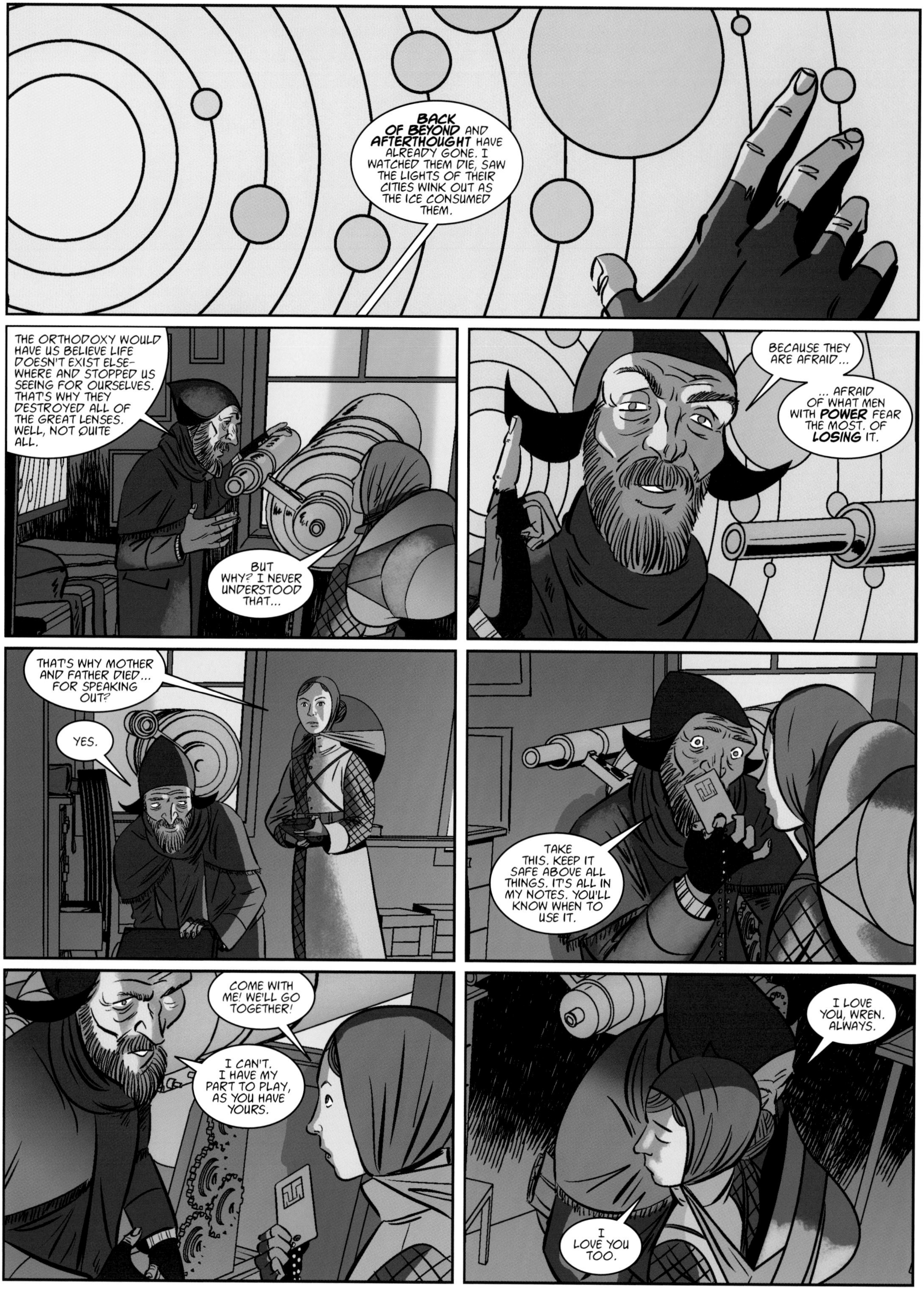
BACK OF BEYOND AND AFTERTHOUGHT HAVE ALREADY GONE. I WATCHED THEM DIE, SAW THE LIGHTS OF THEIR CITIES WINK OUT AS THE ICE CONSUMED THEM.
THE ORTHODOXY WOULD HAVE US BELIEVE LIFE DOESN'T EXIST ELSE-WHERE AND STOPPED US SEEING FOR OURSELVES. THAT'S WHY THEY DESTROYED ALL OF THE GREAT LENSES. WELL, NOT QUITE ALL.
BUT WHY? I NEVER UNDERSTOOD THAT...
BECAUSE THEY ARE AFRAID...
... AFRAID OF WHAT MEN WITH POWER FEAR THE MOST. OF LOSING IT.
THAT'S WHY MOTHER AND FATHER DIED... FOR SPEAKING OUT?
YES.
TAKE THIS. KEEP IT SAFE ABOVE ALL THINGS. IT'S ALL IN MY NOTES. YOU'LL KNOW WHEN TO USE IT.
COME WITH ME! WE'LL GO TOGETHER!
I CAN'T. I HAVE MY PART TO PLAY, AS YOU HAVE YOURS.
I LOVE YOU, WREN. ALWAYS.
I LOVE YOU TOO.

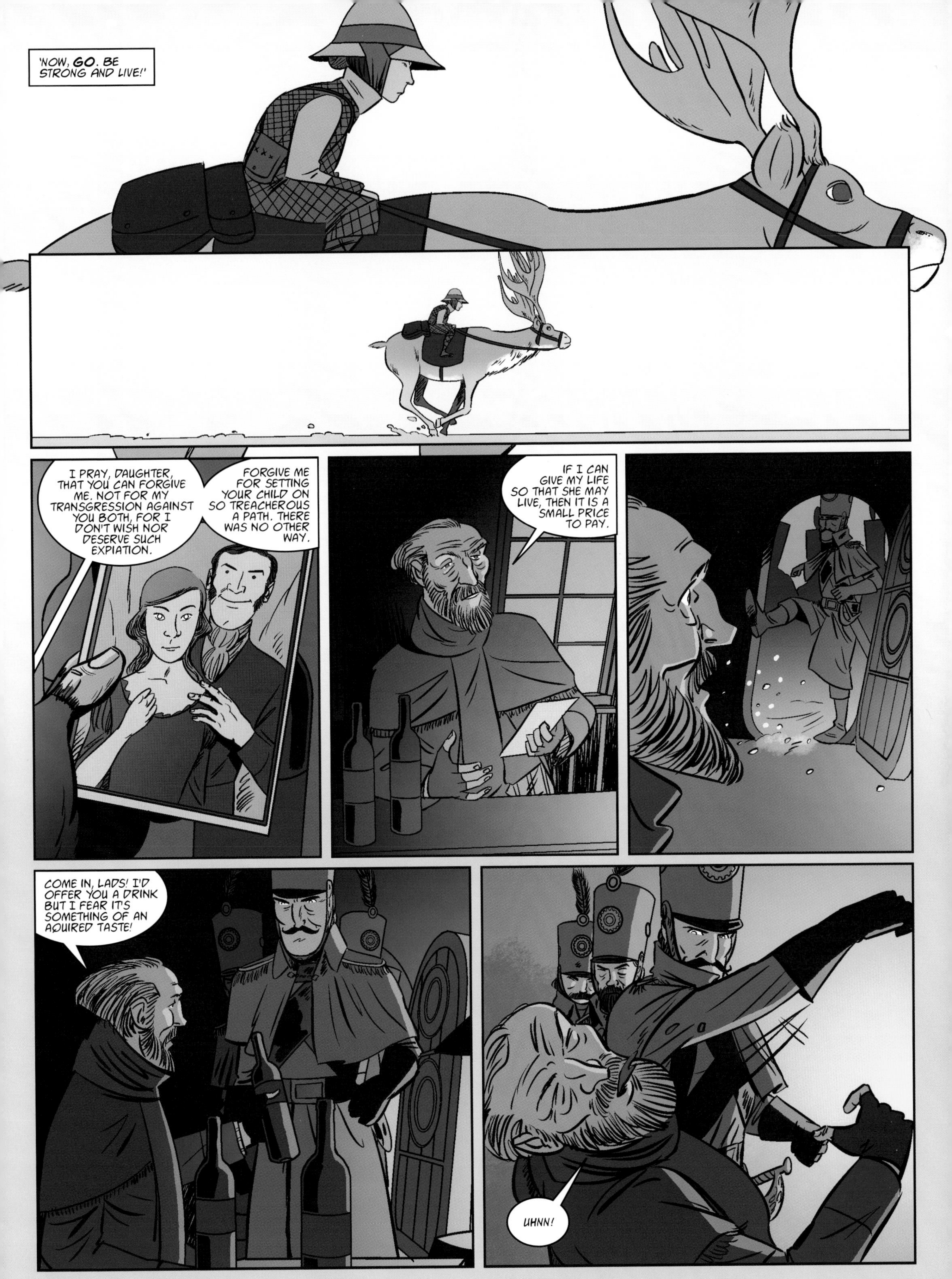
'NOW, GO. BE STRONG AND LIVE!'
I PRAY, DAUGHTER, THAT YOU CAN FORGIVE ME. NOT FOR MY TRANSGRESSION AGAINST YOU BOTH, FOR I DON'T WISH NOR DESERVE SUCH EXPIATION.
FORGIVE ME FOR SETTING YOUR CHILD ON SO TREACHEROUS A PATH. THERE WAS NO OTHER WAY.
IF I CAN GIVE MY LIFE SO THAT SHE MAY LIVE, THEN IT IS A SMALL PRICE TO PAY.
COME IN, LADS! I'D OFFER YOU A DRINK BUT I FEAR IT'S SOMETHING OF AN AQUIRED TASTE!
UHNN!

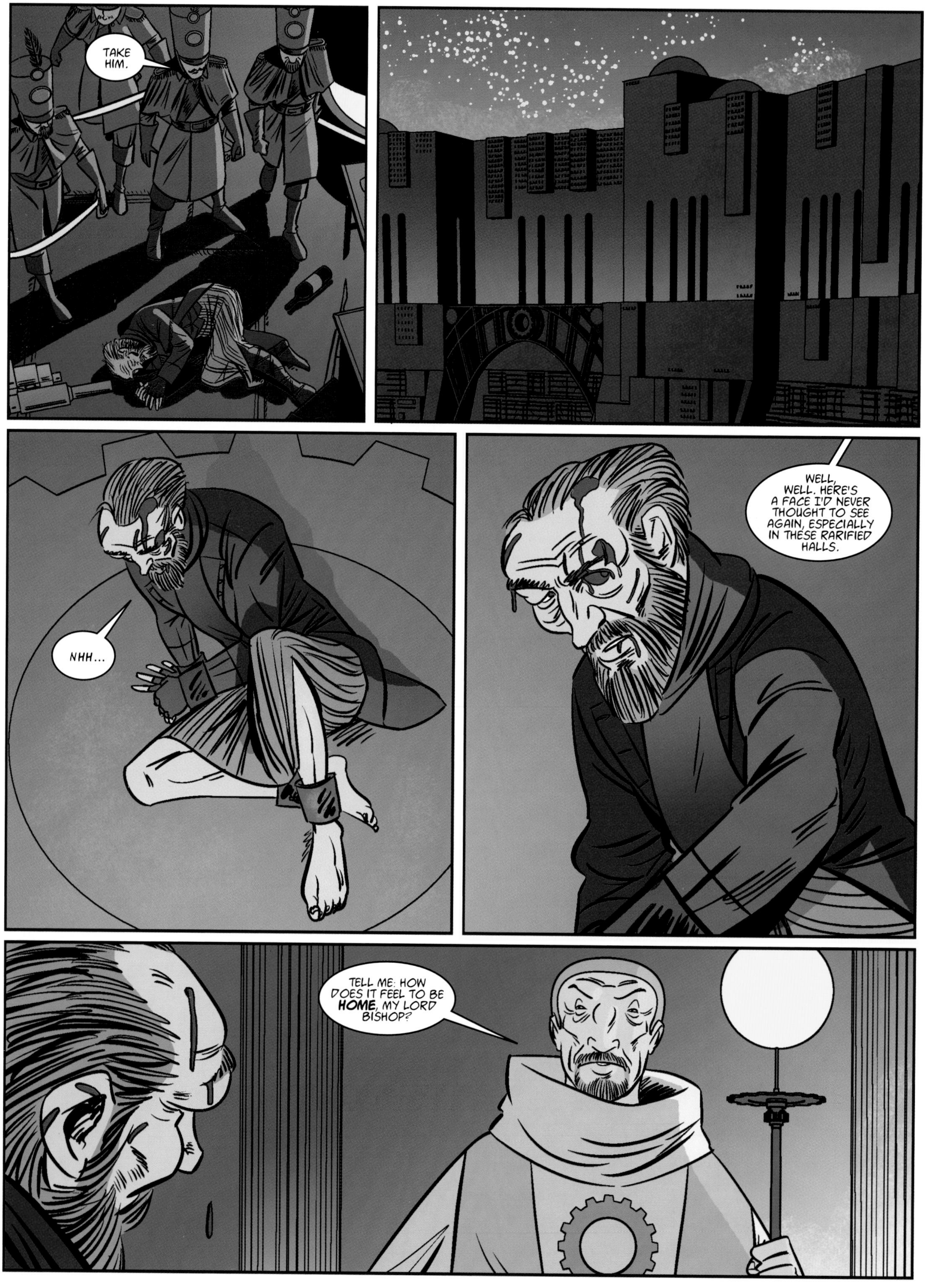
TAKE HIM.
NHH...
WELL, WELL. HERE'S A FACE I'D NEVER THOUGHT TO SEE AGAIN, ESPECIALLY IN THESE RARIFIED HALLS.
TELL ME: HOW DOES IT FEEL TO BE **HOME**, MY LORD BISHOP?

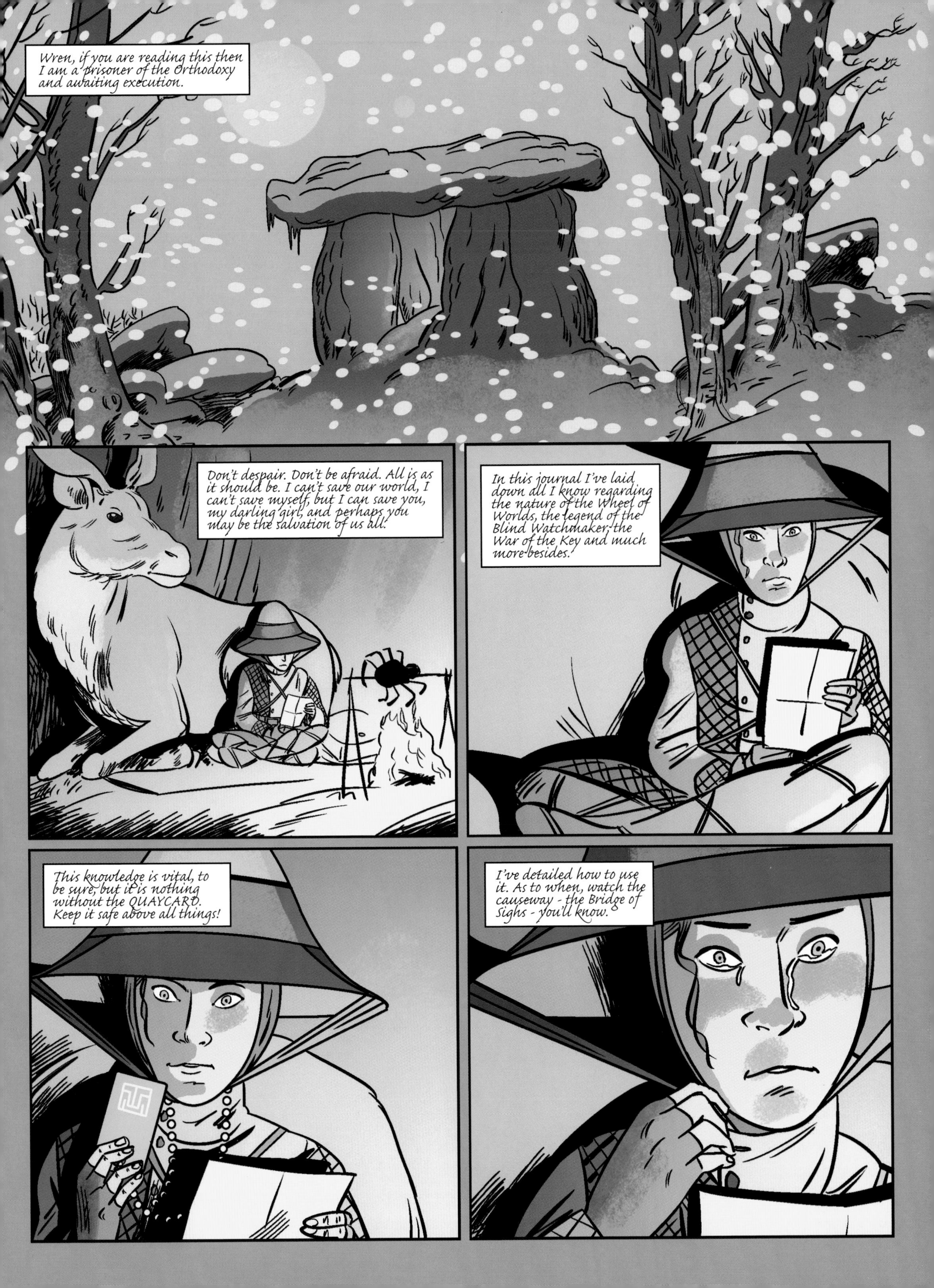
Wren, if you are reading this then I am a prisoner of the Orthodoxy and awaiting execution.
Don't despair. Don't be afraid. All is as it should be. I can't save our world, I can't save myself, but I can save you, my darling girl, and perhaps you may be the salvation of us all.
In this journal I've laid down all I know regarding the nature of the Wheel of Worlds, the legend of the Blind Watchmaker, the War of the Key and much more besides.
This knowledge is vital, to be sure, but it is nothing without the QUAYCARD. Keep it safe above all things!
I've detailed how to use it. As to when, watch the causeway - the Bridge of Sighs - you'll know.

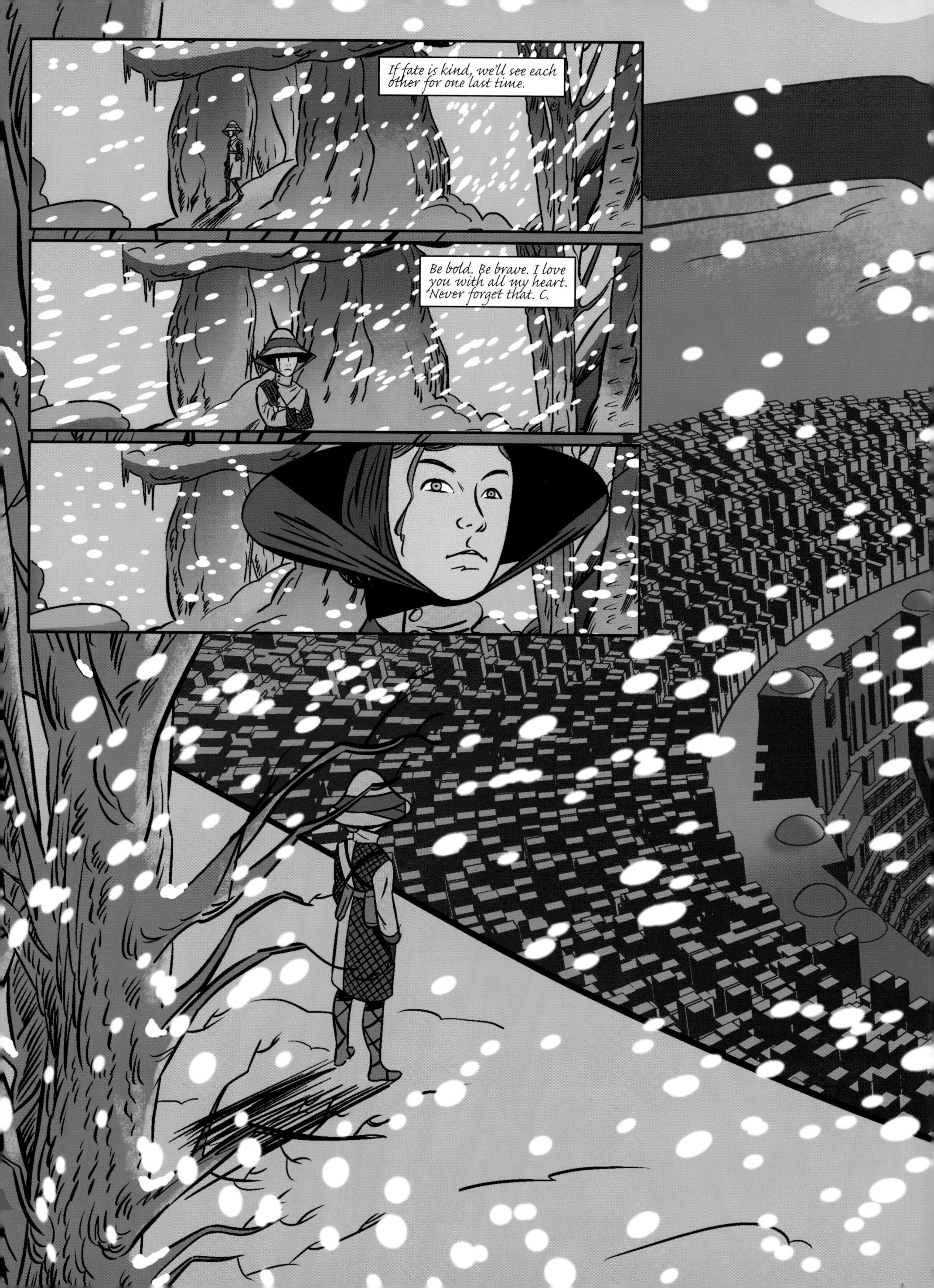
If fate is kind, we'll see each other for one last time.
Be bold. Be brave. I love you with all my heart. Never forget that. C.

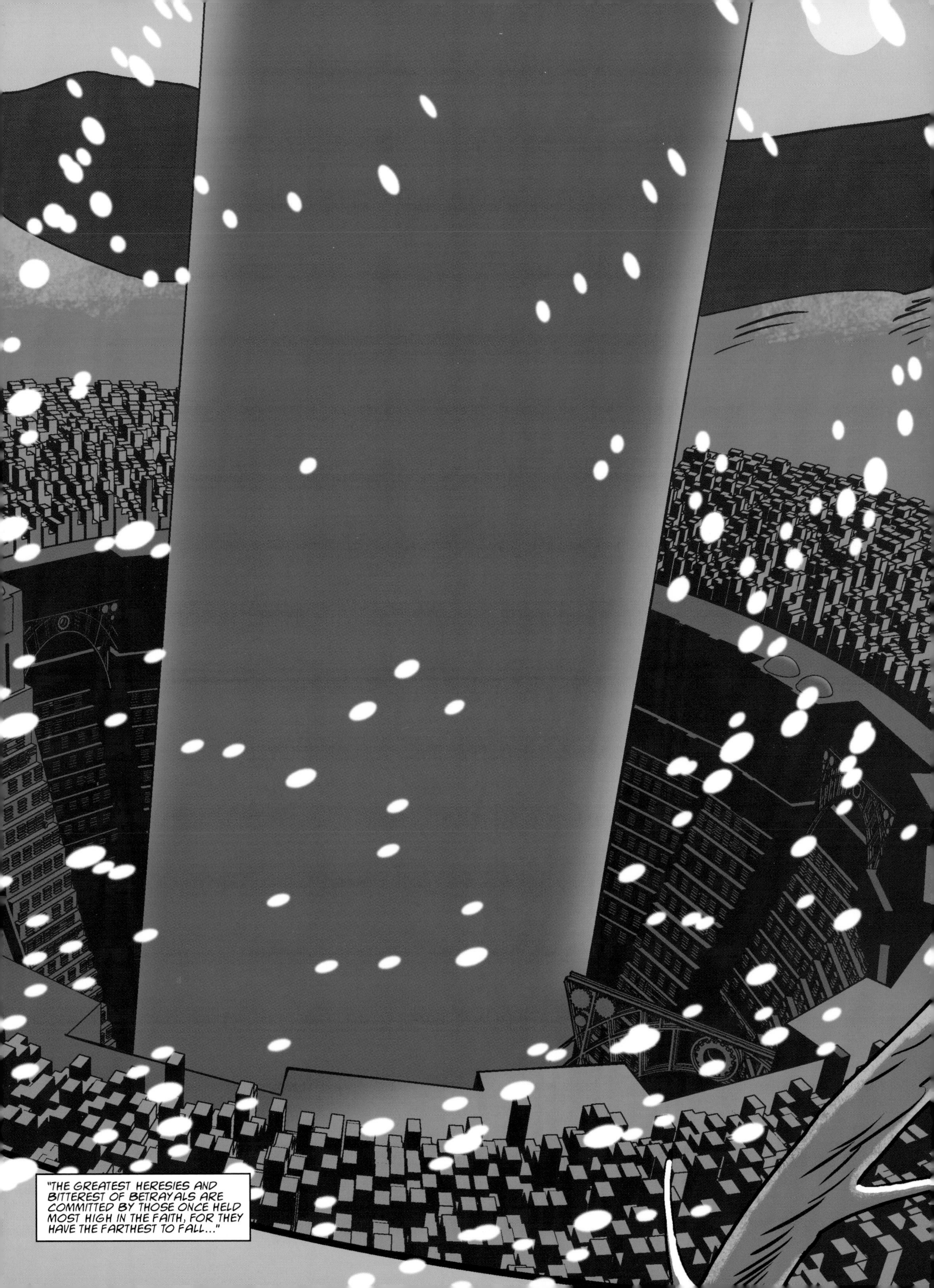
"THE GREATEST HERESIES AND BITTEREST OF BETRAYALS ARE COMMITTED BY THOSE ONCE HELD MOST HIGH IN THE FAITH, FOR THEY HAVE THE FARTHEST TO FALL..."

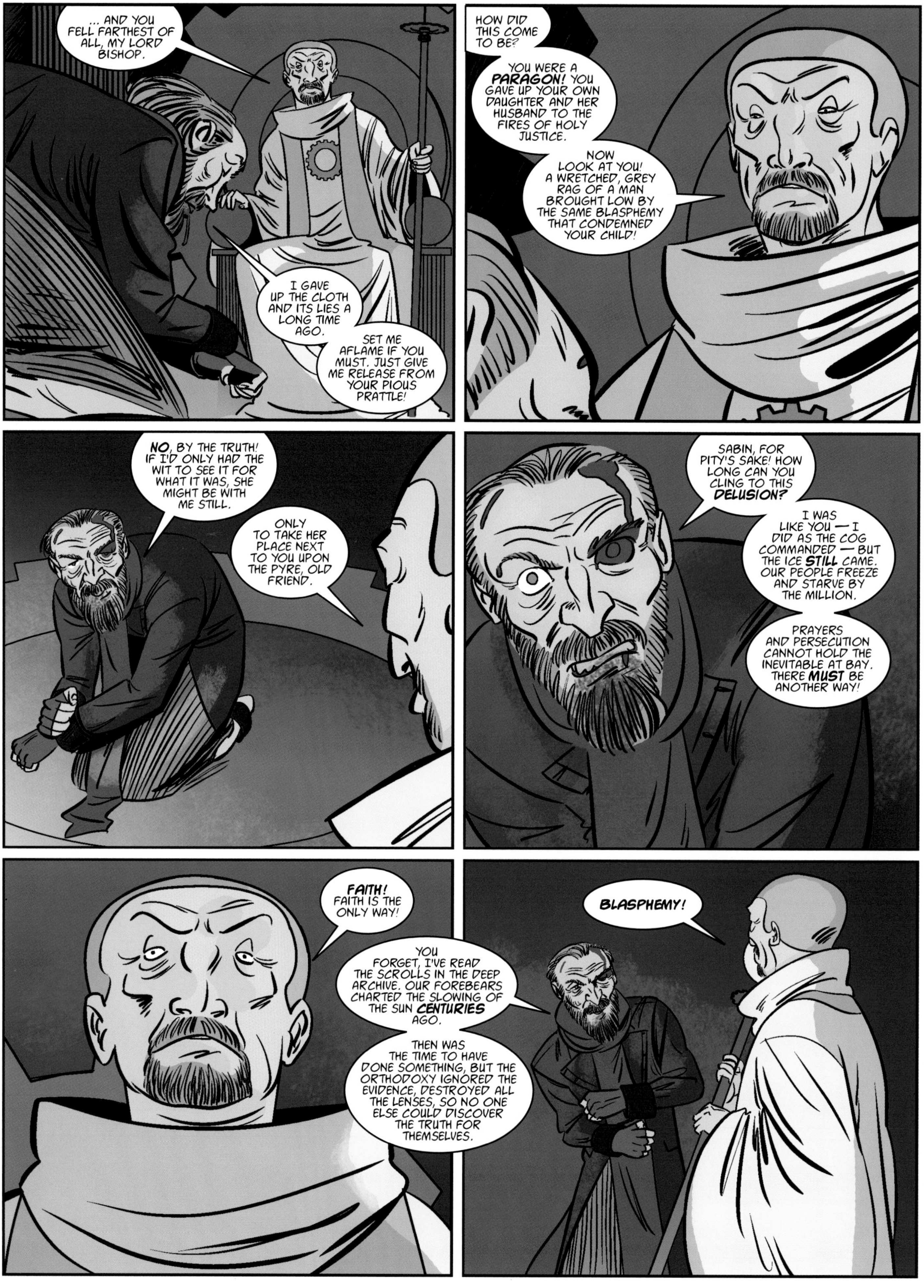
... AND YOU FELL FARTHEST OF ALL, MY LORD BISHOP.
I GAVE UP THE CLOTH AND ITS LIES A LONG TIME AGO.
SET ME AFLAME IF YOU MUST. JUST GIVE ME RELEASE FROM YOUR PIOUS PRATTLE!
HOW DID THIS COME TO BE?
YOU WERE A PARAGON! YOU GAVE UP YOUR OWN DAUGHTER AND HER HUSBAND TO THE FIRES OF HOLY JUSTICE.
NOW LOOK AT YOU! A WRETCHED, GREY RAG OF A MAN BROUGHT LOW BY THE SAME BLASPHEMY THAT CONDEMNED YOUR CHILD!
NO, BY THE TRUTH! IF I'D ONLY HAD THE WIT TO SEE IT FOR WHAT IT WAS, SHE MIGHT BE WITH ME STILL.
ONLY TO TAKE HER PLACE NEXT TO YOU UPON THE PYRE, OLD FRIEND.
SABIN, FOR PITY'S SAKE! HOW LONG CAN YOU CLING TO THIS DELUSION?
I WAS LIKE YOU — I DID AS THE COG COMMANDED — BUT THE ICE STILL CAME. OUR PEOPLE FREEZE AND STARVE BY THE MILLION.
PRAYERS AND PERSECUTION CANNOT HOLD THE INEVITABLE AT BAY. THERE MUST BE ANOTHER WAY!
FAITH! FAITH IS THE ONLY WAY!
YOU FORGET, I'VE READ THE SCROLLS IN THE DEEP ARCHIVE. OUR FOREBEARS CHARTED THE SLOWING OF THE SUN CENTURIES AGO.
THEN WAS THE TIME TO HAVE DONE SOMETHING, BUT THE ORTHODOXY IGNORED THE EVIDENCE, DESTROYED ALL THE LENSES, SO NO ONE ELSE COULD DISCOVER THE TRUTH FOR THEMSELVES.
BLASPHEMY!

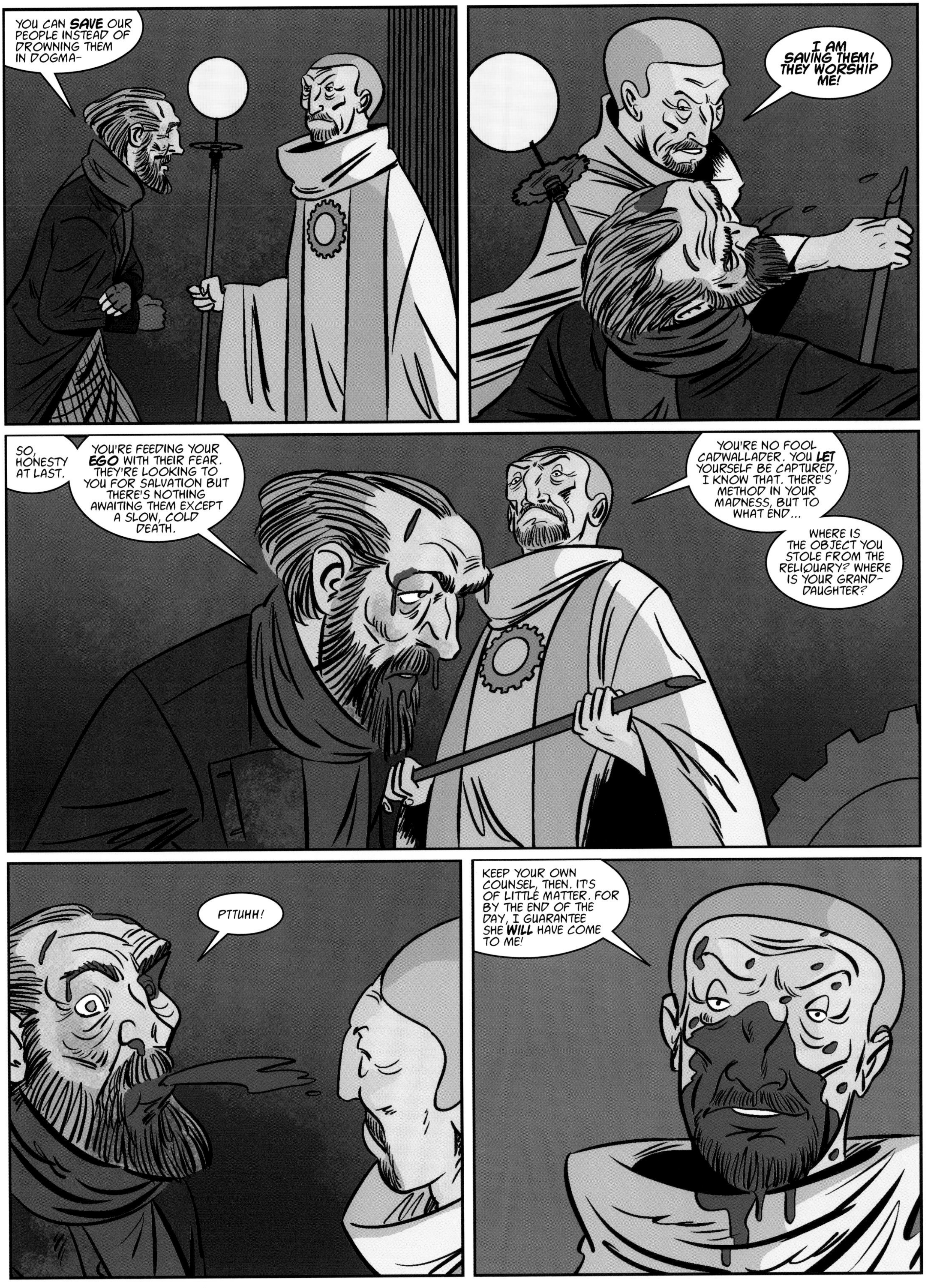

YOU CAN SAVE OUR PEOPLE INSTEAD OF DROWNING THEM IN DOGMA-
I AM SAVING THEM! THEY WORSHIP ME!
SO, HONESTY AT LAST.
YOU'RE FEEDING YOUR EGO WITH THEIR FEAR. THEY'RE LOOKING TO YOU FOR SALVATION BUT THERE'S NOTHING AWAITING THEM EXCEPT A SLOW, COLD DEATH.
YOU'RE NO FOOL CADWALLADER. YOU LET YOURSELF BE CAPTURED, I KNOW THAT. THERE'S METHOD IN YOUR MADNESS, BUT TO WHAT END...
WHERE IS THE OBJECT YOU STOLE FROM THE RELIQUARY? WHERE IS YOUR GRAND-DAUGHTER?
PTTUHH!
KEEP YOUR OWN COUNSEL, THEN. IT'S OF LITTLE MATTER. FOR BY THE END OF THE DAY, I GUARANTEE SHE WILL HAVE COME TO ME!

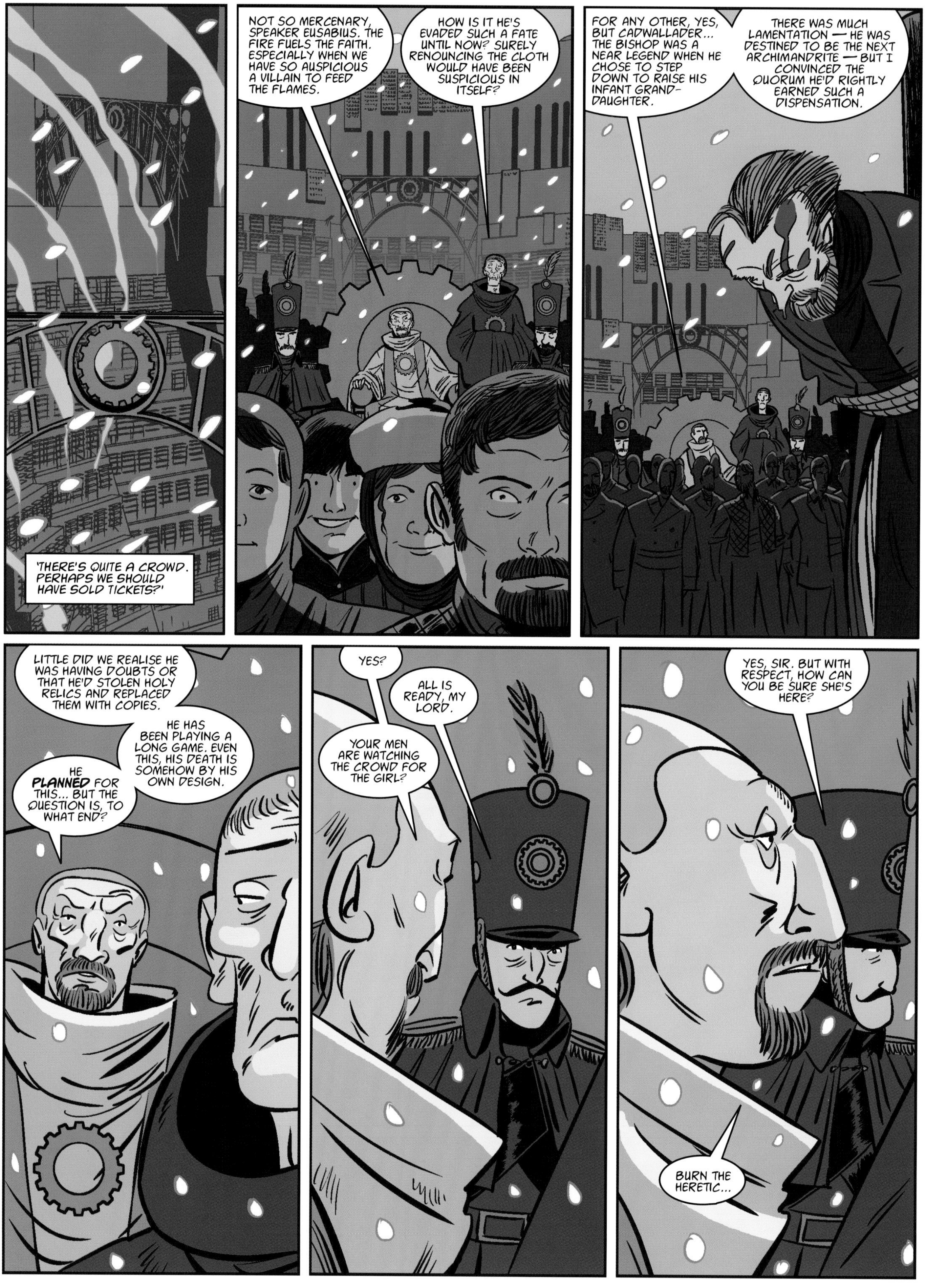
'THERE'S QUITE A CROWD. PERHAPS WE SHOULD HAVE SOLD TICKETS?'
NOT SO MERCENARY, SPEAKER EUSABIUS. THE FIRE FUELS THE FAITH. ESPECIALLY WHEN WE HAVE SO AUSPICIOUS A VILLAIN TO FEED THE FLAMES.
HOW IS IT HE'S EVADED SUCH A FATE UNTIL NOW? SURELY RENOUNCING THE CLOTH WOULD HAVE BEEN SUSPICIOUS IN ITSELF?
FOR ANY OTHER, YES, BUT CADWALLADER... THE BISHOP WAS A NEAR LEGEND WHEN HE CHOSE TO STEP DOWN TO RAISE HIS INFANT GRAND-DAUGHTER.
THERE WAS MUCH LAMENTATION — HE WAS DESTINED TO BE THE NEXT ARCHIMANDRITE — BUT I CONVINCED THE QUORUM HE'D RIGHTLY EARNED SUCH A DISPENSATION.
LITTLE DID WE REALISE HE WAS HAVING DOUBTS OR THAT HE'D STOLEN HOLY RELICS AND REPLACED THEM WITH COPIES.
HE HAS BEEN PLAYING A LONG GAME. EVEN THIS, HIS DEATH IS SOMEHOW BY HIS OWN DESIGN.
HE **PLANNED** FOR THIS... BUT THE QUESTION IS, TO WHAT END?
YES?
ALL IS READY, MY LORD.
YOUR MEN ARE WATCHING THE CROWD FOR THE GIRL?
YES, SIR. BUT WITH RESPECT, HOW CAN YOU BE SURE SHE'S HERE?
BURN THE HERETIC...

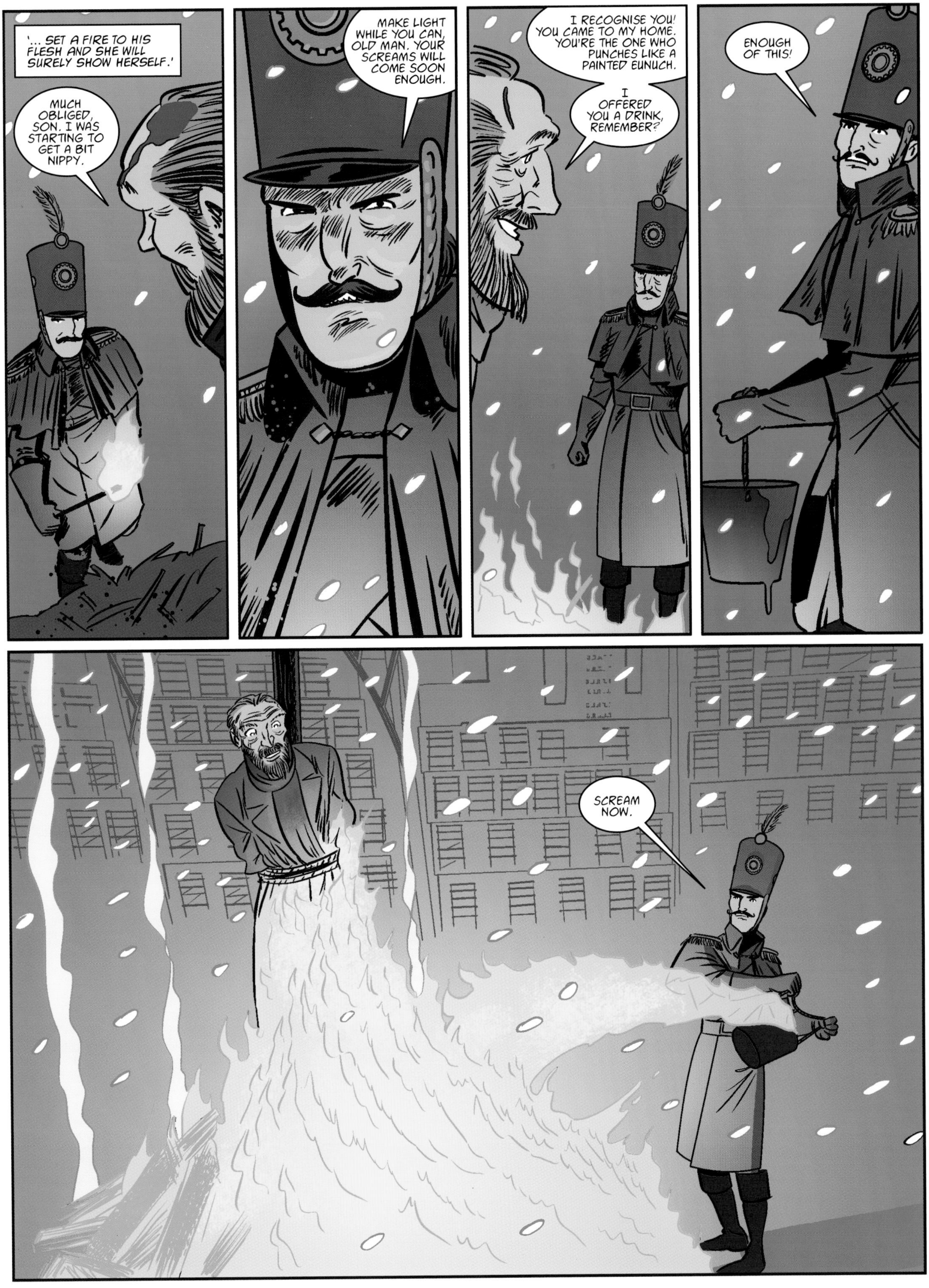
'... SET A FIRE TO HIS FLESH AND SHE WILL SURELY SHOW HERSELF.'
MUCH OBLIGED, SON. I WAS STARTING TO GET A BIT NIPPY.
MAKE LIGHT WHILE YOU CAN, OLD MAN. YOUR SCREAMS WILL COME SOON ENOUGH.
I RECOGNISE YOU! YOU CAME TO MY HOME. YOU'RE THE ONE WHO PUNCHES LIKE A PAINTED EUNUCH.
I OFFERED YOU A DRINK, REMEMBER?
ENOUGH OF THIS!
SCREAM NOW.

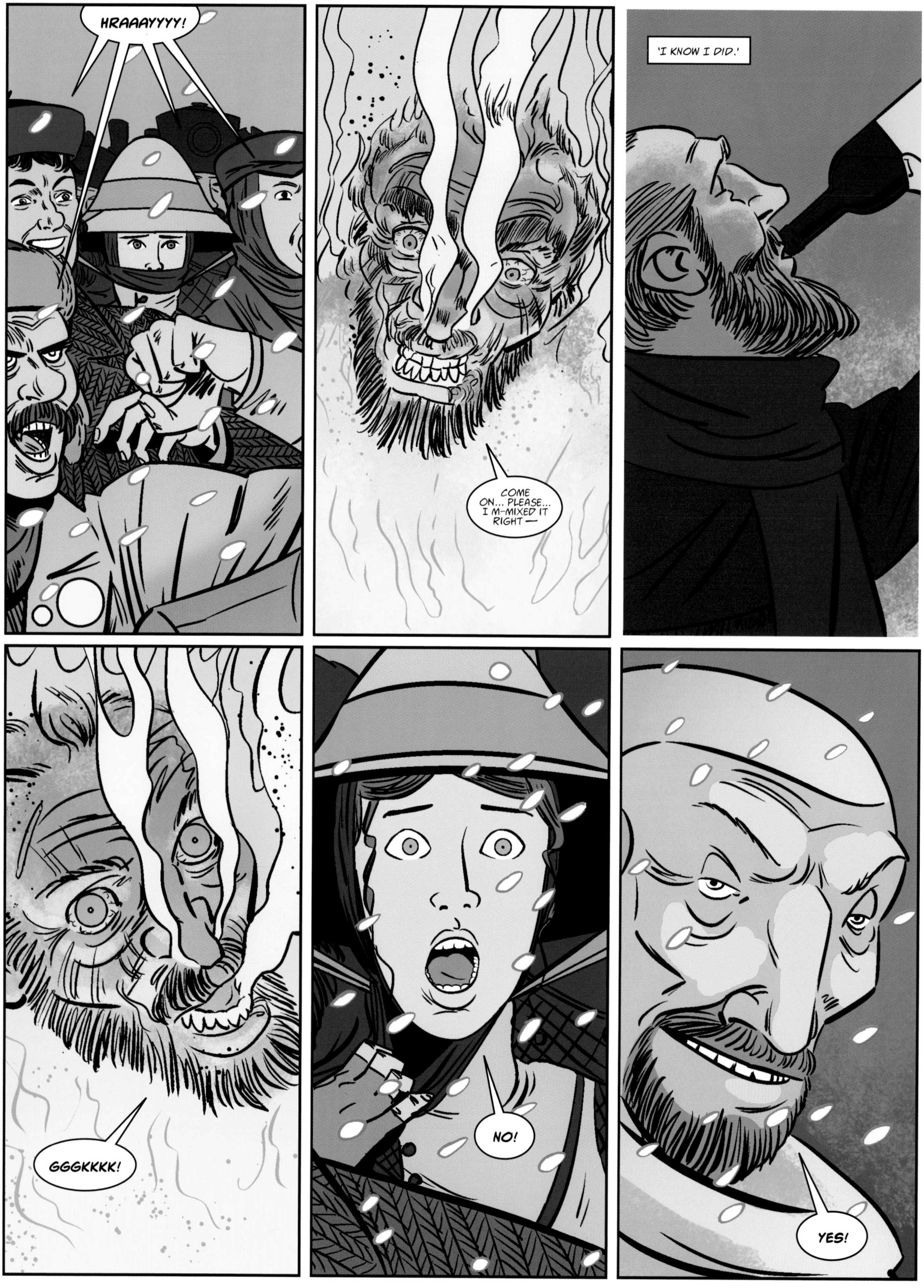
HRAAAYYYY!
COME ON... PLEASE... I M-MIXED IT RIGHT —
'I KNOW I DID.'
GGGKKKK!
NO!
YES!

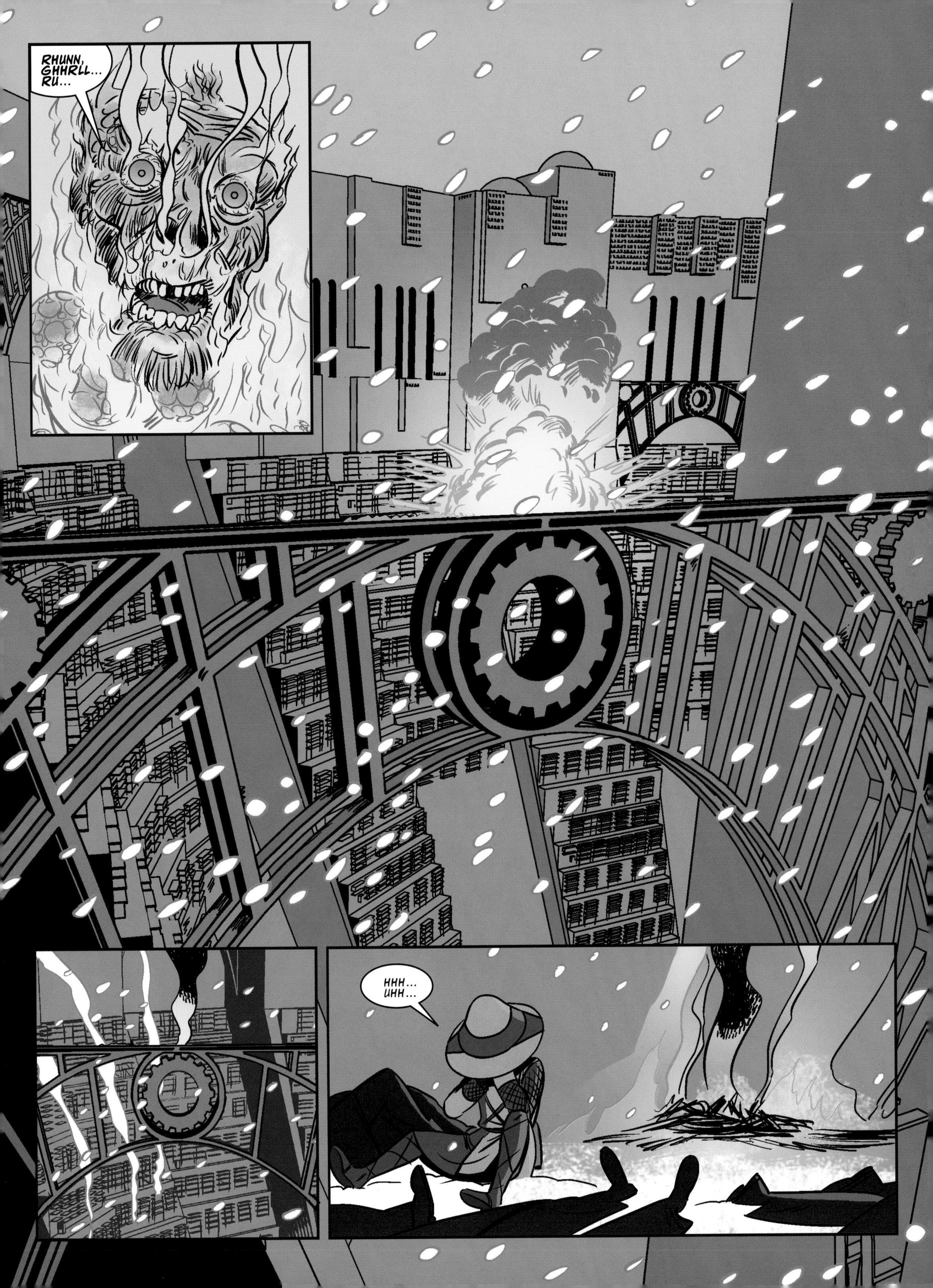
RHUNN, GHHRLL... RU...
HHH... UHH...

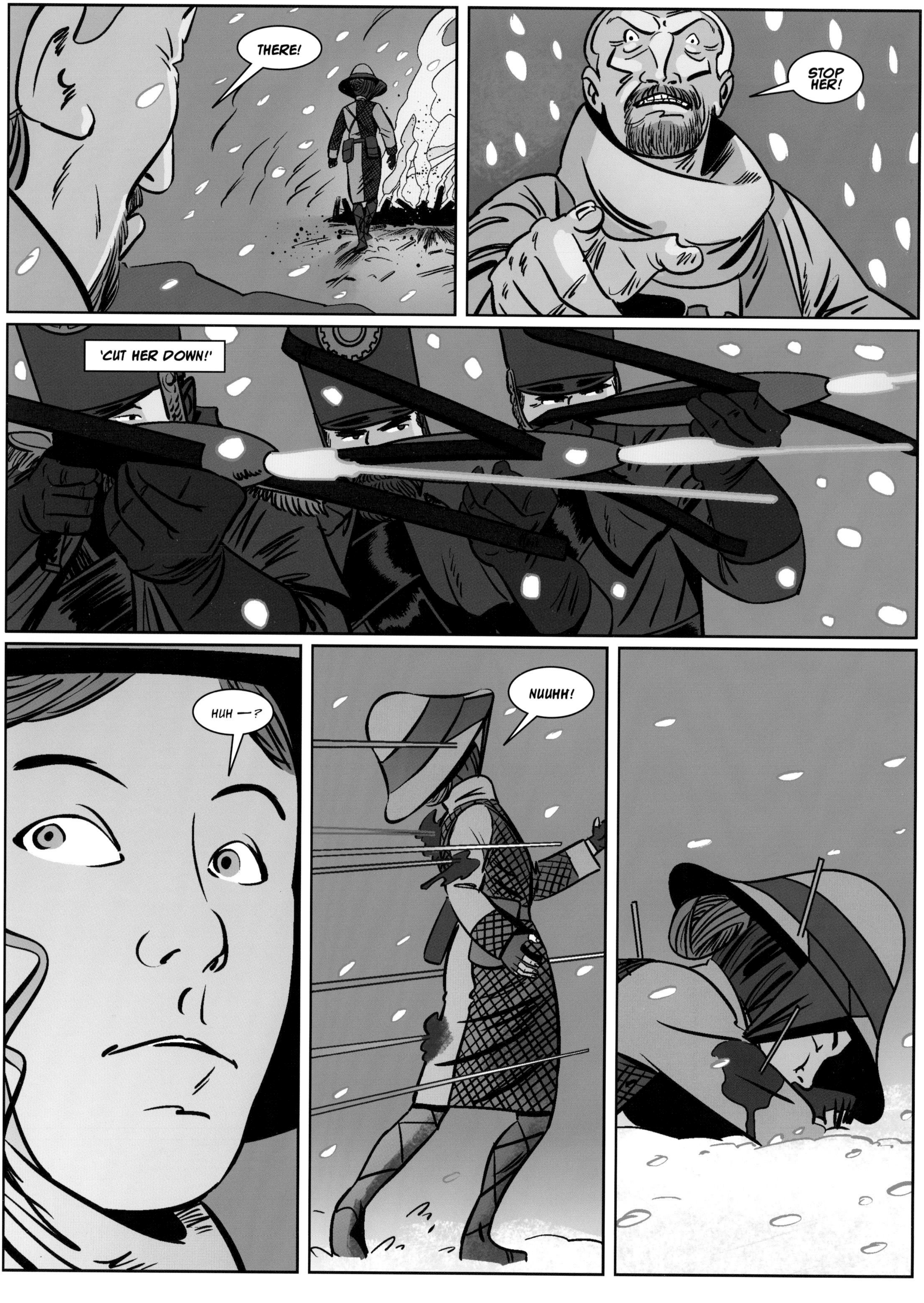
THERE!
STOP HER!
'CUT HER DOWN!'
HUH —?
NUUHH!

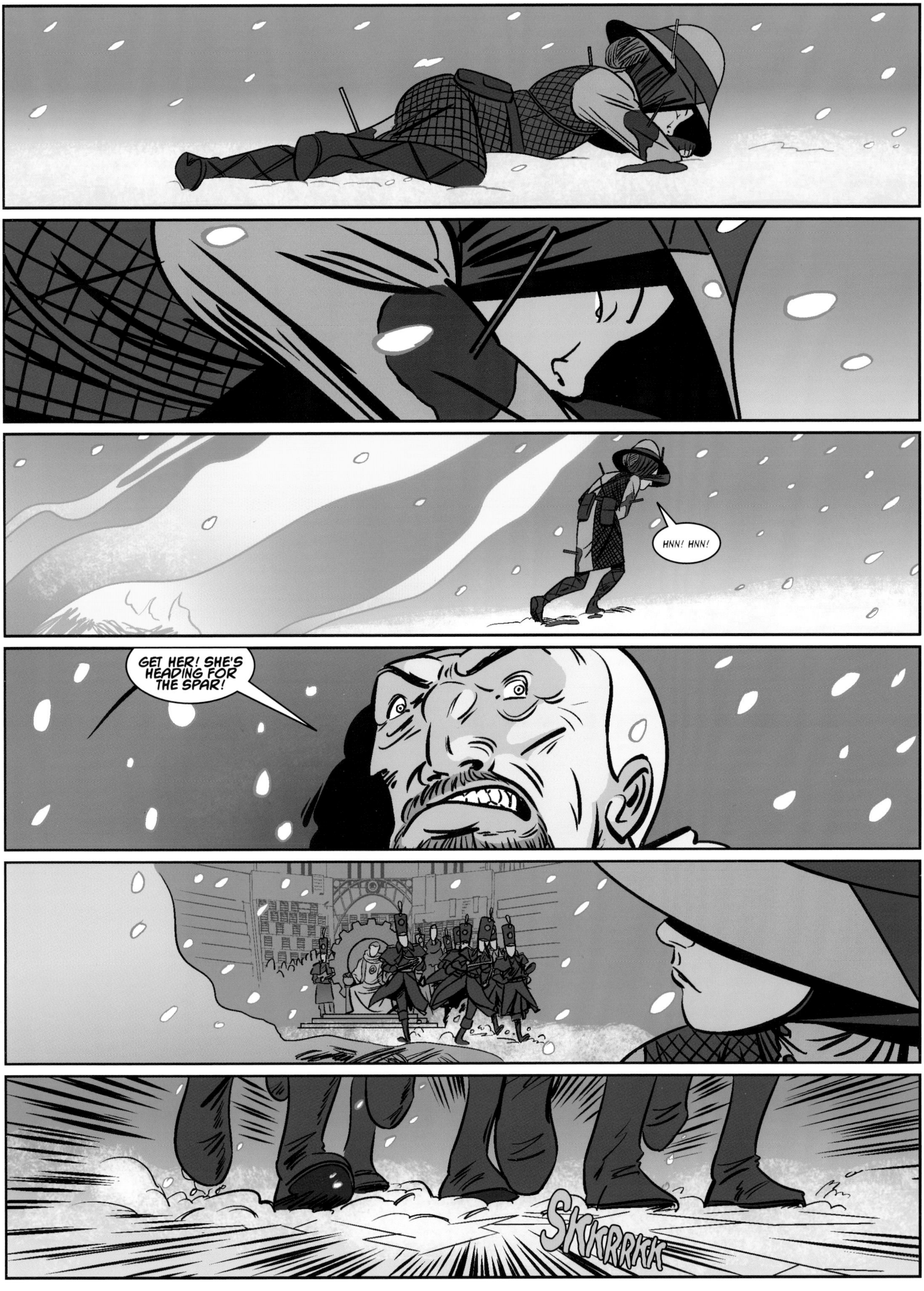
HNN! HNN!
GET HER! SHE'S HEADING FOR THE SPAR!
SKKRRKK

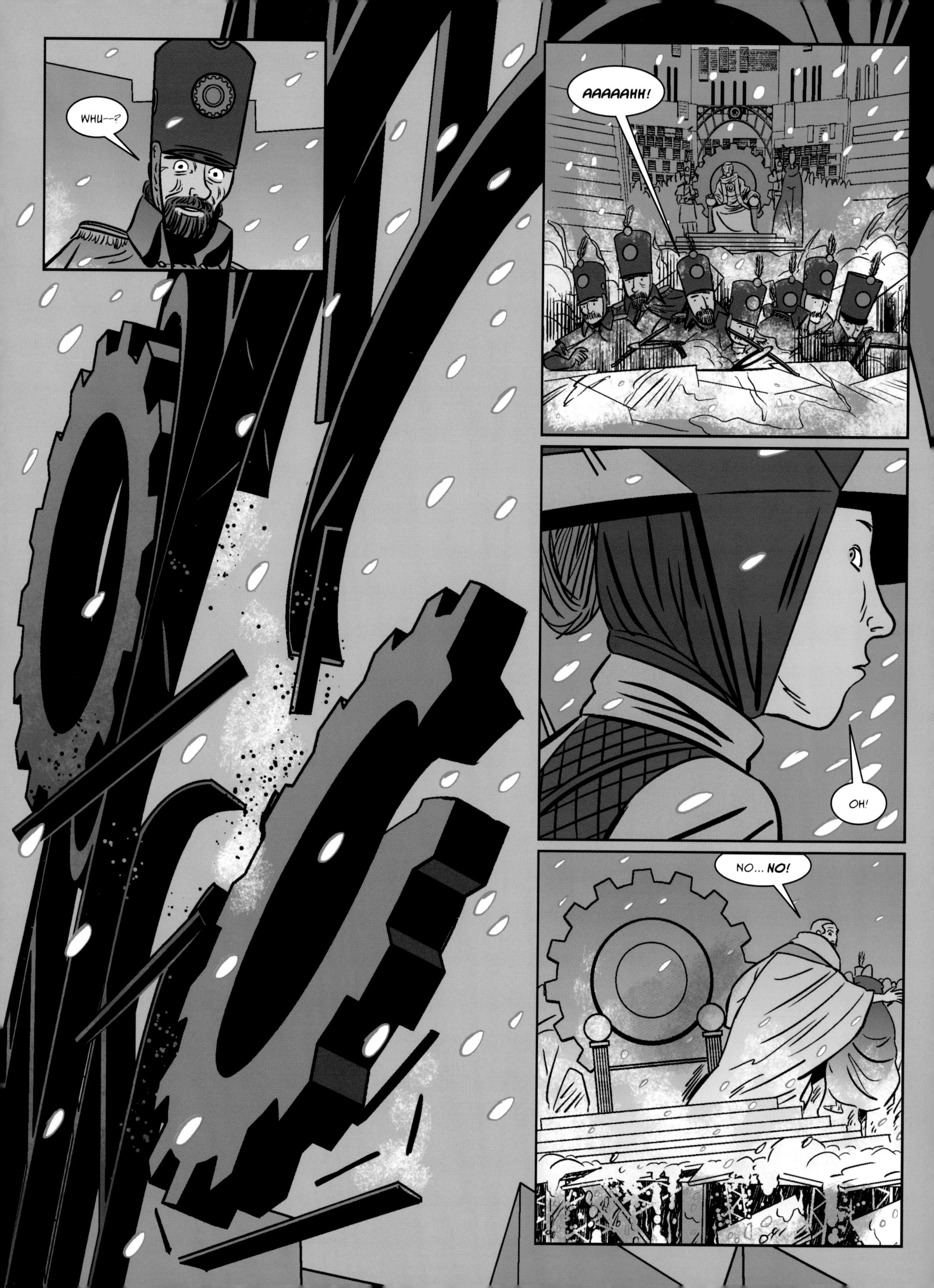
WHU--?
AAAAAHH!
OH!
NO... NO!

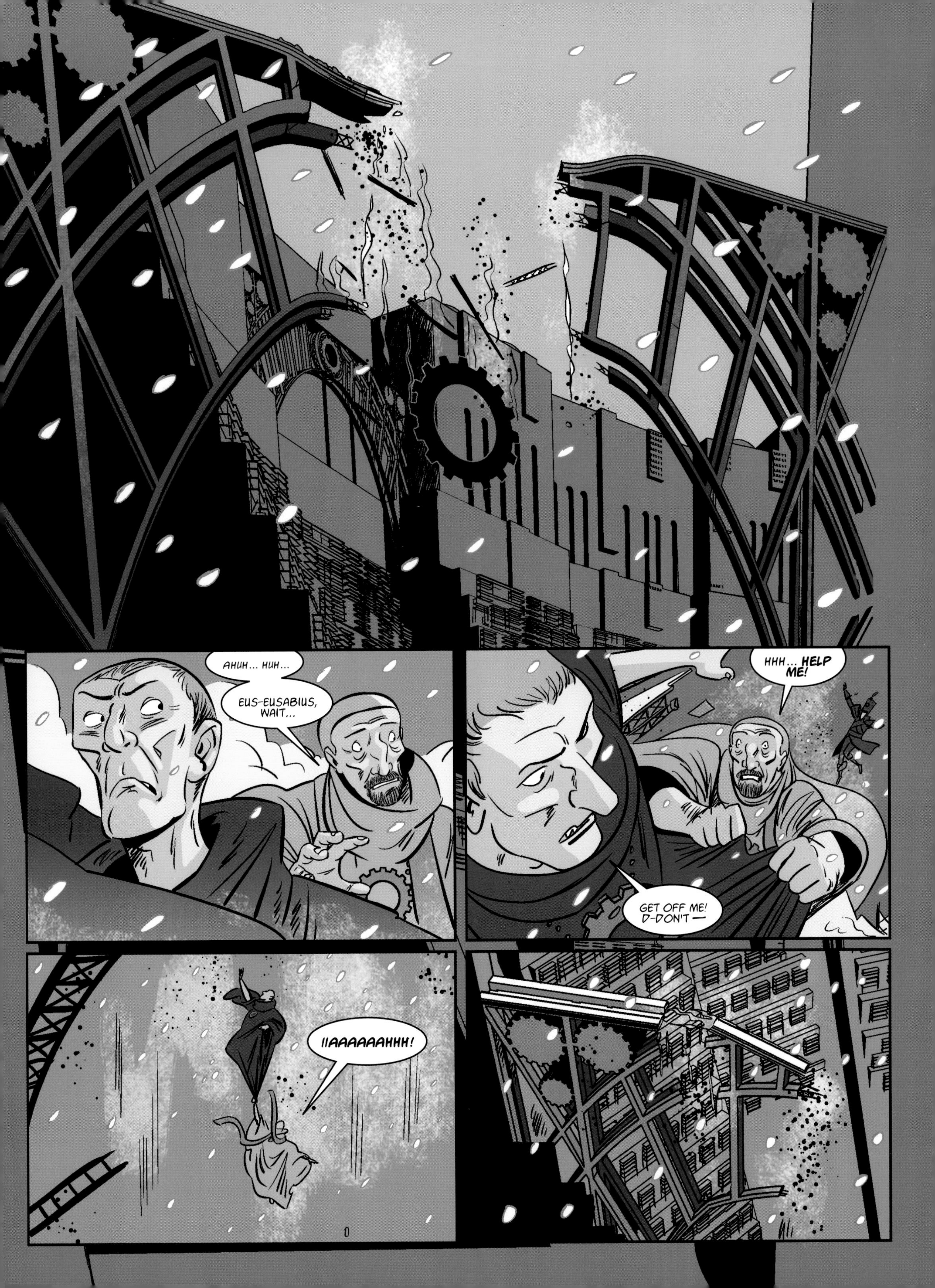
AHUH... HUH...
EUS-EUSABIUS, WAIT...
HHH... HELP ME!
GET OFF ME! D-DON'T —
IIAAAAAAHHH!

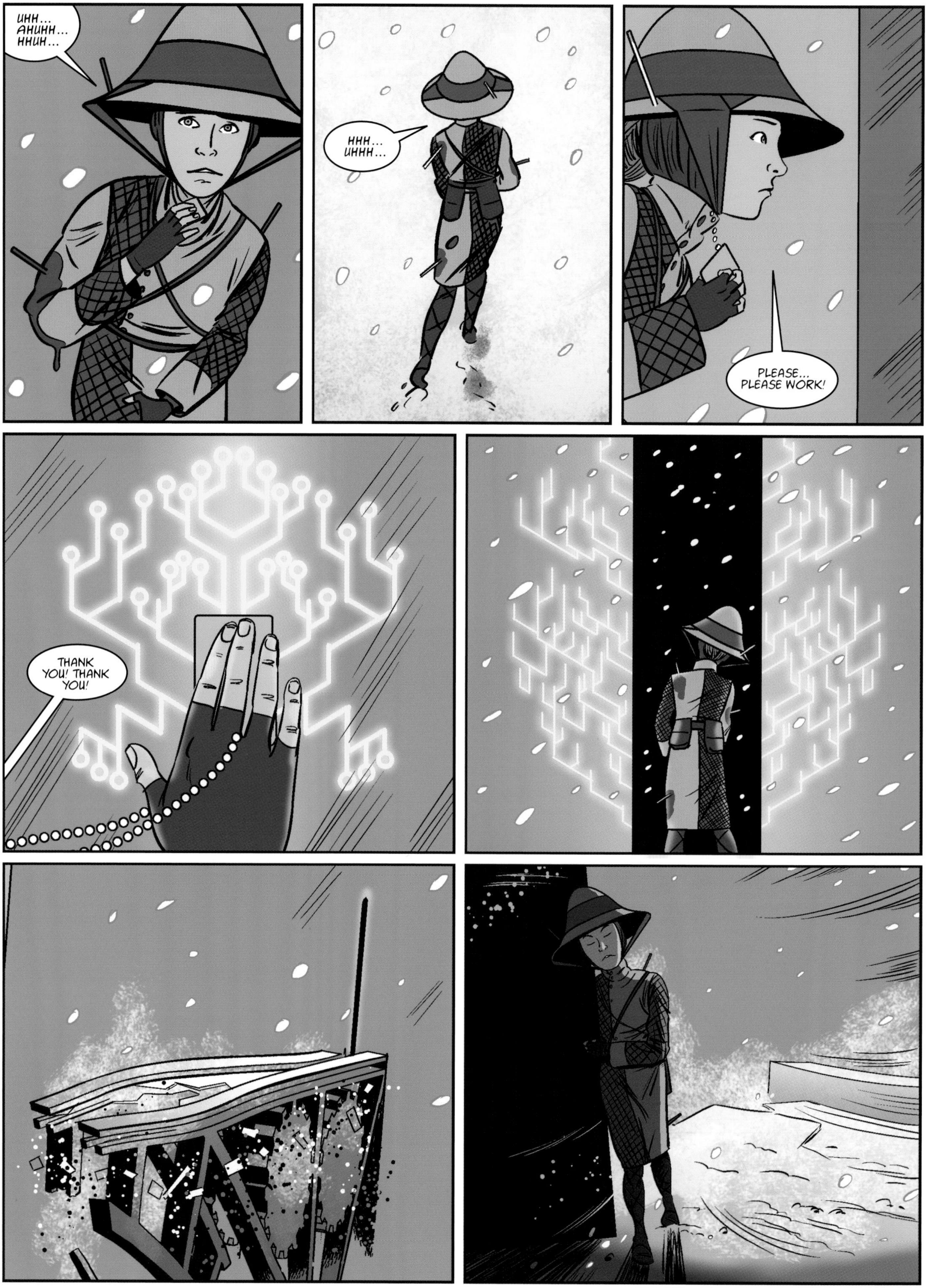
UHH... AHUHH... HHUH...
HHH... UHHH...
PLEASE... PLEASE WORK!
THANK YOU! THANK YOU!

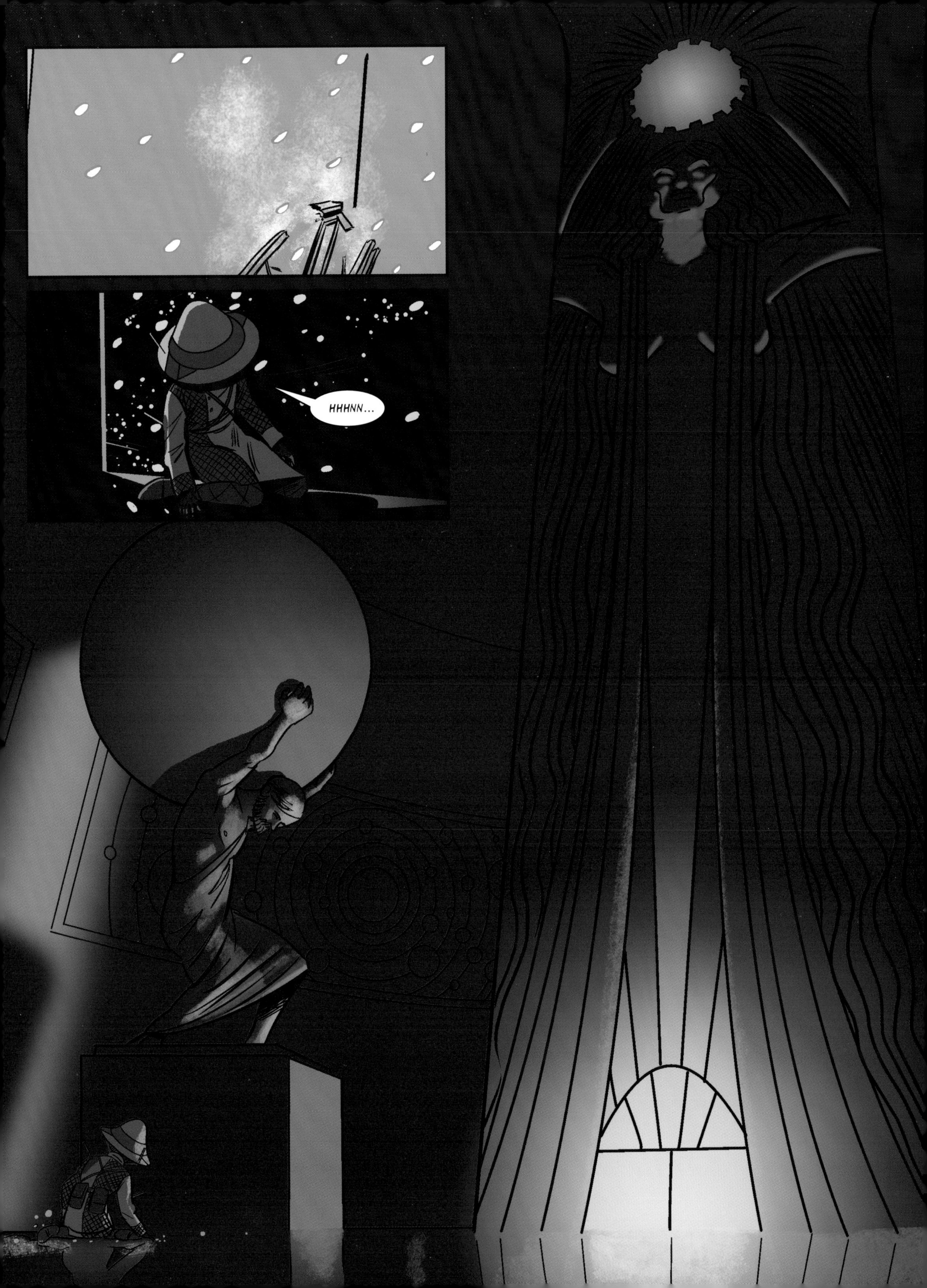
HHHNN...

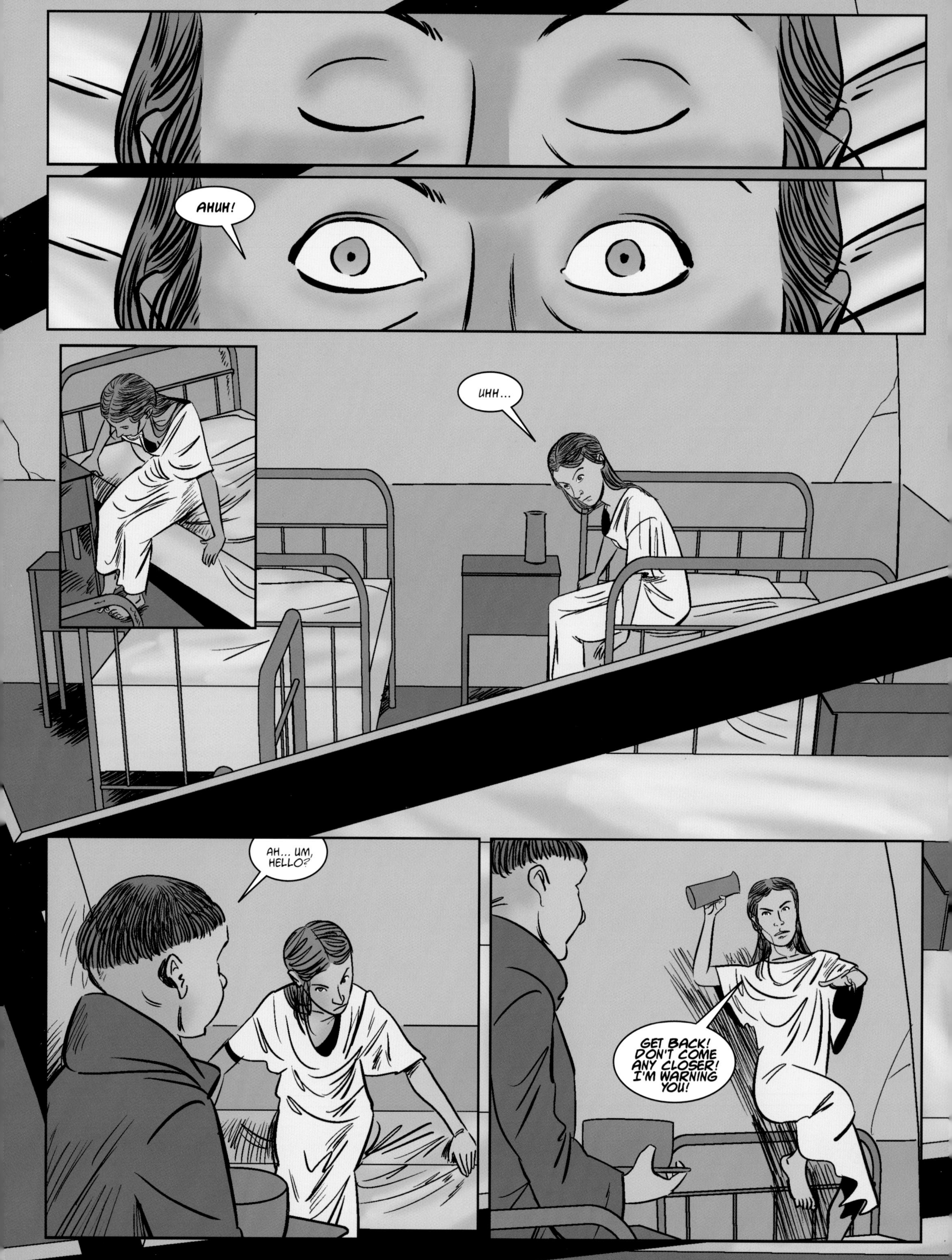
AHUH!
UHH...
AH... UM, HELLO?
GET BACK! DON'T COME ANY CLOSER! I'M WARNING YOU!

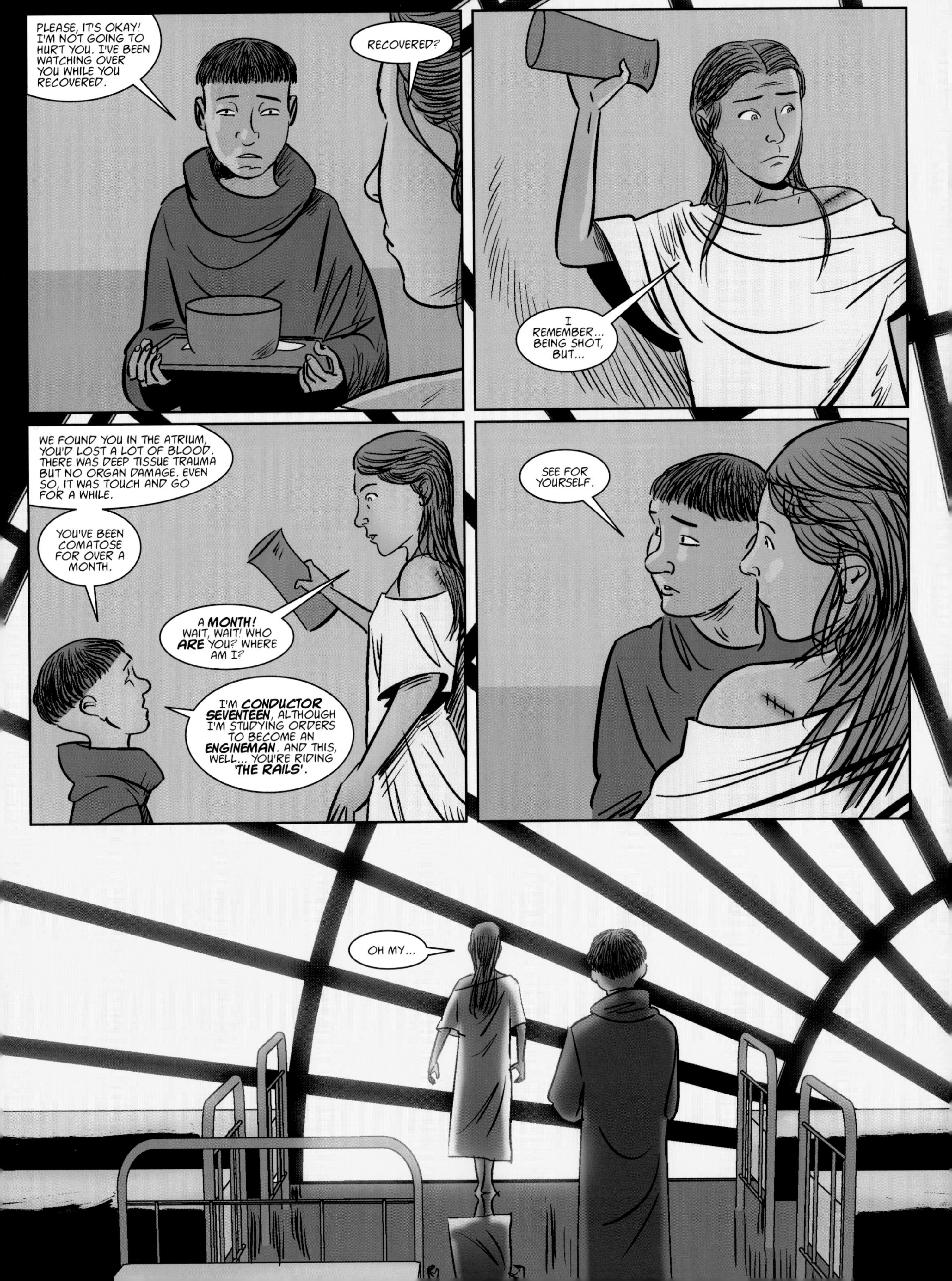
PLEASE, IT'S OKAY! I'M NOT GOING TO HURT YOU. I'VE BEEN WATCHING OVER YOU WHILE YOU RECOVERED.
RECOVERED?
I REMEMBER... BEING SHOT, BUT...
WE FOUND YOU IN THE ATRIUM, YOU'D LOST A LOT OF BLOOD. THERE WAS DEEP TISSUE TRAUMA BUT NO ORGAN DAMAGE. EVEN SO, IT WAS TOUCH AND GO FOR A WHILE.
YOU'VE BEEN COMATOSE FOR OVER A MONTH.
A **MONTH!** WAIT, WAIT! WHO **ARE** YOU? WHERE AM I?
I'M **CONDUCTOR SEVENTEEN**, ALTHOUGH I'M STUDYING ORDERS TO BECOME AN **ENGINEMAN**. AND THIS, WELL... YOU'RE RIDING **'THE RAILS'**.
SEE FOR YOURSELF.
OH MY...

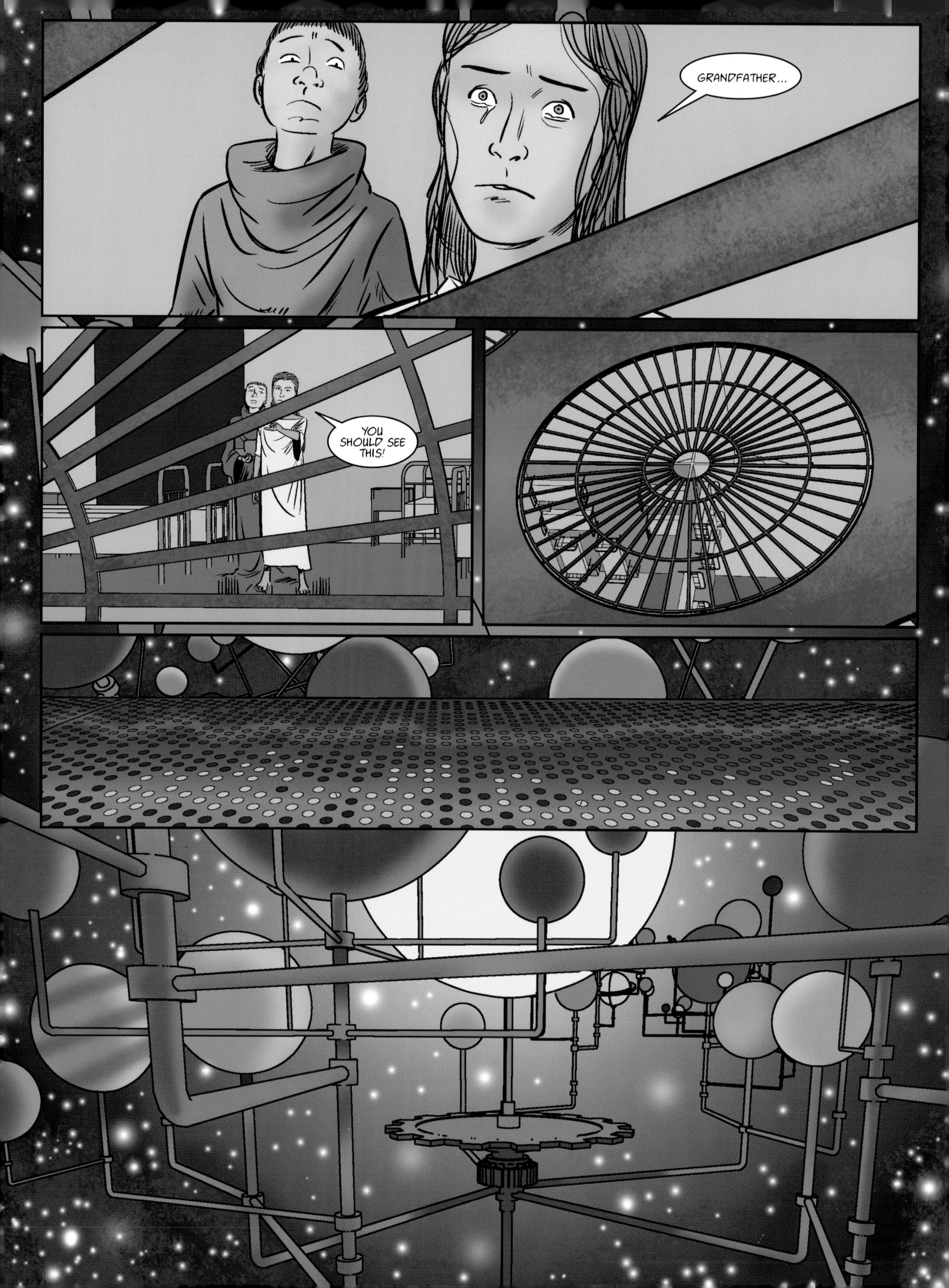
GRANDFATHER...
YOU SHOULD SEE THIS!

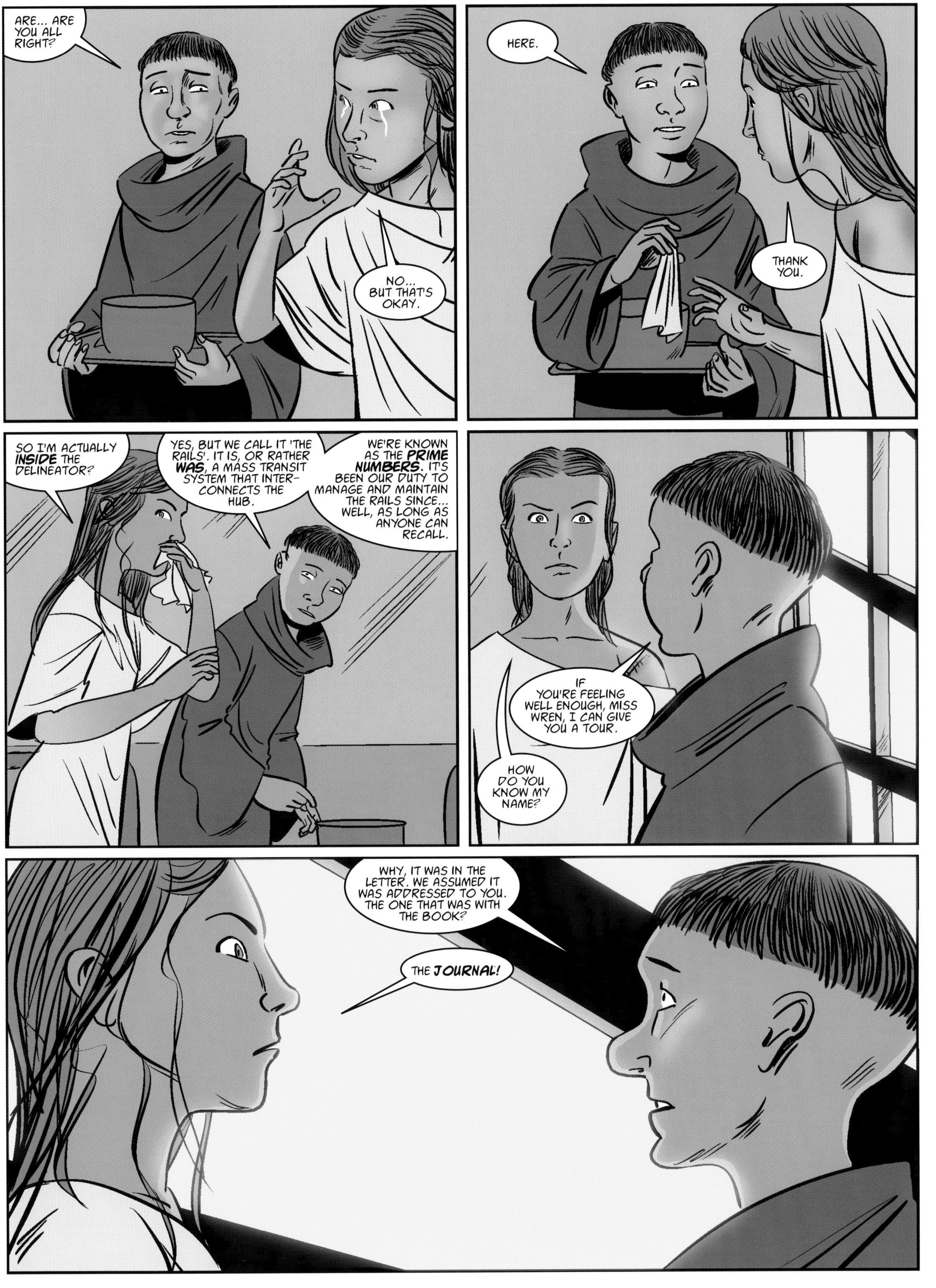
ARE... ARE YOU ALL RIGHT?
NO... BUT THAT'S OKAY.
HERE.
THANK YOU.
SO I'M ACTUALLY **INSIDE** THE DELINEATOR?
YES, BUT WE CALL IT 'THE RAILS'. IT IS, OR RATHER **WAS**, A MASS TRANSIT SYSTEM THAT INTER-CONNECTS THE HUB.
WE'RE KNOWN AS THE **PRIME NUMBERS.** IT'S BEEN OUR DUTY TO MANAGE AND MAINTAIN THE RAILS SINCE... WELL, AS LONG AS ANYONE CAN RECALL.
IF YOU'RE FEELING WELL ENOUGH, MISS WREN, I CAN GIVE YOU A TOUR.
HOW DO YOU KNOW MY NAME?
WHY, IT WAS IN THE LETTER. WE ASSUMED IT WAS ADDRESSED TO YOU. THE ONE THAT WAS WITH THE BOOK?
THE **JOURNAL!**

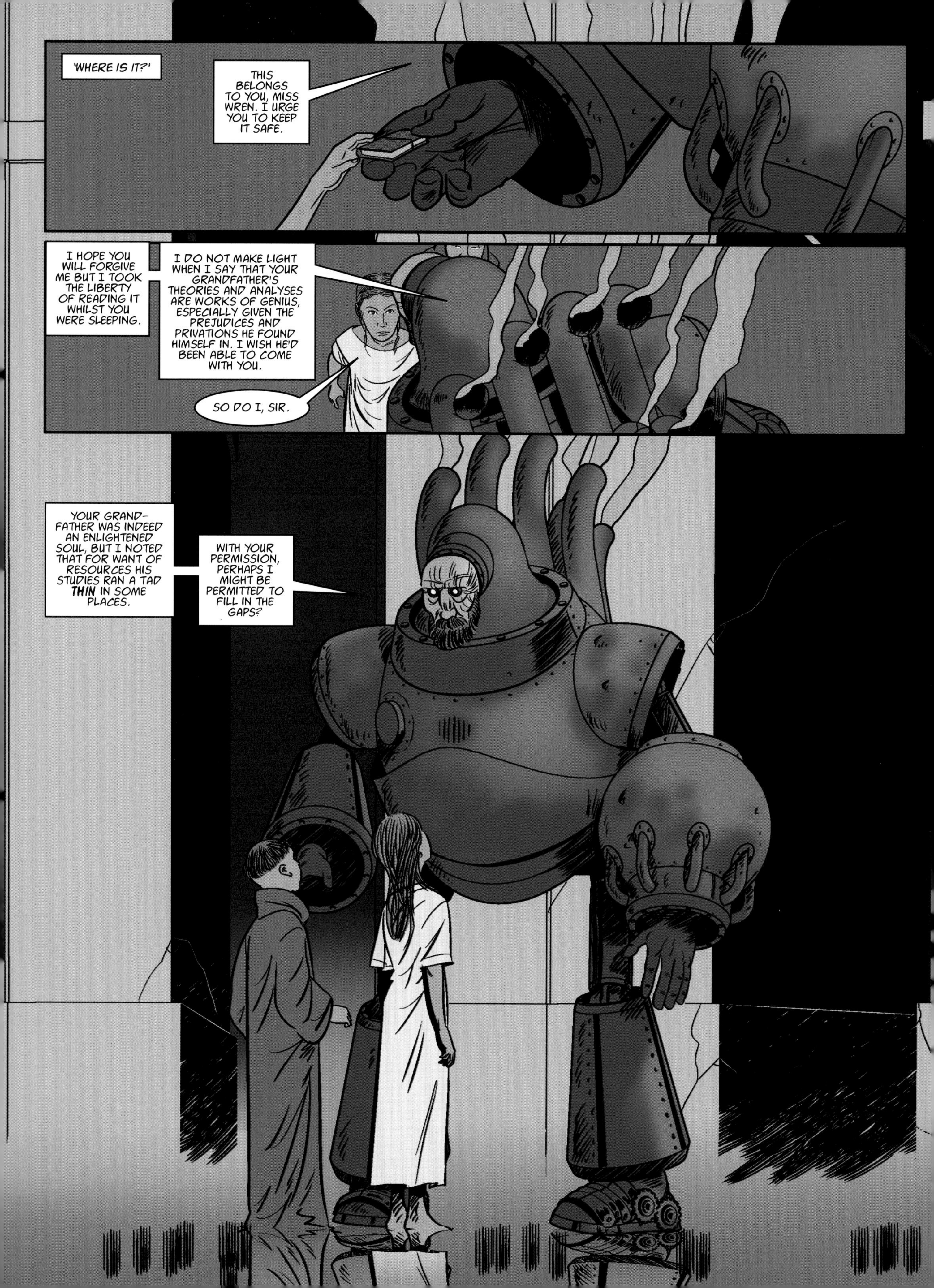
'WHERE IS IT?'
THIS BELONGS TO YOU, MISS WREN. I URGE YOU TO KEEP IT SAFE.
I HOPE YOU WILL FORGIVE ME BUT I TOOK THE LIBERTY OF READING IT WHILST YOU WERE SLEEPING.
I DO NOT MAKE LIGHT WHEN I SAY THAT YOUR GRANDFATHER'S THEORIES AND ANALYSES ARE WORKS OF GENIUS, ESPECIALLY GIVEN THE PREJUDICES AND PRIVATIONS HE FOUND HIMSELF IN. I WISH HE'D BEEN ABLE TO COME WITH YOU.
SO DO I, SIR.
YOUR GRAND-FATHER WAS INDEED AN ENLIGHTENED SOUL, BUT I NOTED THAT FOR WANT OF RESOURCES HIS STUDIES RAN A TAD THIN IN SOME PLACES.
WITH YOUR PERMISSION, PERHAPS I MIGHT BE PERMITTED TO FILL IN THE GAPS?

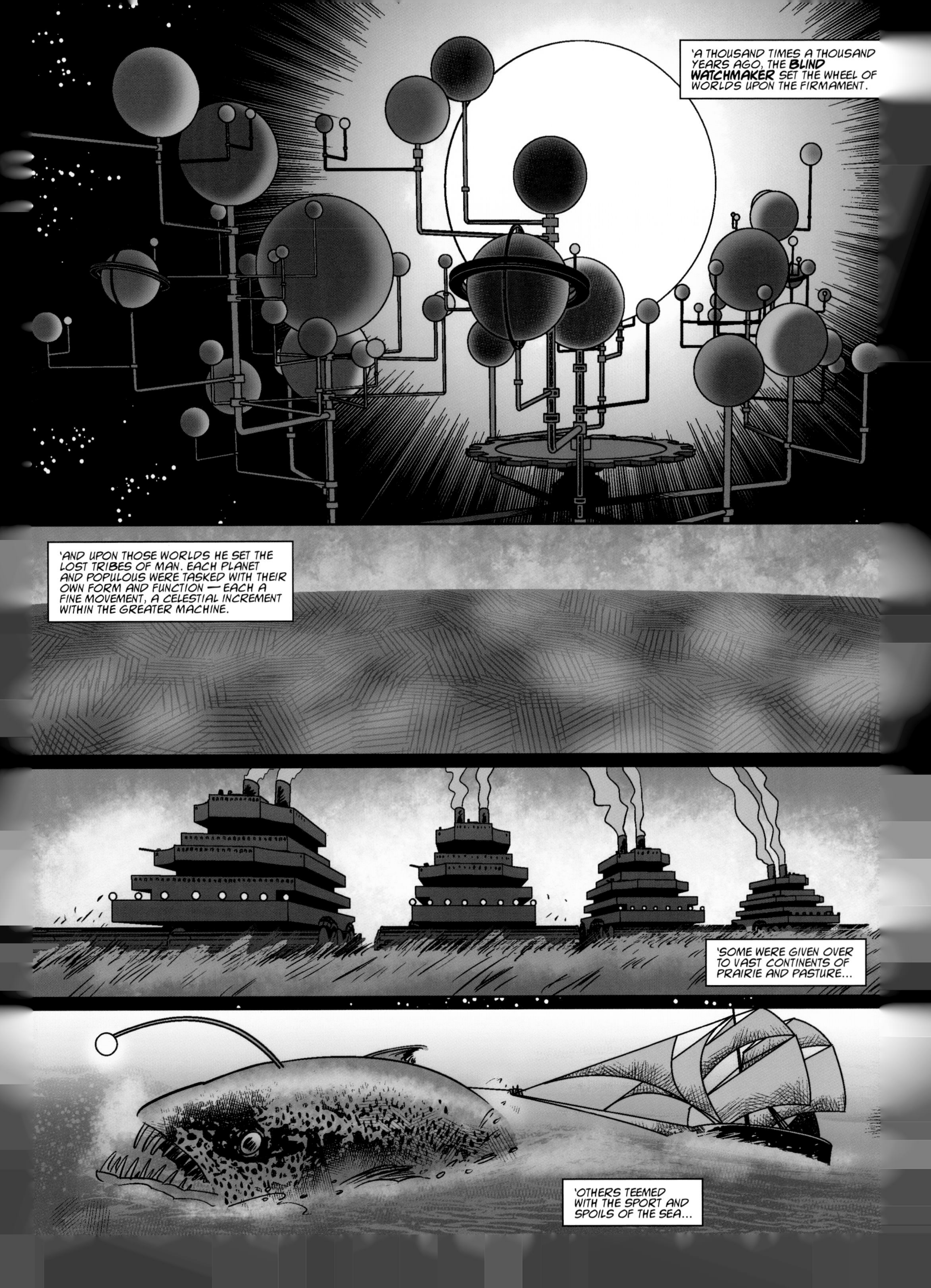
'A THOUSAND TIMES A THOUSAND YEARS AGO, THE BLIND WATCHMAKER SET THE WHEEL OF WORLDS UPON THE FIRMAMENT.
'AND UPON THOSE WORLDS HE SET THE LOST TRIBES OF MAN. EACH PLANET AND POPULOUS WERE TASKED WITH THEIR OWN FORM AND FUNCTION — EACH A FINE MOVEMENT, A CELESTIAL INCREMENT WITHIN THE GREATER MACHINE.
'SOME WERE GIVEN OVER TO VAST CONTINENTS OF PRAIRIE AND PASTURE...
'OTHERS TEEMED WITH THE SPORT AND SPOILS OF THE SEA...

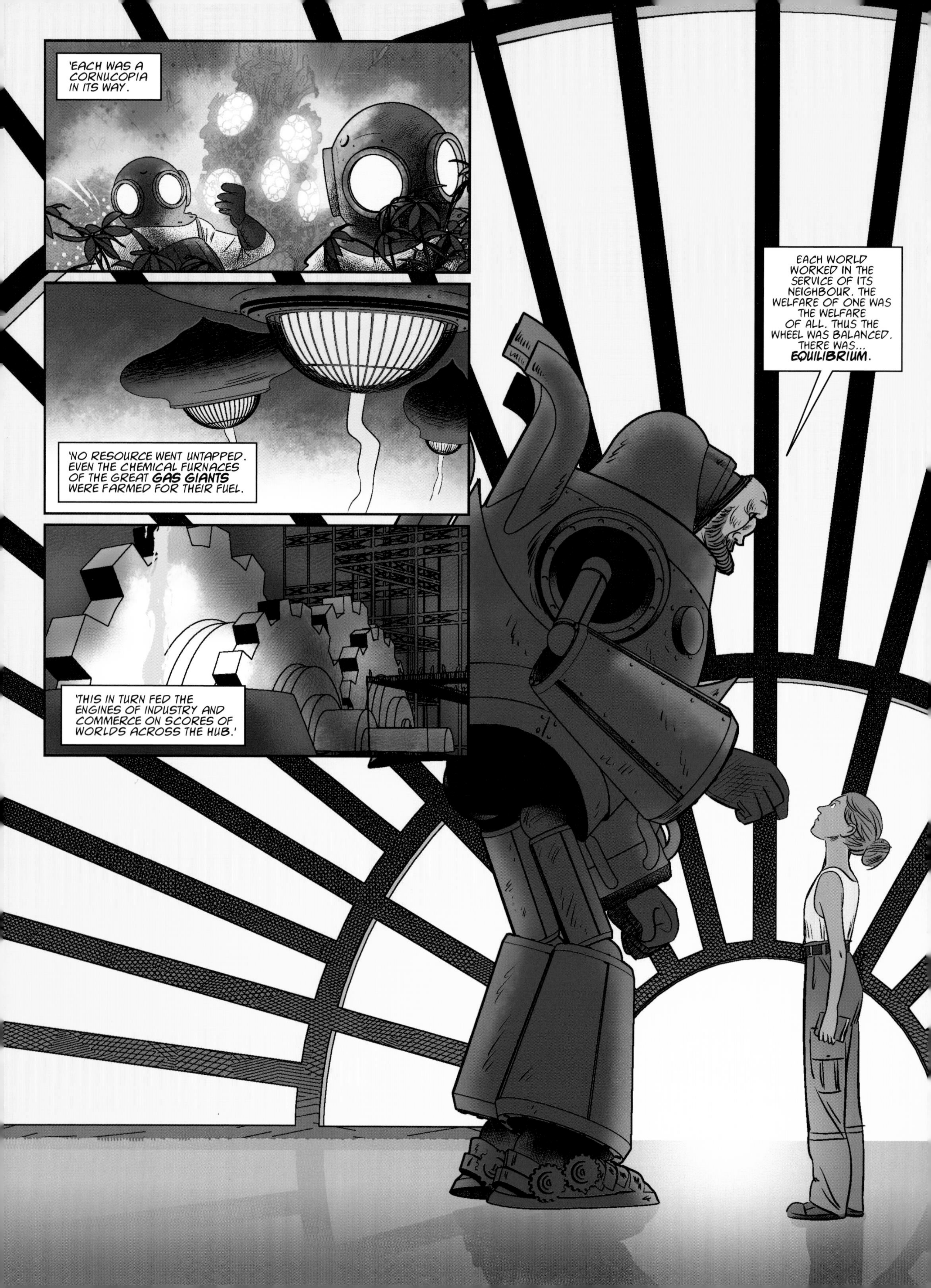
'EACH WAS A CORNUCOPIA IN ITS WAY.
'NO RESOURCE WENT UNTAPPED. EVEN THE CHEMICAL FURNACES OF THE GREAT **GAS GIANTS** WERE FARMED FOR THEIR FUEL.
'THIS IN TURN FED THE ENGINES OF INDUSTRY AND COMMERCE ON SCORES OF WORLDS ACROSS THE HUB.'
EACH WORLD WORKED IN THE SERVICE OF ITS NEIGHBOUR. THE WELFARE OF ONE WAS THE WELFARE OF ALL. THUS THE WHEEL WAS BALANCED. THERE WAS... **EQUILIBRIUM**.

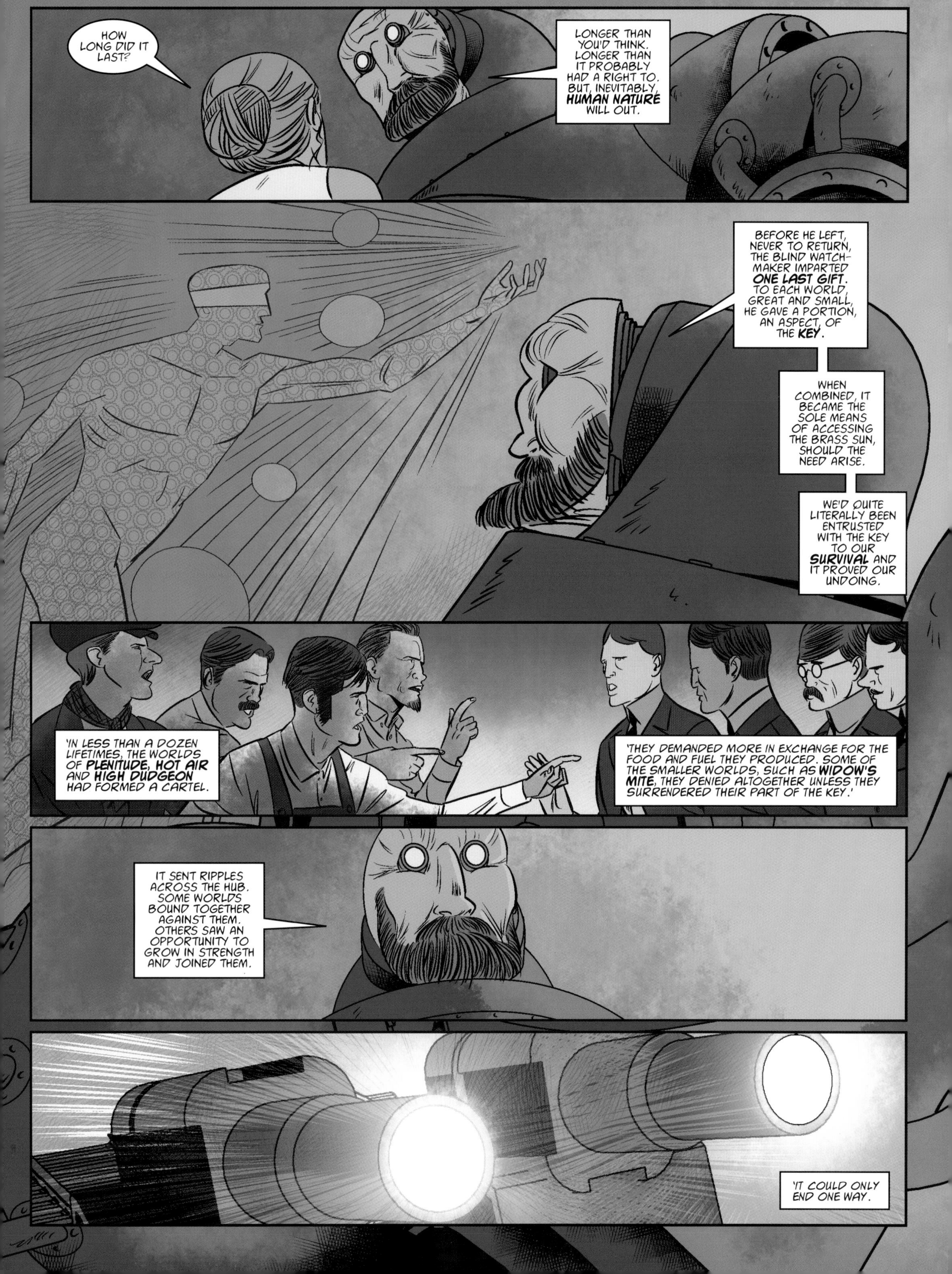
HOW LONG DID IT LAST?
LONGER THAN YOU'D THINK. LONGER THAN IT PROBABLY HAD A RIGHT TO. BUT, INEVITABLY, HUMAN NATURE WILL OUT.
BEFORE HE LEFT, NEVER TO RETURN, THE BLIND WATCH-MAKER IMPARTED ONE LAST GIFT. TO EACH WORLD, GREAT AND SMALL, HE GAVE A PORTION, AN ASPECT, OF THE KEY.
WHEN COMBINED, IT BECAME THE SOLE MEANS OF ACCESSING THE BRASS SUN, SHOULD THE NEED ARISE.
WE'D QUITE LITERALLY BEEN ENTRUSTED WITH THE KEY TO OUR SURVIVAL AND IT PROVED OUR UNDOING.
'IN LESS THAN A DOZEN LIFETIMES, THE WORLDS OF PLENITUDE, HOT AIR AND HIGH DUDGEON HAD FORMED A CARTEL.
'THEY DEMANDED MORE IN EXCHANGE FOR THE FOOD AND FUEL THEY PRODUCED. SOME OF THE SMALLER WORLDS, SUCH AS WIDOW'S MITE, THEY DENIED ALTOGETHER UNLESS THEY SURRENDERED THEIR PART OF THE KEY.'
IT SENT RIPPLES ACROSS THE HUB. SOME WORLDS BOUND TOGETHER AGAINST THEM. OTHERS SAW AN OPPORTUNITY TO GROW IN STRENGTH AND JOINED THEM.
'IT COULD ONLY END ONE WAY.

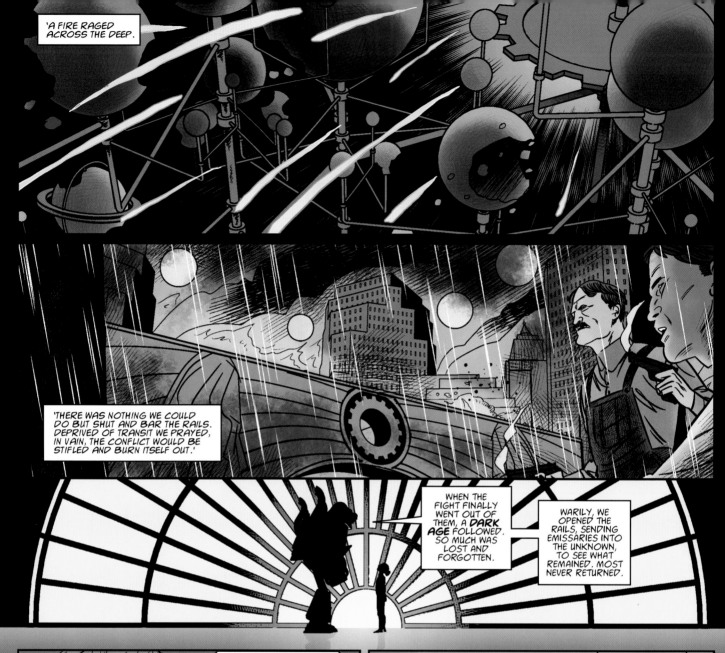

'A FIRE RAGED ACROSS THE DEEP.

'THERE WAS NOTHING WE COULD DO BUT SHUT AND BAR THE RAILS. DEPRIVED OF TRANSIT WE PRAYED, IN VAIN, THE CONFLICT WOULD BE STIFLED AND BURN ITSELF OUT.'

WHEN THE FIGHT FINALLY WENT OUT OF THEM, A **DARK AGE** FOLLOWED. SO MUCH WAS LOST AND FORGOTTEN.

WARILY, WE OPENED THE RAILS, SENDING EMISSARIES INTO THE UNKNOWN, TO SEE WHAT REMAINED. MOST NEVER RETURNED.

THAT'S HOW CADWALLADER FOUND THE **QUAYCARD** IN THE ORTHODOXY ARCHIVE! IT WAS ONE OF YOURS! THEY MUST HAVE TAKEN ONE OF YOUR PEOPLE!

THEY... THEY MUST HAVE KILLED HIM, TOO. I'M SORRY.

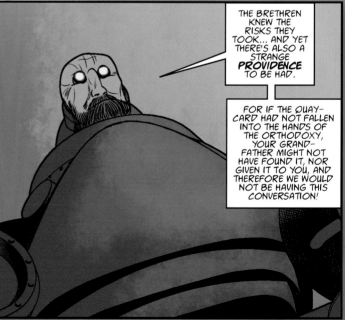

THE BRETHREN KNEW THE RISKS THEY TOOK... AND YET THERE'S ALSO A STRANGE **PROVIDENCE** TO BE HAD.

FOR IF THE QUAY-CARD HAD NOT FALLEN INTO THE HANDS OF THE ORTHODOXY, YOUR GRAND-FATHER MIGHT NOT HAVE FOUND IT, NOR GIVEN IT TO YOU, AND THEREFORE WE WOULD NOT BE HAVING THIS CONVERSATION!

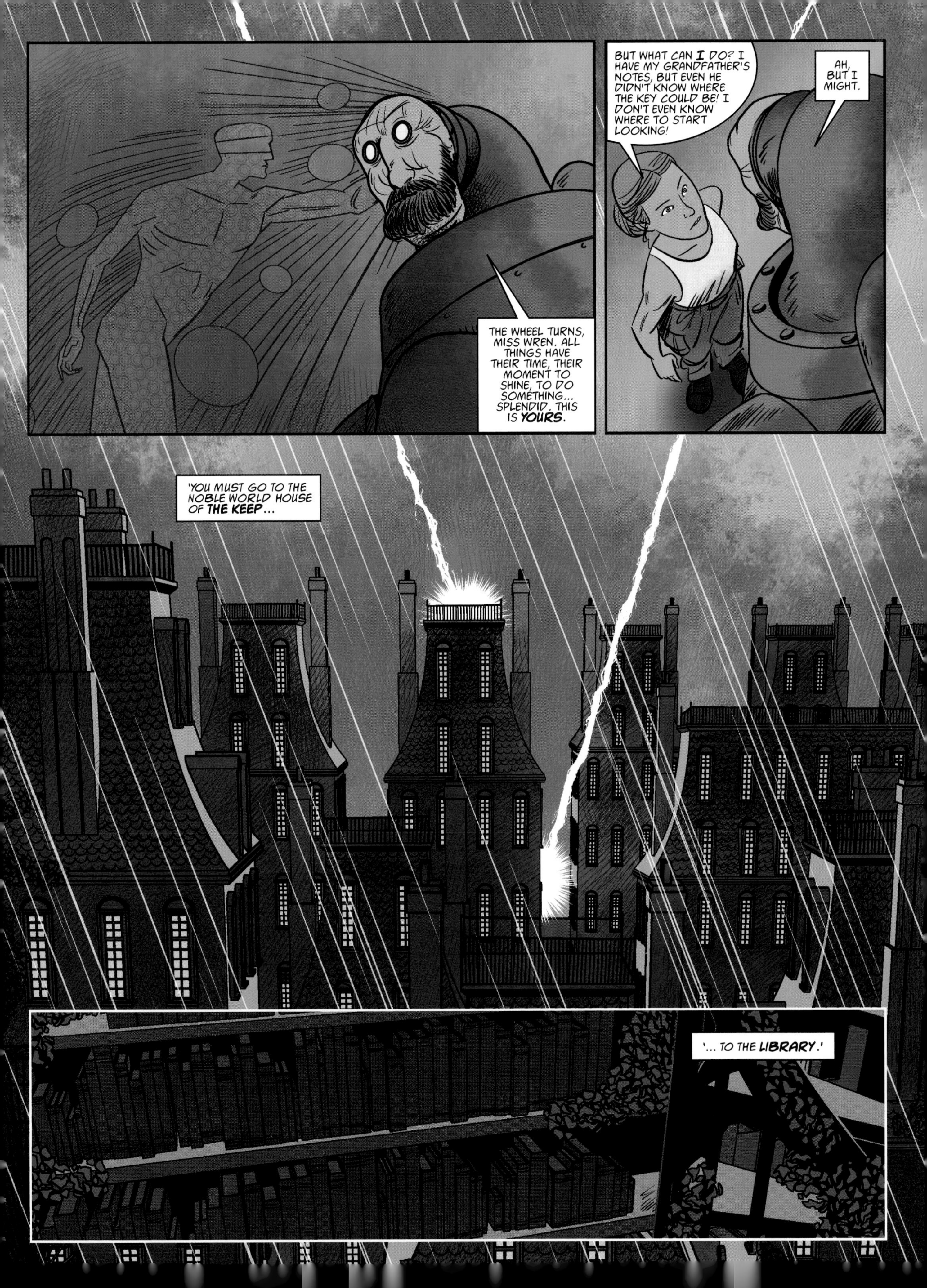
THE WHEEL TURNS, MISS WREN. ALL THINGS HAVE THEIR TIME, THEIR MOMENT TO SHINE, TO DO SOMETHING... SPLENDID. THIS IS YOURS.
BUT WHAT CAN I DO? I HAVE MY GRANDFATHER'S NOTES, BUT EVEN HE DIDN'T KNOW WHERE THE KEY COULD BE! I DON'T EVEN KNOW WHERE TO START LOOKING!
AH, BUT I MIGHT.
'YOU MUST GO TO THE NOBLE WORLD HOUSE OF THE KEEP...
'... TO THE LIBRARY.'

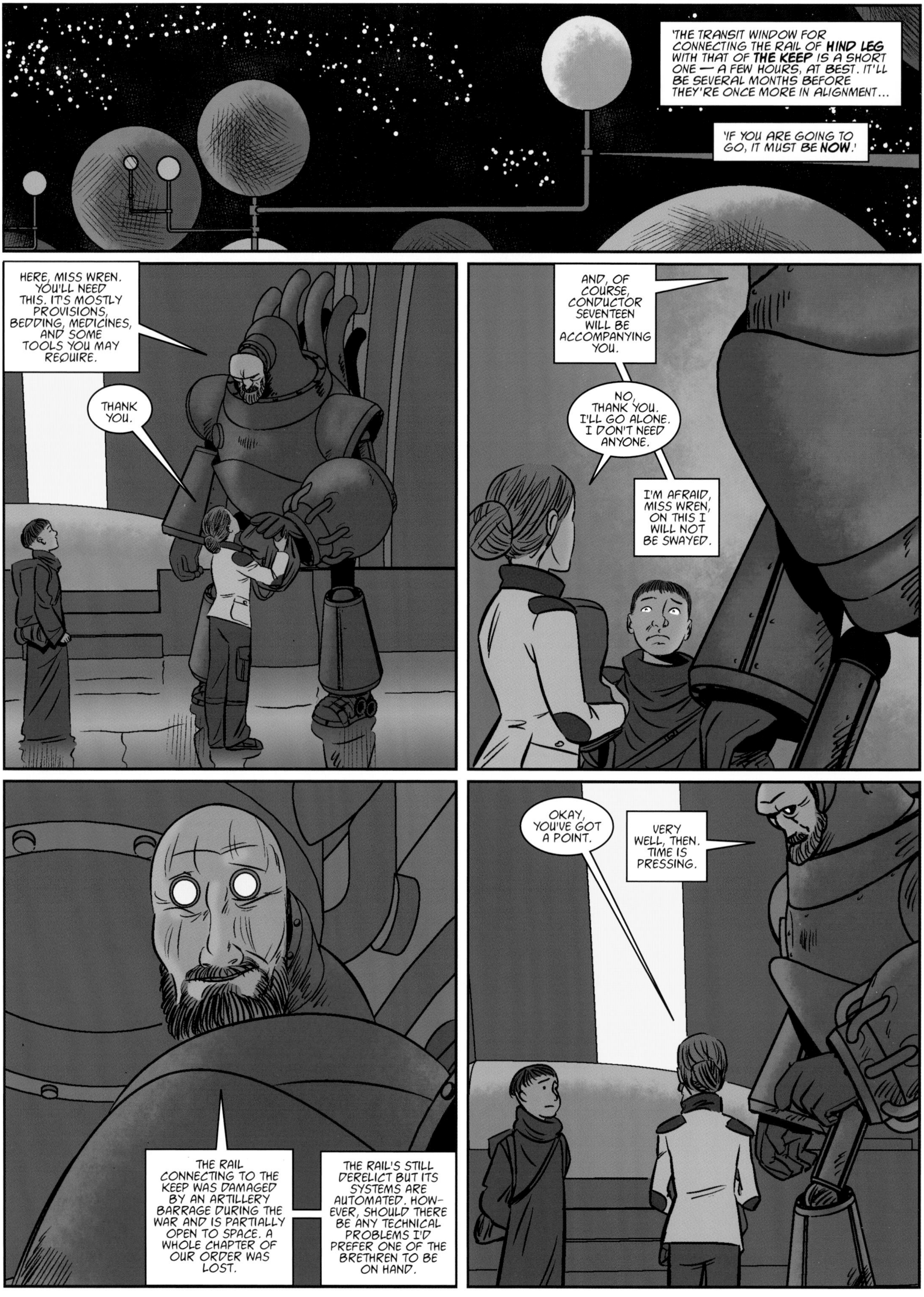
'THE TRANSIT WINDOW FOR CONNECTING THE RAIL OF **HIND LEG** WITH THAT OF **THE KEEP** IS A SHORT ONE — A FEW HOURS, AT BEST. IT'LL BE SEVERAL MONTHS BEFORE THEY'RE ONCE MORE IN ALIGNMENT...
'IF YOU ARE GOING TO GO, IT MUST BE **NOW**.'
HERE, MISS WREN. YOU'LL NEED THIS. IT'S MOSTLY PROVISIONS, BEDDING, MEDICINES, AND SOME TOOLS YOU MAY REQUIRE.
THANK YOU.
AND, OF COURSE, CONDUCTOR SEVENTEEN WILL BE ACCOMPANYING YOU.
NO, THANK YOU. I'LL GO ALONE. I DON'T NEED ANYONE.
I'M AFRAID, MISS WREN, ON THIS I WILL NOT BE SWAYED.
THE RAIL CONNECTING TO THE KEEP WAS DAMAGED BY AN ARTILLERY BARRAGE DURING THE WAR AND IS PARTIALLY OPEN TO SPACE. A WHOLE CHAPTER OF OUR ORDER WAS LOST.
THE RAIL'S STILL DERELICT BUT ITS SYSTEMS ARE AUTOMATED. HOWEVER, SHOULD THERE BE ANY TECHNICAL PROBLEMS I'D PREFER ONE OF THE BRETHREN TO BE ON HAND.
OKAY, YOU'VE GOT A POINT.
VERY WELL, THEN. TIME IS PRESSING.

THIS LOOKS... COSY.

IT'S A **MAINTENANCE BUG**. THE MAIN SHAFT IS TOO BADLY DAMAGED BUT THE ANCILLARY LINES ARE STILL CLEAR... OR THEY WERE.

IT'S BEEN TWO HUNDRED YEARS SINCE THIS WAS USED.

BUT IT WORKS?

OH, IT'S SOUND ENOUGH. IT'S JUST THAT THE LAST PEOPLE WHO USED IT NEVER RETURNED.

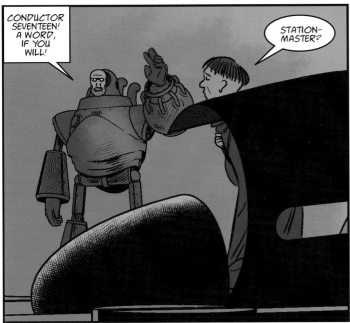

CONDUCTOR SEVENTEEN! A WORD, IF YOU WILL!

STATION-MASTER?

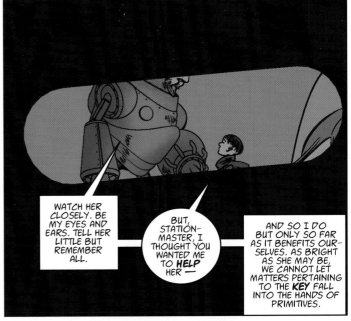

WATCH HER CLOSELY. BE MY EYES AND EARS. TELL HER LITTLE BUT REMEMBER ALL.

BUT, STATION-MASTER, I THOUGHT YOU WANTED ME TO **HELP** HER —

AND SO I DO BUT ONLY SO FAR AS IT BENEFITS OUR-SELVES. AS BRIGHT AS SHE MAY BE, WE CANNOT LET MATTERS PERTAINING TO THE **KEY** FALL INTO THE HANDS OF PRIMITIVES.

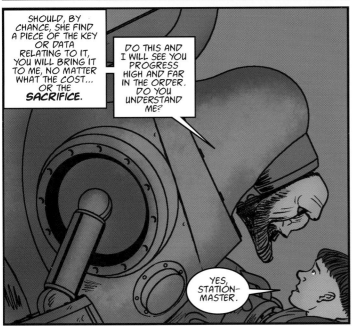

SHOULD, BY CHANCE, SHE FIND A PIECE OF THE KEY OR DATA RELATING TO IT, YOU WILL BRING IT TO ME, NO MATTER WHAT THE COST... OR THE **SACRIFICE**.

DO THIS AND I WILL SEE YOU PROGRESS HIGH AND FAR IN THE ORDER. DO YOU UNDERSTAND ME?

YES, STATION-MASTER.

GOOD LAD. NOW, BEST BE GONE. TICK-TOCK.

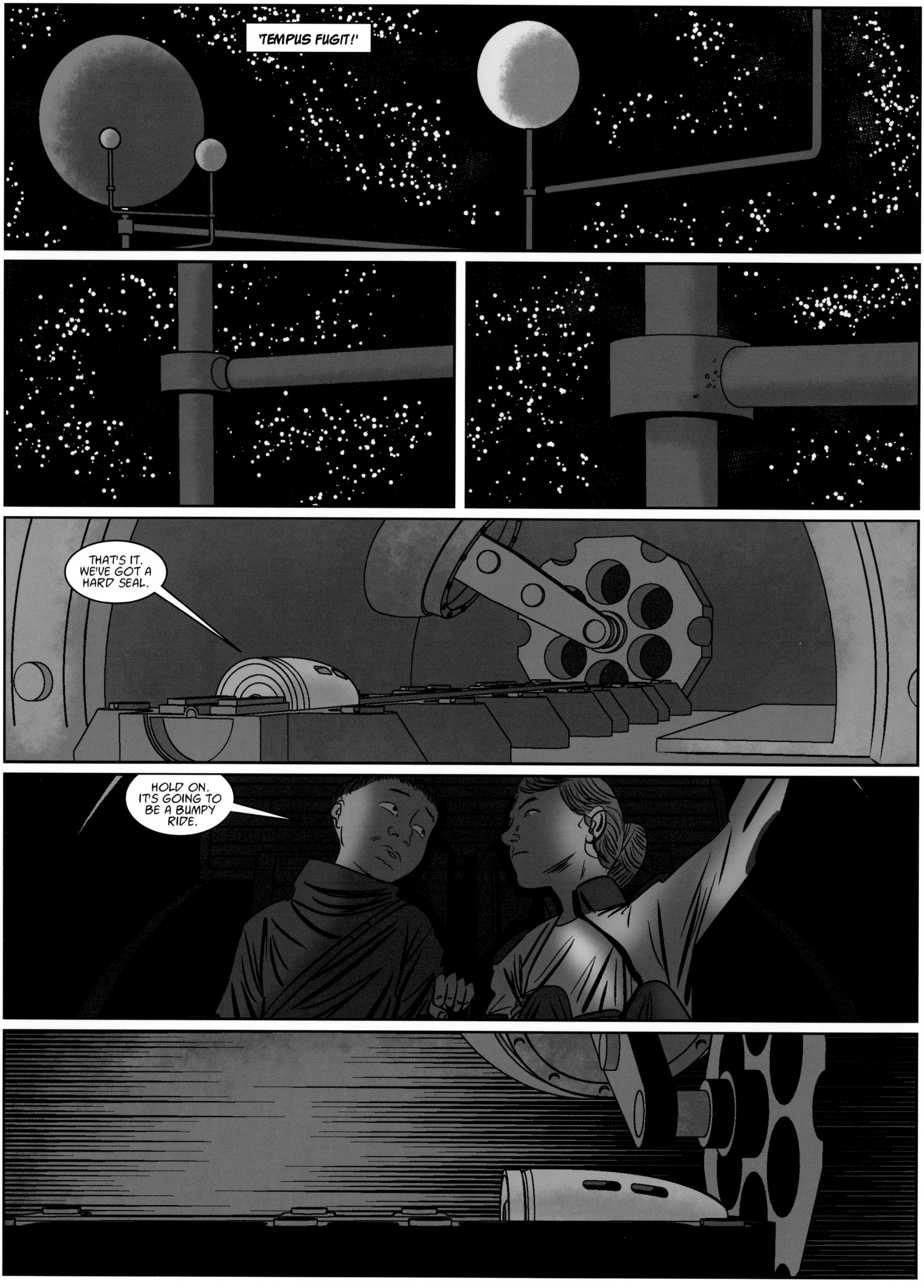
'TEMPUS FUGIT!'
THAT'S IT. WE'VE GOT A HARD SEAL.
HOLD ON. IT'S GOING TO BE A BUMPY RIDE.

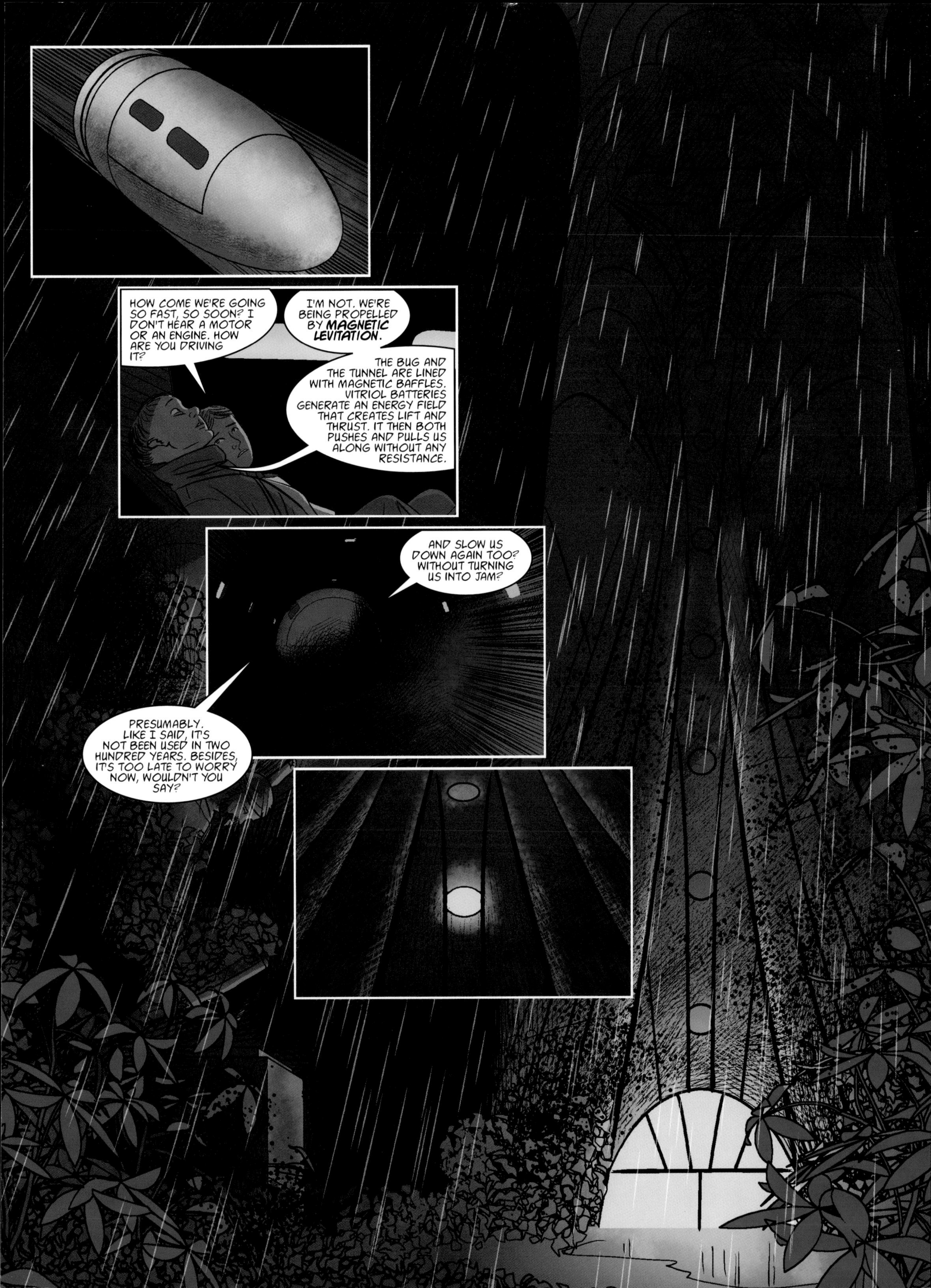
HOW COME WE'RE GOING SO FAST, SO SOON? I DON'T HEAR A MOTOR OR AN ENGINE. HOW ARE YOU DRIVING IT?
I'M NOT. WE'RE BEING PROPELLED BY **MAGNETIC LEVITATION**.
THE BUG AND THE TUNNEL ARE LINED WITH MAGNETIC BAFFLES. VITRIOL BATTERIES GENERATE AN ENERGY FIELD THAT CREATES LIFT AND THRUST. IT THEN BOTH PUSHES AND PULLS US ALONG WITHOUT ANY RESISTANCE.
AND SLOW US DOWN AGAIN TOO? WITHOUT TURNING US INTO JAM?
PRESUMABLY. LIKE I SAID, IT'S NOT BEEN USED IN TWO HUNDRED YEARS. BESIDES, IT'S TOO LATE TO WORRY NOW, WOULDN'T YOU SAY?

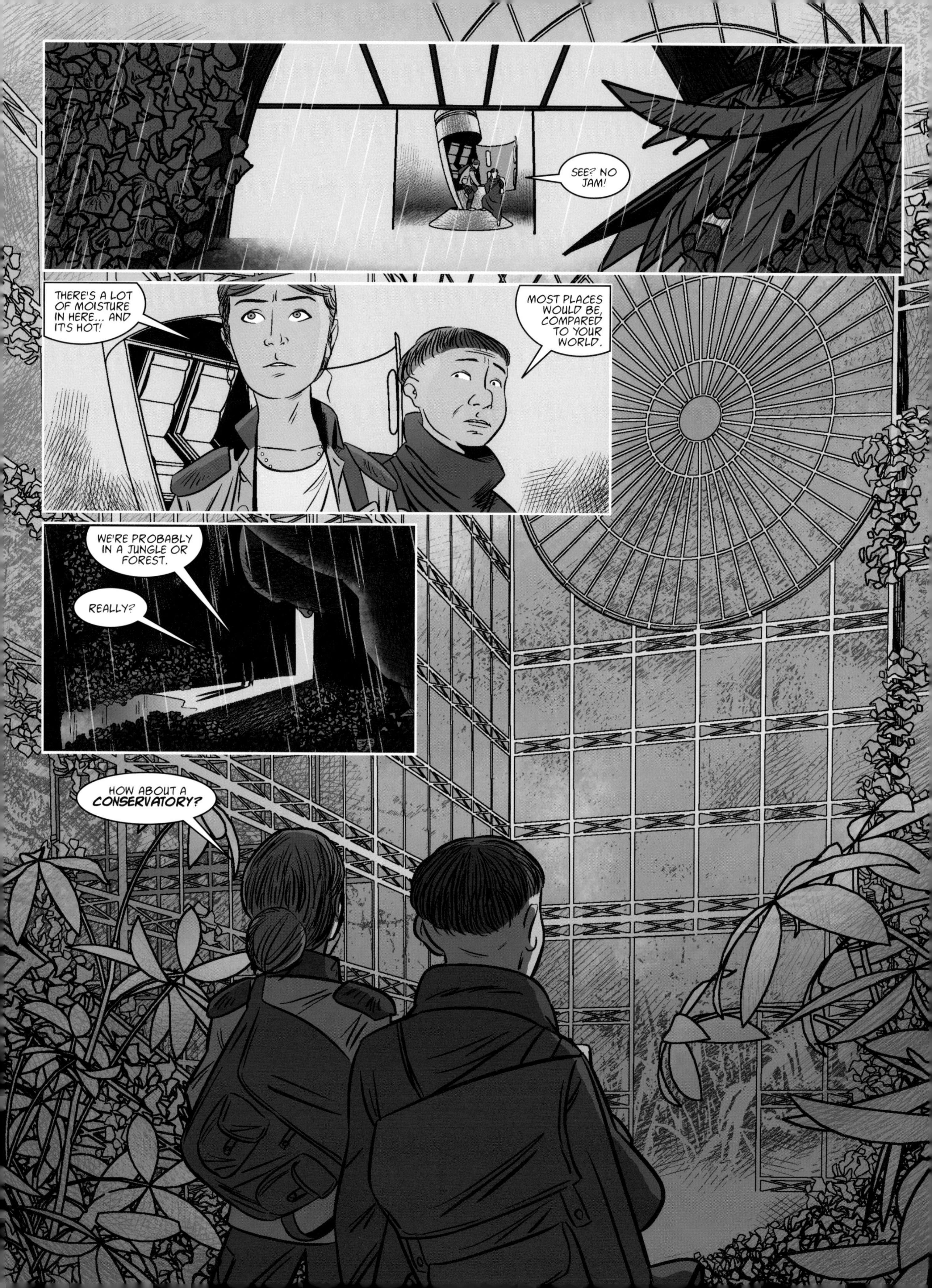
SEE? NO JAM!
THERE'S A LOT OF MOISTURE IN HERE... AND IT'S HOT!
MOST PLACES WOULD BE, COMPARED TO YOUR WORLD.
WE'RE PROBABLY IN A JUNGLE OR FOREST.
REALLY?
HOW ABOUT A CONSERVATORY?

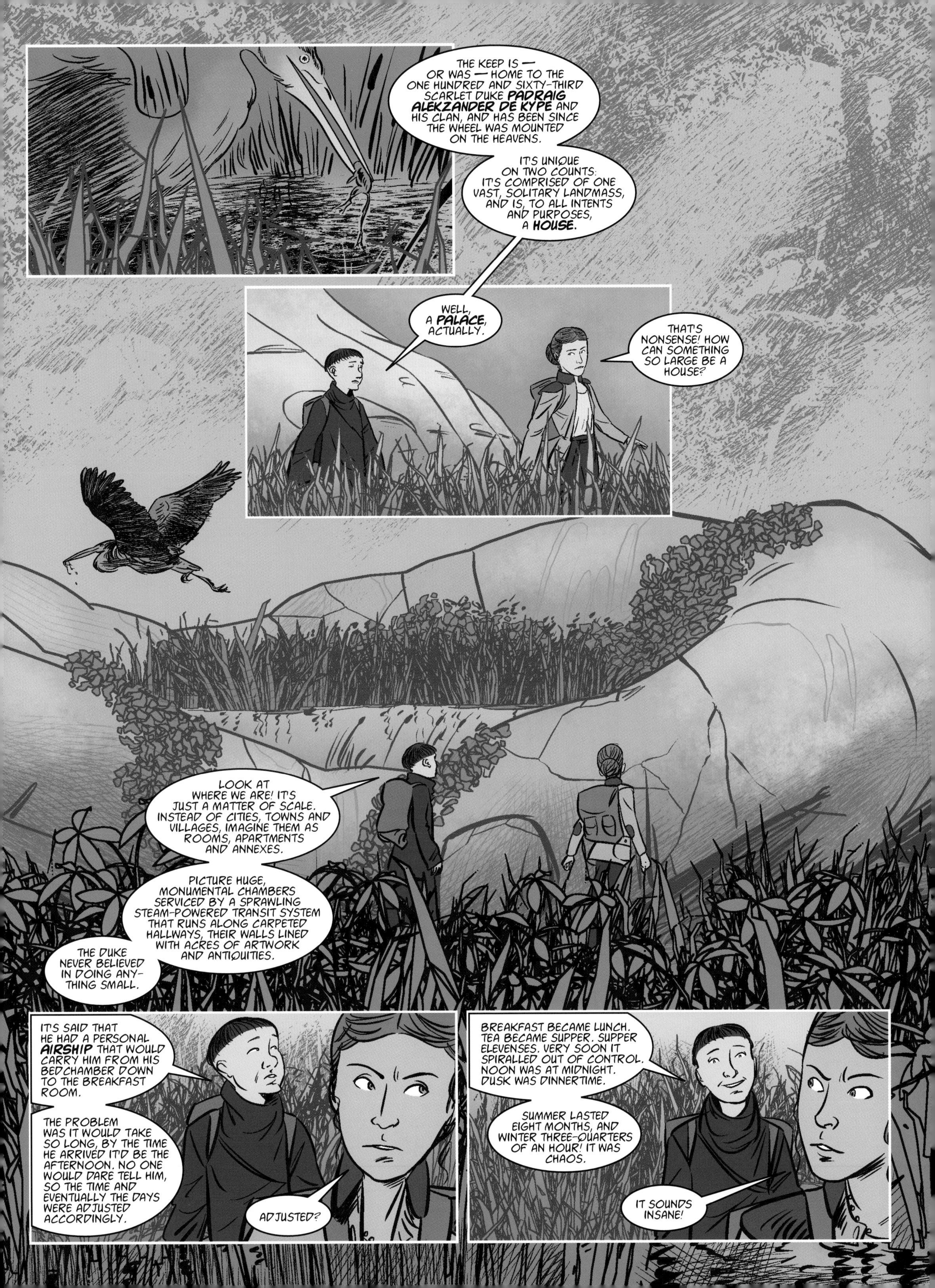
THE KEEP IS — OR WAS — HOME TO THE ONE HUNDRED AND SIXTY-THIRD SCARLET DUKE **PADRAIG ALEKZANDER DE KYPE** AND HIS CLAN, AND HAS BEEN SINCE THE WHEEL WAS MOUNTED ON THE HEAVENS.
IT'S UNIQUE ON TWO COUNTS: IT'S COMPRISED OF ONE VAST, SOLITARY LANDMASS, AND IS, TO ALL INTENTS AND PURPOSES, A **HOUSE.**
WELL, A **PALACE**, ACTUALLY.
THAT'S NONSENSE! HOW CAN SOMETHING SO LARGE BE A HOUSE?
LOOK AT WHERE WE ARE! IT'S JUST A MATTER OF SCALE. INSTEAD OF CITIES, TOWNS AND VILLAGES, IMAGINE THEM AS ROOMS, APARTMENTS AND ANNEXES.
PICTURE HUGE, MONUMENTAL CHAMBERS SERVICED BY A SPRAWLING STEAM-POWERED TRANSIT SYSTEM THAT RUNS ALONG CARPETED HALLWAYS, THEIR WALLS LINED WITH ACRES OF ARTWORK AND ANTIQUITIES.
THE DUKE NEVER BELIEVED IN DOING ANY-THING SMALL.
IT'S SAID THAT HE HAD A PERSONAL **AIRSHIP** THAT WOULD CARRY HIM FROM HIS BEDCHAMBER DOWN TO THE BREAKFAST ROOM.
THE PROBLEM WAS IT WOULD TAKE SO LONG, BY THE TIME HE ARRIVED IT'D BE THE AFTERNOON. NO ONE WOULD DARE TELL HIM, SO THE TIME AND EVENTUALLY THE DAYS WERE ADJUSTED ACCORDINGLY.
ADJUSTED?
BREAKFAST BECAME LUNCH. TEA BECAME SUPPER. SUPPER ELEVENSES. VERY SOON IT SPIRALLED OUT OF CONTROL. NOON WAS AT MIDNIGHT. DUSK WAS DINNERTIME.
SUMMER LASTED EIGHT MONTHS, AND WINTER THREE-QUARTERS OF AN HOUR! IT WAS CHAOS.
IT SOUNDS INSANE!

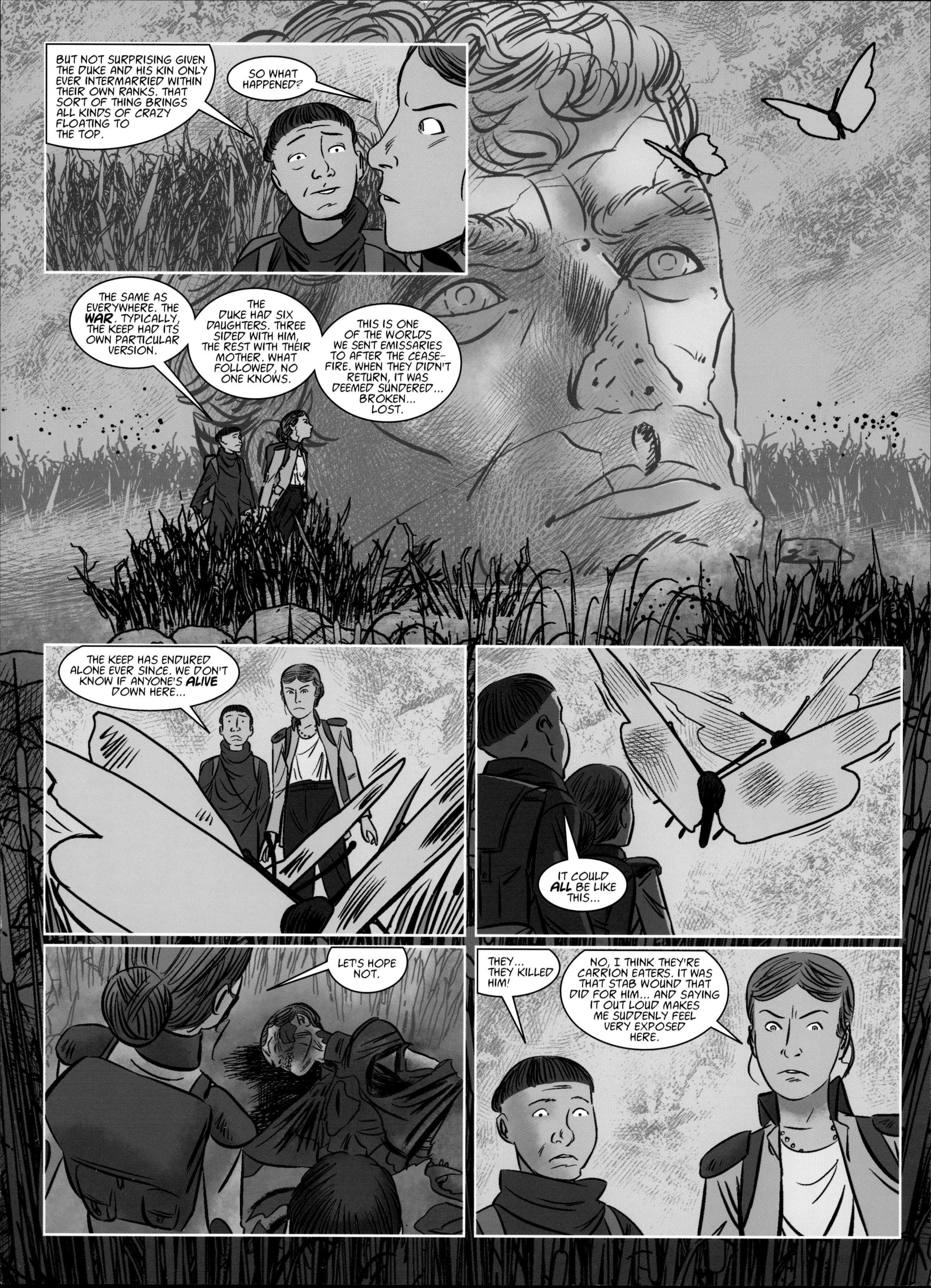
BUT NOT SURPRISING GIVEN THE DUKE AND HIS KIN ONLY EVER INTERMARRIED WITHIN THEIR OWN RANKS. THAT SORT OF THING BRINGS ALL KINDS OF CRAZY FLOATING TO THE TOP.
SO WHAT HAPPENED?
THE SAME AS EVERYWHERE. THE **WAR**. TYPICALLY, THE KEEP HAD ITS OWN PARTICULAR VERSION.
THE DUKE HAD SIX DAUGHTERS. THREE SIDED WITH HIM, THE REST WITH THEIR MOTHER. WHAT FOLLOWED, NO ONE KNOWS.
THIS IS ONE OF THE WORLDS WE SENT EMISSARIES TO AFTER THE CEASE-FIRE. WHEN THEY DIDN'T RETURN, IT WAS DEEMED SUNDERED... BROKEN... LOST.
THE KEEP HAS ENDURED ALONE EVER SINCE. WE DON'T KNOW IF ANYONE'S **ALIVE** DOWN HERE...
IT COULD **ALL** BE LIKE THIS...
LET'S HOPE NOT.
THEY... THEY KILLED HIM!
NO, I THINK THEY'RE CARRION EATERS. IT WAS THAT STAB WOUND THAT DID FOR HIM... AND SAYING IT OUT LOUD MAKES ME SUDDENLY FEEL VERY EXPOSED HERE.

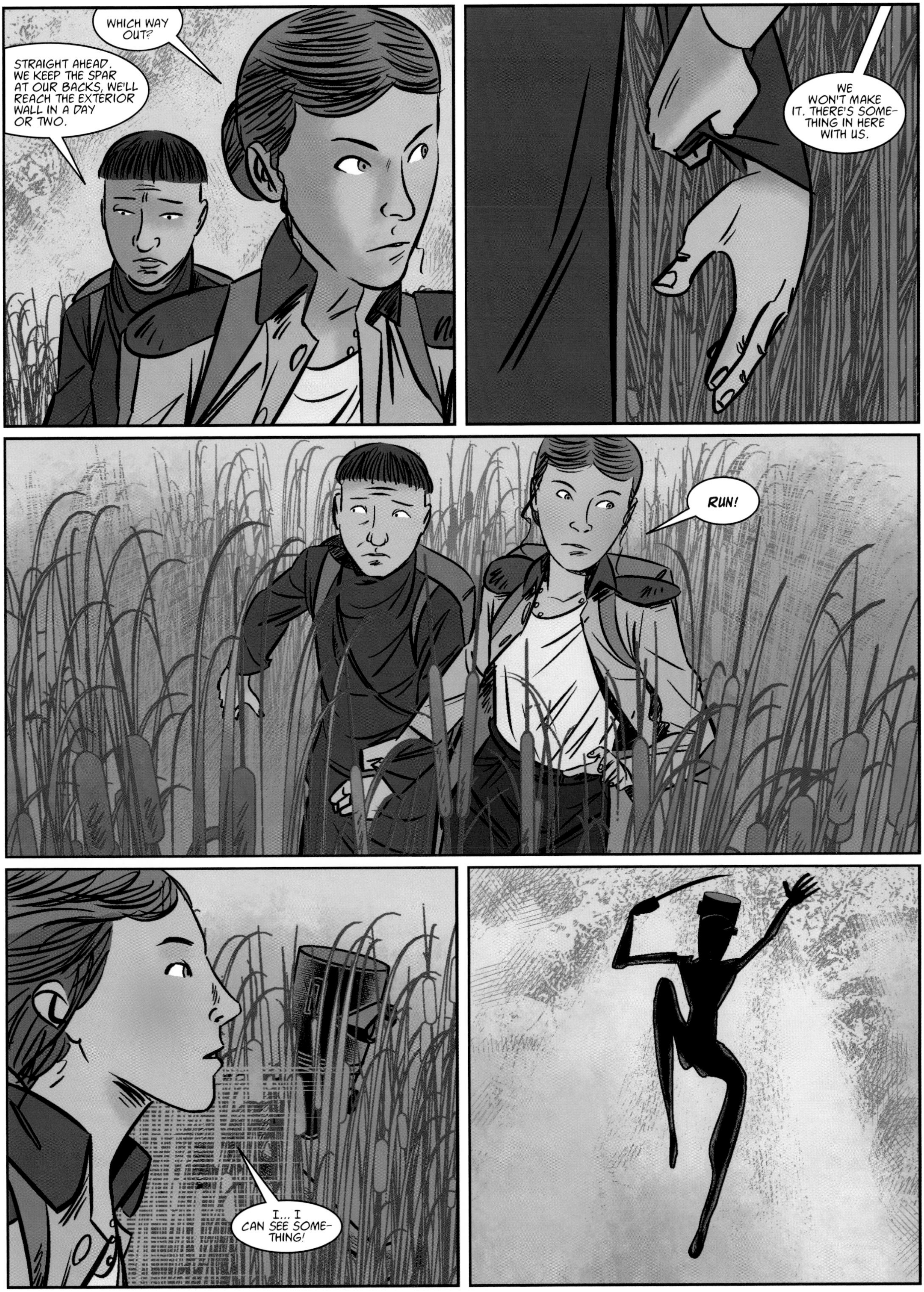
WHICH WAY OUT?
STRAIGHT AHEAD. WE KEEP THE SPAR AT OUR BACKS, WE'LL REACH THE EXTERIOR WALL IN A DAY OR TWO.
WE WON'T MAKE IT. THERE'S SOME-THING IN HERE WITH US.
RUN!
I... I CAN SEE SOME-THING!

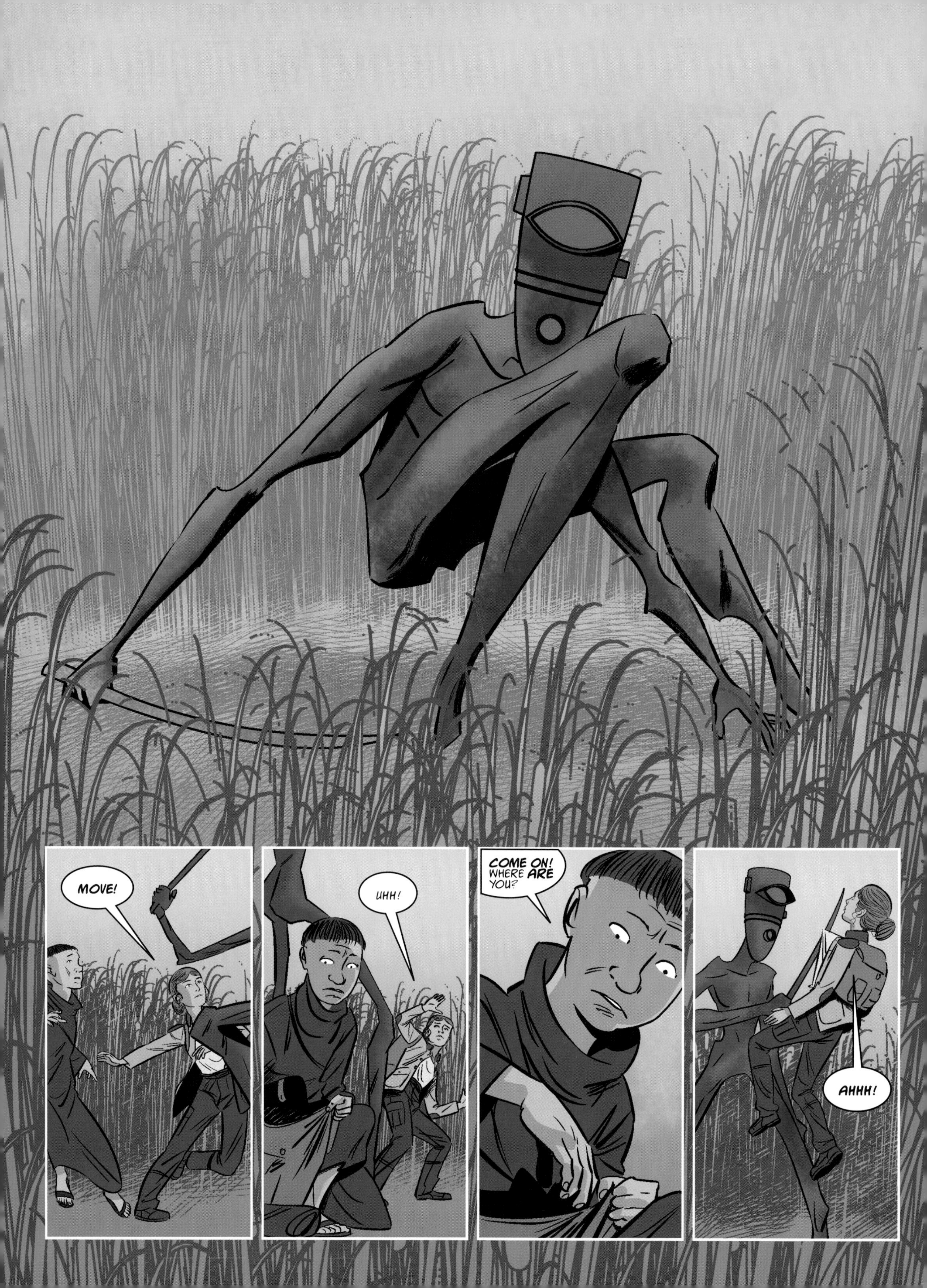
MOVE!
UHH!
COME ON! WHERE ARE YOU?
AHHH!

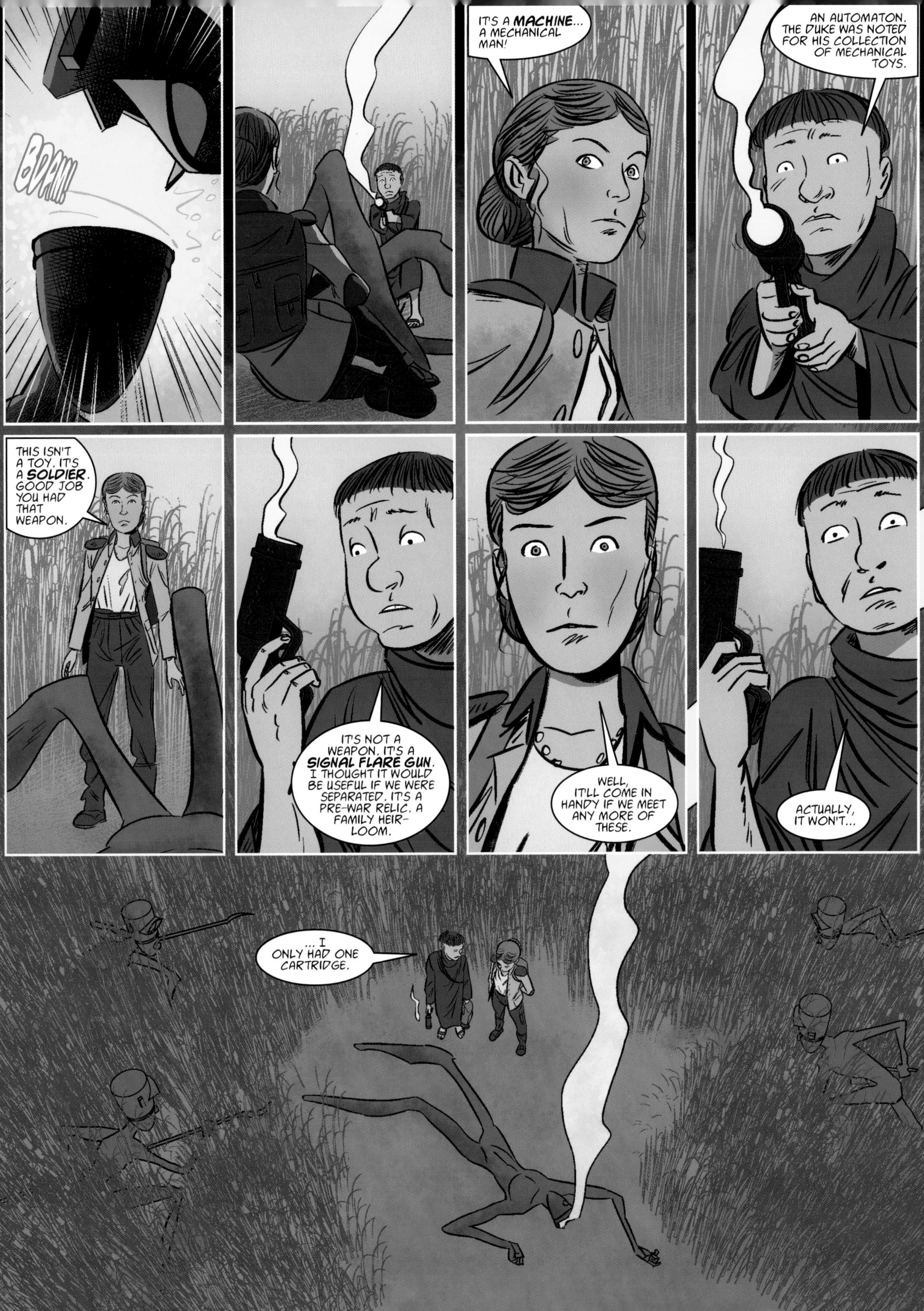
BDAM!
IT'S A MACHINE... A MECHANICAL MAN!
AN AUTOMATON. THE DUKE WAS NOTED FOR HIS COLLECTION OF MECHANICAL TOYS.
THIS ISN'T A TOY. IT'S A SOLDIER. GOOD JOB YOU HAD THAT WEAPON.
IT'S NOT A WEAPON. IT'S A SIGNAL FLARE GUN. I THOUGHT IT WOULD BE USEFUL IF WE WERE SEPARATED. IT'S A PRE-WAR RELIC. A FAMILY HEIR-LOOM.
WELL, IT'LL COME IN HANDY IF WE MEET ANY MORE OF THESE.
ACTUALLY, IT WON'T...
... I ONLY HAD ONE CARTRIDGE.

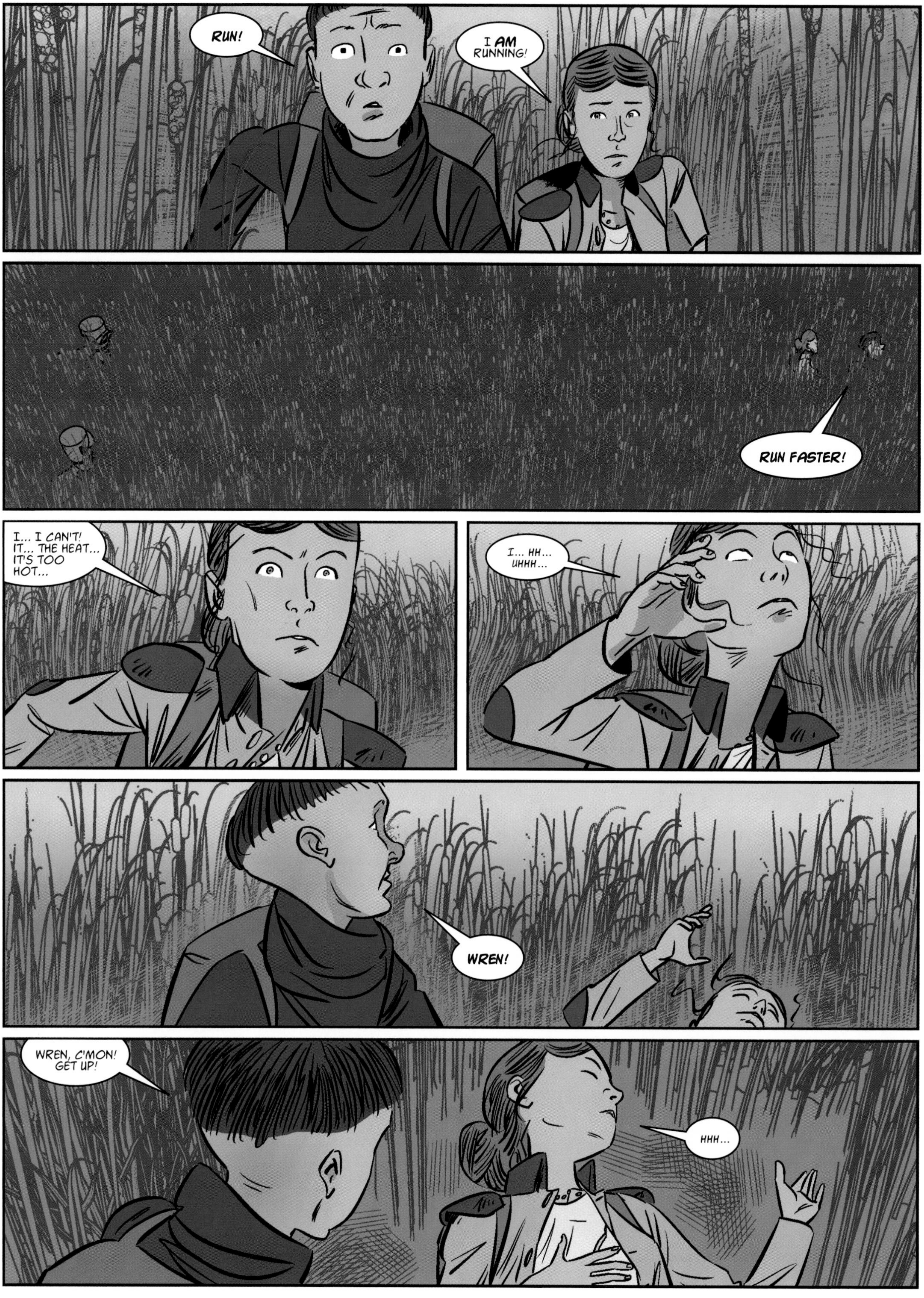
RUN!
I AM RUNNING!
RUN FASTER!
I... I CAN'T! IT... THE HEAT... IT'S TOO HOT...
I... HH... UHHH...
WREN!
WREN, C'MON! GET UP!
HHH...

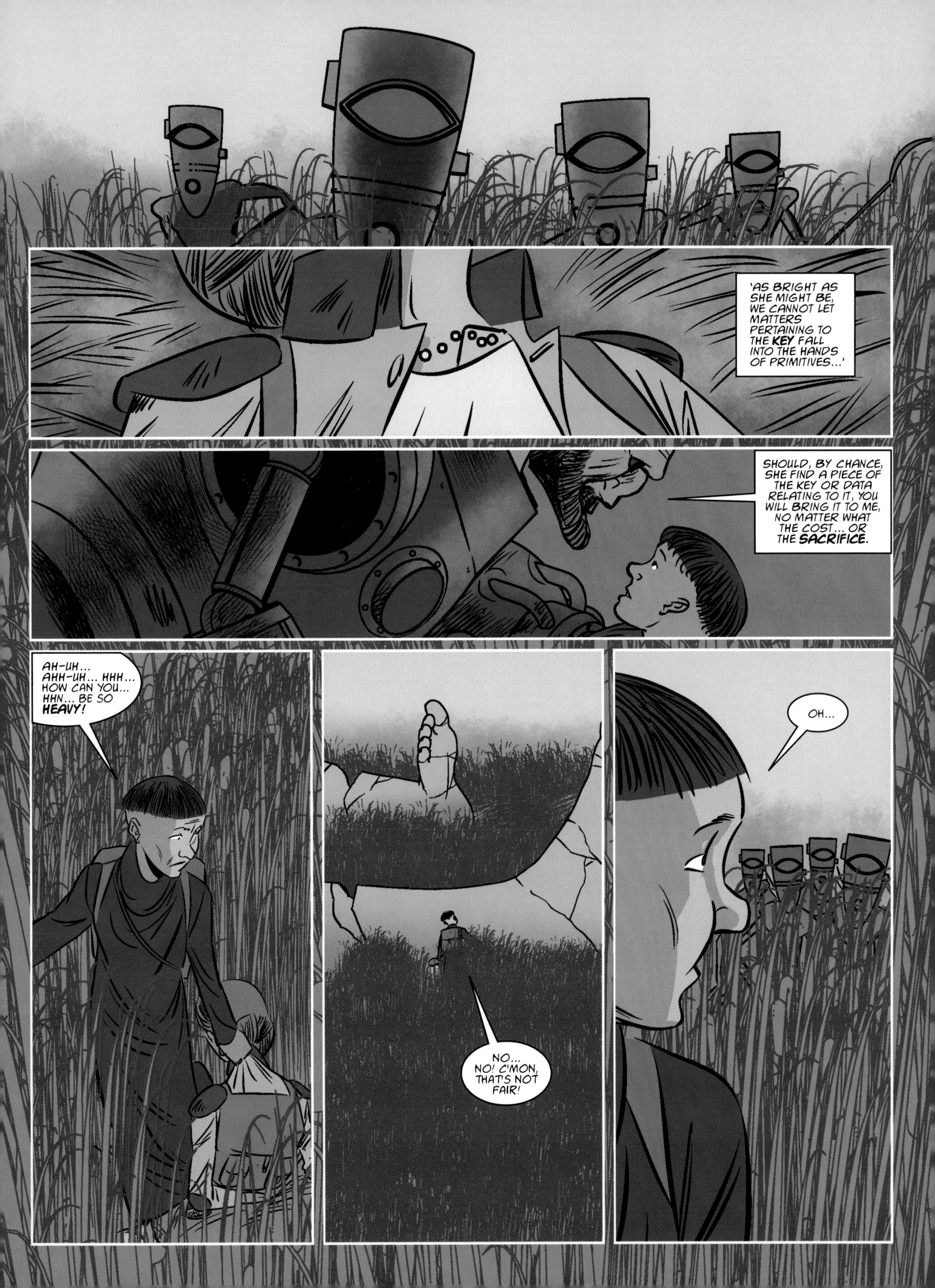
'AS BRIGHT AS SHE MIGHT BE, WE CANNOT LET MATTERS PERTAINING TO THE **KEY** FALL INTO THE HANDS OF PRIMITIVES...'
SHOULD, BY CHANCE, SHE FIND A PIECE OF THE KEY OR DATA RELATING TO IT, YOU WILL BRING IT TO ME, NO MATTER WHAT THE COST... OR THE **SACRIFICE**.
AH-UH... AHH-UH... HHH... HOW CAN YOU... HHN... BE SO **HEAVY**!
NO... NO! C'MON, THAT'S NOT FAIR!
OH...

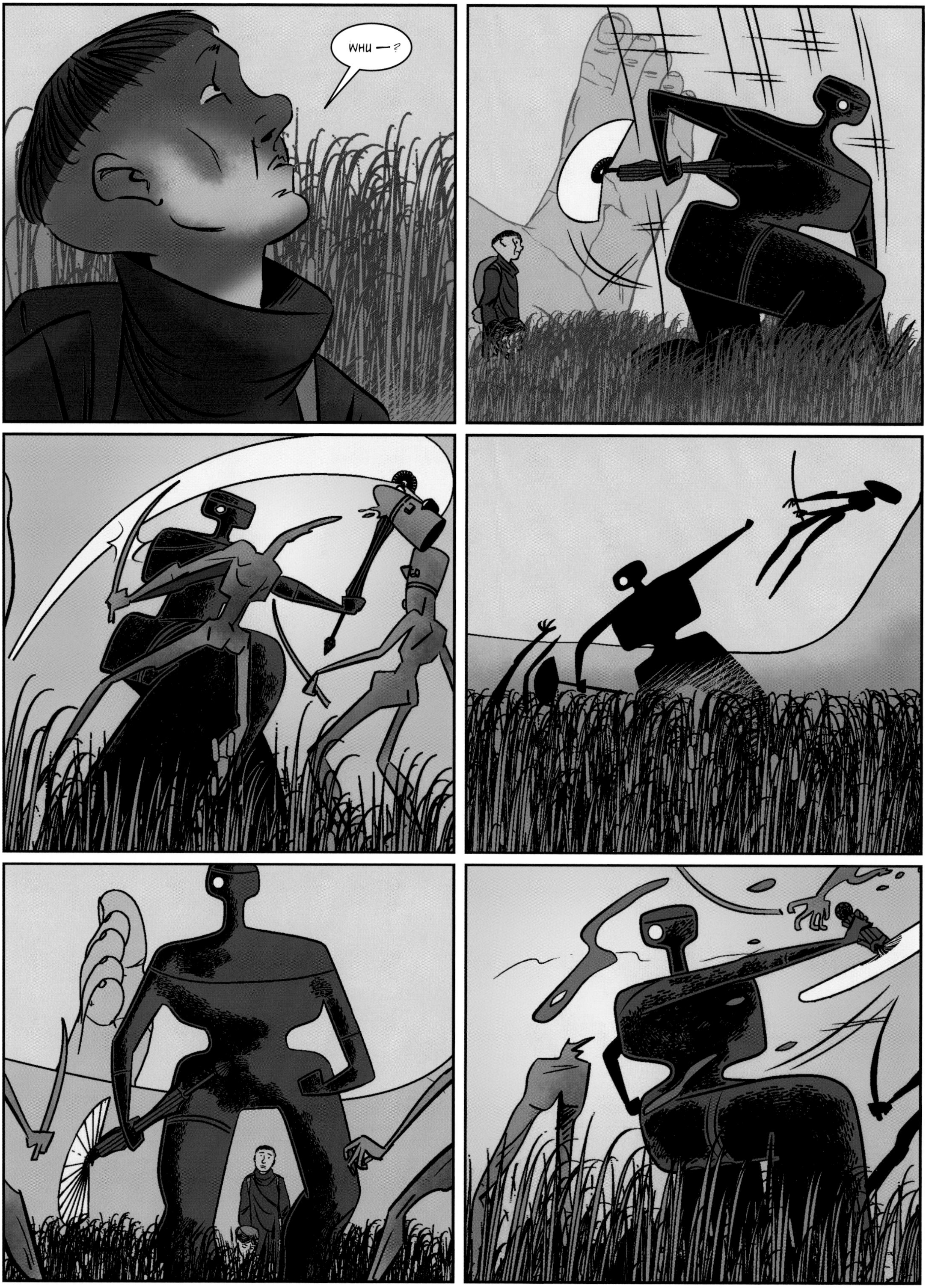
WHU —?

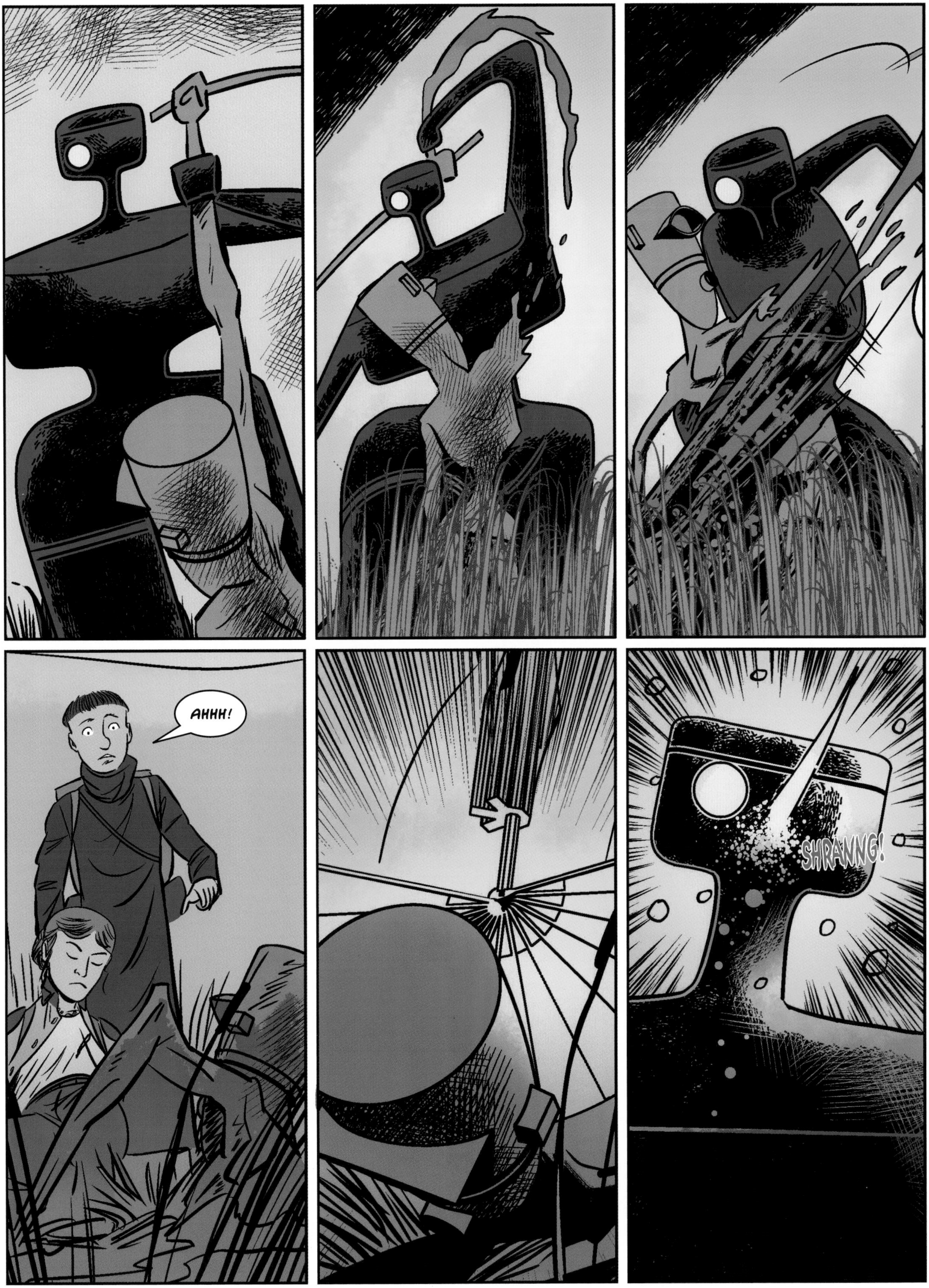
AHHH!
SHRANNG!

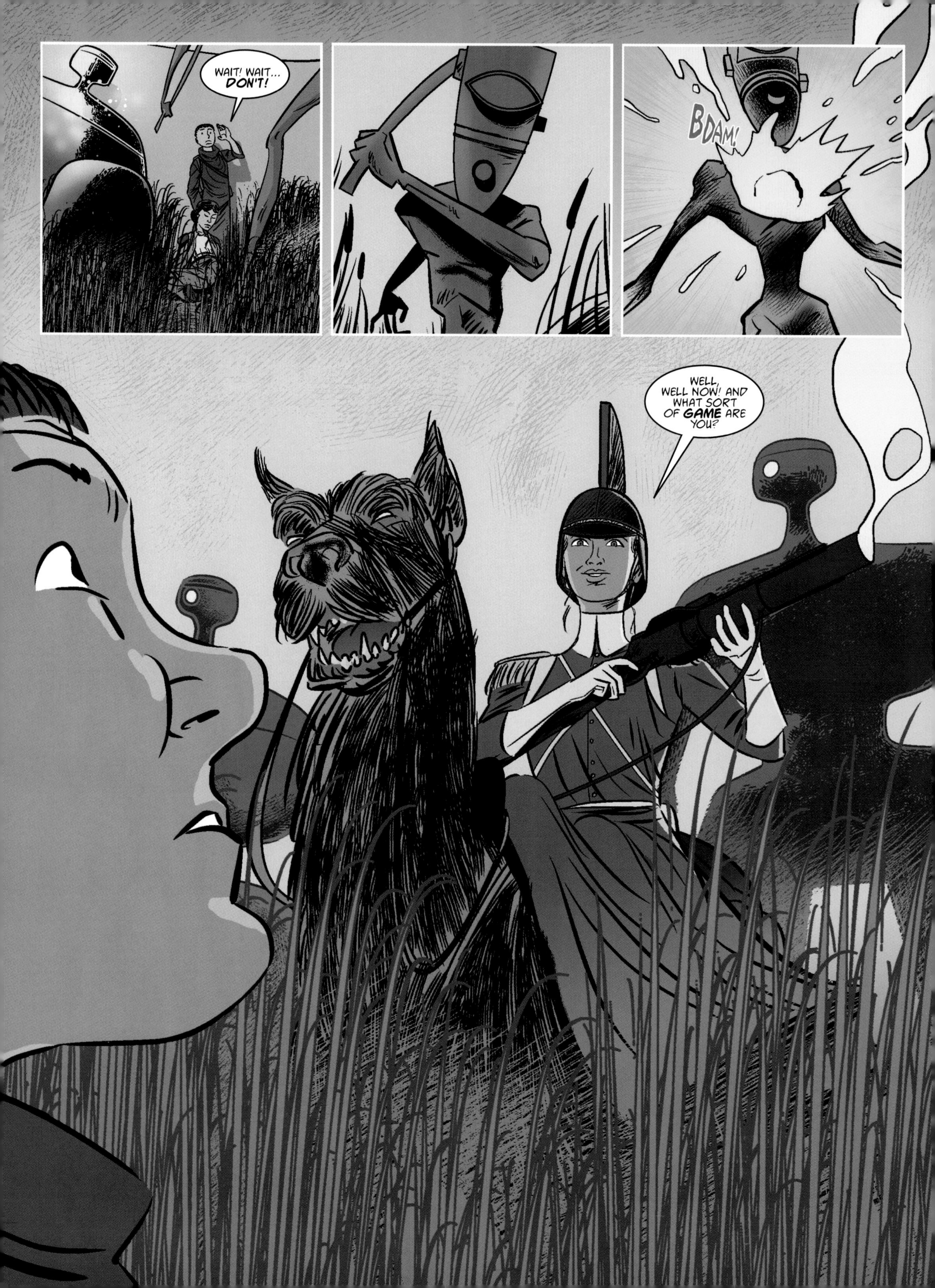
WAIT! WAIT... DON'T!
BDAM!
WELL, WELL NOW! AND WHAT SORT OF GAME ARE YOU?

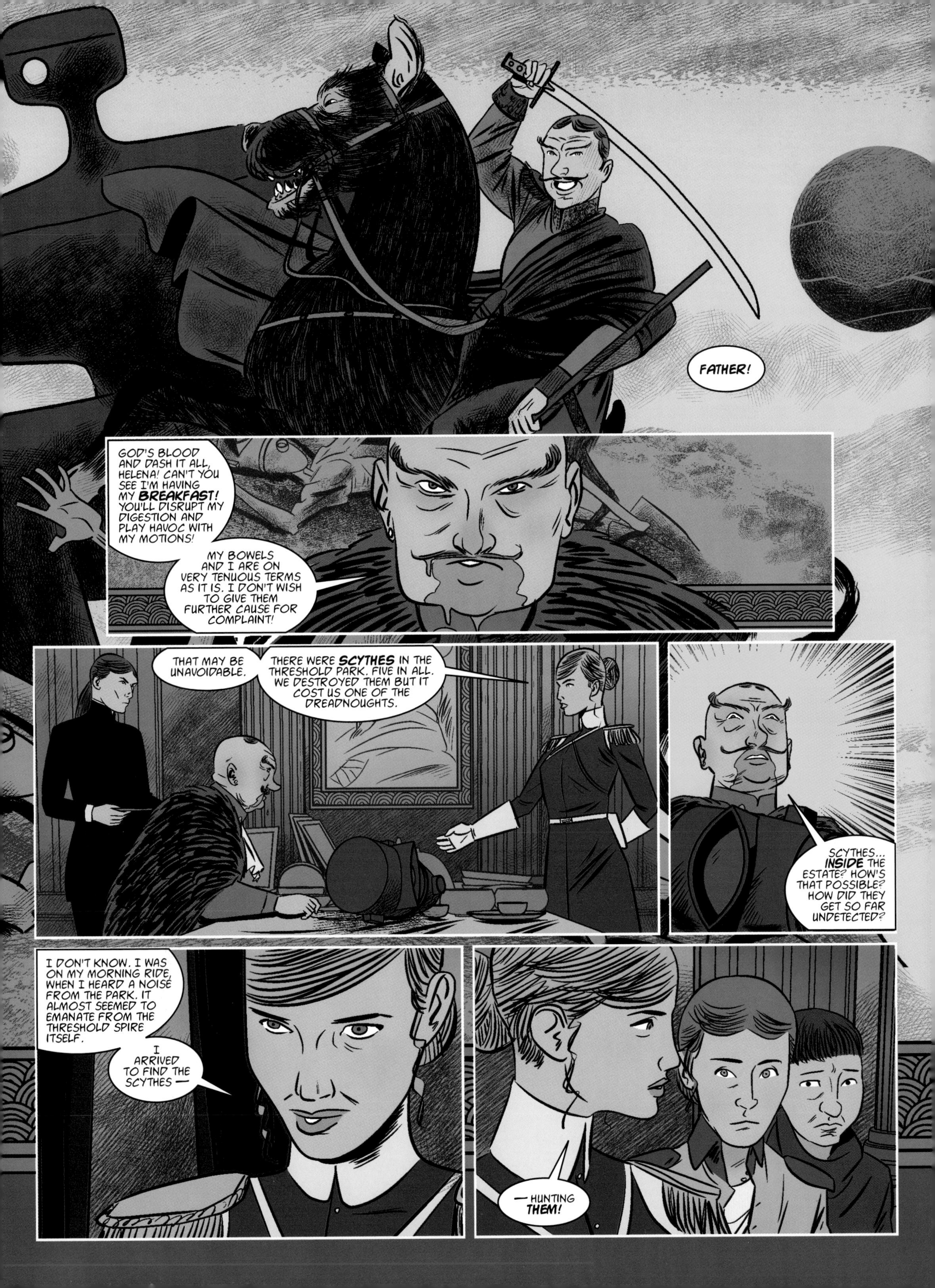

FATHER!
GOD'S BLOOD AND DASH IT ALL, HELENA! CAN'T YOU SEE I'M HAVING MY BREAKFAST! YOU'LL DISRUPT MY DIGESTION AND PLAY HAVOC WITH MY MOTIONS!
MY BOWELS AND I ARE ON VERY TENUOUS TERMS AS IT IS. I DON'T WISH TO GIVE THEM FURTHER CAUSE FOR COMPLAINT!
THAT MAY BE UNAVOIDABLE.
THERE WERE SCYTHES IN THE THRESHOLD PARK. FIVE IN ALL. WE DESTROYED THEM BUT IT COST US ONE OF THE DREADNOUGHTS.
SCYTHES... INSIDE THE ESTATE? HOW'S THAT POSSIBLE? HOW DID THEY GET SO FAR UNDETECTED?
I DON'T KNOW. I WAS ON MY MORNING RIDE, WHEN I HEARD A NOISE FROM THE PARK. IT ALMOST SEEMED TO EMANATE FROM THE THRESHOLD SPIRE ITSELF.
I ARRIVED TO FIND THE SCYTHES —
— HUNTING THEM!

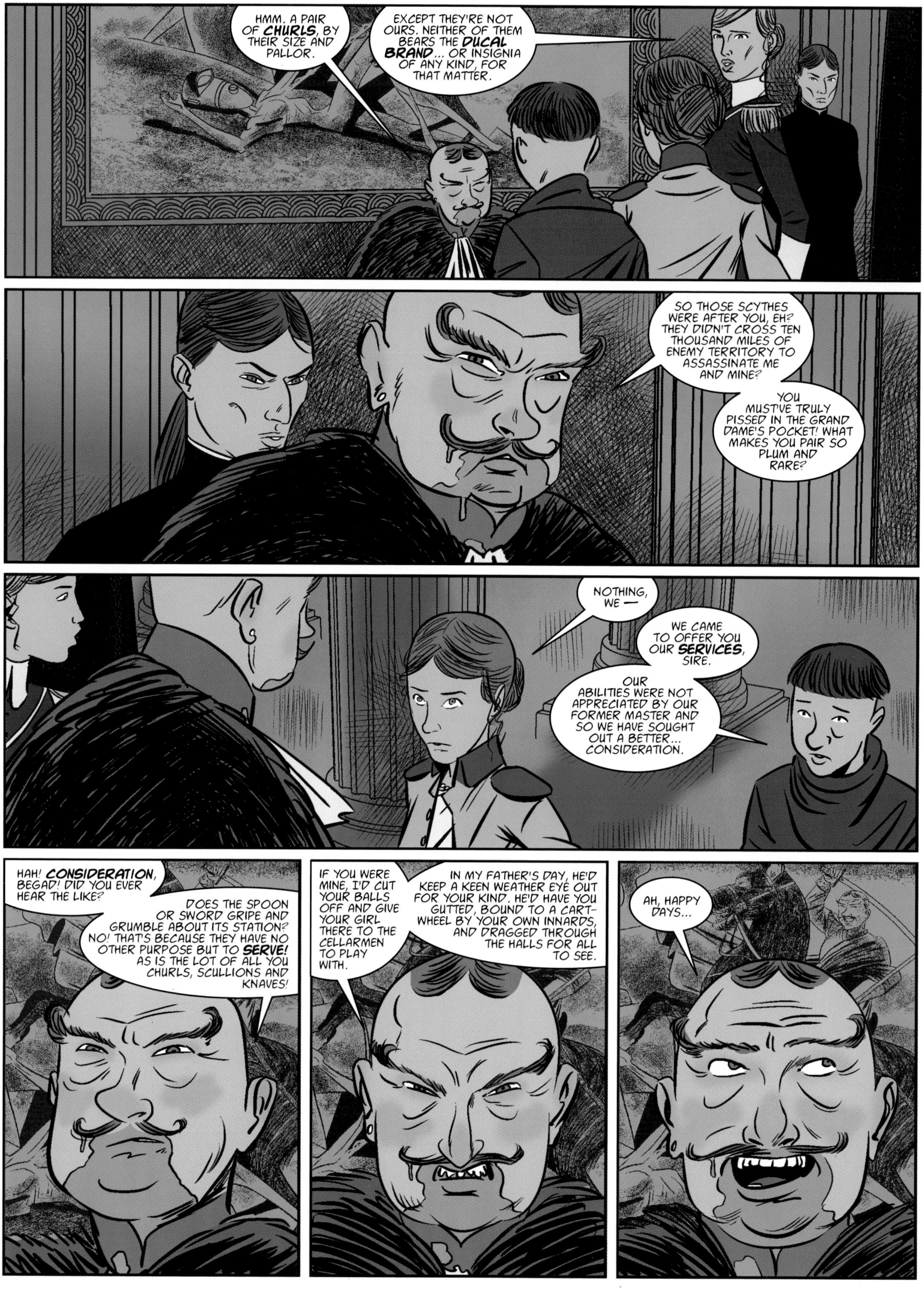
HMM. A PAIR OF CHURLS, BY THEIR SIZE AND PALLOR.
EXCEPT THEY'RE NOT OURS. NEITHER OF THEM BEARS THE DUCAL BRAND... OR INSIGNIA OF ANY KIND, FOR THAT MATTER.
SO THOSE SCYTHES WERE AFTER YOU, EH? THEY DIDN'T CROSS TEN THOUSAND MILES OF ENEMY TERRITORY TO ASSASSINATE ME AND MINE?
YOU MUST'VE TRULY PISSED IN THE GRAND DAME'S POCKET! WHAT MAKES YOU PAIR SO PLUM AND RARE?
NOTHING, WE —
WE CAME TO OFFER YOU OUR SERVICES, SIRE.
OUR ABILITIES WERE NOT APPRECIATED BY OUR FORMER MASTER AND SO WE HAVE SOUGHT OUT A BETTER... CONSIDERATION.
HAH! CONSIDERATION, BEGAD! DID YOU EVER HEAR THE LIKE?
DOES THE SPOON OR SWORD GRIPE AND GRUMBLE ABOUT ITS STATION? NO! THAT'S BECAUSE THEY HAVE NO OTHER PURPOSE BUT TO SERVE! AS IS THE LOT OF ALL YOU CHURLS, SCULLIONS AND KNAVES!
IF YOU WERE MINE, I'D CUT YOUR BALLS OFF AND GIVE YOUR GIRL THERE TO THE CELLARMEN TO PLAY WITH.
IN MY FATHER'S DAY, HE'D KEEP A KEEN WEATHER EYE OUT FOR YOUR KIND. HE'D HAVE YOU GUTTED, BOUND TO A CART-WHEEL BY YOUR OWN INNARDS, AND DRAGGED THROUGH THE HALLS FOR ALL TO SEE.
AH, HAPPY DAYS...

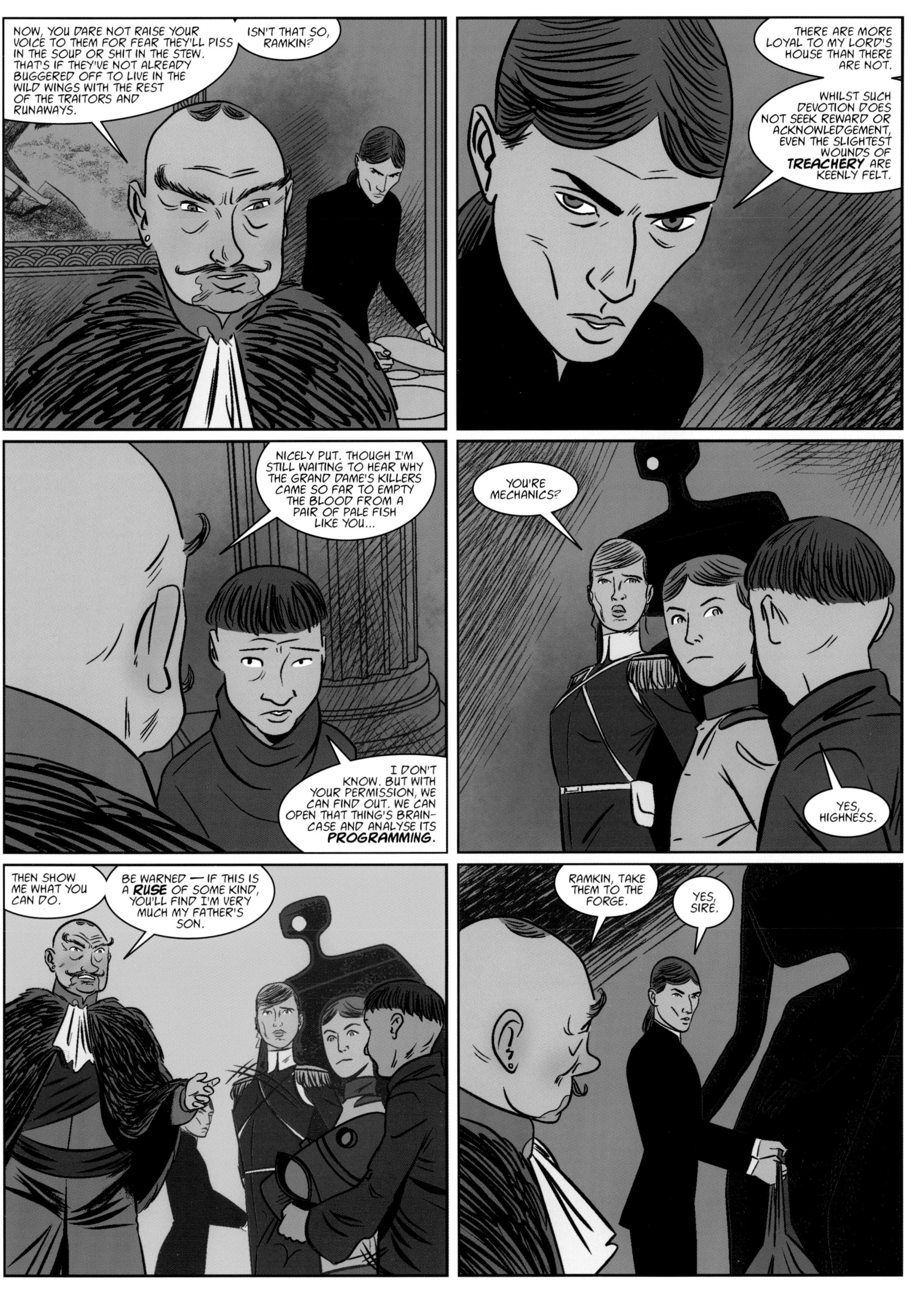
NOW, YOU DARE NOT RAISE YOUR VOICE TO THEM FOR FEAR THEY'LL PISS IN THE SOUP OR SHIT IN THE STEW. THAT'S IF THEY'VE NOT ALREADY BUGGERED OFF TO LIVE IN THE WILD WINGS WITH THE REST OF THE TRAITORS AND RUNAWAYS.
ISN'T THAT SO, RAMKIN?
THERE ARE MORE LOYAL TO MY LORD'S HOUSE THAN THERE ARE NOT.
WHILST SUCH DEVOTION DOES NOT SEEK REWARD OR ACKNOWLEDGEMENT, EVEN THE SLIGHTEST WOUNDS OF TREACHERY ARE KEENLY FELT.
NICELY PUT. THOUGH I'M STILL WAITING TO HEAR WHY THE GRAND DAME'S KILLERS CAME SO FAR TO EMPTY THE BLOOD FROM A PAIR OF PALE FISH LIKE YOU...
I DON'T KNOW. BUT WITH YOUR PERMISSION, WE CAN FIND OUT. WE CAN OPEN THAT THING'S BRAIN-CASE AND ANALYSE ITS PROGRAMMING.
YOU'RE MECHANICS?
YES, HIGHNESS.
THEN SHOW ME WHAT YOU CAN DO.
BE WARNED — IF THIS IS A RUSE OF SOME KIND, YOU'LL FIND I'M VERY MUCH MY FATHER'S SON.
RAMKIN, TAKE THEM TO THE FORGE.
YES, SIRE.

FOLLOW ME.

FATHER? WHAT IS IT?

BE ON YOUR GUARD, MY GIRL. MUCH OF THIS DOES NOT SIT RIGHT WITH ME. THERE ARE ANGLES AS YET UNCOVERED. THE SCYTHES MAY BE SCRAP...

'...BUT I FEAR THERE ARE WOLVES IN THE FOLD.'

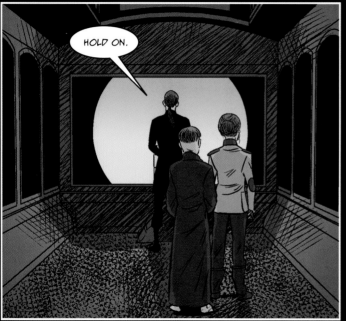

HOLD ON.

UH...

OH... LOOK AT THAT!

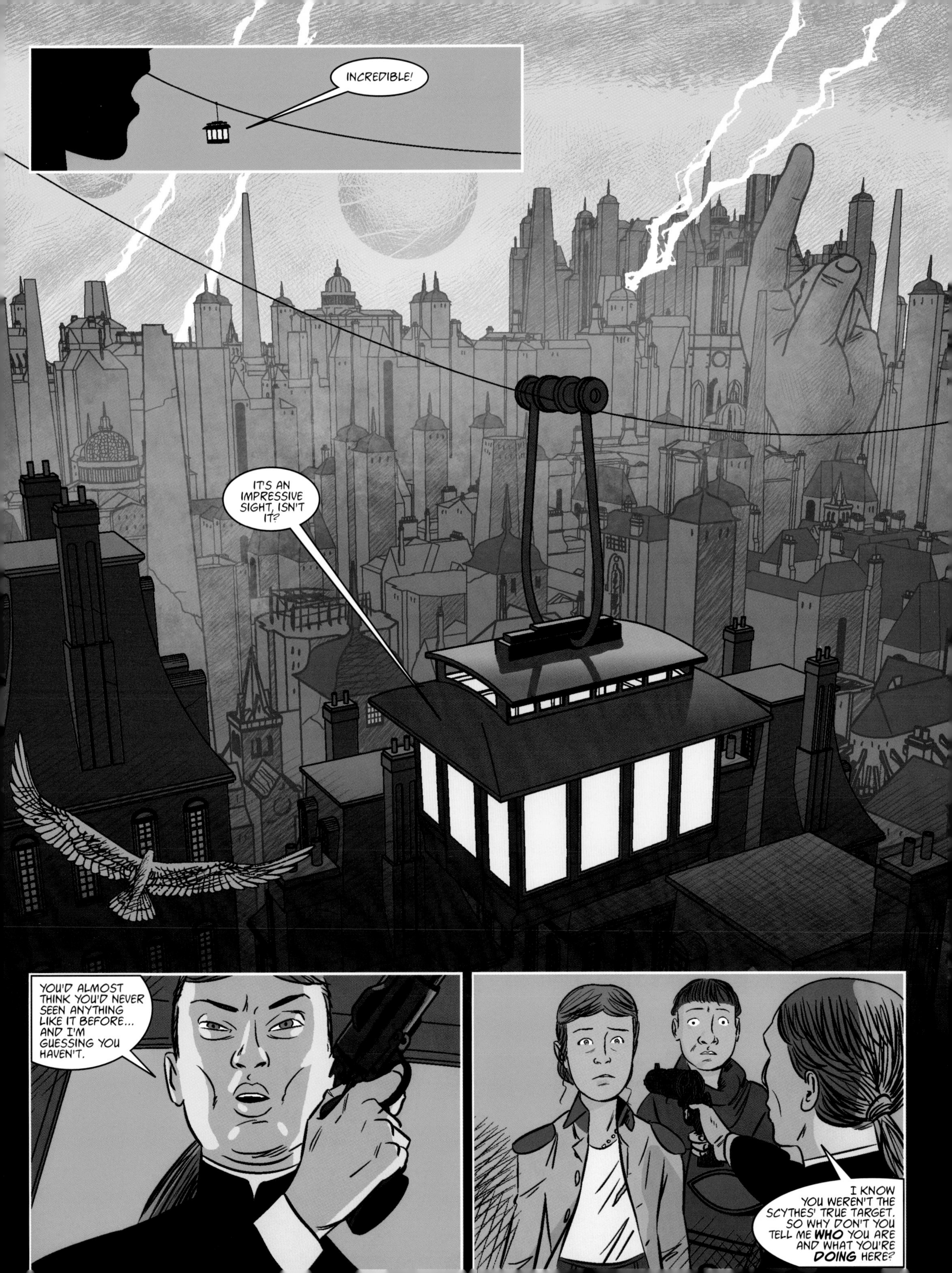
INCREDIBLE!
IT'S AN IMPRESSIVE SIGHT, ISN'T IT?
YOU'D ALMOST THINK YOU'D NEVER SEEN ANYTHING LIKE IT BEFORE... AND I'M GUESSING YOU HAVEN'T.
I KNOW YOU WEREN'T THE SCYTHES' TRUE TARGET. SO WHY DON'T YOU TELL ME **WHO** YOU ARE AND WHAT YOU'RE **DOING** HERE?

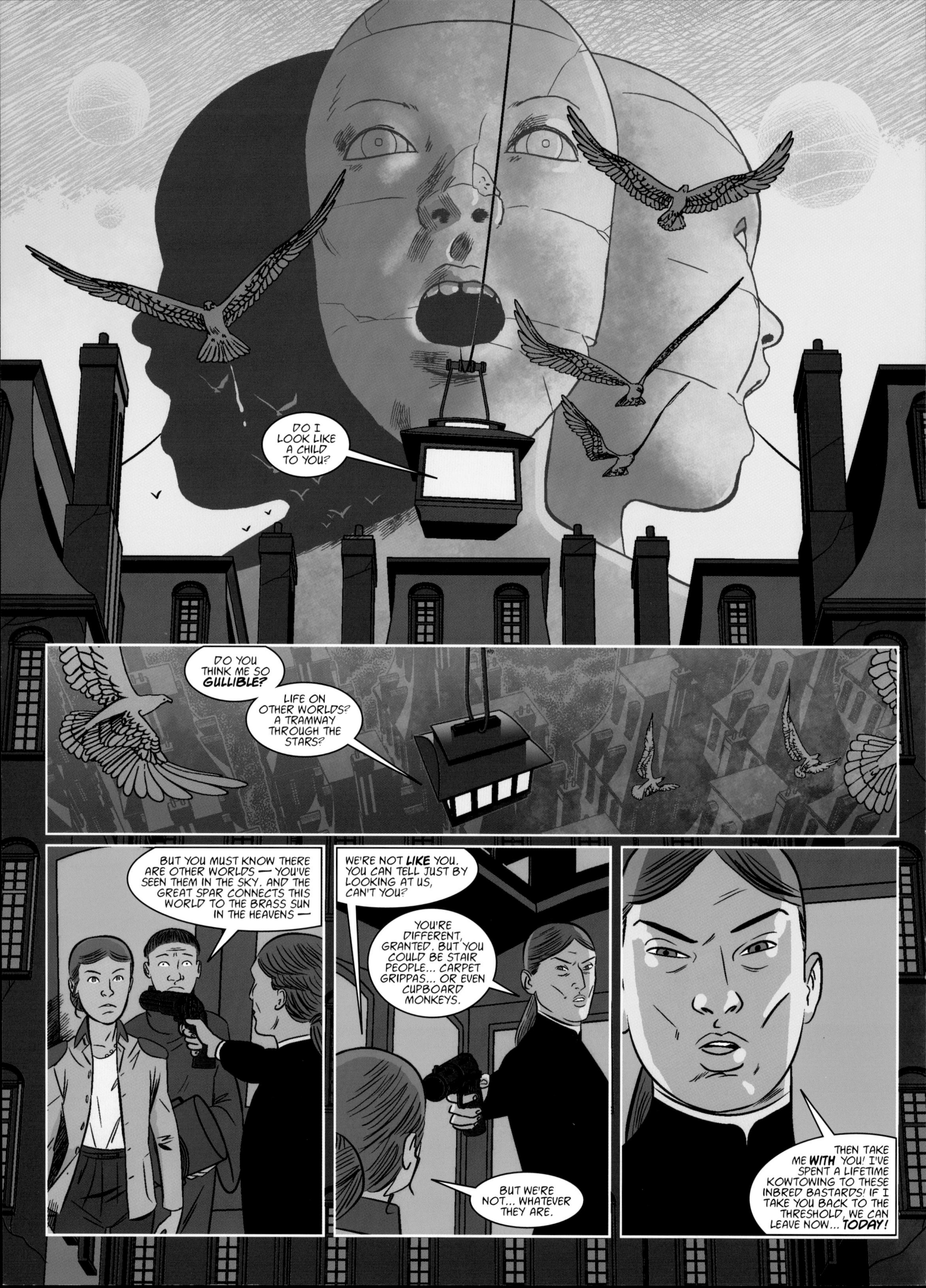
DO I LOOK LIKE A CHILD TO YOU?
DO YOU THINK ME SO **GULLIBLE?**
LIFE ON OTHER WORLDS? A TRAMWAY THROUGH THE STARS?
BUT YOU MUST KNOW THERE ARE OTHER WORLDS — YOU'VE SEEN THEM IN THE SKY. AND THE GREAT SPAR CONNECTS THIS WORLD TO THE BRASS SUN IN THE HEAVENS —
WE'RE NOT **LIKE** YOU. YOU CAN TELL JUST BY LOOKING AT US, CAN'T YOU?
YOU'RE DIFFERENT, GRANTED. BUT YOU COULD BE STAIR PEOPLE... CARPET GRIPPAS... OR EVEN CUPBOARD MONKEYS.
BUT WE'RE NOT... WHATEVER THEY ARE.
THEN TAKE ME **WITH** YOU! I'VE SPENT A LIFETIME KOWTOWING TO THESE INBRED BASTARDS! IF I TAKE YOU BACK TO THE THRESHOLD, WE CAN LEAVE NOW... ***TODAY!***

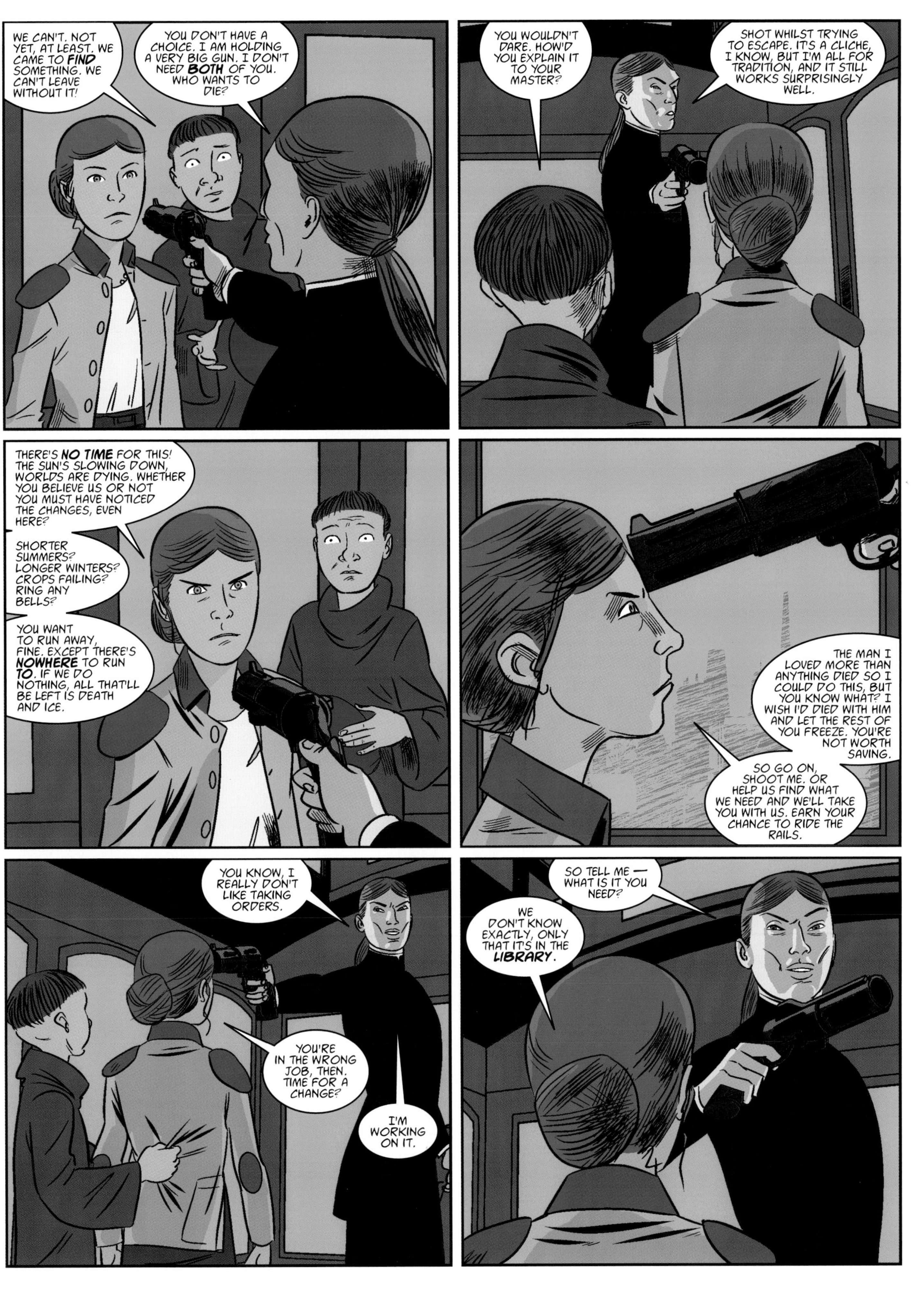

WE CAN'T. NOT YET, AT LEAST. WE CAME TO **FIND** SOMETHING. WE CAN'T LEAVE WITHOUT IT!
YOU DON'T HAVE A CHOICE. I AM HOLDING A VERY BIG GUN. I DON'T NEED **BOTH** OF YOU. WHO WANTS TO DIE?
YOU WOULDN'T DARE. HOW'D YOU EXPLAIN IT TO YOUR MASTER?
SHOT WHILST TRYING TO ESCAPE. IT'S A CLICHE, I KNOW, BUT I'M ALL FOR TRADITION, AND IT STILL WORKS SURPRISINGLY WELL.
THERE'S **NO TIME** FOR THIS! THE SUN'S SLOWING DOWN, WORLDS ARE DYING. WHETHER YOU BELIEVE US OR NOT YOU MUST HAVE NOTICED THE CHANGES, EVEN HERE?
SHORTER SUMMERS? LONGER WINTERS? CROPS FAILING? RING ANY BELLS?
YOU WANT TO RUN AWAY, FINE. EXCEPT THERE'S **NOWHERE** TO RUN **TO**. IF WE DO NOTHING, ALL THAT'LL BE LEFT IS DEATH AND ICE.
THE MAN I LOVED MORE THAN ANYTHING DIED SO I COULD DO THIS, BUT YOU KNOW WHAT? I WISH I'D DIED WITH HIM AND LET THE REST OF YOU FREEZE. YOU'RE NOT WORTH SAVING.
SO GO ON, SHOOT ME. OR HELP US FIND WHAT WE NEED AND WE'LL TAKE YOU WITH US. EARN YOUR CHANCE TO RIDE THE RAILS.
YOU KNOW, I REALLY DON'T LIKE TAKING ORDERS.
YOU'RE IN THE WRONG JOB, THEN. TIME FOR A CHANGE?
I'M WORKING ON IT.
SO TELL ME — WHAT IS IT YOU NEED?
WE DON'T KNOW EXACTLY, ONLY THAT IT'S IN THE **LIBRARY**.

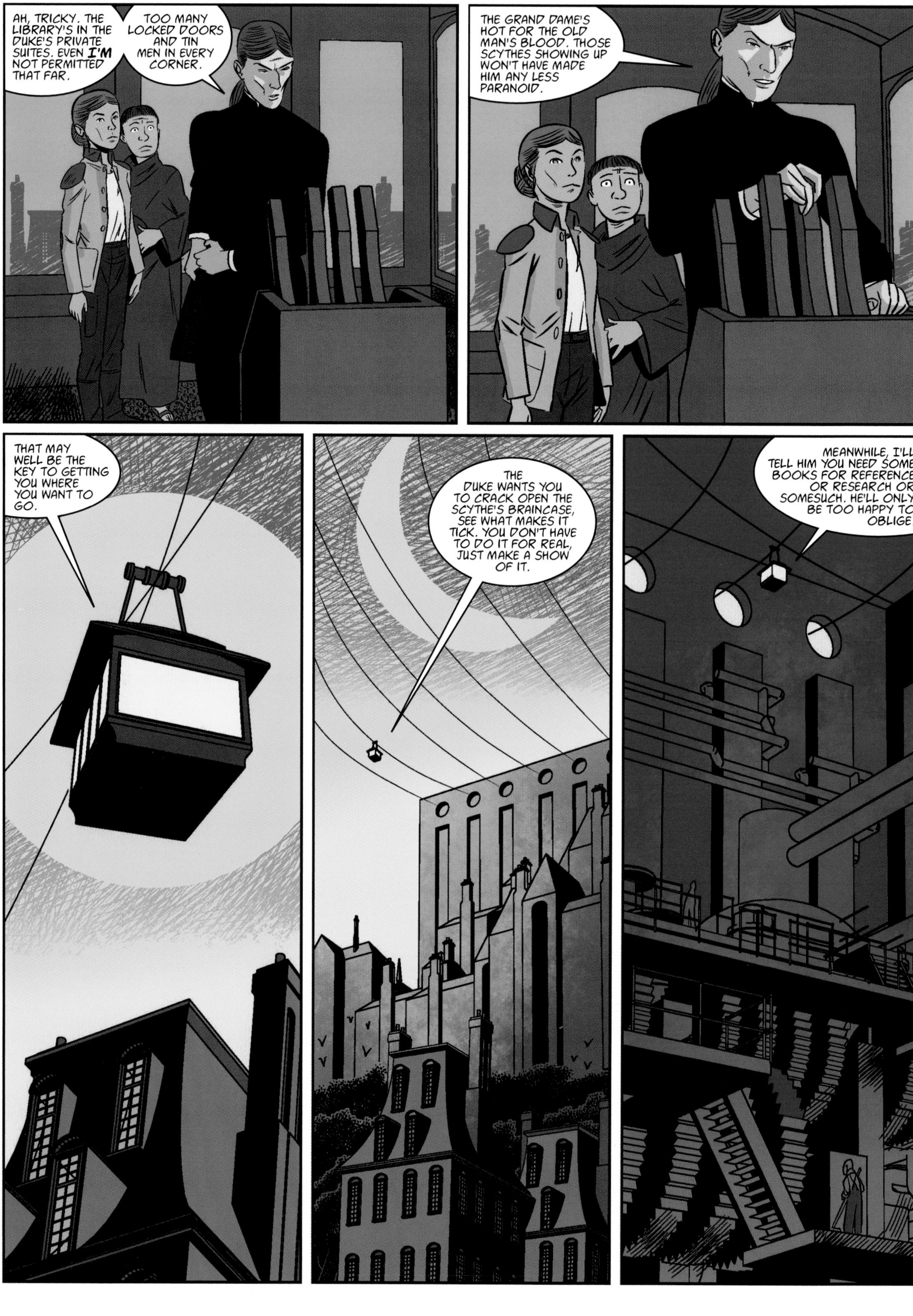
AH, TRICKY. THE LIBRARY'S IN THE DUKE'S PRIVATE SUITES. EVEN I'M NOT PERMITTED THAT FAR.
TOO MANY LOCKED DOORS AND TIN MEN IN EVERY CORNER.
THE GRAND DAME'S HOT FOR THE OLD MAN'S BLOOD. THOSE SCYTHES SHOWING UP WON'T HAVE MADE HIM ANY LESS PARANOID.
THAT MAY WELL BE THE KEY TO GETTING YOU WHERE YOU WANT TO GO.
THE DUKE WANTS YOU TO CRACK OPEN THE SCYTHE'S BRAINCASE, SEE WHAT MAKES IT TICK. YOU DON'T HAVE TO DO IT FOR REAL, JUST MAKE A SHOW OF IT.
MEANWHILE, I'LL TELL HIM YOU NEED SOME BOOKS FOR REFERENCE OR RESEARCH OR SOMESUCH. HE'LL ONLY BE TOO HAPPY TO OBLIGE.

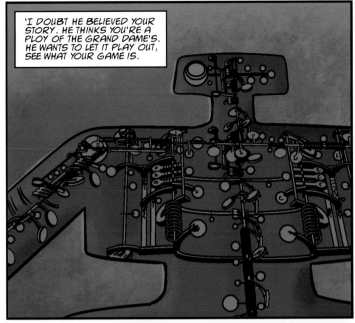

'I DOUBT HE BELIEVED YOUR STORY. HE THINKS YOU'RE A PLOY OF THE GRAND DAME'S. HE WANTS TO LET IT PLAY OUT, SEE WHAT YOUR GAME IS.

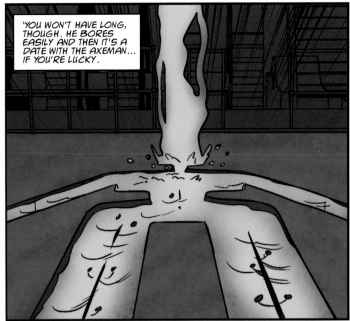

'YOU WON'T HAVE LONG, THOUGH. HE BORES EASILY AND THEN IT'S A DATE WITH THE AXEMAN... IF YOU'RE LUCKY.

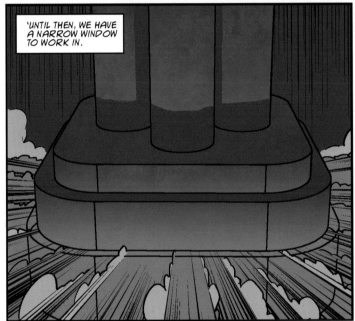

'UNTIL THEN, WE HAVE A NARROW WINDOW TO WORK IN.

'SO IT'S BEST TO STRIKE WHILST THE IRON'S HOT.'

CAN YOU DO IT?

DO WE HAVE A CHOICE?

'ELLO, 'ELLO! WHAT'S OCCURIN'? I HAIN'T GOT NO DOCKETS FOR DISEMBARKCATIONS HEREABOUTS!

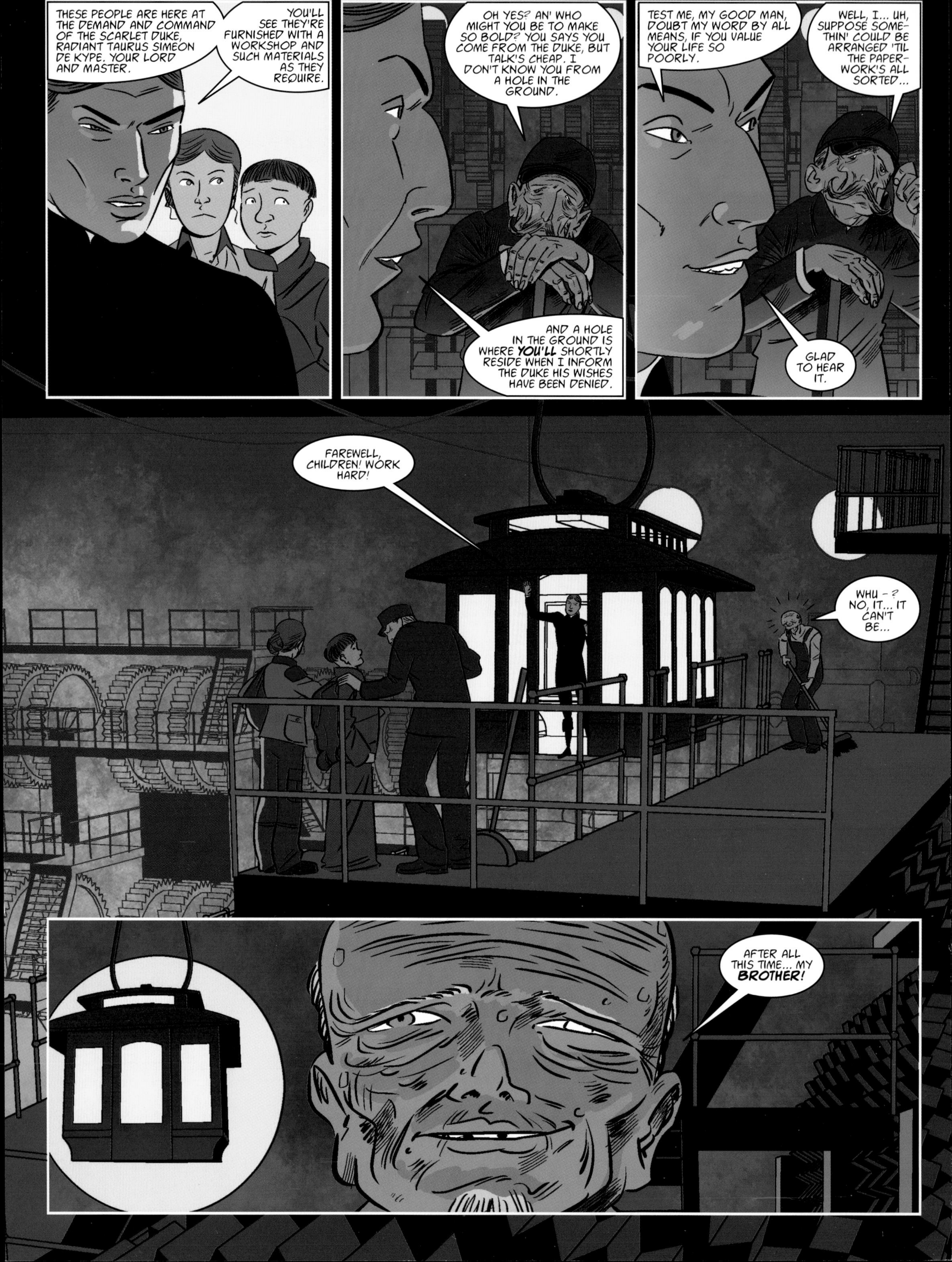

THESE PEOPLE ARE HERE AT THE DEMAND AND COMMAND OF THE SCARLET DUKE, RADIANT TAURUS SIMEON DE KYPE. YOUR LORD AND MASTER.
YOU'LL SEE THEY'RE FURNISHED WITH A WORKSHOP AND SUCH MATERIALS AS THEY REQUIRE.
OH YES? AN' WHO MIGHT YOU BE TO MAKE SO BOLD? YOU SAYS YOU COME FROM THE DUKE, BUT TALK'S CHEAP. I DON'T KNOW YOU FROM A HOLE IN THE GROUND.
AND A HOLE IN THE GROUND IS WHERE **YOU'LL** SHORTLY RESIDE WHEN I INFORM THE DUKE HIS WISHES HAVE BEEN DENIED.
TEST ME, MY GOOD MAN, DOUBT MY WORD BY ALL MEANS, IF YOU VALUE YOUR LIFE SO POORLY.
WELL, I... UH, SUPPOSE SOME-THIN' COULD BE ARRANGED 'TIL THE PAPER-WORK'S ALL SORTED...
GLAD TO HEAR IT.
FAREWELL, CHILDREN! WORK HARD!
WHU - ? NO, IT... IT CAN'T BE...
AFTER ALL THIS TIME... MY **BROTHER**!

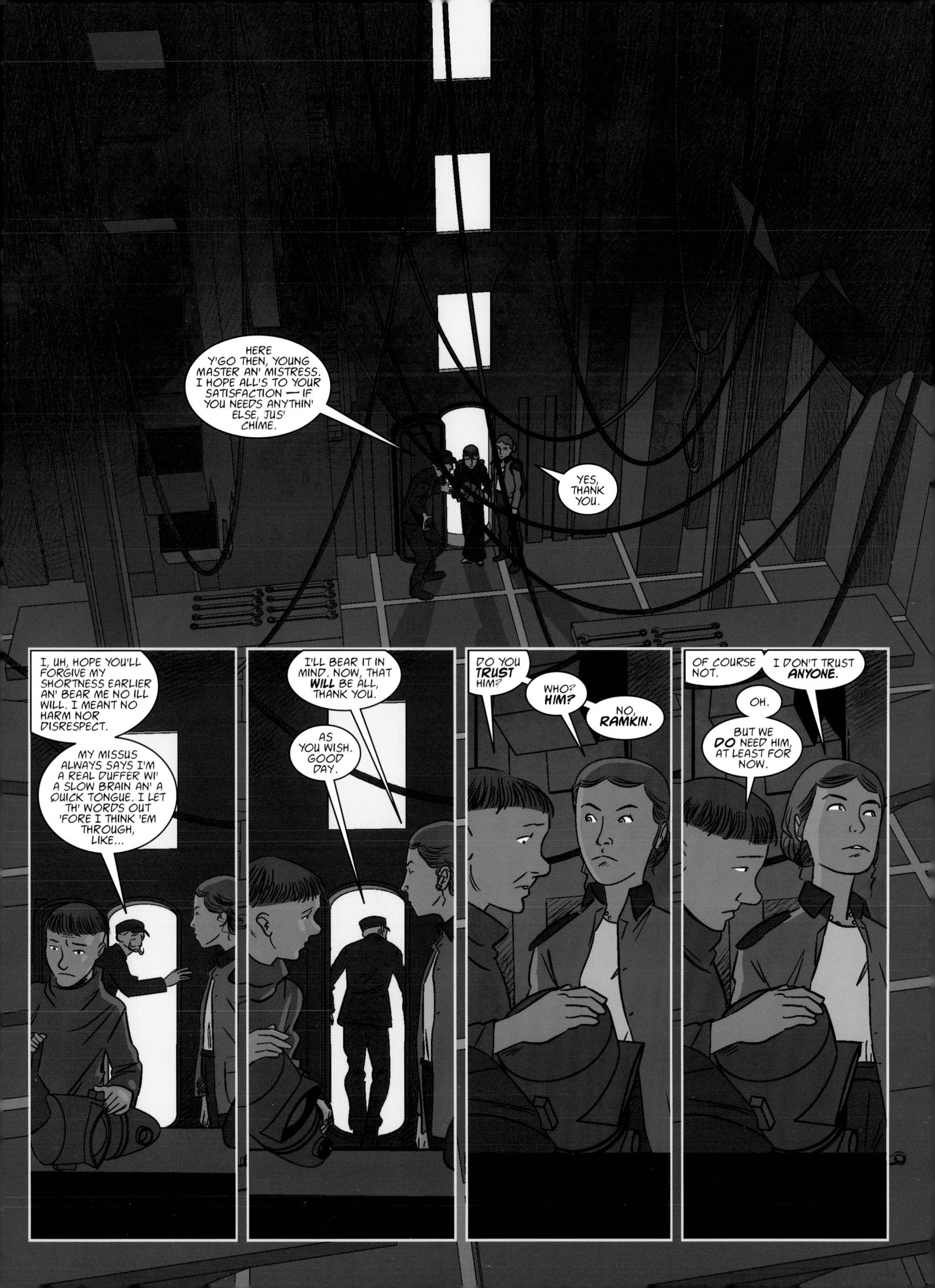
HERE Y'GO THEN, YOUNG MASTER AN' MISTRESS. I HOPE ALL'S TO YOUR SATISFACTION — IF YOU NEEDS ANYTHIN' ELSE, JUS' CHIME.
YES, THANK YOU.
I, UH, HOPE YOU'LL FORGIVE MY SHORTNESS EARLIER AN' BEAR ME NO ILL WILL. I MEANT NO HARM NOR DISRESPECT.
MY MISSUS ALWAYS SAYS I'M A REAL DUFFER WI' A SLOW BRAIN AN' A QUICK TONGUE. I LET TH' WORDS OUT 'FORE I THINK 'EM THROUGH, LIKE...
I'LL BEAR IT IN MIND. NOW, THAT WILL BE ALL, THANK YOU.
AS YOU WISH. GOOD DAY.
DO YOU TRUST HIM?
WHO? HIM?
NO, RAMKIN.
OF COURSE NOT.
I DON'T TRUST ANYONE.
OH.
BUT WE DO NEED HIM, AT LEAST FOR NOW.

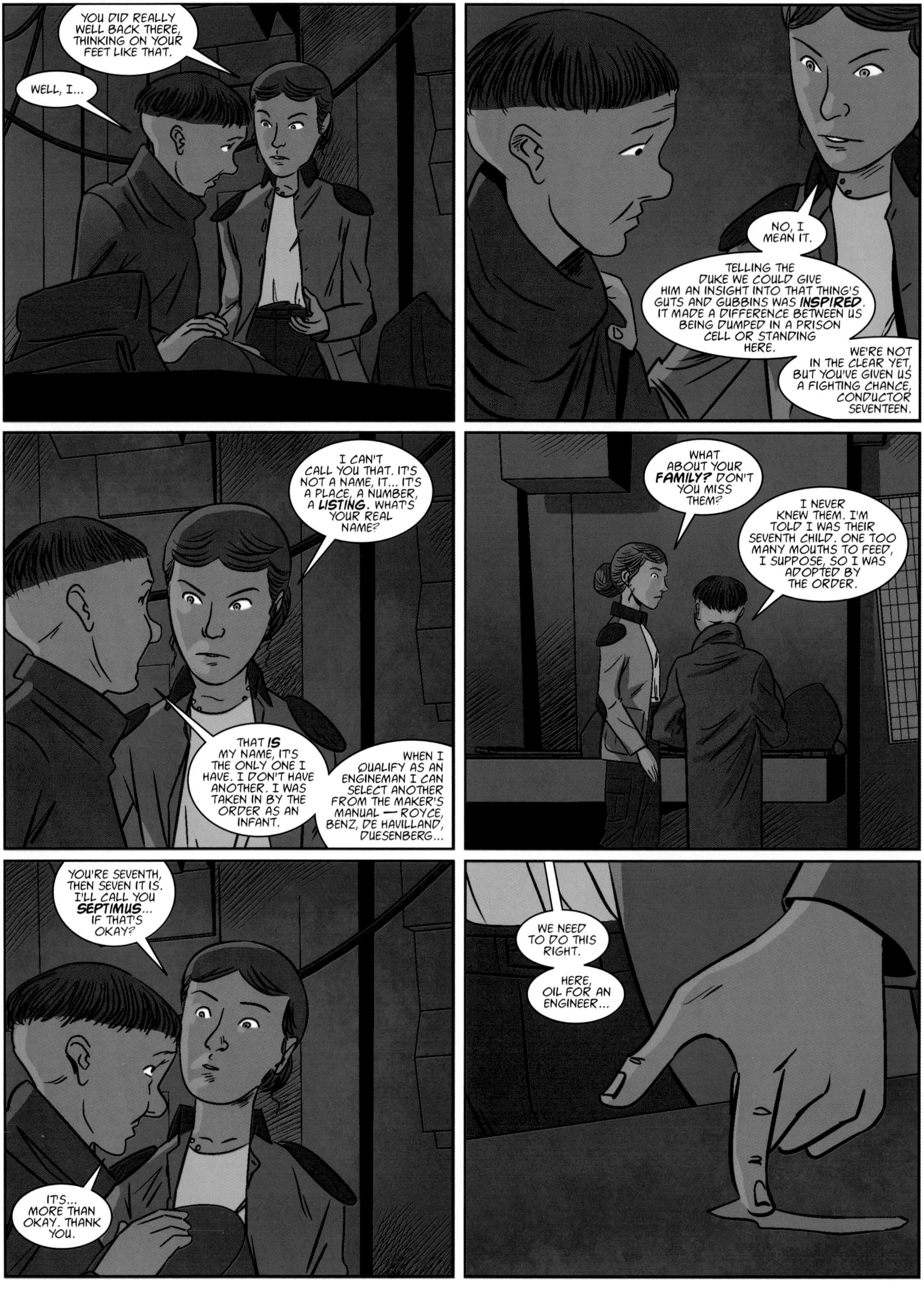
YOU DID REALLY WELL BACK THERE, THINKING ON YOUR FEET LIKE THAT.
WELL, I...
NO, I MEAN IT.
TELLING THE DUKE WE COULD GIVE HIM AN INSIGHT INTO THAT THING'S GUTS AND GUBBINS WAS INSPIRED. IT MADE A DIFFERENCE BETWEEN US BEING DUMPED IN A PRISON CELL OR STANDING HERE.
WE'RE NOT IN THE CLEAR YET, BUT YOU'VE GIVEN US A FIGHTING CHANCE, CONDUCTOR SEVENTEEN.
I CAN'T CALL YOU THAT. IT'S NOT A NAME, IT... IT'S A PLACE, A NUMBER, A LISTING. WHAT'S YOUR REAL NAME?
THAT IS MY NAME, IT'S THE ONLY ONE I HAVE. I DON'T HAVE ANOTHER. I WAS TAKEN IN BY THE ORDER AS AN INFANT.
WHEN I QUALIFY AS AN ENGINEMAN I CAN SELECT ANOTHER FROM THE MAKER'S MANUAL — ROYCE, BENZ, DE HAVILLAND, DUESENBERG...
WHAT ABOUT YOUR FAMILY? DON'T YOU MISS THEM?
I NEVER KNEW THEM. I'M TOLD I WAS THEIR SEVENTH CHILD. ONE TOO MANY MOUTHS TO FEED, I SUPPOSE, SO I WAS ADOPTED BY THE ORDER.
YOU'RE SEVENTH, THEN SEVEN IT IS. I'LL CALL YOU SEPTIMUS... IF THAT'S OKAY?
IT'S... MORE THAN OKAY. THANK YOU.
WE NEED TO DO THIS RIGHT.
HERE, OIL FOR AN ENGINEER...

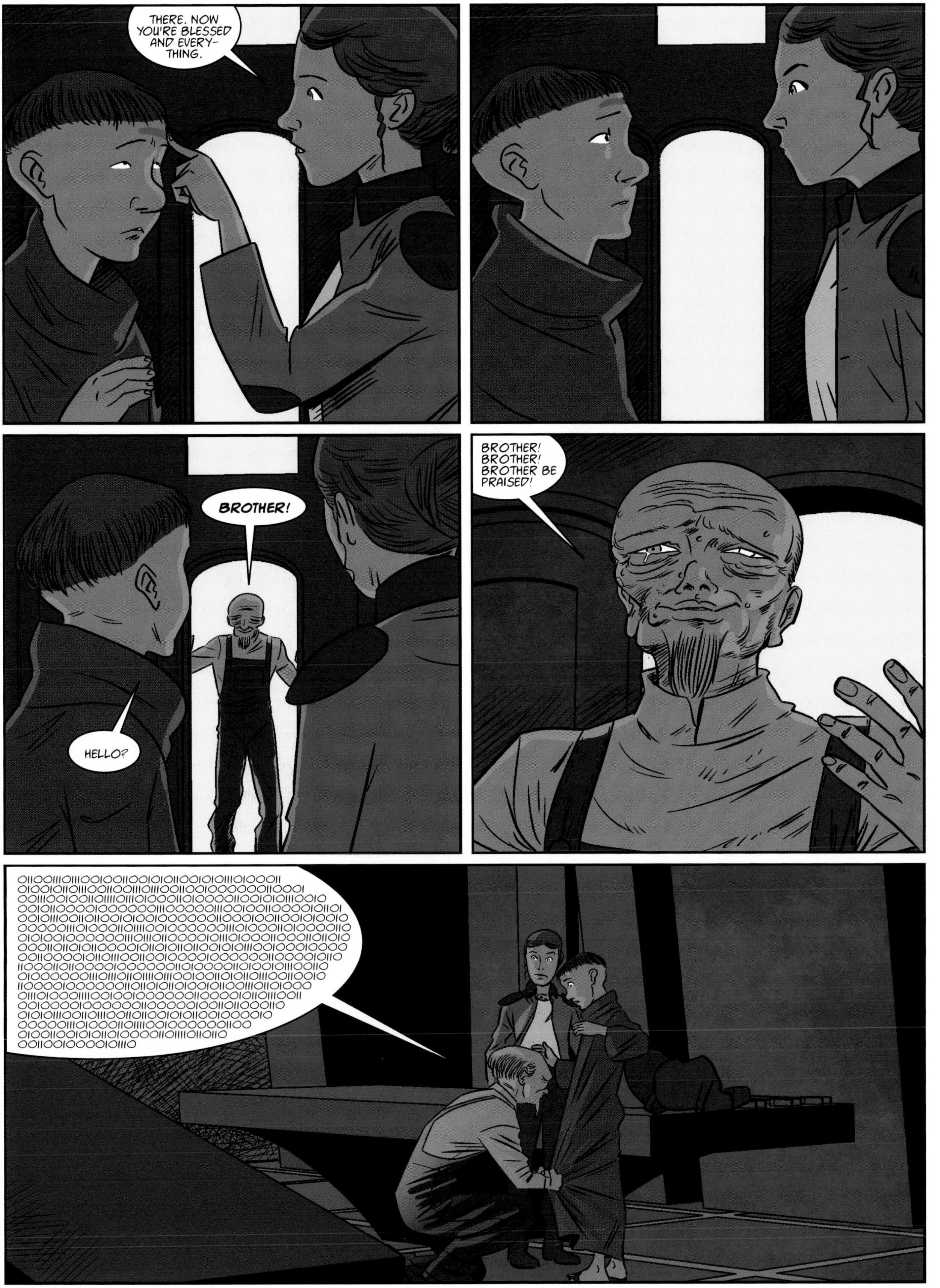
THERE. NOW YOU'RE BLESSED AND EVERY-THING.
BROTHER!
HELLO?
BROTHER! BROTHER! BROTHER BE PRAISED!
0110011101110010011001010110010101110100011
010010110111001100111011100110010000001100001
0011100100110111101110100011010000110010101110010
00101100000100000000111000000111001001100000101101
0010111001101100101001000000001100010011001010010
00000111010000110111100100000000111010000110100000110
0101001000000001110111011000001011101000011000011011010
0001101101011000001011010110110010101110010000100000
00110000010110111001100100000100000000110000010110
1100011011000001000000001101000001101001011100110
01000000001110111011011110111001001101011011100110010
1100001000000001101101011010010110011101101000
01110100001111001001000000001100000101101110011
00100000100000000110000000100110110000110
01010111001101110011011001010110010000010
000001110100001101111001000000001100
0100110010101101000001101110110110
001100100000101110

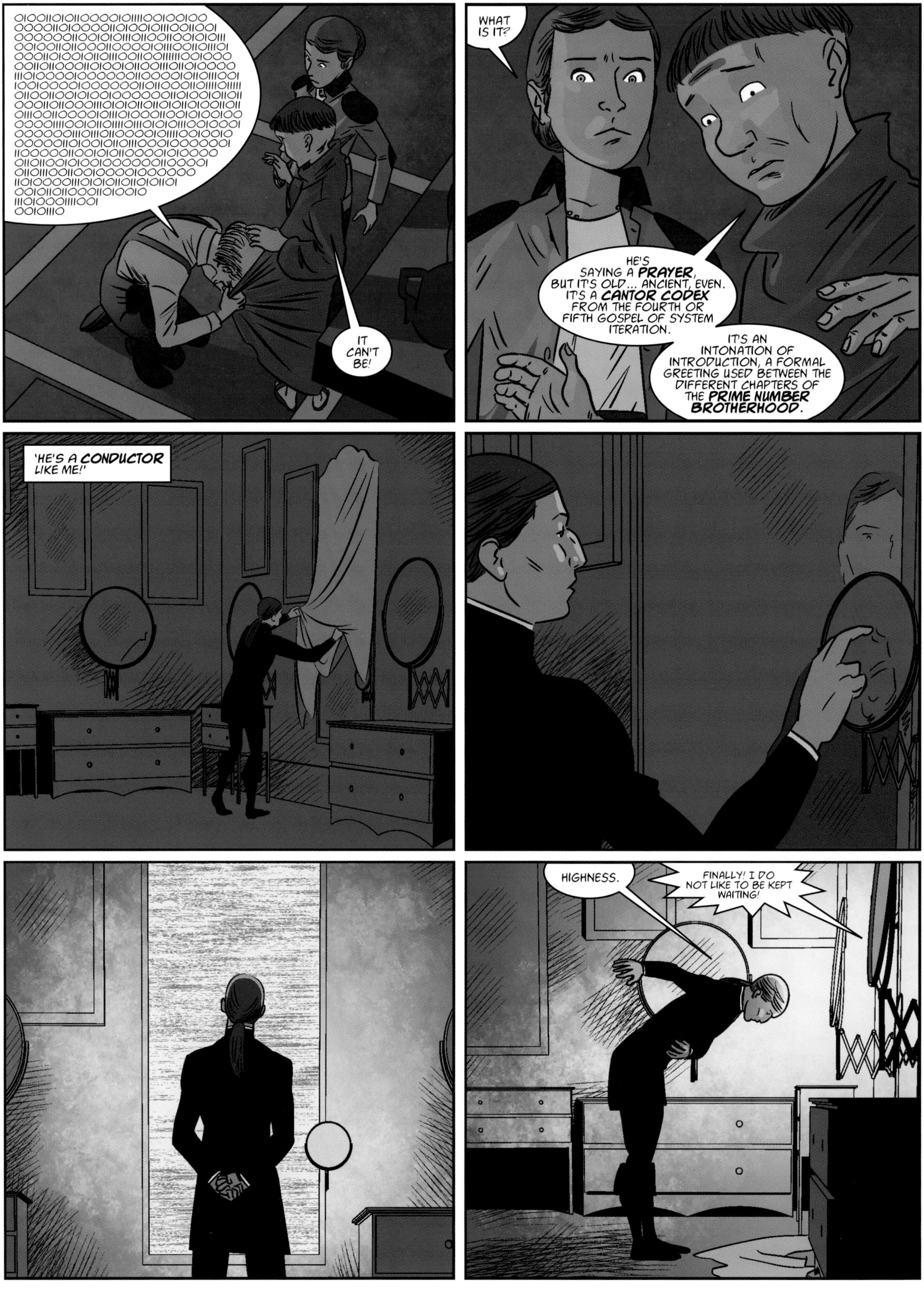

01001101011000001011100100100
0000110100000110100101110011001
0000000110010101110110011001010111
001001101100001100000101110011011101
00011010010110111001100111110010000
0011011000011010010110011101101000000
1110100000100000001100000101101110001
100100000100000000110110000110111101111
0110011001010100100000000110100101101 1
000110110000111010101101101011010011011
0111001100000101110100001100101001001 00
0000011110010110111101110101011100100001
000000011101110110000001011110010010
000000110100101101110001000000001
1100000011001010110000010100000
01101100101001000000000110000001
0110111001100100000010000000
1101000001110101011011010110 1
0010110110000110100100 10
111010001111001
00101110
IT CAN'T BE!
WHAT IS IT?
HE'S SAYING A **PRAYER**, BUT IT'S OLD... ANCIENT, EVEN. IT'S A **CANTOR CODEX** FROM THE FOURTH OR FIFTH GOSPEL OF SYSTEM ITERATION.
IT'S AN INTONATION OF INTRODUCTION, A FORMAL GREETING USED BETWEEN THE DIFFERENT CHAPTERS OF THE **PRIME NUMBER BROTHERHOOD**.
'HE'S A **CONDUCTOR** LIKE ME!'
HIGHNESS.
FINALLY! I DO NOT LIKE TO BE KEPT WAITING!

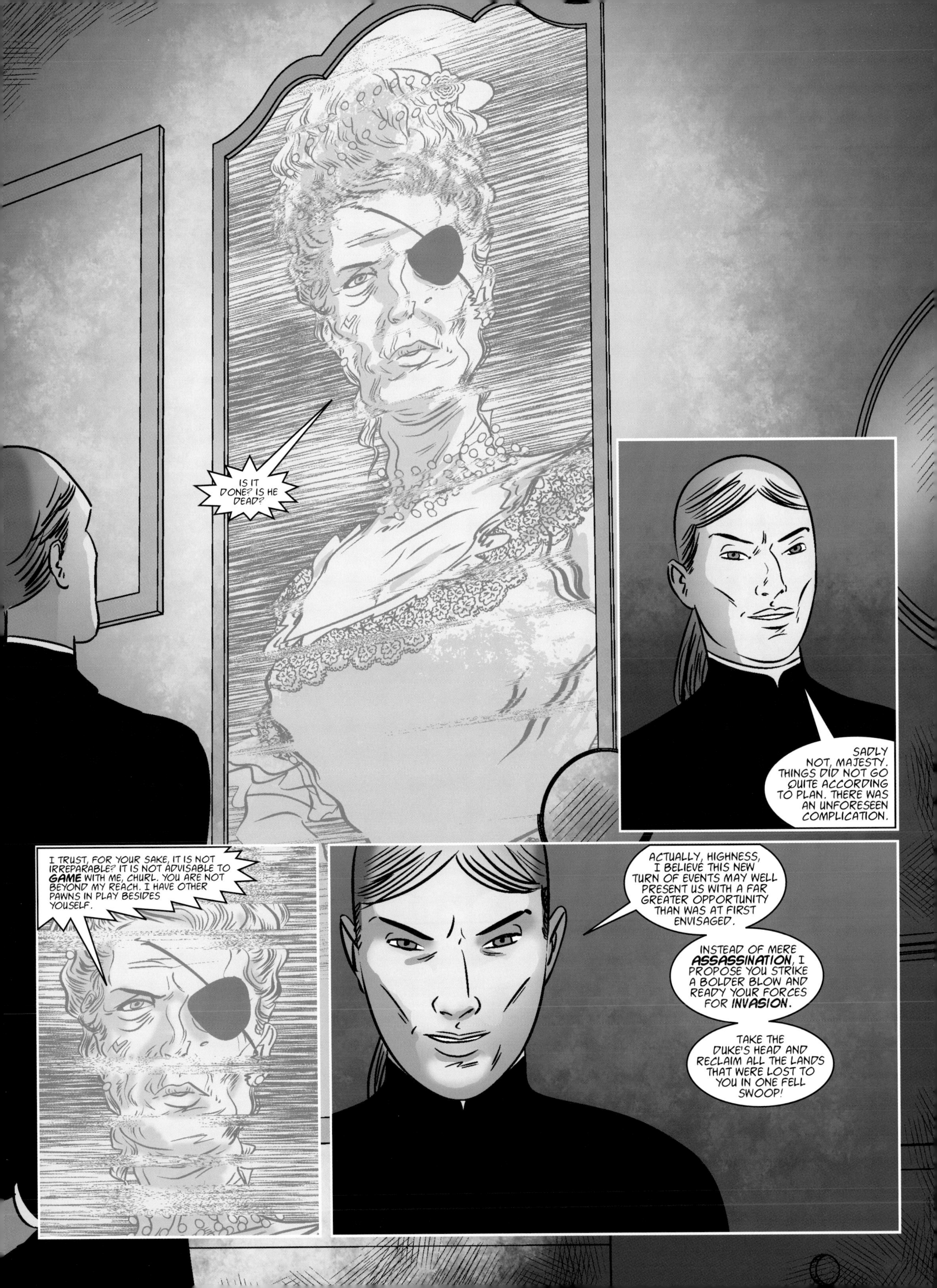
IS IT DONE? IS HE DEAD?
SADLY NOT, MAJESTY. THINGS DID NOT GO QUITE ACCORDING TO PLAN. THERE WAS AN UNFORESEEN COMPLICATION.
I TRUST, FOR YOUR SAKE, IT IS NOT IRREPARABLE? IT IS NOT ADVISABLE TO GAME WITH ME, CHURL. YOU ARE NOT BEYOND MY REACH. I HAVE OTHER PAWNS IN PLAY BESIDES YOUSELF.
ACTUALLY, HIGHNESS, I BELIEVE THIS NEW TURN OF EVENTS MAY WELL PRESENT US WITH A FAR GREATER OPPORTUNITY THAN WAS AT FIRST ENVISAGED.
INSTEAD OF MERE ASSASSINATION, I PROPOSE YOU STRIKE A BOLDER BLOW AND READY YOUR FORCES FOR INVASION.
TAKE THE DUKE'S HEAD AND RECLAIM ALL THE LANDS THAT WERE LOST TO YOU IN ONE FELL SWOOP!

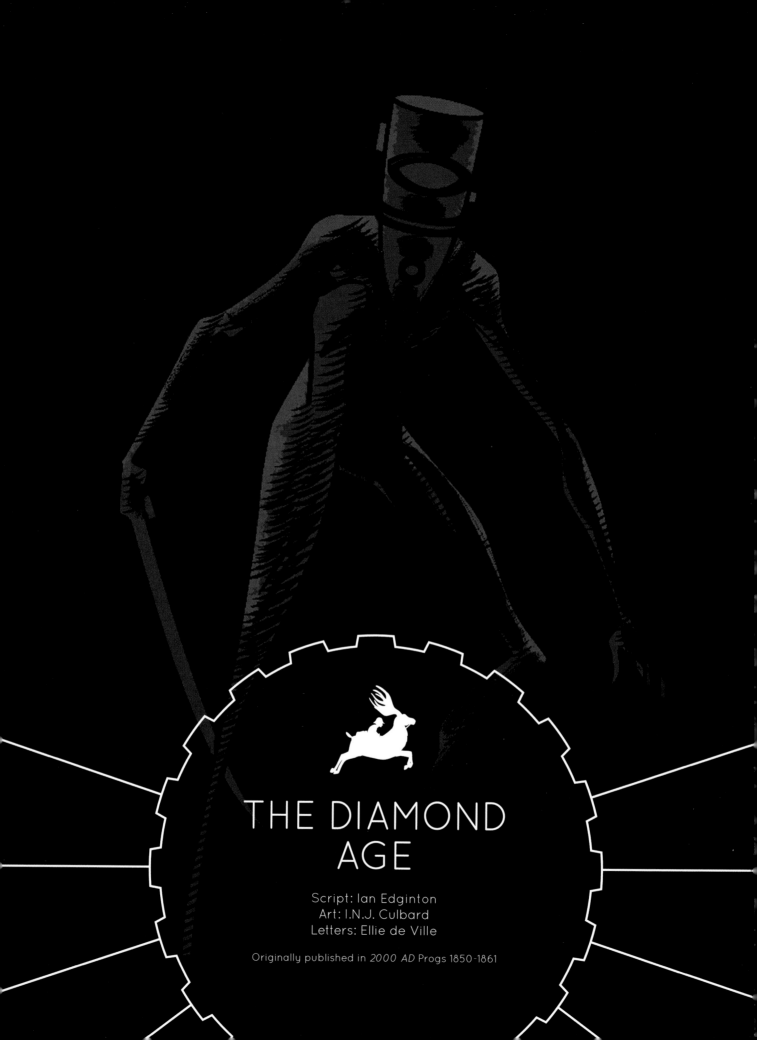

THE DIAMOND
AGE

Script: Ian Edginton
Art: I.N.J. Culbard
Letters: Ellie de Ville

Originally published in *2000 AD* Progs 1850-1861

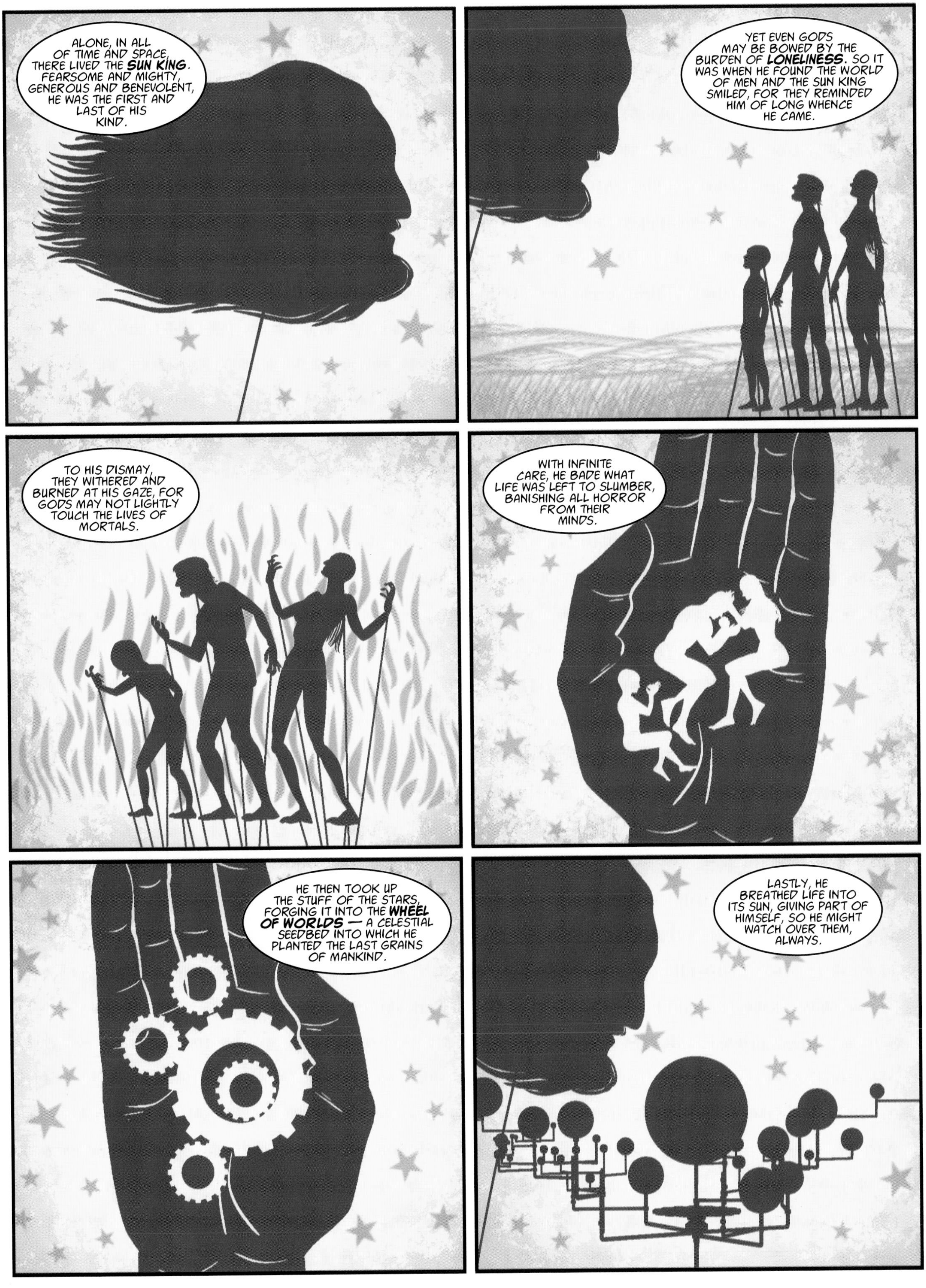
ALONE, IN ALL OF TIME AND SPACE, THERE LIVED THE SUN KING. FEARSOME AND MIGHTY, GENEROUS AND BENEVOLENT, HE WAS THE FIRST AND LAST OF HIS KIND.
YET EVEN GODS MAY BE BOWED BY THE BURDEN OF LONELINESS. SO IT WAS WHEN HE FOUND THE WORLD OF MEN AND THE SUN KING SMILED, FOR THEY REMINDED HIM OF LONG WHENCE HE CAME.
TO HIS DISMAY, THEY WITHERED AND BURNED AT HIS GAZE, FOR GODS MAY NOT LIGHTLY TOUCH THE LIVES OF MORTALS.
WITH INFINITE CARE, HE BADE WHAT LIFE WAS LEFT TO SLUMBER, BANISHING ALL HORROR FROM THEIR MINDS.
HE THEN TOOK UP THE STUFF OF THE STARS, FORGING IT INTO THE WHEEL OF WORLDS — A CELESTIAL SEEDBED INTO WHICH HE PLANTED THE LAST GRAINS OF MANKIND.
LASTLY, HE BREATHED LIFE INTO ITS SUN, GIVING PART OF HIMSELF, SO HE MIGHT WATCH OVER THEM, ALWAYS.

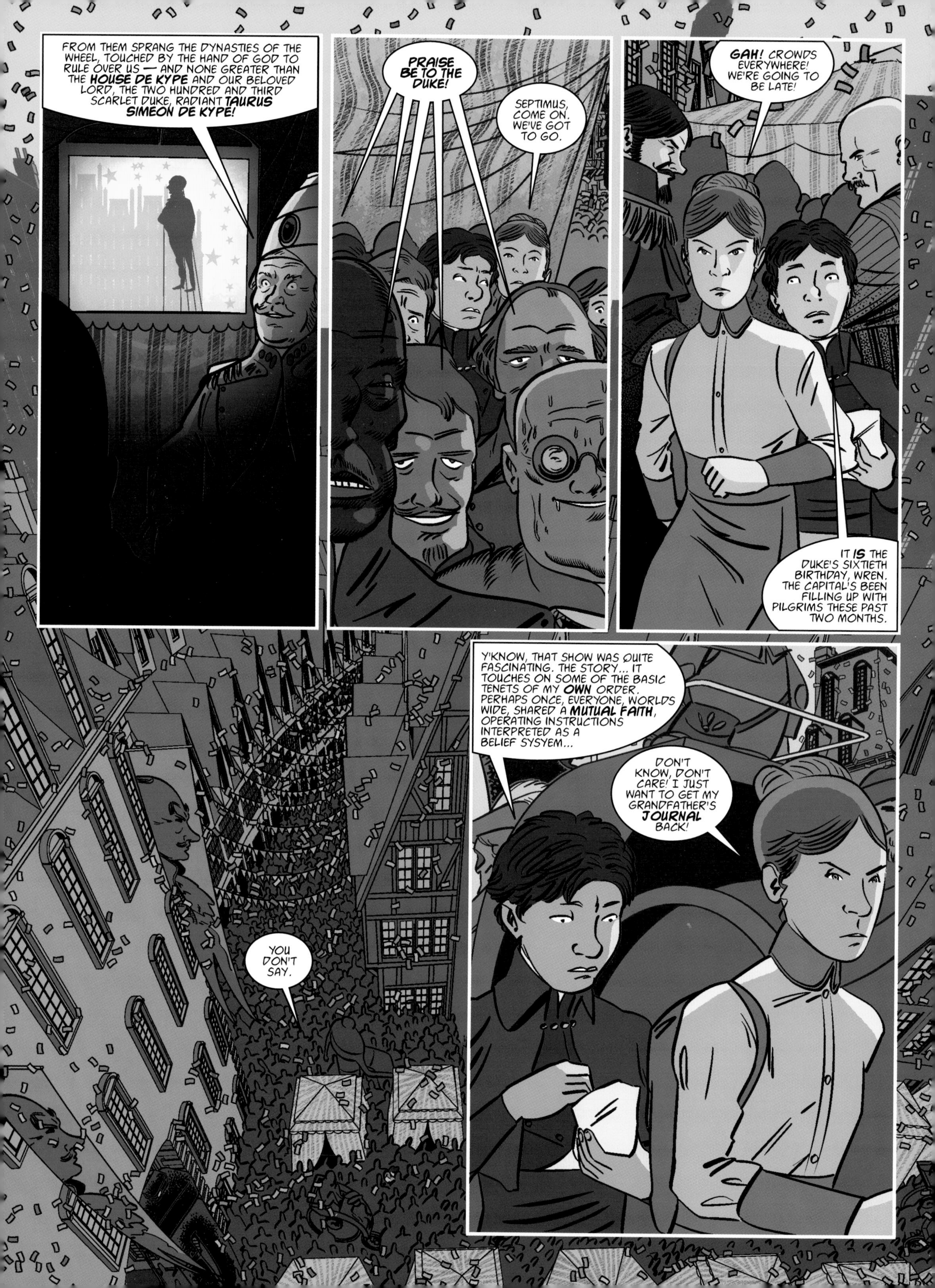
FROM THEM SPRANG THE DYNASTIES OF THE WHEEL, TOUCHED BY THE HAND OF GOD TO RULE OVER US — AND NONE GREATER THAN THE HOUSE DE KYPE AND OUR BELOVED LORD, THE TWO HUNDRED AND THIRD SCARLET DUKE, RADIANT TAURUS SIMEON DE KYPE!
PRAISE BE TO THE DUKE!
SEPTIMUS, COME ON. WE'VE GOT TO GO.
GAH! CROWDS EVERYWHERE! WE'RE GOING TO BE LATE!
IT IS THE DUKE'S SIXTIETH BIRTHDAY, WREN. THE CAPITAL'S BEEN FILLING UP WITH PILGRIMS THESE PAST TWO MONTHS.
Y'KNOW, THAT SHOW WAS QUITE FASCINATING. THE STORY... IT TOUCHES ON SOME OF THE BASIC TENETS OF MY OWN ORDER. PERHAPS ONCE, EVERYONE, WORLDS WIDE, SHARED A MUTUAL FAITH, OPERATING INSTRUCTIONS INTERPRETED AS A BELIEF SYSYEM...
DON'T KNOW, DON'T CARE! I JUST WANT TO GET MY GRANDFATHER'S JOURNAL BACK!
YOU DON'T SAY.

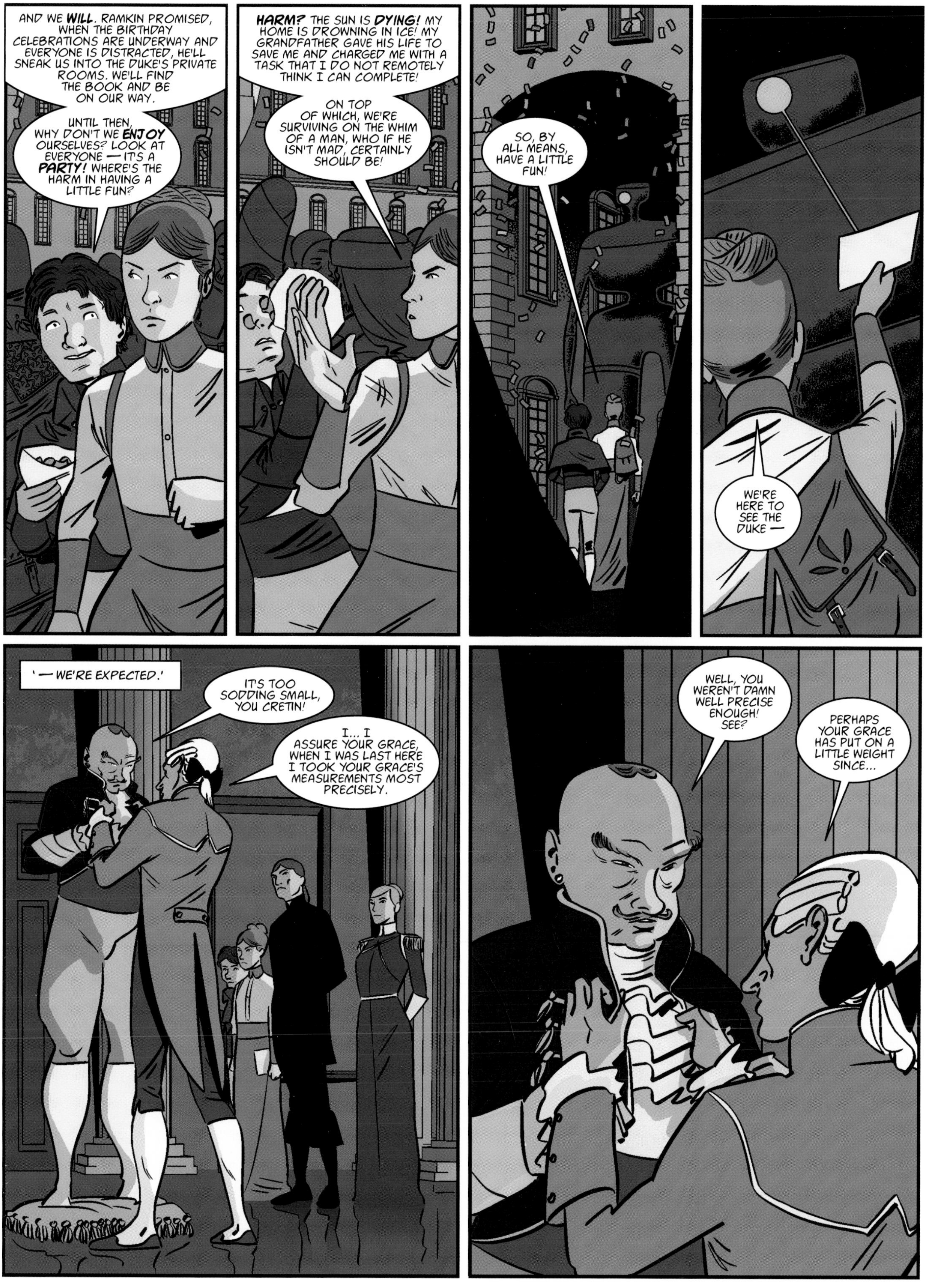

AND WE WILL. RAMKIN PROMISED, WHEN THE BIRTHDAY CELEBRATIONS ARE UNDERWAY AND EVERYONE IS DISTRACTED, HE'LL SNEAK US INTO THE DUKE'S PRIVATE ROOMS. WE'LL FIND THE BOOK AND BE ON OUR WAY.
UNTIL THEN, WHY DON'T WE ENJOY OURSELVES? LOOK AT EVERYONE — IT'S A PARTY! WHERE'S THE HARM IN HAVING A LITTLE FUN?
HARM? THE SUN IS DYING! MY HOME IS DROWNING IN ICE! MY GRANDFATHER GAVE HIS LIFE TO SAVE ME AND CHARGED ME WITH A TASK THAT I DO NOT REMOTELY THINK I CAN COMPLETE!
ON TOP OF WHICH, WE'RE SURVIVING ON THE WHIM OF A MAN, WHO IF HE ISN'T MAD, CERTAINLY SHOULD BE!
SO, BY ALL MEANS, HAVE A LITTLE FUN!
WE'RE HERE TO SEE THE DUKE —
'— WE'RE EXPECTED.'
IT'S TOO SODDING SMALL, YOU CRETIN!
I... I ASSURE YOUR GRACE, WHEN I WAS LAST HERE I TOOK YOUR GRACE'S MEASUREMENTS MOST PRECISELY.
WELL, YOU WEREN'T DAMN WELL PRECISE ENOUGH! SEE?
PERHAPS YOUR GRACE HAS PUT ON A LITTLE WEIGHT SINCE...

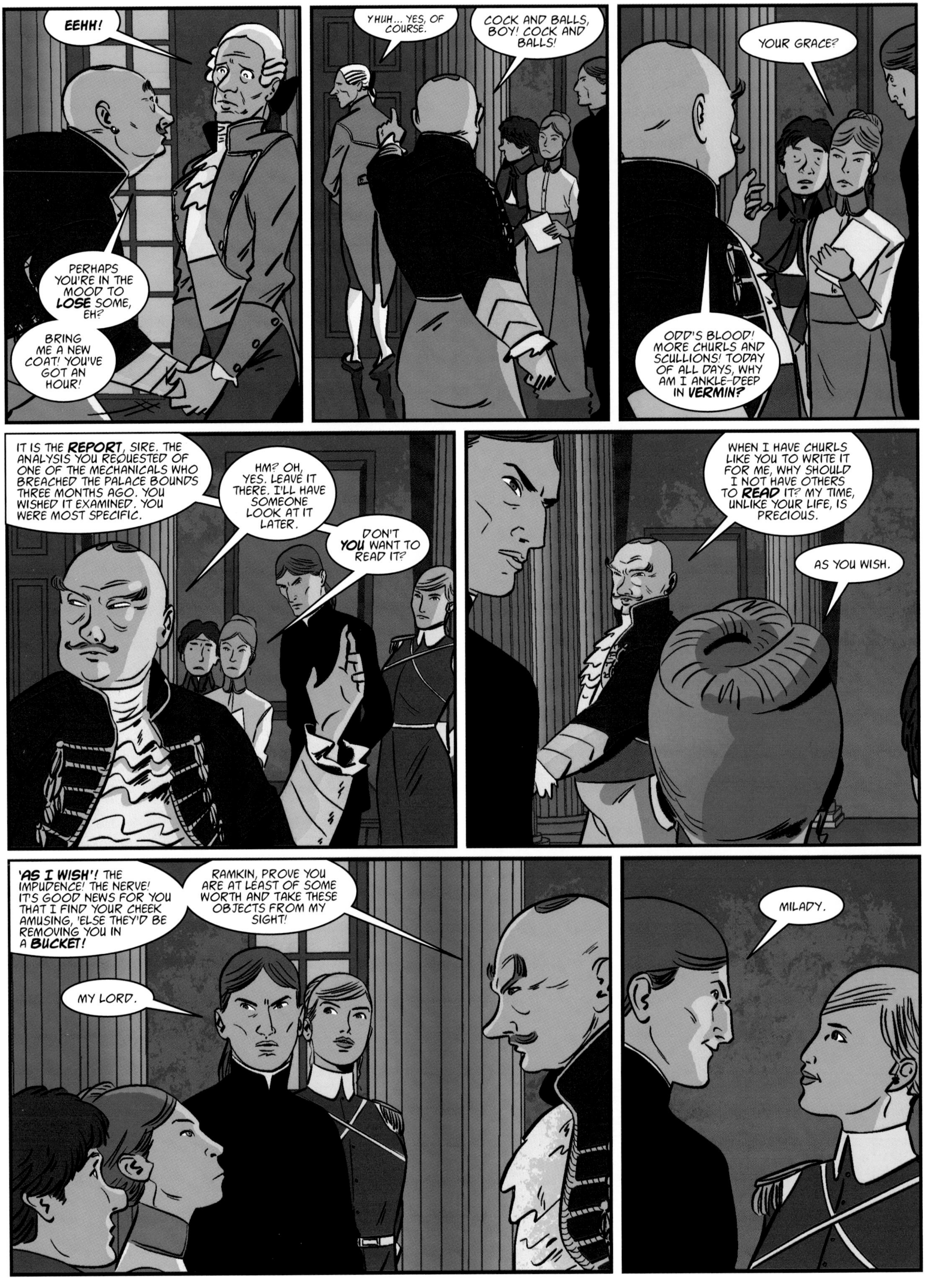
EEHH!
PERHAPS YOU'RE IN THE MOOD TO LOSE SOME, EH?
BRING ME A NEW COAT! YOU'VE GOT AN HOUR!
YHUH... YES, OF COURSE.
COCK AND BALLS, BOY! COCK AND BALLS!
YOUR GRACE?
ODD'S BLOOD! MORE CHURLS AND SCULLIONS! TODAY OF ALL DAYS, WHY AM I ANKLE-DEEP IN VERMIN?
IT IS THE REPORT, SIRE. THE ANALYSIS YOU REQUESTED OF ONE OF THE MECHANICALS WHO BREACHED THE PALACE BOUNDS THREE MONTHS AGO. YOU WISHED IT EXAMINED. YOU WERE MOST SPECIFIC.
HM? OH, YES. LEAVE IT THERE. I'LL HAVE SOMEONE LOOK AT IT LATER.
DON'T YOU WANT TO READ IT?
WHEN I HAVE CHURLS LIKE YOU TO WRITE IT FOR ME, WHY SHOULD I NOT HAVE OTHERS TO READ IT? MY TIME, UNLIKE YOUR LIFE, IS PRECIOUS.
AS YOU WISH.
'AS I WISH'! THE IMPUDENCE! THE NERVE! IT'S GOOD NEWS FOR YOU THAT I FIND YOUR CHEEK AMUSING, 'ELSE THEY'D BE REMOVING YOU IN A BUCKET!
RAMKIN, PROVE YOU ARE AT LEAST OF SOME WORTH AND TAKE THESE OBJECTS FROM MY SIGHT!
MY LORD.
MILADY.

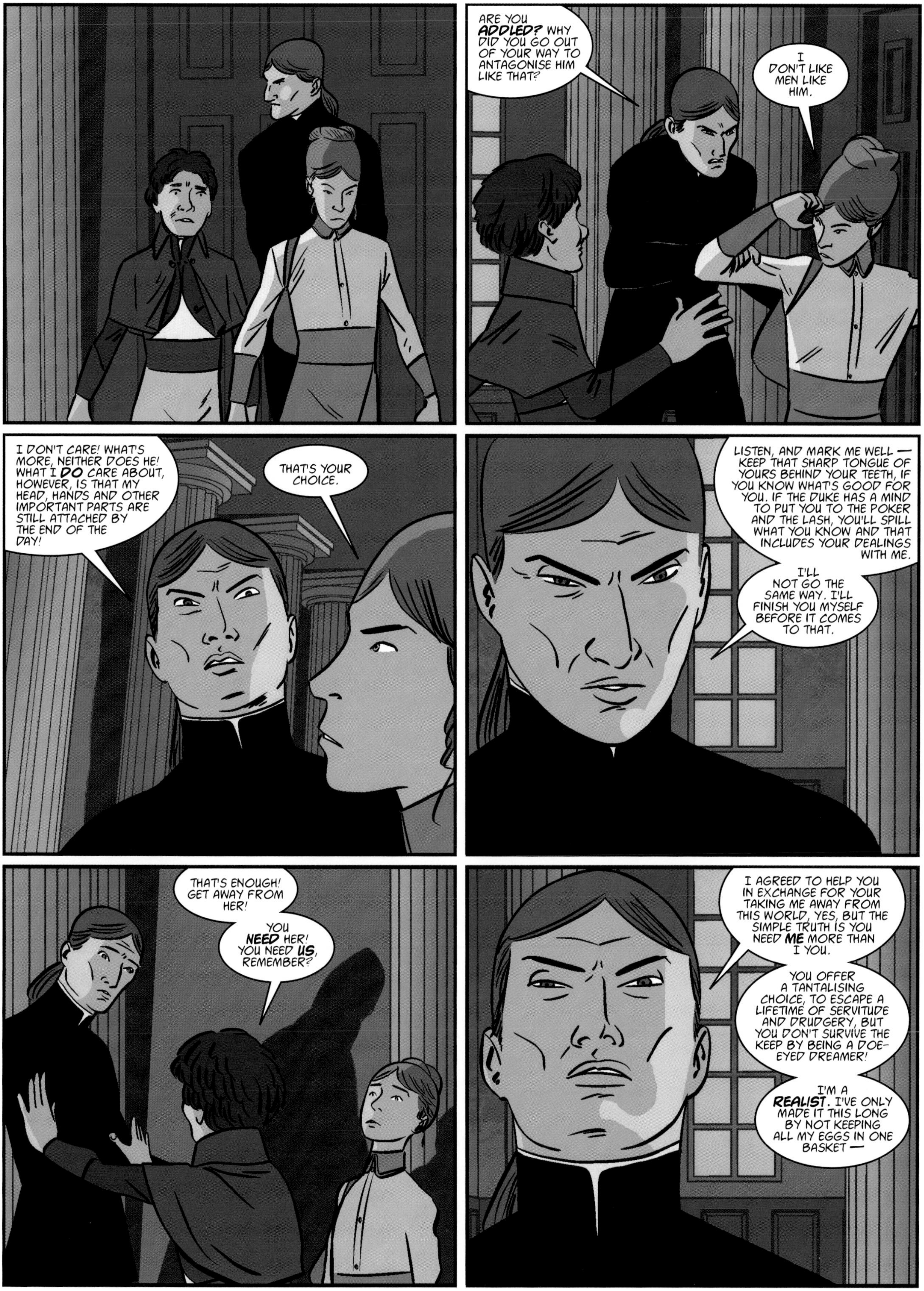
ARE YOU ADDLED? WHY DID YOU GO OUT OF YOUR WAY TO ANTAGONISE HIM LIKE THAT?
I DON'T LIKE MEN LIKE HIM.
I DON'T CARE! WHAT'S MORE, NEITHER DOES HE! WHAT I DO CARE ABOUT, HOWEVER, IS THAT MY HEAD, HANDS AND OTHER IMPORTANT PARTS ARE STILL ATTACHED BY THE END OF THE DAY!
THAT'S YOUR CHOICE.
LISTEN, AND MARK ME WELL — KEEP THAT SHARP TONGUE OF YOURS BEHIND YOUR TEETH, IF YOU KNOW WHAT'S GOOD FOR YOU. IF THE DUKE HAS A MIND TO PUT YOU TO THE POKER AND THE LASH, YOU'LL SPILL WHAT YOU KNOW AND THAT INCLUDES YOUR DEALINGS WITH ME.
I'LL NOT GO THE SAME WAY. I'LL FINISH YOU MYSELF BEFORE IT COMES TO THAT.
THAT'S ENOUGH! GET AWAY FROM HER!
YOU NEED HER! YOU NEED US, REMEMBER?
I AGREED TO HELP YOU IN EXCHANGE FOR YOUR TAKING ME AWAY FROM THIS WORLD, YES, BUT THE SIMPLE TRUTH IS YOU NEED ME MORE THAN I YOU.
YOU OFFER A TANTALISING CHOICE, TO ESCAPE A LIFETIME OF SERVITUDE AND DRUDGERY, BUT YOU DON'T SURVIVE THE KEEP BY BEING A DOE-EYED DREAMER!
I'M A REALIST. I'VE ONLY MADE IT THIS LONG BY NOT KEEPING ALL MY EGGS IN ONE BASKET —

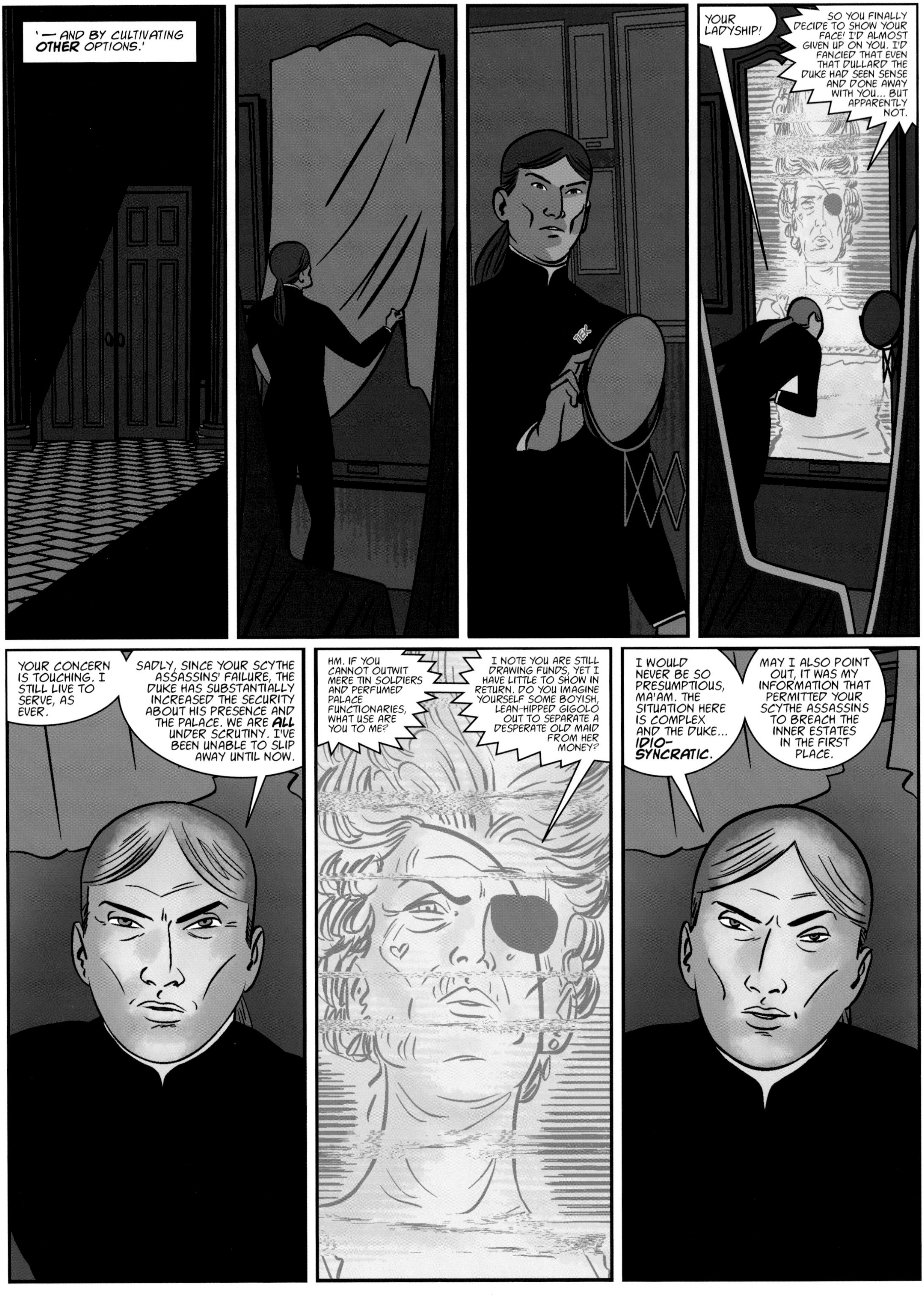
'— AND BY CULTIVATING OTHER OPTIONS.'
YOUR LADYSHIP!
SO YOU FINALLY DECIDE TO SHOW YOUR FACE! I'D ALMOST GIVEN UP ON YOU. I'D FANCIED THAT EVEN THAT DULLARD THE DUKE HAD SEEN SENSE AND DONE AWAY WITH YOU... BUT APPARENTLY NOT.
YOUR CONCERN IS TOUCHING. I STILL LIVE TO SERVE, AS EVER.
SADLY, SINCE YOUR SCYTHE ASSASSINS' FAILURE, THE DUKE HAS SUBSTANTIALLY INCREASED THE SECURITY ABOUT HIS PRESENCE AND THE PALACE. WE ARE ALL UNDER SCRUTINY. I'VE BEEN UNABLE TO SLIP AWAY UNTIL NOW.
HM. IF YOU CANNOT OUTWIT MERE TIN SOLDIERS AND PERFUMED PALACE FUNCTIONARIES, WHAT USE ARE YOU TO ME?
I NOTE YOU ARE STILL DRAWING FUNDS, YET I HAVE LITTLE TO SHOW IN RETURN. DO YOU IMAGINE YOURSELF SOME BOYISH, LEAN-HIPPED GIGOLO OUT TO SEPARATE A DESPERATE OLD MAID FROM HER MONEY?
I WOULD NEVER BE SO PRESUMPTIOUS, MA'AM. THE SITUATION HERE IS COMPLEX AND THE DUKE... IDIO-SYNCRATIC.
MAY I ALSO POINT OUT, IT WAS MY INFORMATION THAT PERMITTED YOUR SCYTHE ASSASSINS TO BREACH THE INNER ESTATES IN THE FIRST PLACE.
TEK

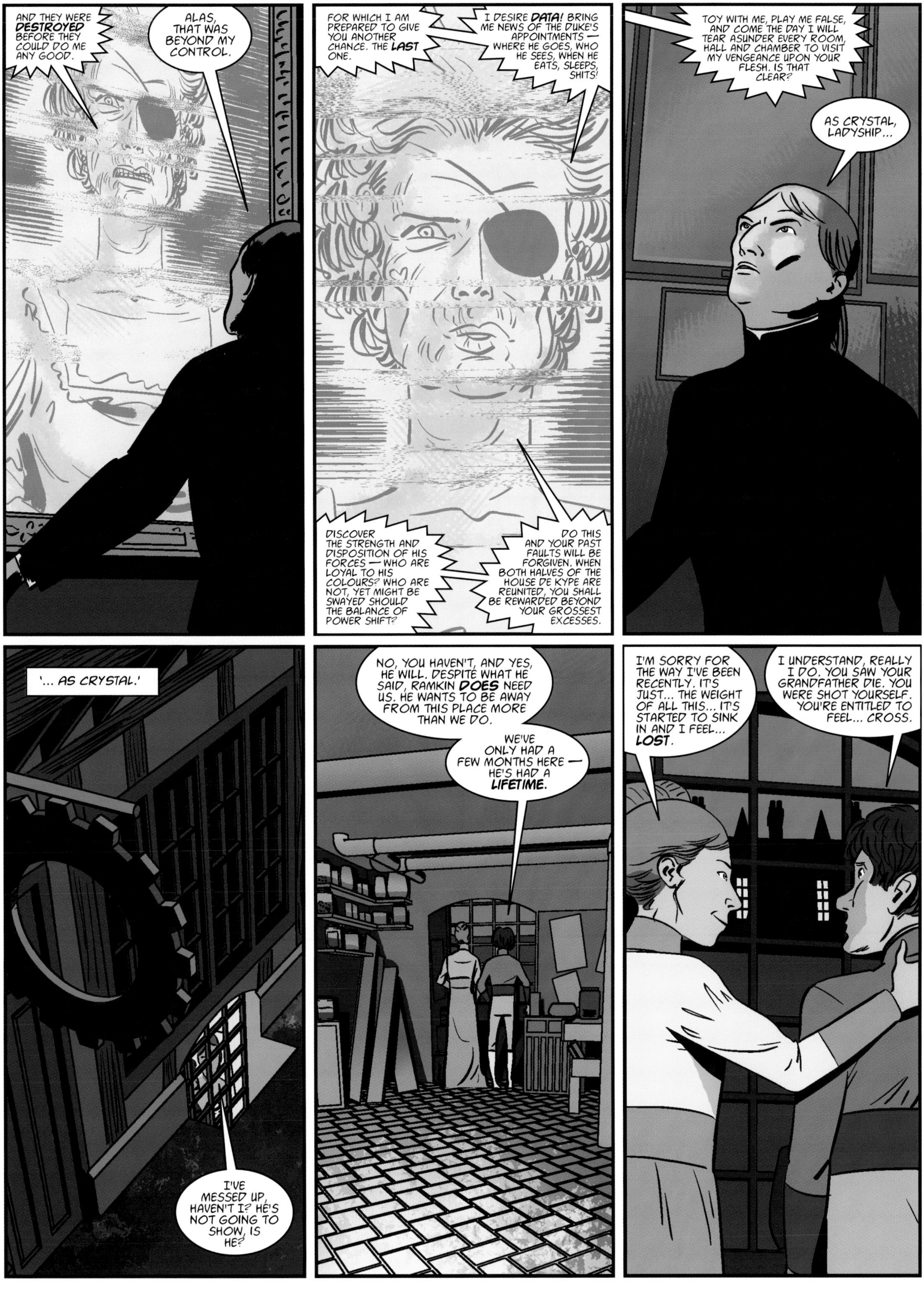
AND THEY WERE DESTROYED BEFORE THEY COULD DO ME ANY GOOD.
ALAS, THAT WAS BEYOND MY CONTROL.
FOR WHICH I AM PREPARED TO GIVE YOU ANOTHER CHANCE. THE LAST ONE.
I DESIRE DATA! BRING ME NEWS OF THE DUKE'S APPOINTMENTS — WHERE HE GOES, WHO HE SEES, WHEN HE EATS, SLEEPS, SHITS!
DISCOVER THE STRENGTH AND DISPOSITION OF HIS FORCES — WHO ARE LOYAL TO HIS COLOURS? WHO ARE NOT, YET MIGHT BE SWAYED SHOULD THE BALANCE OF POWER SHIFT?
DO THIS AND YOUR PAST FAULTS WILL BE FORGIVEN. WHEN BOTH HALVES OF THE HOUSE DE KYPE ARE REUNITED, YOU SHALL BE REWARDED BEYOND YOUR GROSSEST EXCESSES.
TOY WITH ME, PLAY ME FALSE, AND COME THE DAY I WILL TEAR ASUNDER EVERY ROOM, HALL AND CHAMBER TO VISIT MY VENGEANCE UPON YOUR FLESH. IS THAT CLEAR?
AS CRYSTAL, LADYSHIP...
'... AS CRYSTAL.'
I'VE MESSED UP, HAVEN'T I? HE'S NOT GOING TO SHOW, IS HE?
NO, YOU HAVEN'T, AND YES, HE WILL. DESPITE WHAT HE SAID, RAMKIN DOES NEED US. HE WANTS TO BE AWAY FROM THIS PLACE MORE THAN WE DO.
WE'VE ONLY HAD A FEW MONTHS HERE — HE'S HAD A LIFETIME.
I'M SORRY FOR THE WAY I'VE BEEN RECENTLY. IT'S JUST... THE WEIGHT OF ALL THIS... IT'S STARTED TO SINK IN AND I FEEL... LOST.
I UNDERSTAND, REALLY I DO. YOU SAW YOUR GRANDFATHER DIE. YOU WERE SHOT YOURSELF. YOU'RE ENTITLED TO FEEL... CROSS.

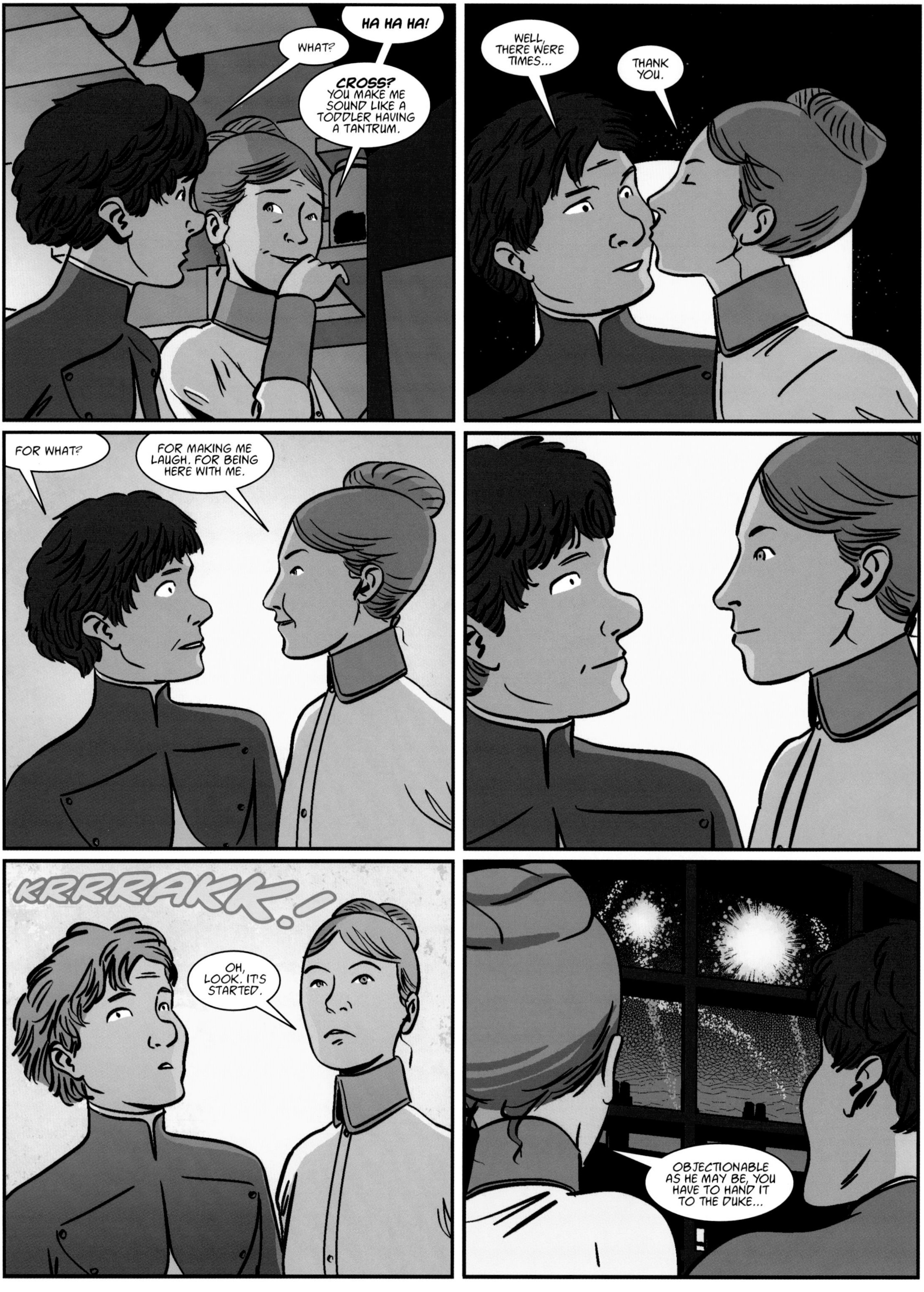
WHAT?
HA HA HA!
CROSS? YOU MAKE ME SOUND LIKE A TODDLER HAVING A TANTRUM.
WELL, THERE WERE TIMES...
THANK YOU.
FOR WHAT?
FOR MAKING ME LAUGH. FOR BEING HERE WITH ME.
KRRRAKK.!
OH, LOOK. IT'S STARTED.
OBJECTIONABLE AS HE MAY BE, YOU HAVE TO HAND IT TO THE DUKE...

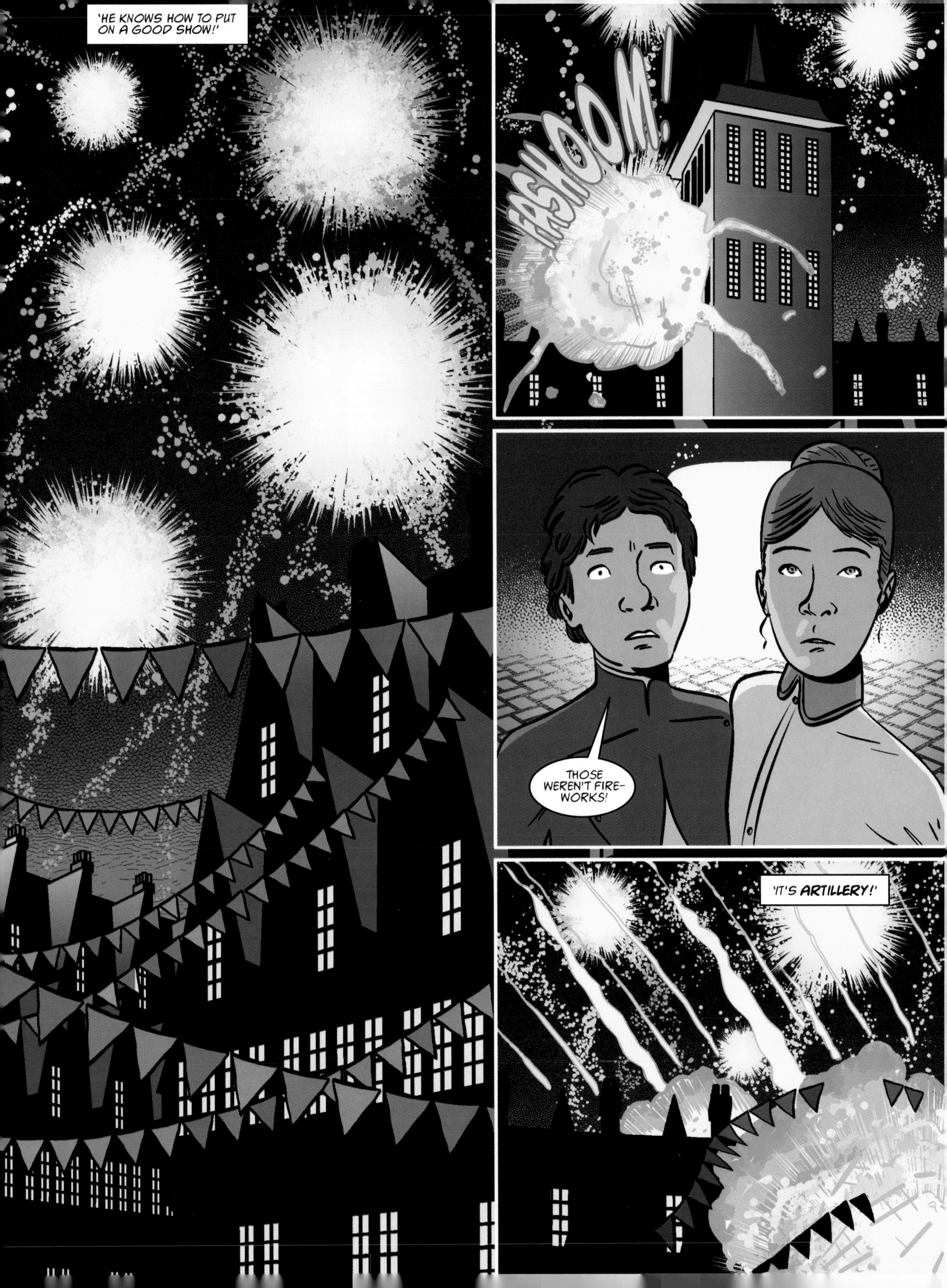
'HE KNOWS HOW TO PUT ON A GOOD SHOW!'
FASHOOM!
THOSE WEREN'T FIRE-WORKS!
'IT'S ARTILLERY!'

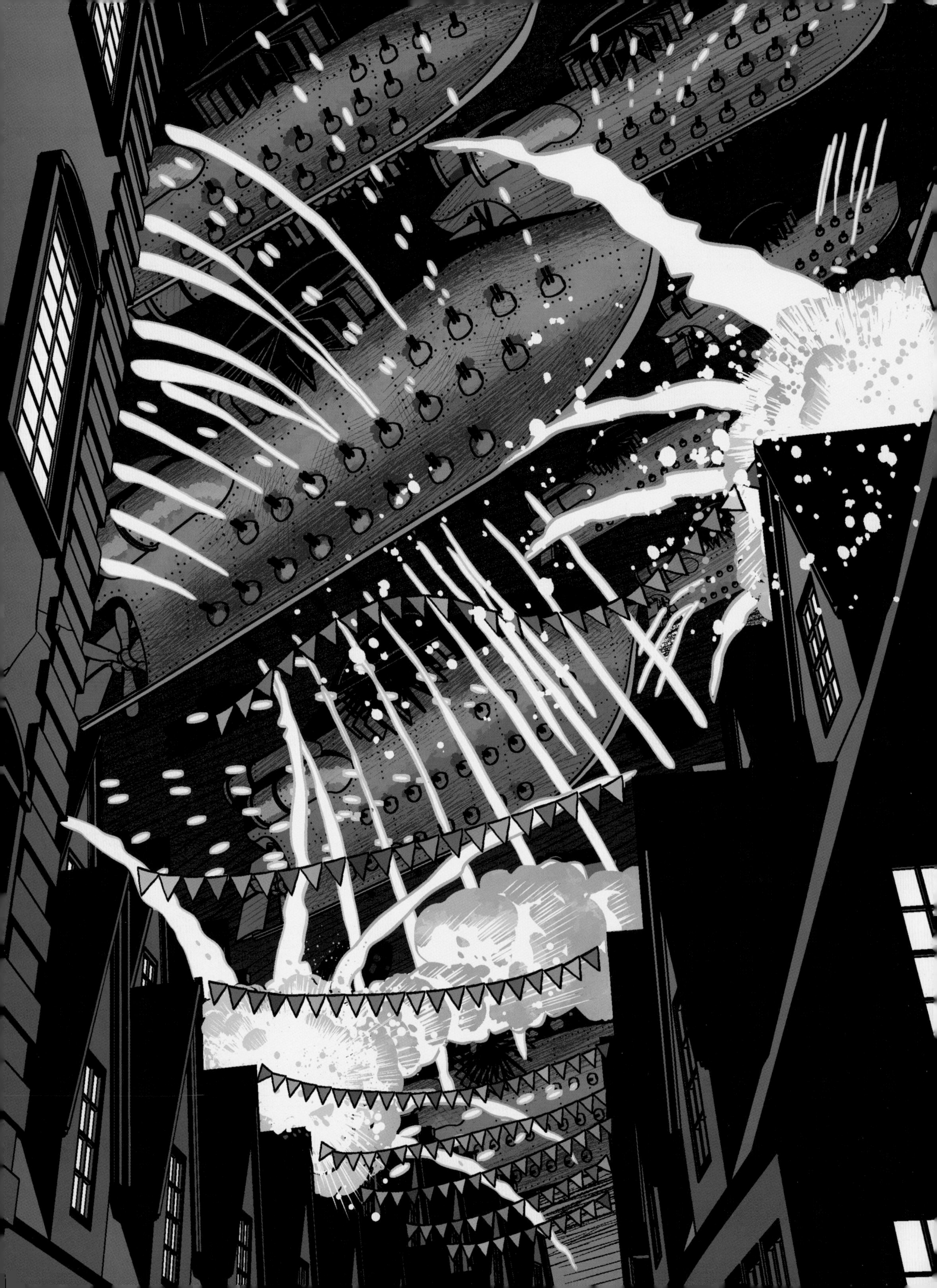

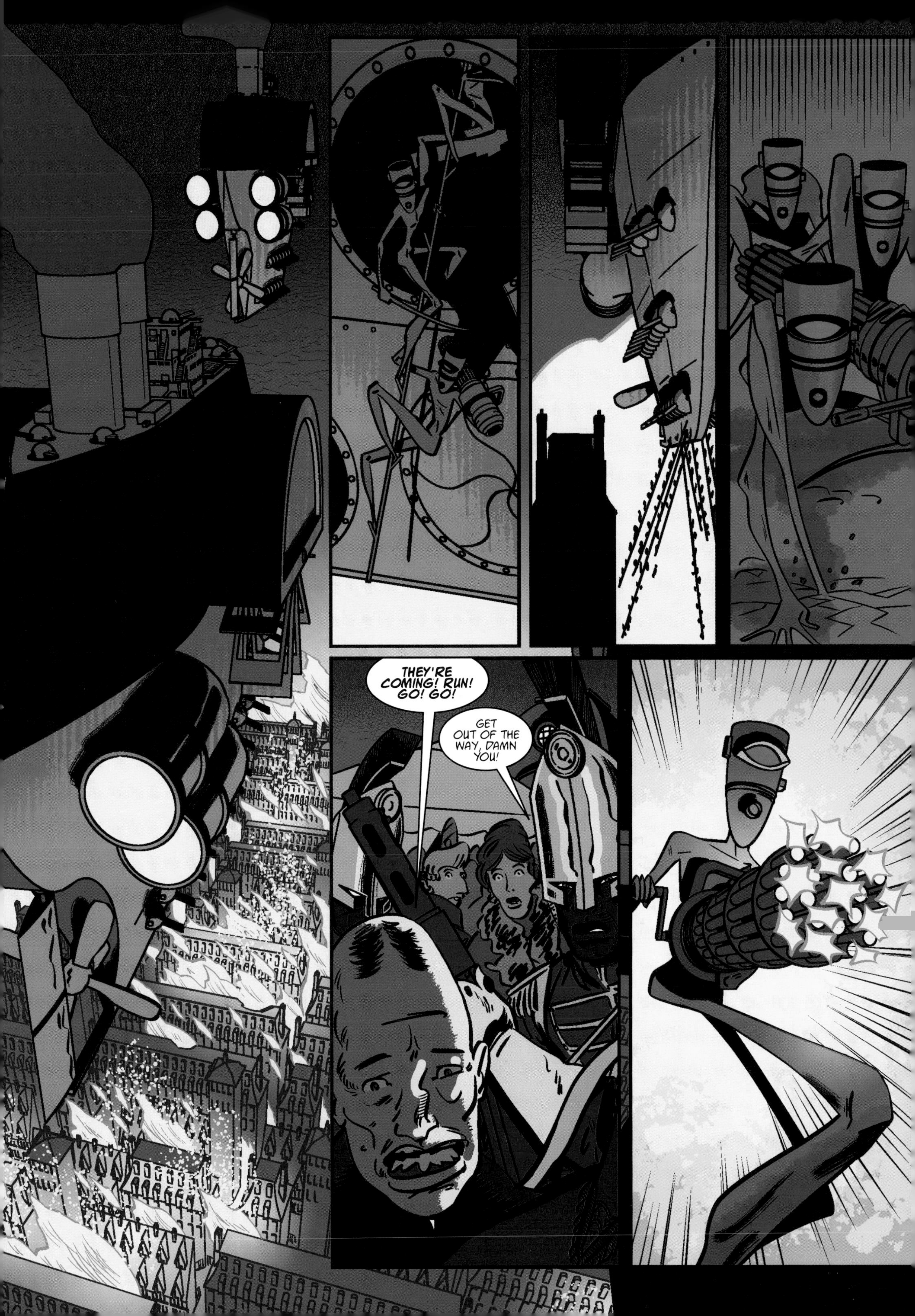
THEY'RE COMING! RUN! GO! GO!
GET OUT OF THE WAY, DAMN YOU!

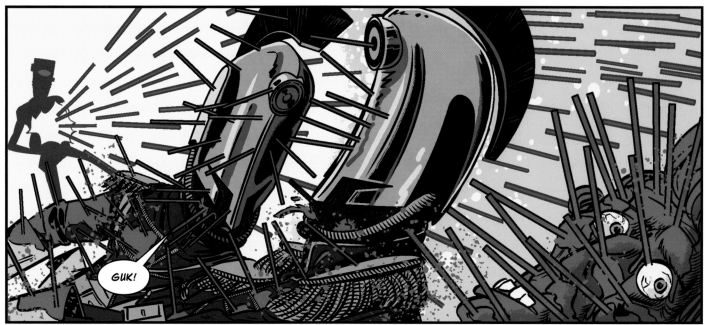

GUK!

NO... DON'T...

IT'S NO GOOD. WE'LL NOT MAKE IT HALFWAY TO THE PALACE BEFORE THEY DO.

YOU SURE THAT'S WHERE THEY'RE GOING?

WHERE ELSE IS THERE THAT MATTERS? THEY WANT THE DUKE — I WANT MY GRANDFATHER'S BOOK. WE HAVE TO GET THERE FIRST!

WHAT ABOUT RAMKIN?

DON'T HOLD YOUR BREATH. WE'VE SEEN THE LAST OF HIM. WE'LL FIND THE JOURNAL WITHOUT HIM.

WELL, I THINK I'VE FOUND US A SAFER ROUTE. QUICKER, AT LEAST.

WHERE?

UP THERE, OVER THE TOP. IT'S ALMOST A CLEAR RUN, GIVE OR TAKE.

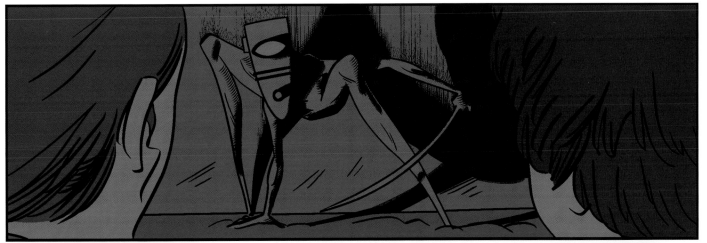

GET BEHIND ME! HURRY!

BDAM

AREN'T YOU FULL OF SURPRISES! I THOUGHT THEY TOOK YOUR WEAPON WHEN WE GOT HERE.

THEY DID. I MADE ANOTHER.

JUST BECAUSE I'M NICE DOESN'T MEAN I'M STUPID.

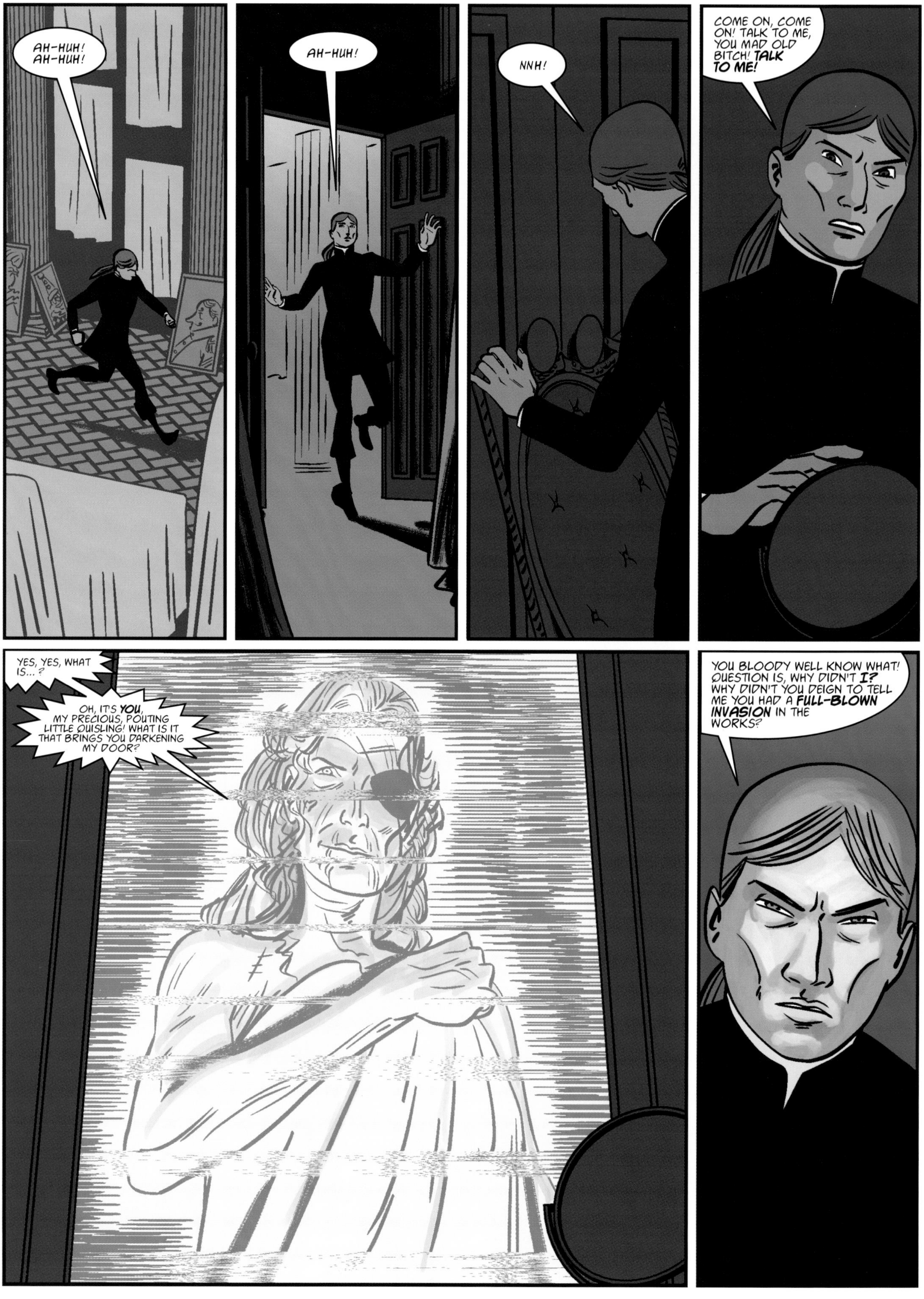
AH-HUH! AH-HUH!
AH-HUH!
NNH!
COME ON, COME ON! TALK TO ME, YOU MAD OLD BITCH! **TALK TO ME!**
YES, YES, WHAT IS... ?
OH, IT'S ***YOU***, MY PRECIOUS, POUTING LITTLE QUISLING! WHAT IS IT THAT BRINGS YOU DARKENING MY DOOR?
YOU BLOODY WELL KNOW WHAT! QUESTION IS, WHY DIDN'T ***I?*** WHY DIDN'T YOU DEIGN TO TELL ME YOU HAD A ***FULL-BLOWN INVASION*** IN THE WORKS?

YOU REALLY HAVE TO **ASK?** YOU BETRAYED YOUR LORD AND MASTER TO ME FOR A PURSE FULL OF SHINY SILVER. WHAT MANNER OF **LOYALTY** IS THAT, HM?

HOW DO I KNOW YOU WOULDN'T TURN THE TABLES AND DO THE SAME TO ME?

BUT I DIDN'T... I WOULDN'T!

MORE FOOL YOU!

DID YOU REALLY IMAGINE YOUR-SELF THE ONLY GAME IN TOWN, LITTLE BOY? THAT YOU WERE SO SMART? WHAT DID YOU THINK WAS GOING TO HAPPEN — THAT I'D LET A SLY LITTLE CHURL LIKE YOU SIT AT MY RIGHT HAND?

YOU WERE NEVER ANYTHING MORE THAN A **PAWN**, DARLING. I HAVE OTHER PIECES IN PLAY BESIDES YOURSELF AND YOU HAVE JUST RUN OUT OF MOVES.

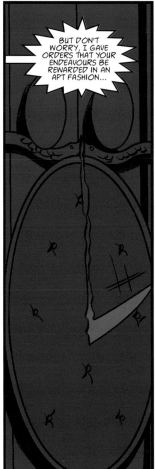

BUT DON'T WORRY, I GAVE ORDERS THAT YOUR ENDEAVOURS BE REWARDED IN AN APT FASHION...

... KNIGHT TAKES PAWN!

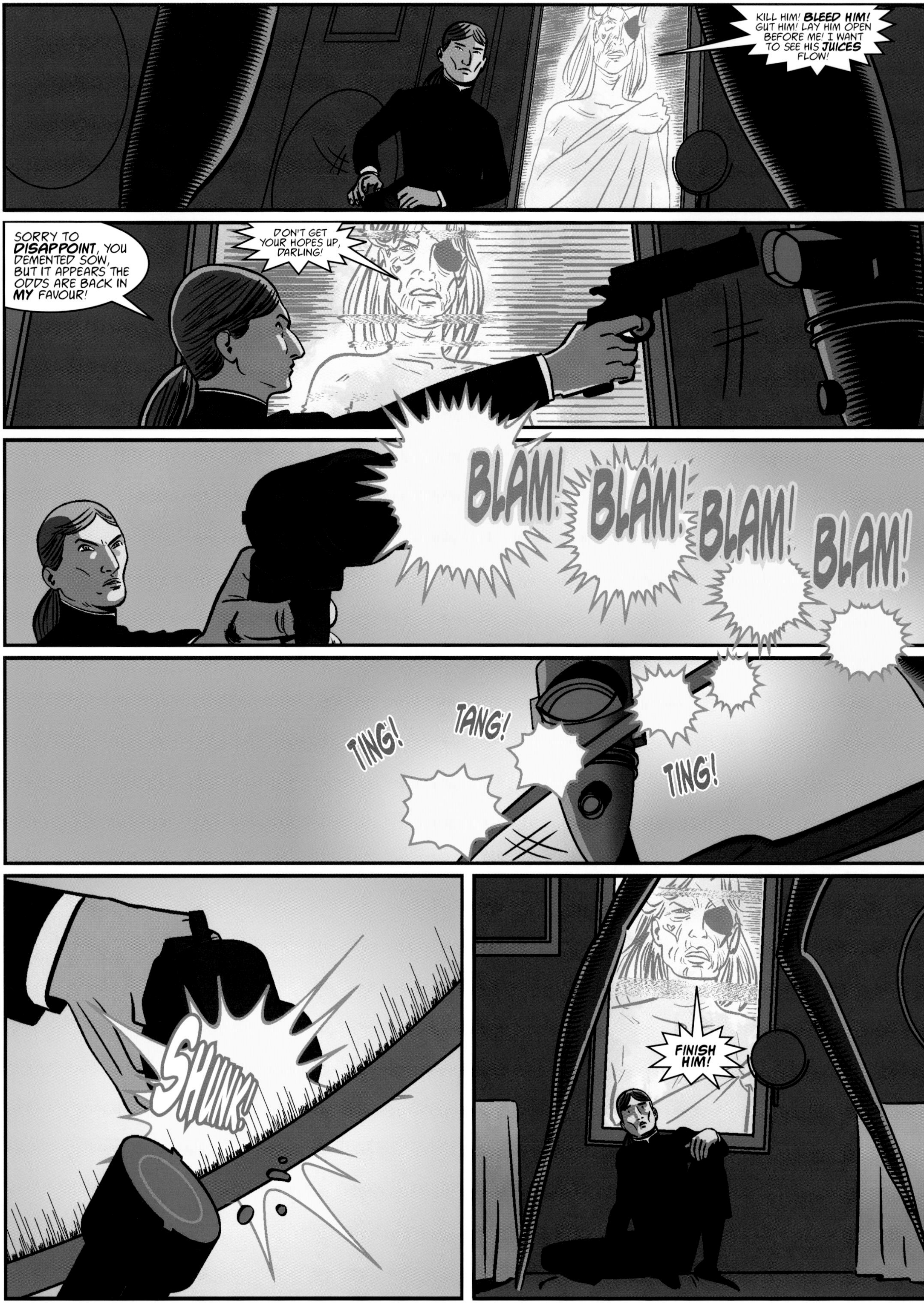
KILL HIM! BLEED HIM! GUT HIM! LAY HIM OPEN BEFORE ME! I WANT TO SEE HIS JUICES FLOW!
SORRY TO DISAPPOINT, YOU DEMENTED SOW, BUT IT APPEARS THE ODDS ARE BACK IN MY FAVOUR!
DON'T GET YOUR HOPES UP, DARLING!
BLAM! BLAM! BLAM! BLAM!
TING! TANG! TING!
SHUNK!
FINISH HIM!

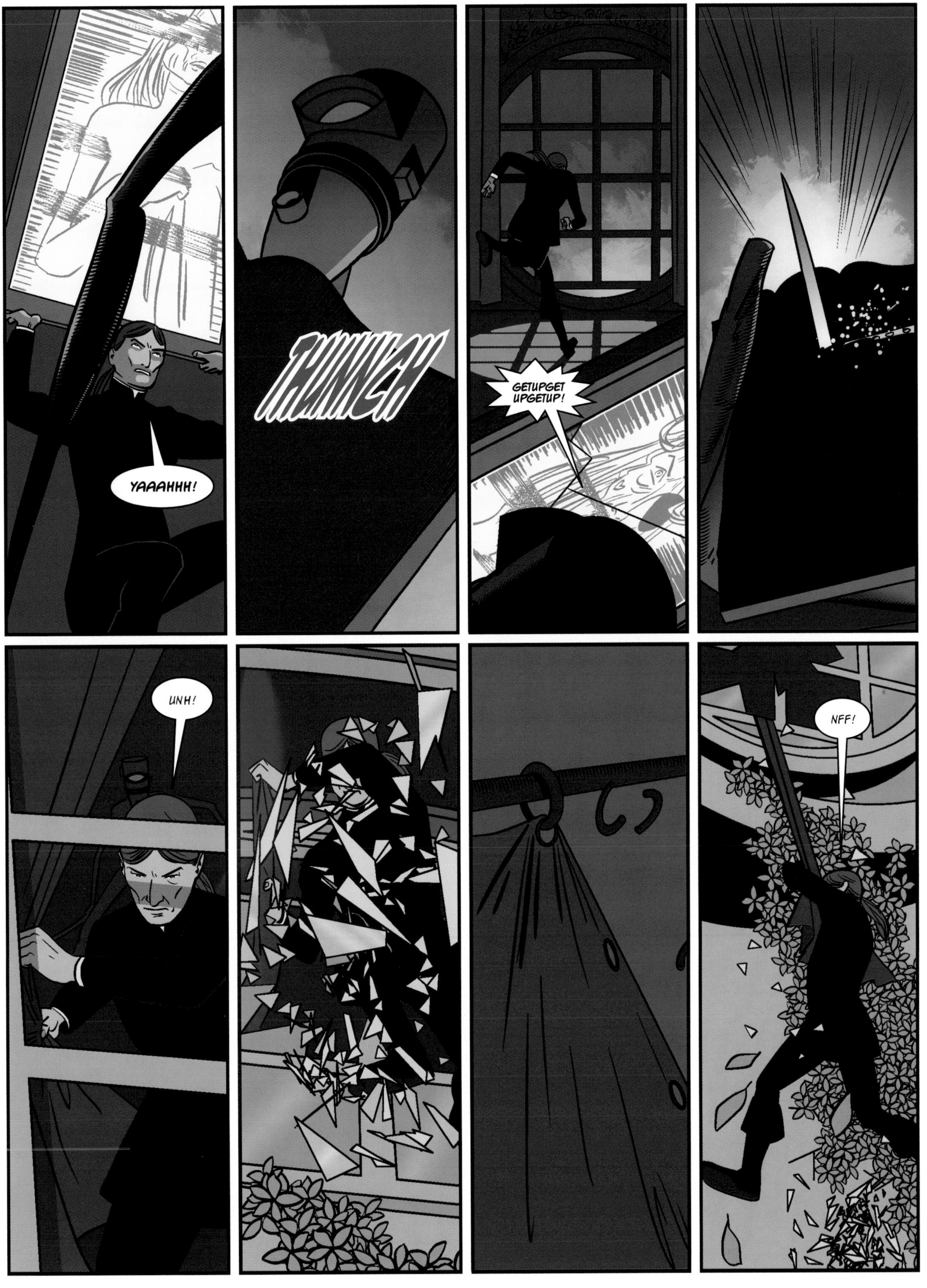
YAAAHHH!
THUNNCH
GETUPGET UPGETUP!
UNH!
NFF!

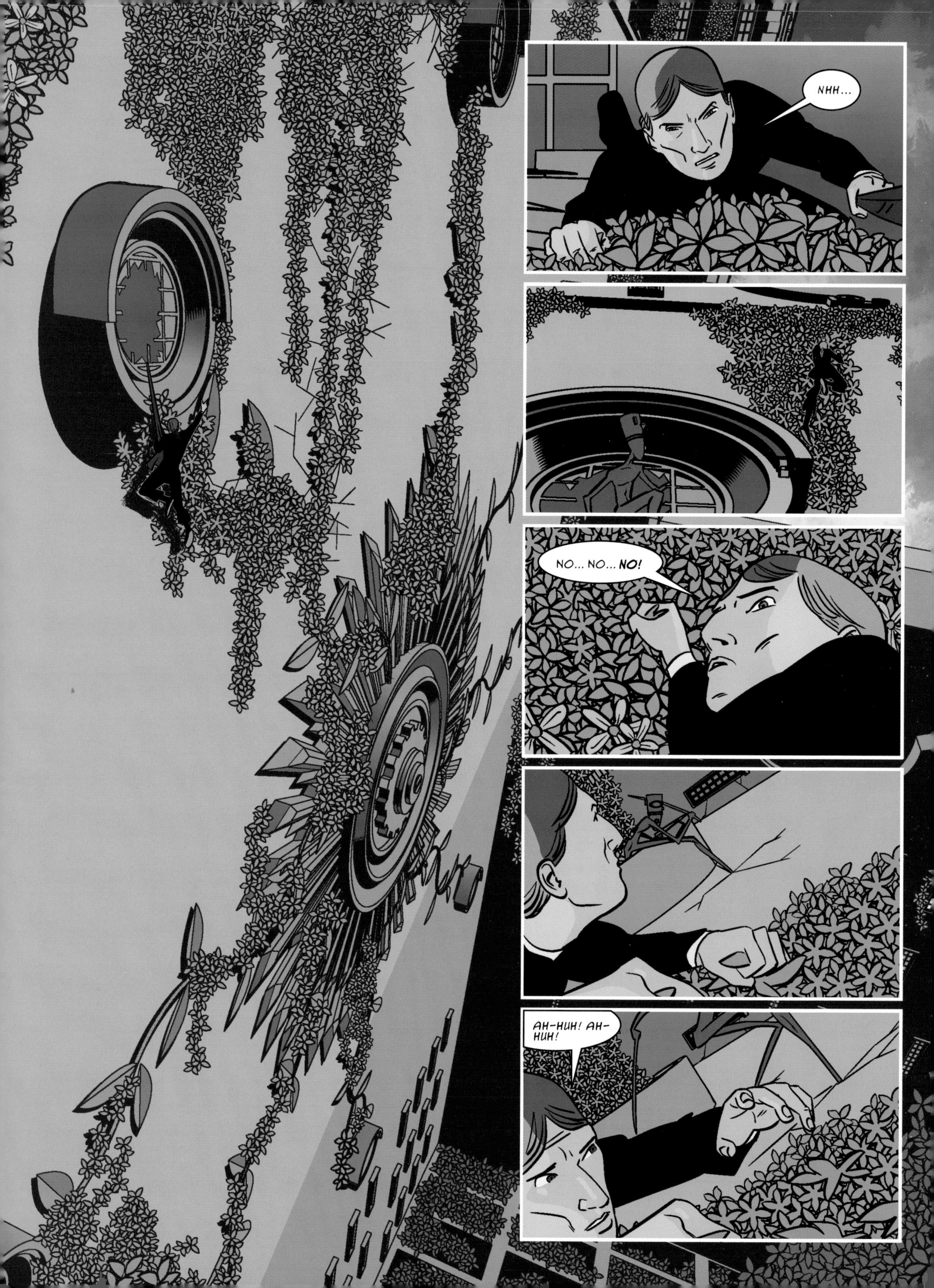
NHH...
NO... NO... NO!
AH-HUH! AH-HUH!

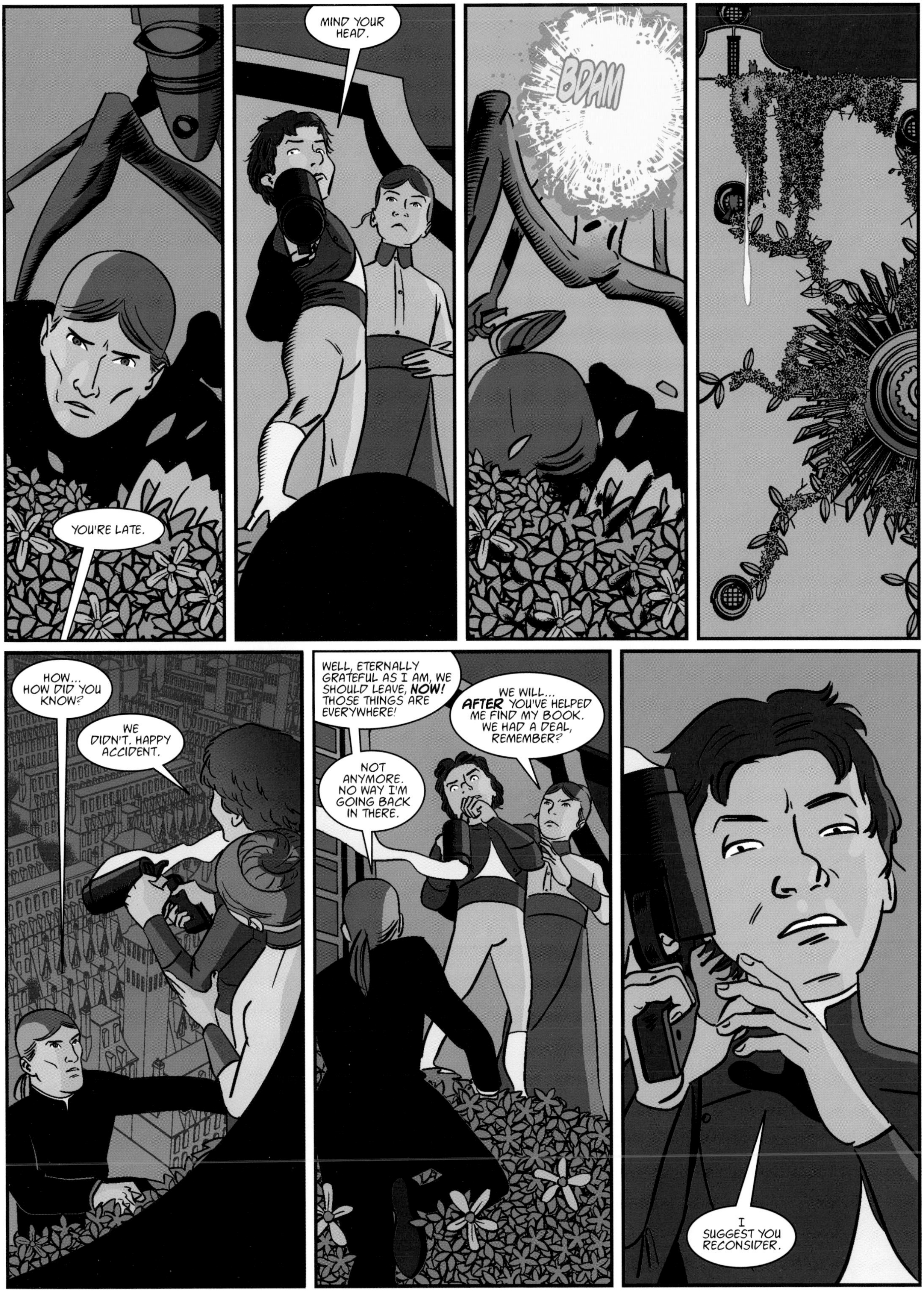
YOU'RE LATE.
MIND YOUR HEAD.
BDAM
HOW... HOW DID YOU KNOW?
WE DIDN'T. HAPPY ACCIDENT.
WELL, ETERNALLY GRATEFUL AS I AM, WE SHOULD LEAVE, NOW! THOSE THINGS ARE EVERYWHERE!
WE WILL... AFTER YOU'VE HELPED ME FIND MY BOOK. WE HAD A DEAL, REMEMBER?
NOT ANYMORE. NO WAY I'M GOING BACK IN THERE.
I SUGGEST YOU RECONSIDER.

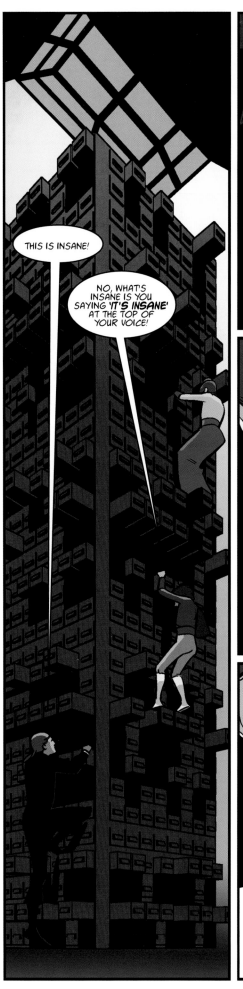

THIS IS INSANE!

NO, WHAT'S INSANE IS YOU SAYING 'IT'S INSANE' AT THE TOP OF YOUR VOICE!

YOU KNOW, I GET IT. I REALLY DO. THE GUN. THE ATTITUDE. YOU WANT TO IMPRESS YOUR GIRLFRIEND...

IT'S NOT LIKE THAT! I MEAN... SHE'S NOT...

AND SHE NEVER WILL BE, OLD SON. NOTHING MATTERS TO HER EXCEPT WHAT'S IN THAT DAMN **BOOK**.

YOU'RE WASTING YOUR TIME, SO SPARE US ALL AND STOP PLAYING THE PRAT, EH?

WHERE ARE WE?

THE DUKE'S APARTMENTS. THIS IS WHERE HE KEEPS HIS TUESDAY-EVENING DRESS CUFFLINKS, BUT SINCE HE **ABOLISHED** TUESDAY TEN YEARS AGO NO ONE'S BEEN HERE SINCE.

WE'VE GOT THE PLACE TO OURSELVES...

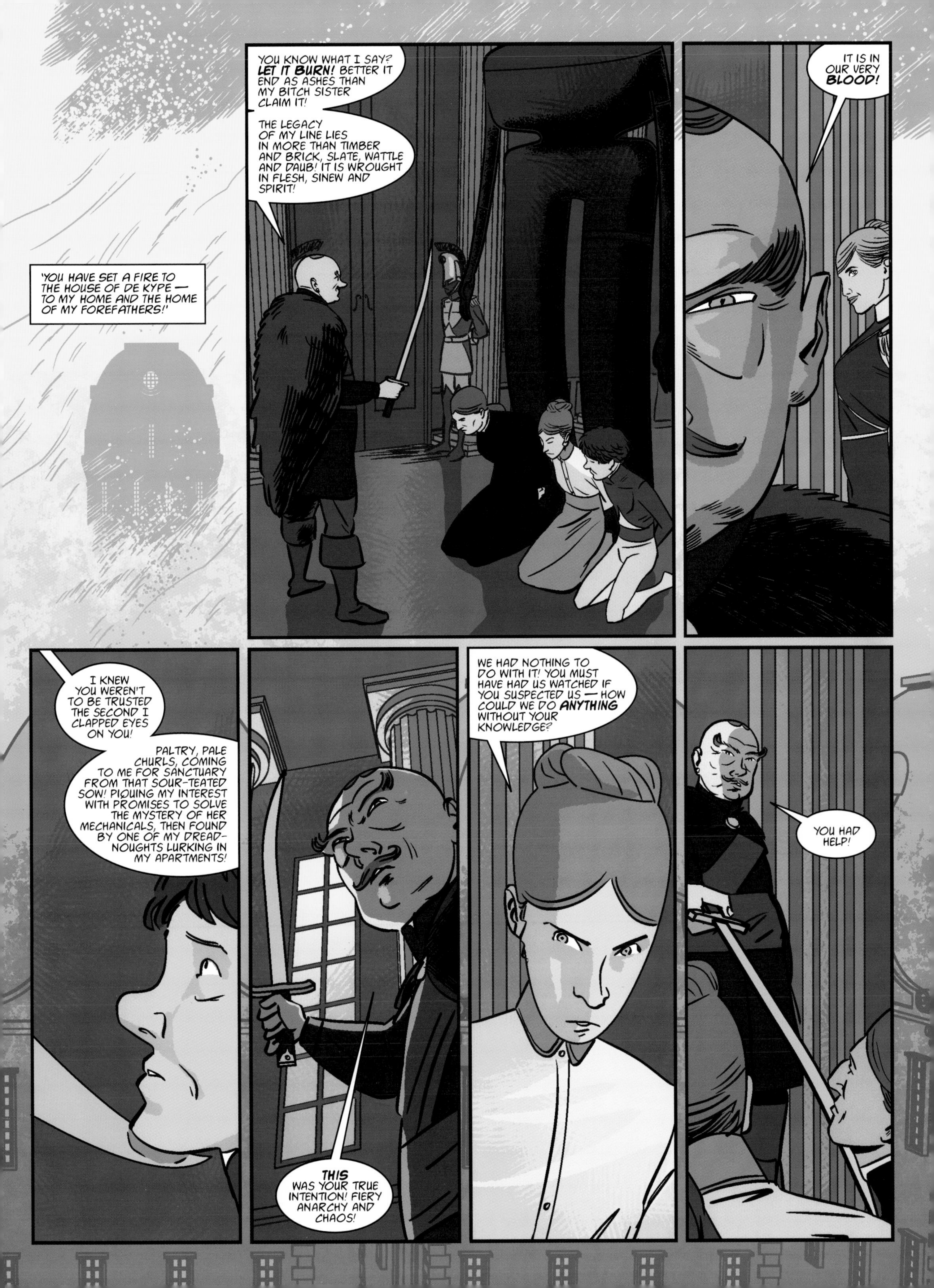
'YOU HAVE SET A FIRE TO THE HOUSE OF DE KYPE — TO MY HOME AND THE HOME OF MY FOREFATHERS!'
YOU KNOW WHAT I SAY? LET IT BURN! BETTER IT END AS ASHES THAN MY BITCH SISTER CLAIM IT!
THE LEGACY OF MY LINE LIES IN MORE THAN TIMBER AND BRICK, SLATE, WATTLE AND DAUB! IT IS WROUGHT IN FLESH, SINEW AND SPIRIT!
IT IS IN OUR VERY BLOOD!
I KNEW YOU WEREN'T TO BE TRUSTED THE SECOND I CLAPPED EYES ON YOU!
PALTRY, PALE CHURLS, COMING TO ME FOR SANCTUARY FROM THAT SOUR-TEATED SOW! PIQUING MY INTEREST WITH PROMISES TO SOLVE THE MYSTERY OF HER MECHANICALS, THEN FOUND BY ONE OF MY DREAD-NOUGHTS LURKING IN MY APARTMENTS!
THIS WAS YOUR TRUE INTENTION! FIERY ANARCHY AND CHAOS!
WE HAD NOTHING TO DO WITH IT! YOU MUST HAVE HAD US WATCHED IF YOU SUSPECTED US — HOW COULD WE DO ANYTHING WITHOUT YOUR KNOWLEDGE?
YOU HAD HELP!

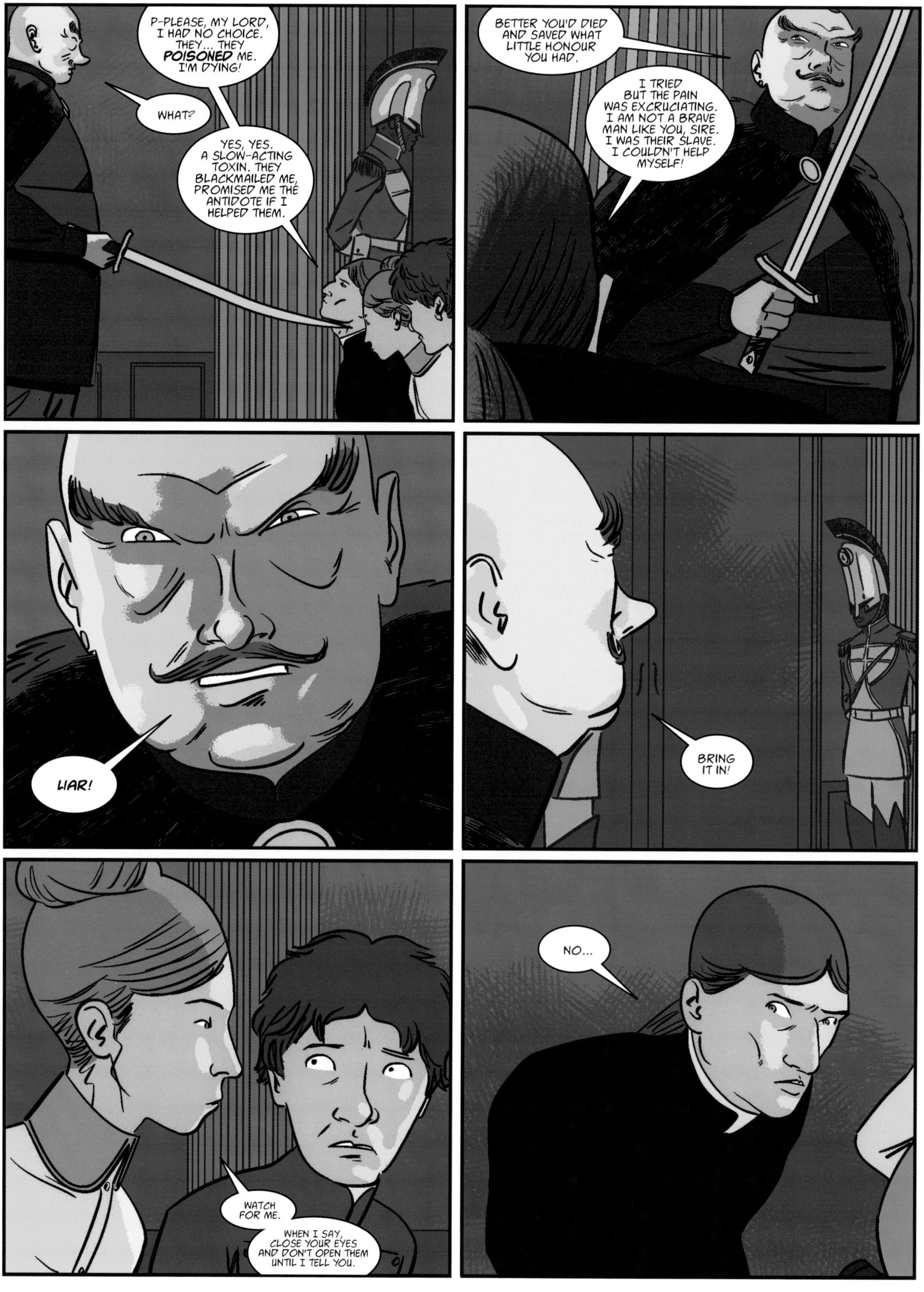
P-PLEASE, MY LORD, I HAD NO CHOICE. THEY... THEY POISONED ME. I'M DYING!
WHAT?
YES, YES. A SLOW-ACTING TOXIN. THEY BLACKMAILED ME, PROMISED ME THE ANTIDOTE IF I HELPED THEM.
BETTER YOU'D DIED AND SAVED WHAT LITTLE HONOUR YOU HAD.
I TRIED BUT THE PAIN WAS EXCRUCIATING. I AM NOT A BRAVE MAN LIKE YOU, SIRE. I WAS THEIR SLAVE. I COULDN'T HELP MYSELF!
LIAR!
BRING IT IN!
WATCH FOR ME.
WHEN I SAY, CLOSE YOUR EYES AND DON'T OPEN THEM UNTIL I TELL YOU.
NO...

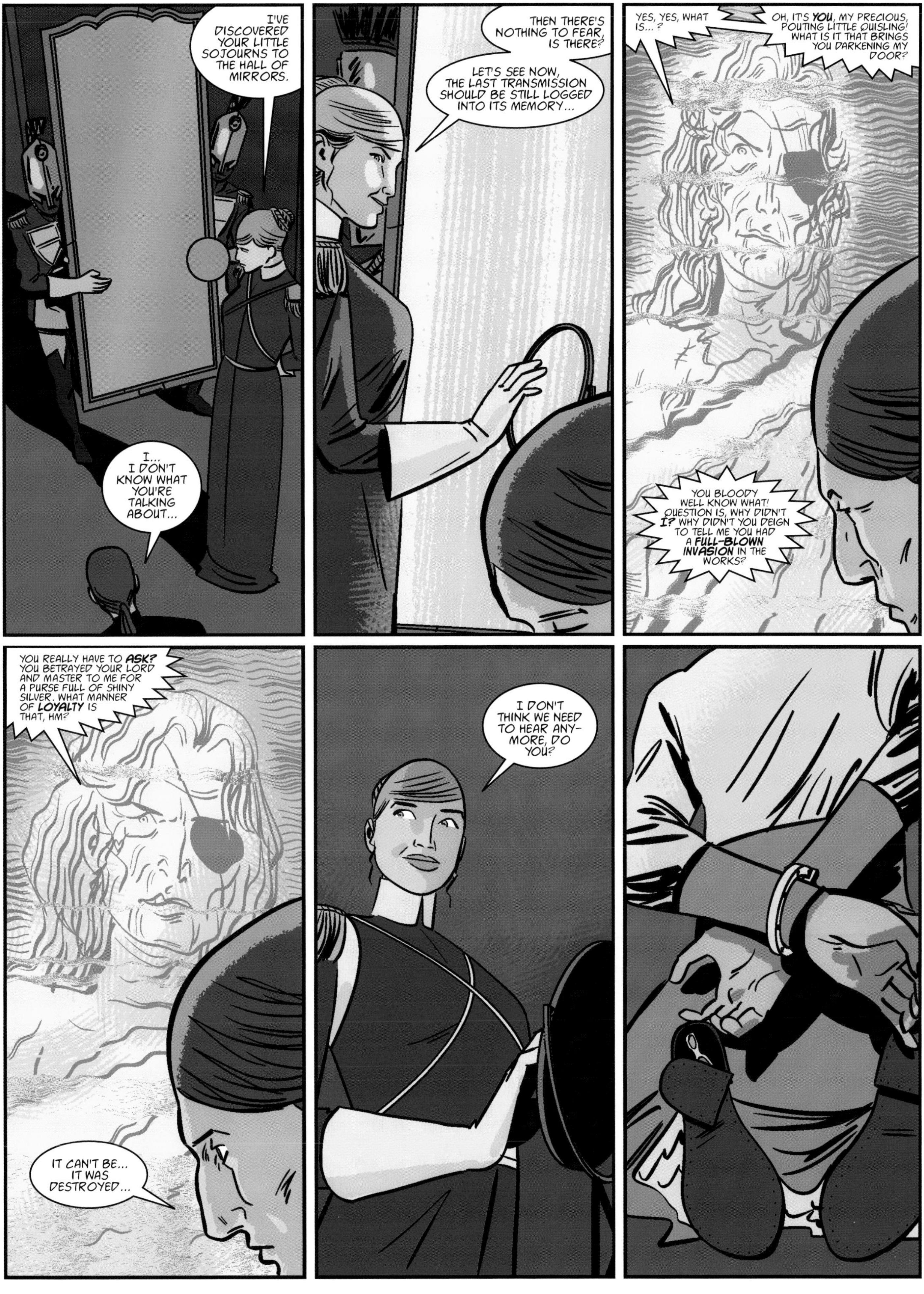

I'VE DISCOVERED YOUR LITTLE SOJOURNS TO THE HALL OF MIRRORS.
I... I DON'T KNOW WHAT YOU'RE TALKING ABOUT...
THEN THERE'S NOTHING TO FEAR, IS THERE?
LET'S SEE NOW, THE LAST TRANSMISSION SHOULD BE STILL LOGGED INTO ITS MEMORY...
YES, YES, WHAT IS... ?
OH, IT'S **YOU**, MY PRECIOUS, POUTING LITTLE QUISLING! WHAT IS IT THAT BRINGS YOU DARKENING MY DOOR?
YOU BLOODY WELL KNOW WHAT! QUESTION IS, WHY DIDN'T **I?** WHY DIDN'T YOU DEIGN TO TELL ME YOU HAD A **FULL-BLOWN INVASION** IN THE WORKS?
YOU REALLY HAVE TO **ASK?** YOU BETRAYED YOUR LORD AND MASTER TO ME FOR A PURSE FULL OF SHINY SILVER. WHAT MANNER OF **LOYALTY** IS THAT, HM?
IT CAN'T BE... IT WAS DESTROYED...
I DON'T THINK WE NEED TO HEAR ANY-MORE, DO YOU?

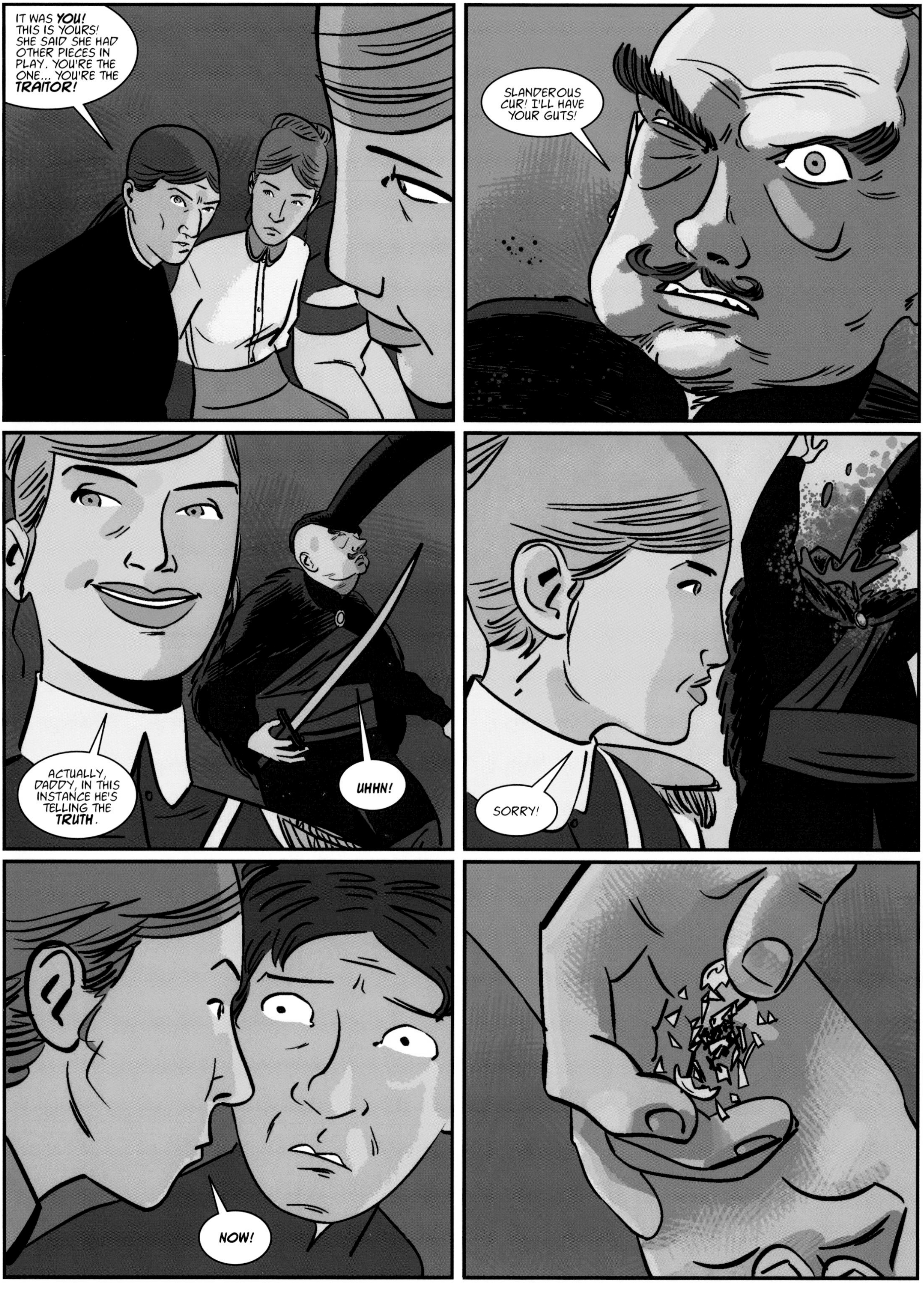
IT WAS YOU! THIS IS YOURS! SHE SAID SHE HAD OTHER PIECES IN PLAY. YOU'RE THE ONE... YOU'RE THE TRAITOR!
SLANDEROUS CUR! I'LL HAVE YOUR GUTS!
ACTUALLY, DADDY, IN THIS INSTANCE HE'S TELLING THE TRUTH.
UHHN!
SORRY!
NOW!

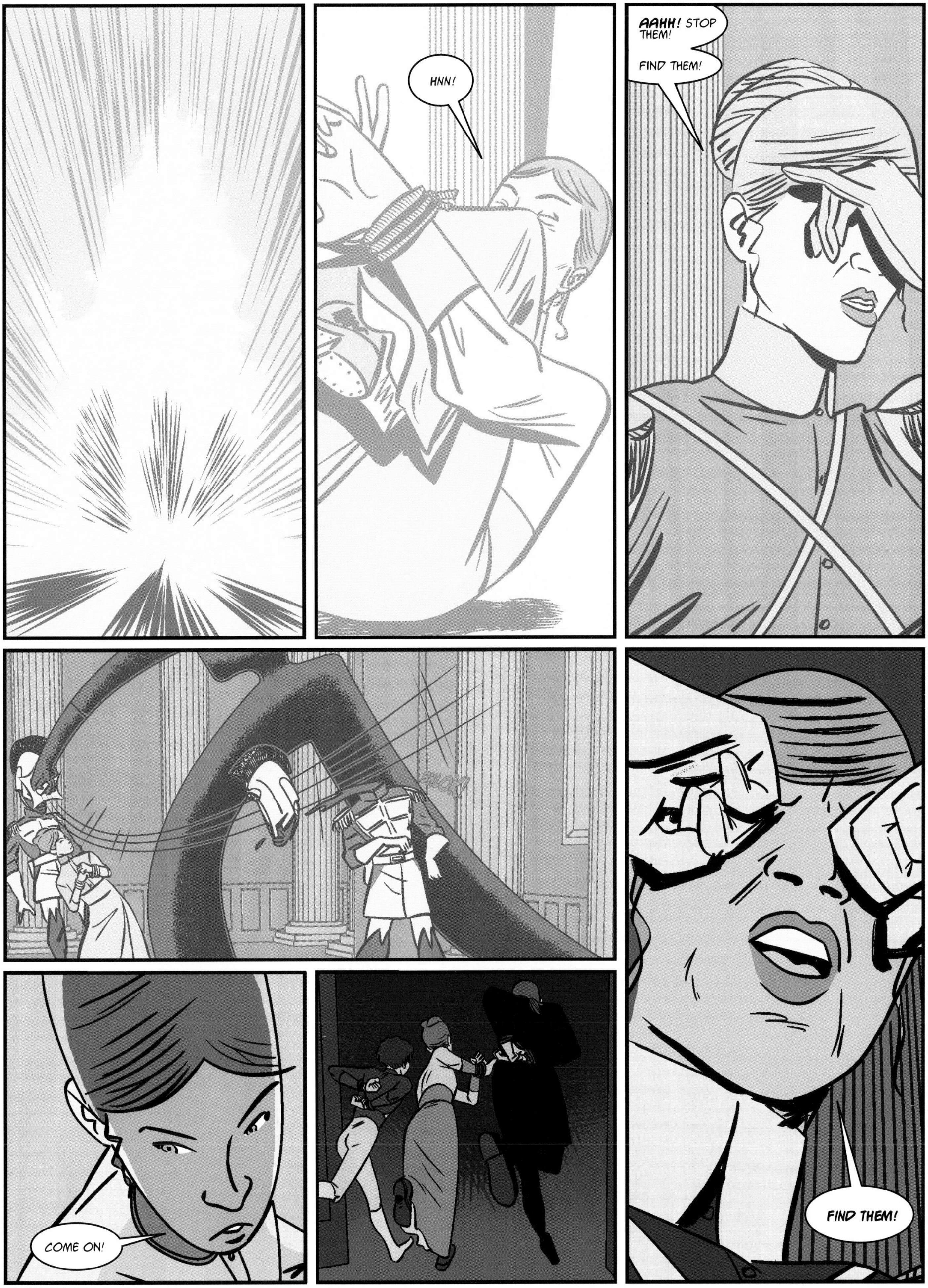
HNN!
AAHH! STOP THEM!
FIND THEM!
SHLOK!
FIND THEM!
COME ON!

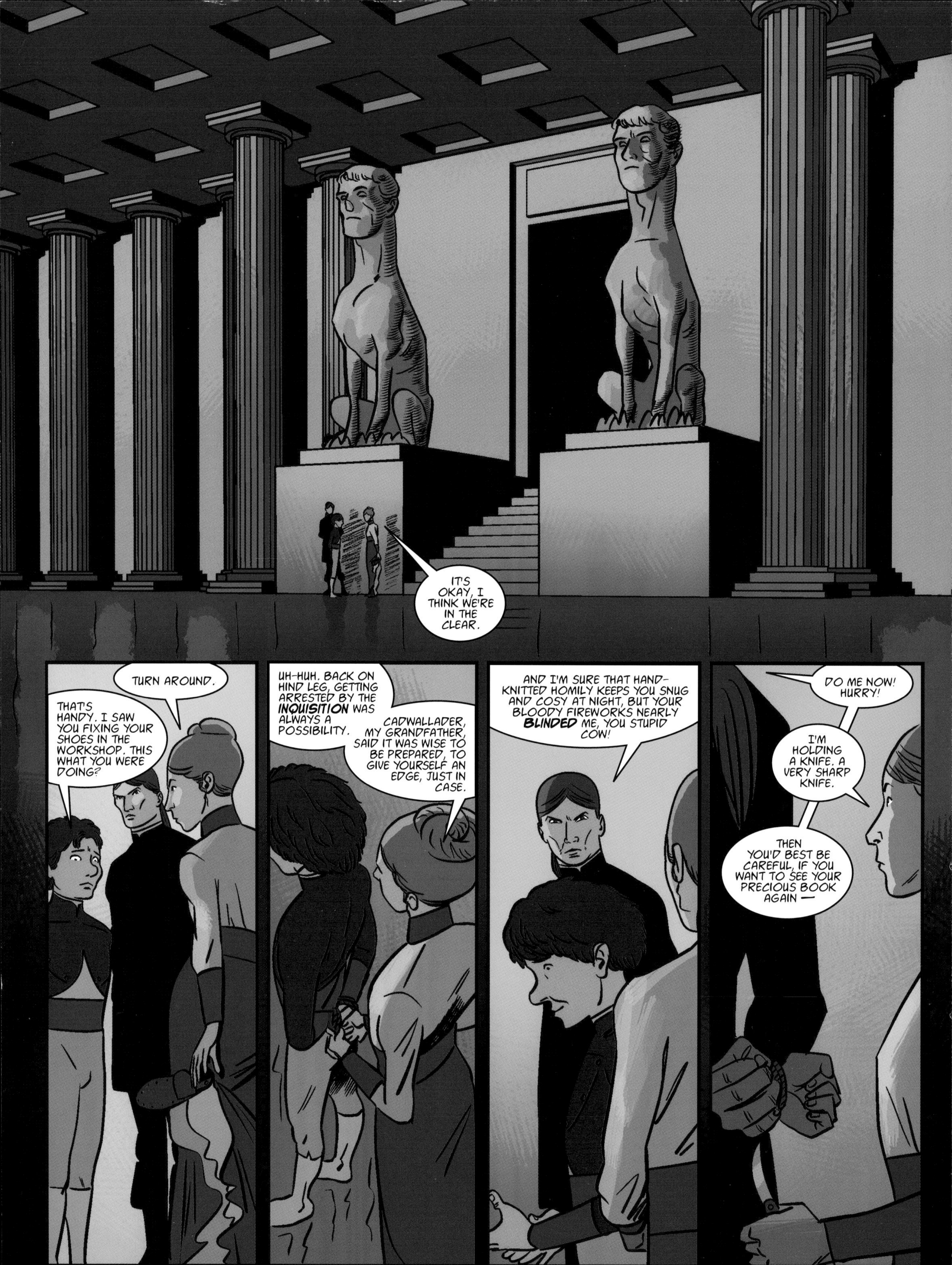
IT'S OKAY, I THINK WE'RE IN THE CLEAR.
TURN AROUND.
THAT'S HANDY. I SAW YOU FIXING YOUR SHOES IN THE WORKSHOP. THIS WHAT YOU WERE DOING?
UH-HUH. BACK ON HIND LEG, GETTING ARRESTED BY THE INQUISITION WAS ALWAYS A POSSIBILITY.
CADWALLADER, MY GRANDFATHER, SAID IT WAS WISE TO BE PREPARED, TO GIVE YOURSELF AN EDGE, JUST IN CASE.
AND I'M SURE THAT HAND-KNITTED HOMILY KEEPS YOU SNUG AND COSY AT NIGHT, BUT YOUR BLOODY FIREWORKS NEARLY BLINDED ME, YOU STUPID COW!
DO ME NOW! HURRY!
I'M HOLDING A KNIFE. A VERY SHARP KNIFE.
THEN YOU'D BEST BE CAREFUL, IF YOU WANT TO SEE YOUR PRECIOUS BOOK AGAIN —

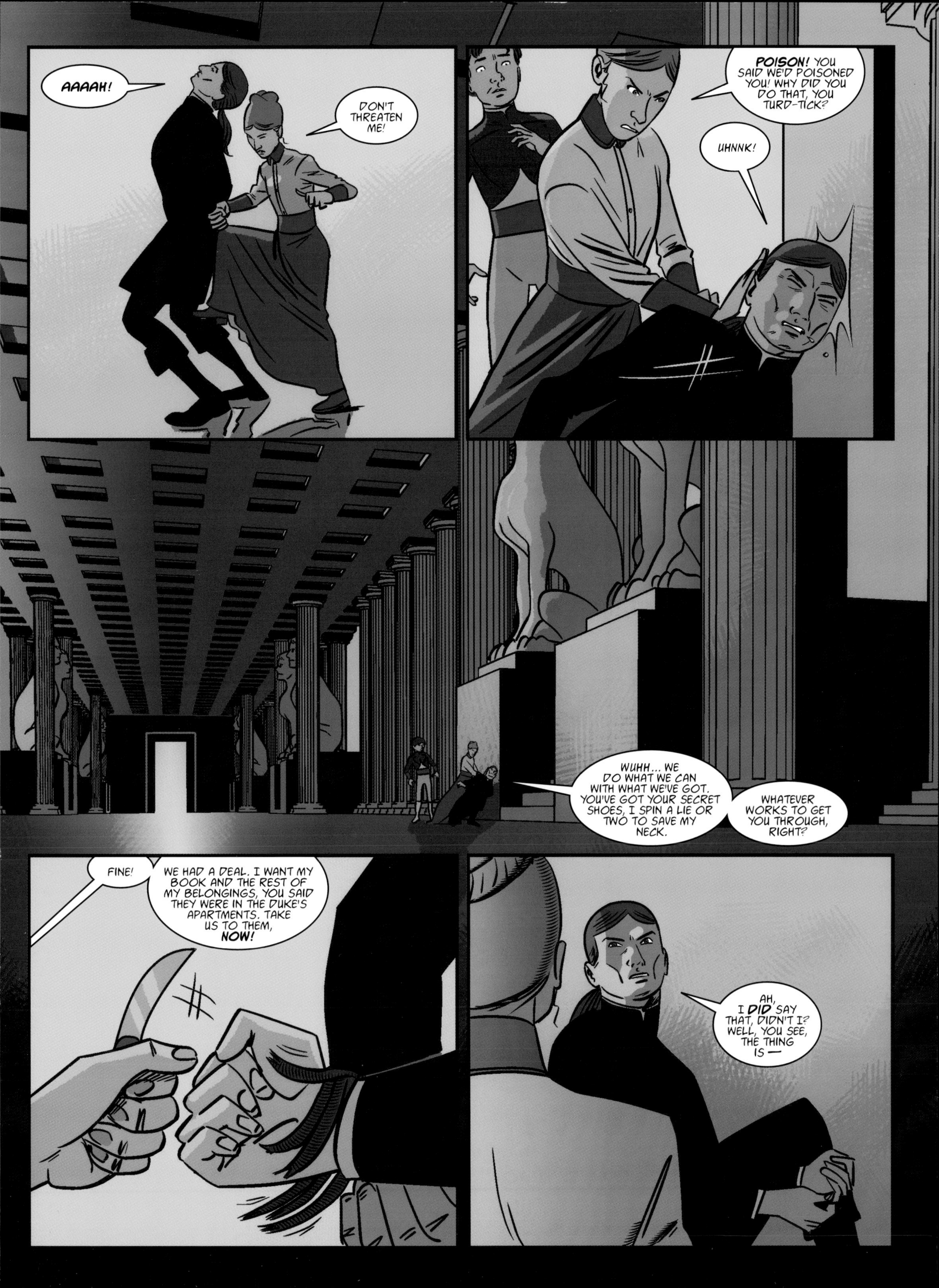

AAAAH!
DON'T THREATEN ME!
POISON! YOU SAID WE'D POISONED YOU! WHY DID YOU DO THAT, YOU TURD-TICK?
UHNNK!
WUHH... WE DO WHAT WE CAN WITH WHAT WE'VE GOT. YOU'VE GOT YOUR SECRET SHOES, I SPIN A LIE OR TWO TO SAVE MY NECK.
WHATEVER WORKS TO GET YOU THROUGH, RIGHT?
FINE!
WE HAD A DEAL. I WANT MY BOOK AND THE REST OF MY BELONGINGS, YOU SAID THEY WERE IN THE DUKE'S APARTMENTS. TAKE US TO THEM, NOW!
AH, I DID SAY THAT, DIDN'T I? WELL, YOU SEE, THE THING IS —

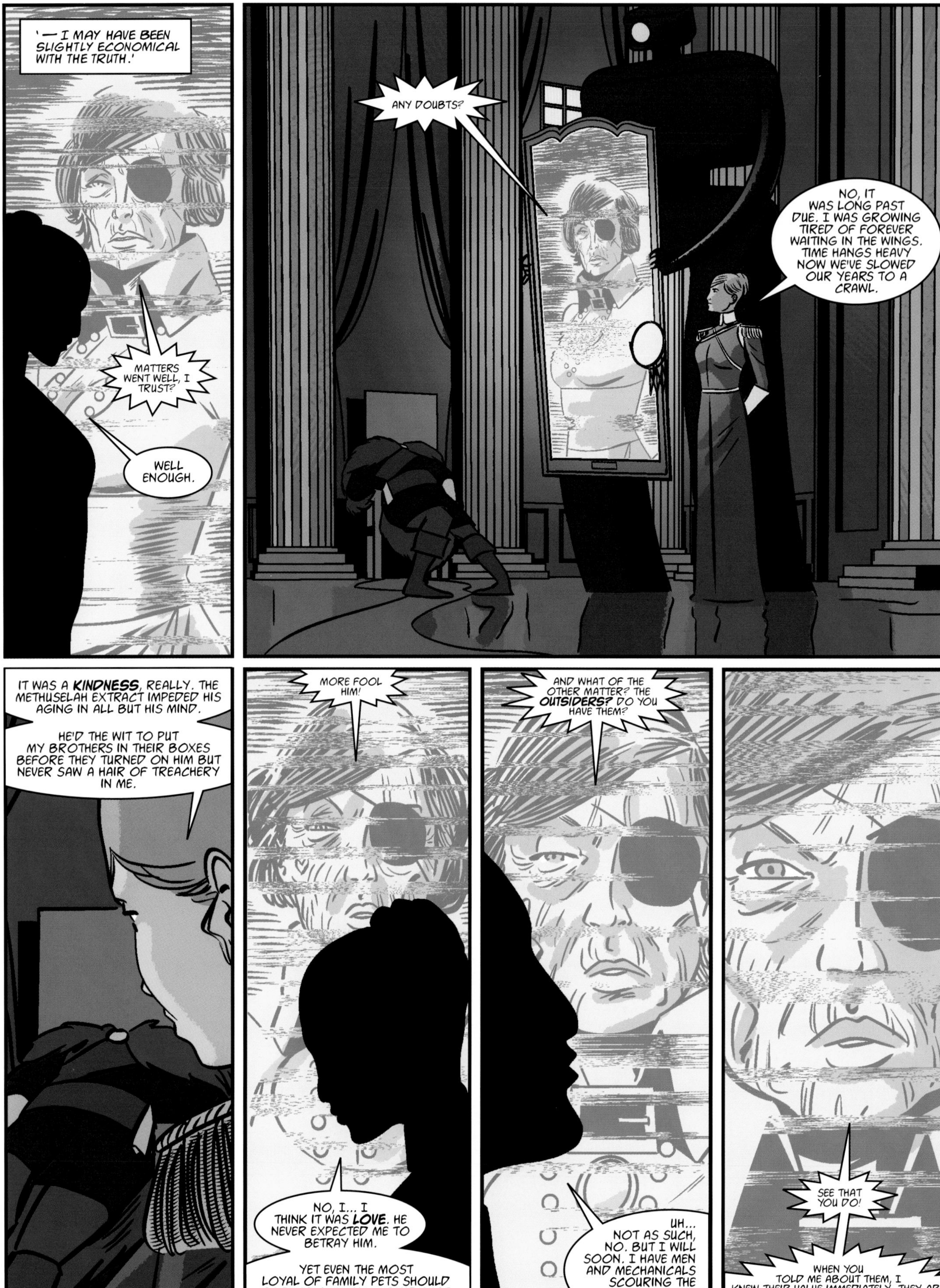
'— I MAY HAVE BEEN SLIGHTLY ECONOMICAL WITH THE TRUTH.'
MATTERS WENT WELL, I TRUST?
WELL ENOUGH.
ANY DOUBTS?
NO, IT WAS LONG PAST DUE. I WAS GROWING TIRED OF FOREVER WAITING IN THE WINGS. TIME HANGS HEAVY NOW WE'VE SLOWED OUR YEARS TO A CRAWL.
IT WAS A KINDNESS, REALLY. THE METHUSELAH EXTRACT IMPEDED HIS AGING IN ALL BUT HIS MIND.
HE'D THE WIT TO PUT MY BROTHERS IN THEIR BOXES BEFORE THEY TURNED ON HIM BUT NEVER SAW A HAIR OF TREACHERY IN ME.
MORE FOOL HIM!
NO, I... I THINK IT WAS LOVE. HE NEVER EXPECTED ME TO BETRAY HIM.
YET EVEN THE MOST LOYAL OF FAMILY PETS SHOULD BE PUT DOWN ONCE THEIR BEST YEARS ARE BEHIND THEM.
AND WHAT OF THE OTHER MATTER? THE OUTSIDERS? DO YOU HAVE THEM?
UH... NOT AS SUCH, NO. BUT I WILL SOON. I HAVE MEN AND MECHANICALS SCOURING THE HALLS FOR THEM AS WE SPEAK.
SEE THAT YOU DO!
WHEN YOU TOLD ME ABOUT THEM, I KNEW THEIR VALUE IMMEDIATELY. THEY ARE THE VERY REASON I HAVE COMMITTED MY RESOURCES TO THIS INVASION.

I DON'T UNDER-STAND... THIS **ISN'T** ABOUT UNITING OUR DIVIDED HOUSE?

THE HOUSE DE KYPE IS A MOULDERING RUIN! IF IT IS TO STAGNATE NO FURTHER WE MUST LOOK TO THE **STARS** FOR SALVATION.

WE HAVE FORGOTTEN MUCH AND HAVE A LONG WAY TO CRAWL BACK INTO THE LIGHT.

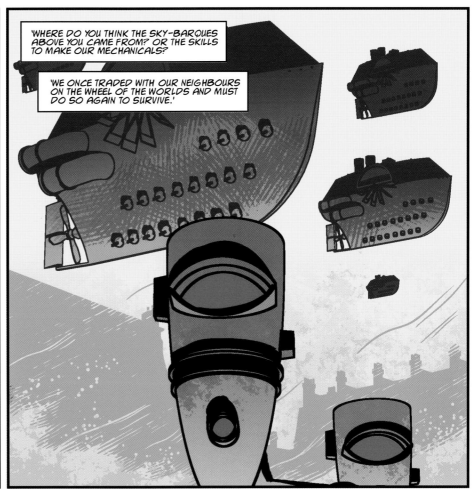

'WHERE DO YOU THINK THE SKY-BARQUES ABOVE YOU CAME FROM? OR THE SKILLS TO MAKE OUR MECHANICALS?

'WE ONCE TRADED WITH OUR NEIGHBOURS ON THE WHEEL OF THE WORLDS AND MUST DO SO AGAIN TO SURVIVE.'

IF THEY ARE FROM OFF-WORLD, AS I SUSPECT, WE MUST PRESS THEM INTO SERVICE. YOU HAVE THE GIRL'S EFFECTS?

YES, AUNT, I DO.

'MY FATHER KEPT THEM SECURED IN HIS PRIVATE ROOMS.'

YOU HAD THEM **ALL THIS TIME?**

YES... NO. WELL, NOT ON ME. THE DUKE JUST LEFT IT LYING AROUND. I SWAPPED IT FOR A SIMILAR ONE WHEN I GOT THE CHANCE.

HE NEVER NOTICED. I DON'T THINK HE COULD TELL ONE BOOK FROM ANOTHER.

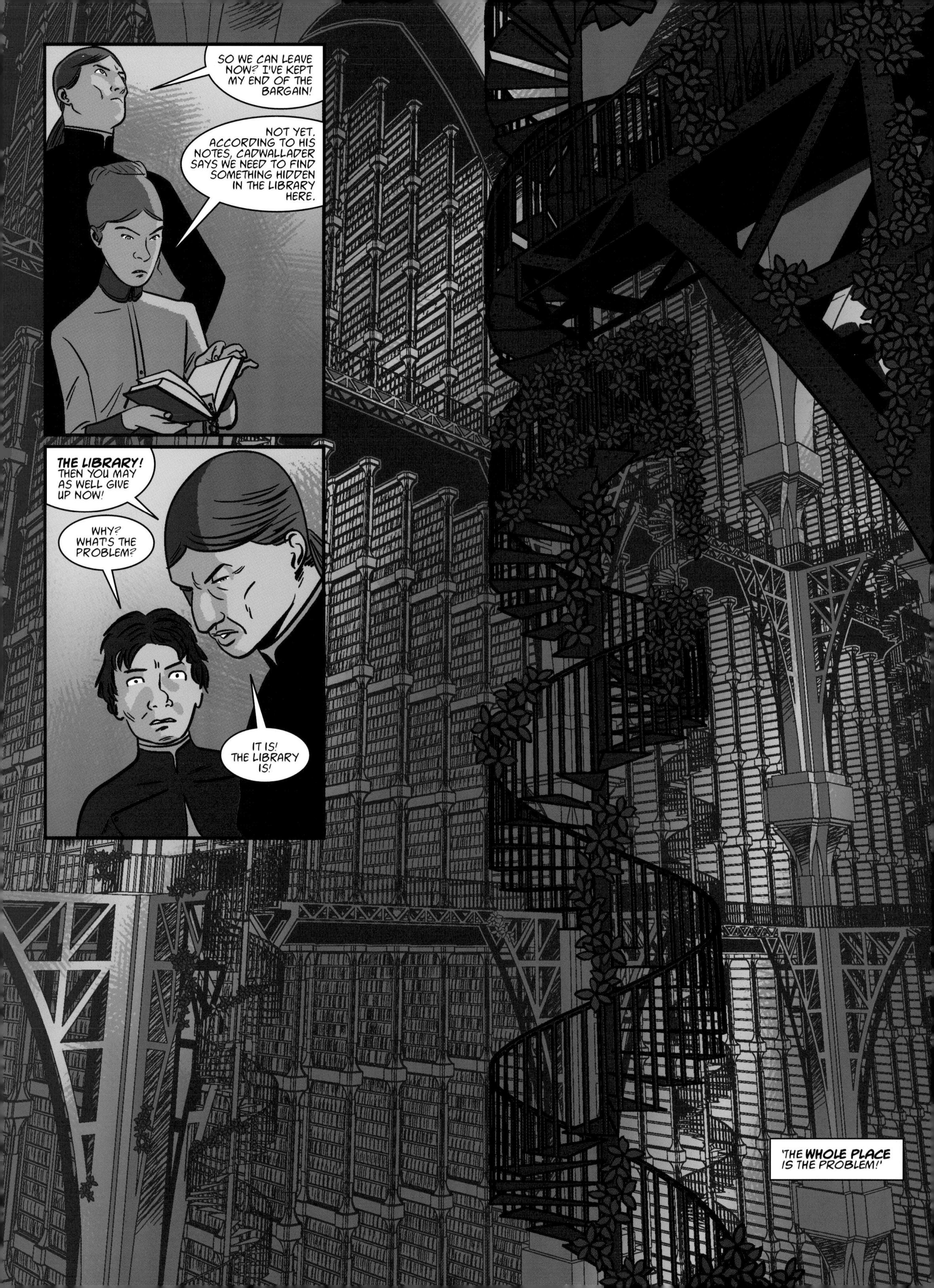
SO WE CAN LEAVE NOW? I'VE KEPT MY END OF THE BARGAIN!
NOT YET. ACCORDING TO HIS NOTES, CADWALLADER SAYS WE NEED TO FIND SOMETHING HIDDEN IN THE LIBRARY HERE.
THE LIBRARY! THEN YOU MAY AS WELL GIVE UP NOW!
WHY? WHAT'S THE PROBLEM?
IT IS! THE LIBRARY IS!
'THE **WHOLE PLACE** IS THE PROBLEM!'

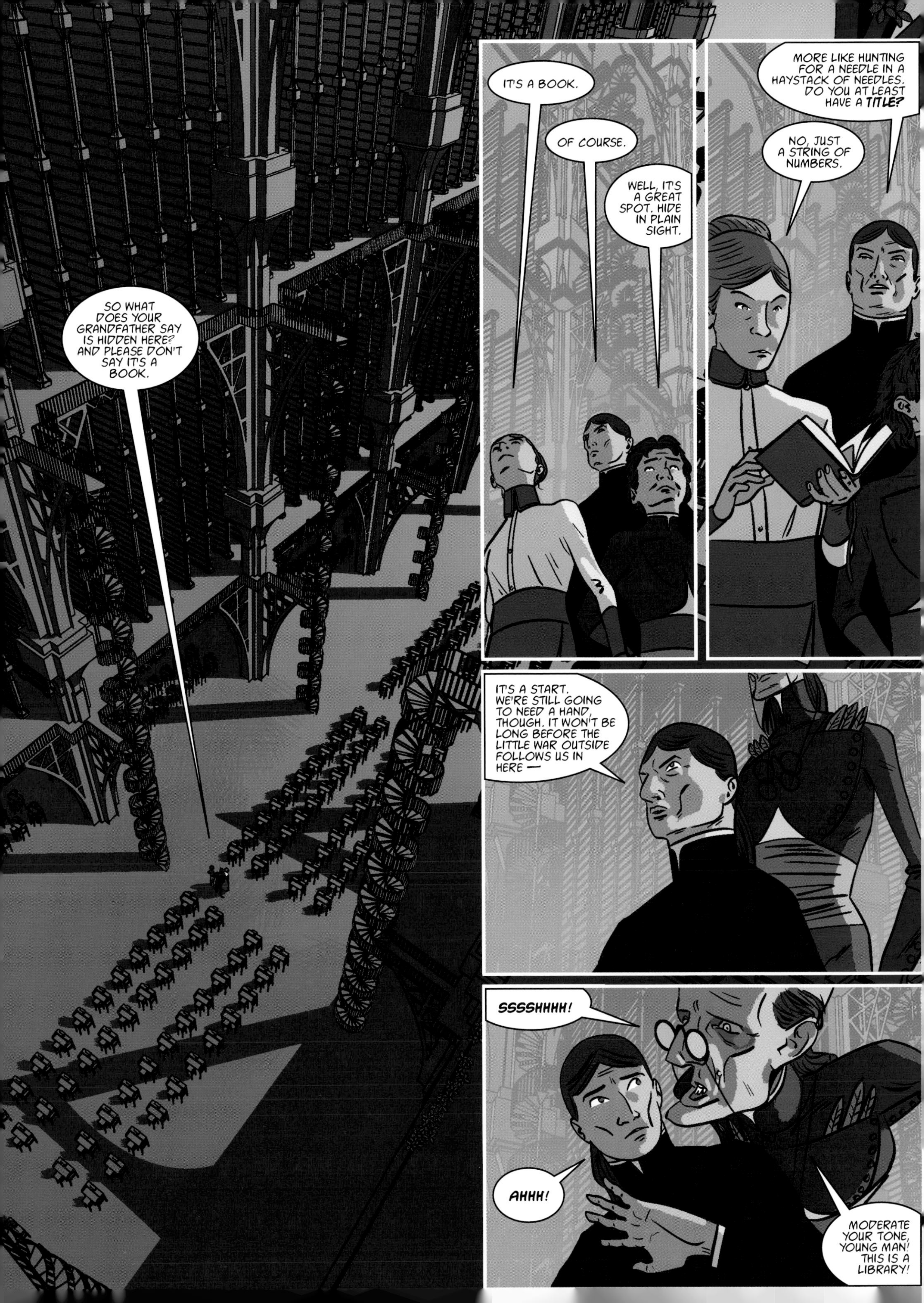
SO WHAT DOES YOUR GRANDFATHER SAY IS HIDDEN HERE? AND PLEASE DON'T SAY IT'S A BOOK.
IT'S A BOOK.
OF COURSE.
WELL, IT'S A GREAT SPOT. HIDE IN PLAIN SIGHT.
MORE LIKE HUNTING FOR A NEEDLE IN A HAYSTACK OF NEEDLES. DO YOU AT LEAST HAVE A TITLE?
NO, JUST A STRING OF NUMBERS.
IT'S A START. WE'RE STILL GOING TO NEED A HAND, THOUGH. IT WON'T BE LONG BEFORE THE LITTLE WAR OUTSIDE FOLLOWS US IN HERE —
SSSSHHHH!
AHHH!
MODERATE YOUR TONE, YOUNG MAN! THIS IS A LIBRARY!

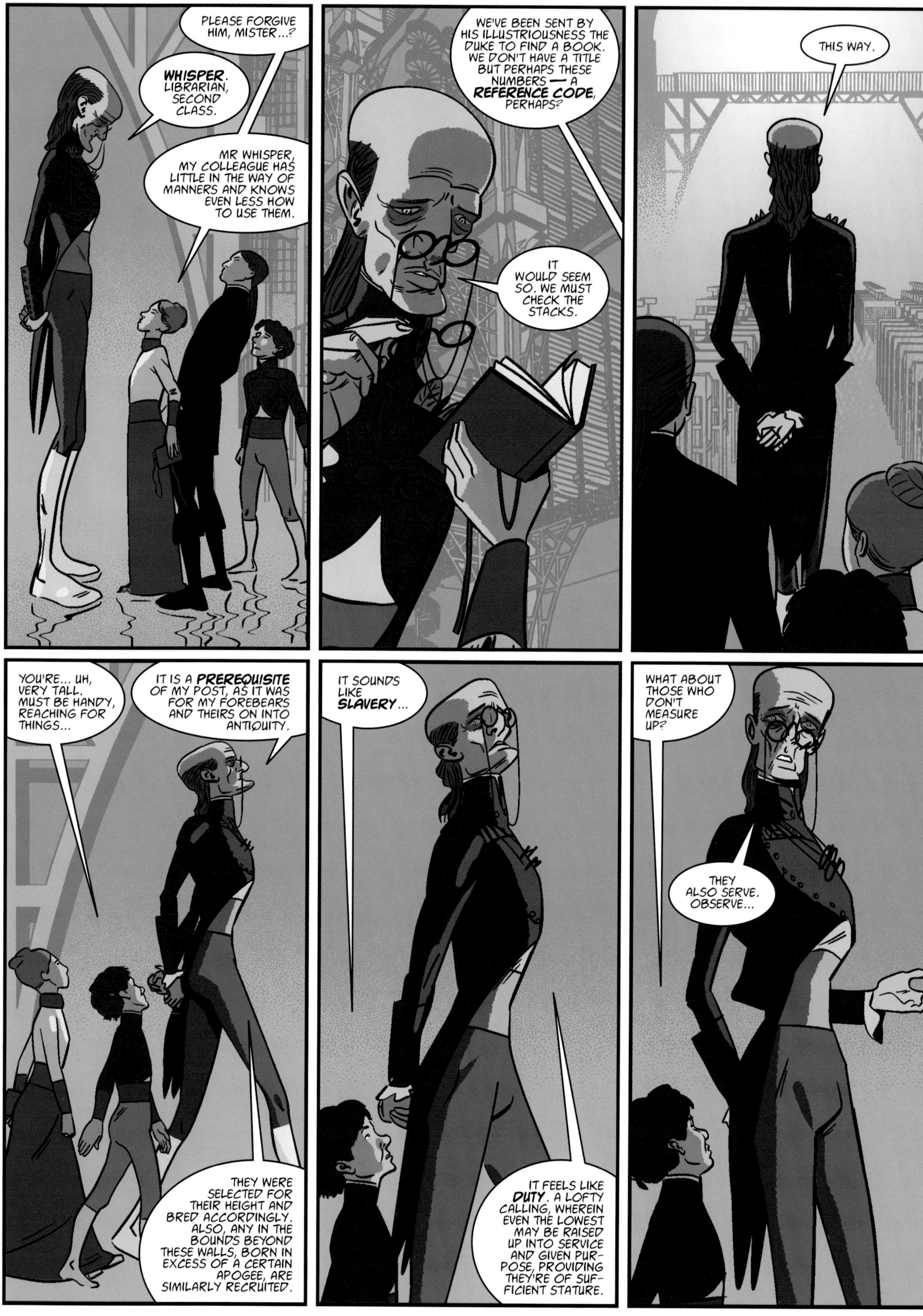
PLEASE FORGIVE HIM, MISTER...?
WHISPER. LIBRARIAN, SECOND CLASS.
MR WHISPER, MY COLLEAGUE HAS LITTLE IN THE WAY OF MANNERS AND KNOWS EVEN LESS HOW TO USE THEM.
WE'VE BEEN SENT BY HIS **ILLUSTRIOUSNESS** THE DUKE TO FIND A BOOK. WE DON'T HAVE A TITLE BUT PERHAPS THESE NUMBERS — A **REFERENCE CODE**, PERHAPS?
IT WOULD SEEM SO. WE MUST CHECK THE STACKS.
THIS WAY.
YOU'RE... UH, VERY TALL. MUST BE HANDY, REACHING FOR THINGS...
IT IS A **PREREQUISITE** OF MY POST, AS IT WAS FOR MY FOREBEARS AND THEIRS ON INTO ANTIQUITY.
THEY WERE SELECTED FOR THEIR HEIGHT AND BRED ACCORDINGLY. ALSO, ANY IN THE BOUNDS BEYOND THESE WALLS, BORN IN EXCESS OF A CERTAIN APOGEE, ARE SIMILARLY RECRUITED.
IT SOUNDS LIKE **SLAVERY**...
IT FEELS LIKE **DUTY**. A LOFTY CALLING, WHEREIN EVEN THE LOWEST MAY BE RAISED UP INTO SERVICE AND GIVEN PURPOSE, PROVIDING THEY'RE OF SUFFICIENT STATURE.
WHAT ABOUT THOSE WHO DON'T MEASURE UP?
THEY ALSO SERVE. OBSERVE...

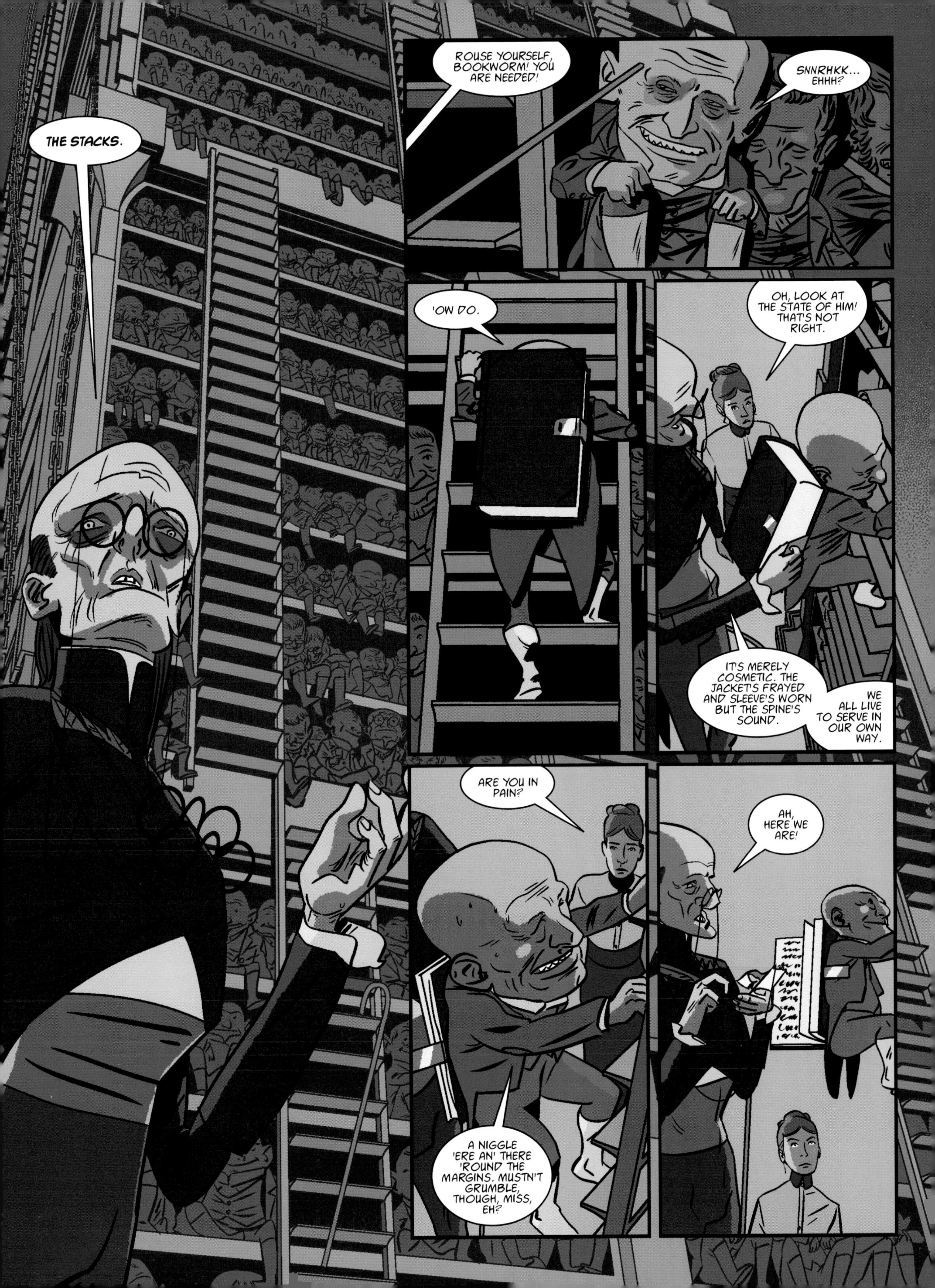
THE STACKS.
ROUSE YOURSELF, BOOKWORM! YOU ARE NEEDED!
SNNRHKK... EHHH?
'OW DO.
OH, LOOK AT THE STATE OF HIM! THAT'S NOT RIGHT.
IT'S MERELY COSMETIC. THE JACKET'S FRAYED AND SLEEVE'S WORN BUT THE SPINE'S SOUND.
WE ALL LIVE TO SERVE IN OUR OWN WAY.
ARE YOU IN PAIN?
A NIGGLE 'ERE AN' THERE 'ROUND THE MARGINS. MUSTN'T GRUMBLE, THOUGH, MISS, EH?
AH, HERE WE ARE!

WON'T BE A JIFFY!

THERE ARE SO MANY BOOKS HERE! IMAGINE THE WEALTH OF KNOWLEDGE THEY MUST CONTAIN!

INDEED. WHY, THERE IS AN ENTIRE **WING** WHOSE WORKS ARE CONCERNED WITH AN EGG THE DUKE'S GREAT GRANDFATHER ONCE HAD FOR BREAKFAST.

AN **EGG?**

OH YES. VOLUMES UPON VOLUMES ON ITS COLOUR AND CONSISTENCY. GREAT PHILOSOPHICAL TRACTS ON ITS SHAPE AND LUSTRE. REAMS OF HISTORICAL OBSERVATIONS ON ITS INFLUENCE ON THE GREAT MAN'S MOOD AND DIGESTION.

WHY, I DO BELIEVE A MAGNIFICENT BRONZE WAS EVEN STRUCK COMMEMORATING THE BIRD WHO LAID IT.

THEN, OF COURSE, THERE IS THE GREAT MATRIARCH'S ANNEX, WHICH DOCUMENTS IN THE MINUTEST DETAIL HER LIFETIME OF **BODILY EXPULSIONS** AND **ASSOCIATED EFFLUVIA.**

IS THAT **IT?** ALL THESE COPIOUS RESOURCES DEDICATED TO THE BLATHER AND BOWEL MOVEMENTS OF ONE FAMILY? A MONUMENT TO THEIR **EGO?**

CALM YOURSELF. THIS ISN'T THE PLACE OR TIME.

IS THERE ANYTHING ABOUT THE **WHEEL OF WORLDS?** OR THE **WAR?** OR **THE KEEP** ITSELF?

NO, WHY SHOULD THERE BE? THAT IS NOT THE LIBRARY'S PURPOSE.

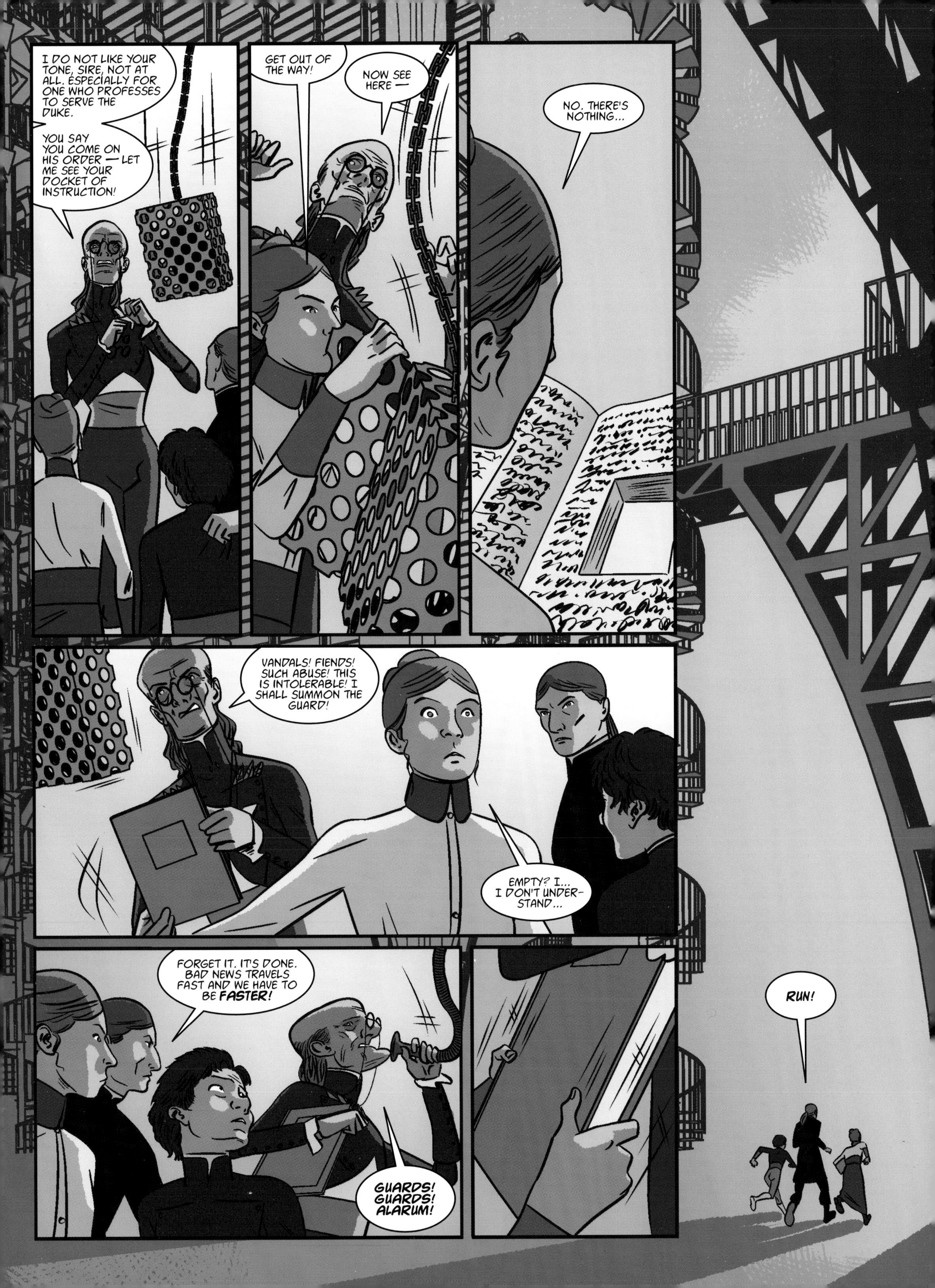
I DO NOT LIKE YOUR TONE, SIRE, NOT AT ALL. ESPECIALLY FOR ONE WHO PROFESSES TO SERVE THE DUKE.
YOU SAY YOU COME ON HIS ORDER — LET ME SEE YOUR DOCKET OF INSTRUCTION!
GET OUT OF THE WAY!
NOW SEE HERE —
NO. THERE'S NOTHING...
VANDALS! FIENDS! SUCH ABUSE! THIS IS INTOLERABLE! I SHALL SUMMON THE GUARD!
EMPTY? I... I DON'T UNDER-STAND...
FORGET IT. IT'S DONE. BAD NEWS TRAVELS FAST AND WE HAVE TO BE FASTER!
GUARDS! GUARDS! ALARUM!
RUN!

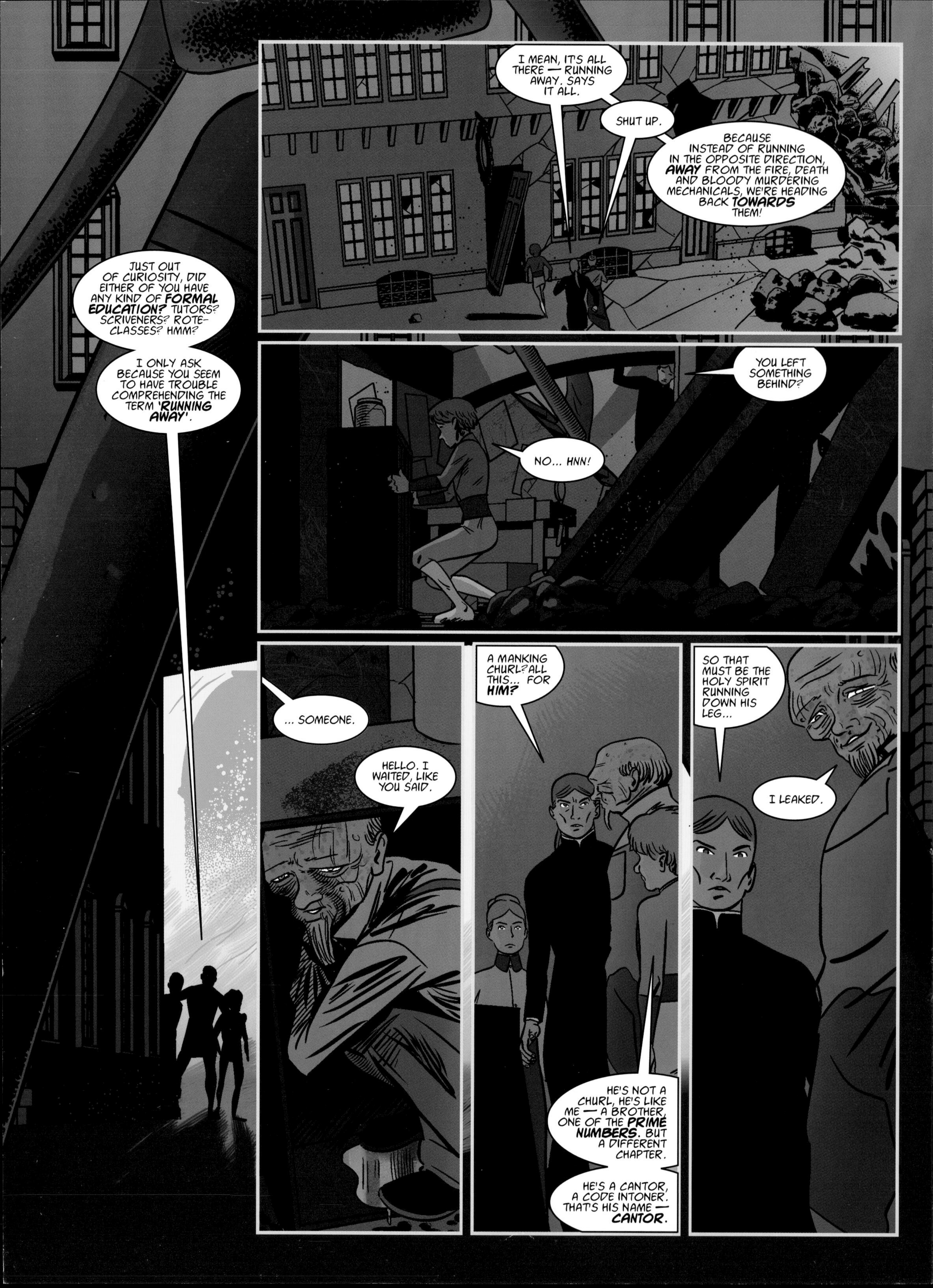
I MEAN, IT'S ALL THERE — RUNNING AWAY. SAYS IT ALL.
SHUT UP.
BECAUSE INSTEAD OF RUNNING IN THE OPPOSITE DIRECTION, AWAY FROM THE FIRE, DEATH AND BLOODY MURDERING MECHANICALS, WE'RE HEADING BACK TOWARDS THEM!
JUST OUT OF CURIOSITY, DID EITHER OF YOU HAVE ANY KIND OF FORMAL EDUCATION? TUTORS? SCRIVENERS? ROTE-CLASSES? HMM?
I ONLY ASK BECAUSE YOU SEEM TO HAVE TROUBLE COMPREHENDING THE TERM 'RUNNING AWAY'.
YOU LEFT SOMETHING BEHIND?
NO... HNN!
... SOMEONE.
HELLO. I WAITED, LIKE YOU SAID.
A MANKING CHURL? ALL THIS... FOR HIM?
HE'S NOT A CHURL, HE'S LIKE ME — A BROTHER, ONE OF THE PRIME NUMBERS. BUT A DIFFERENT CHAPTER.
HE'S A CANTOR, A CODE INTONER. THAT'S HIS NAME — CANTOR.
SO THAT MUST BE THE HOLY SPIRIT RUNNING DOWN HIS LEG...
I LEAKED.

WE'RE DONE HERE. RAMKIN, TAKE US TO THE THRESHOLD SPIRE. WE'RE LEAVING.

WHATEVER MY GRANDFATHER MEANT US TO FIND IS GONE. IT'S BEEN A WASTE OF TIME. HE DIED FOR NOTHING.

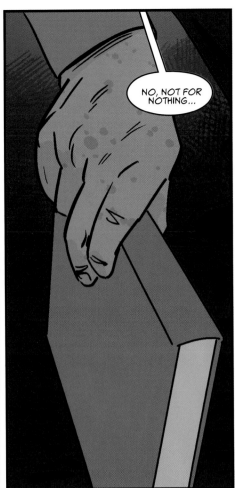

NO, NOT FOR NOTHING...

... YOU WERE SIMPLY LOOKING IN THE WRONG PLACE.

HTTT!

WREN!

SHE'S FINE, DON'T WORRY. SHE'S JUST COMPILING.

THAT'S A BIG WORD FOR A TROUSER-WETTER.

AH, YES. I'M AFRAID I SHOULD'VE TAKEN BETTER CARE OF HIM, BUT TIME'S TAKEN ITS TOLL ON BOTH OF US.

I'VE BEEN IN SLEEP MODE FOR SO LONG... SO MUCH HAS PASSED ME BY. IT WAS ONLY THE SIGHT OF THE BOOK THAT WOKE ME.

DID YOU UNDERSTAND ANY OF THAT?

HE'S A PART OF THE KEY. I'D GUESS AN OPERATING SYSTEM MONITOR, AN INSTRUCTIONAL MATRIX.

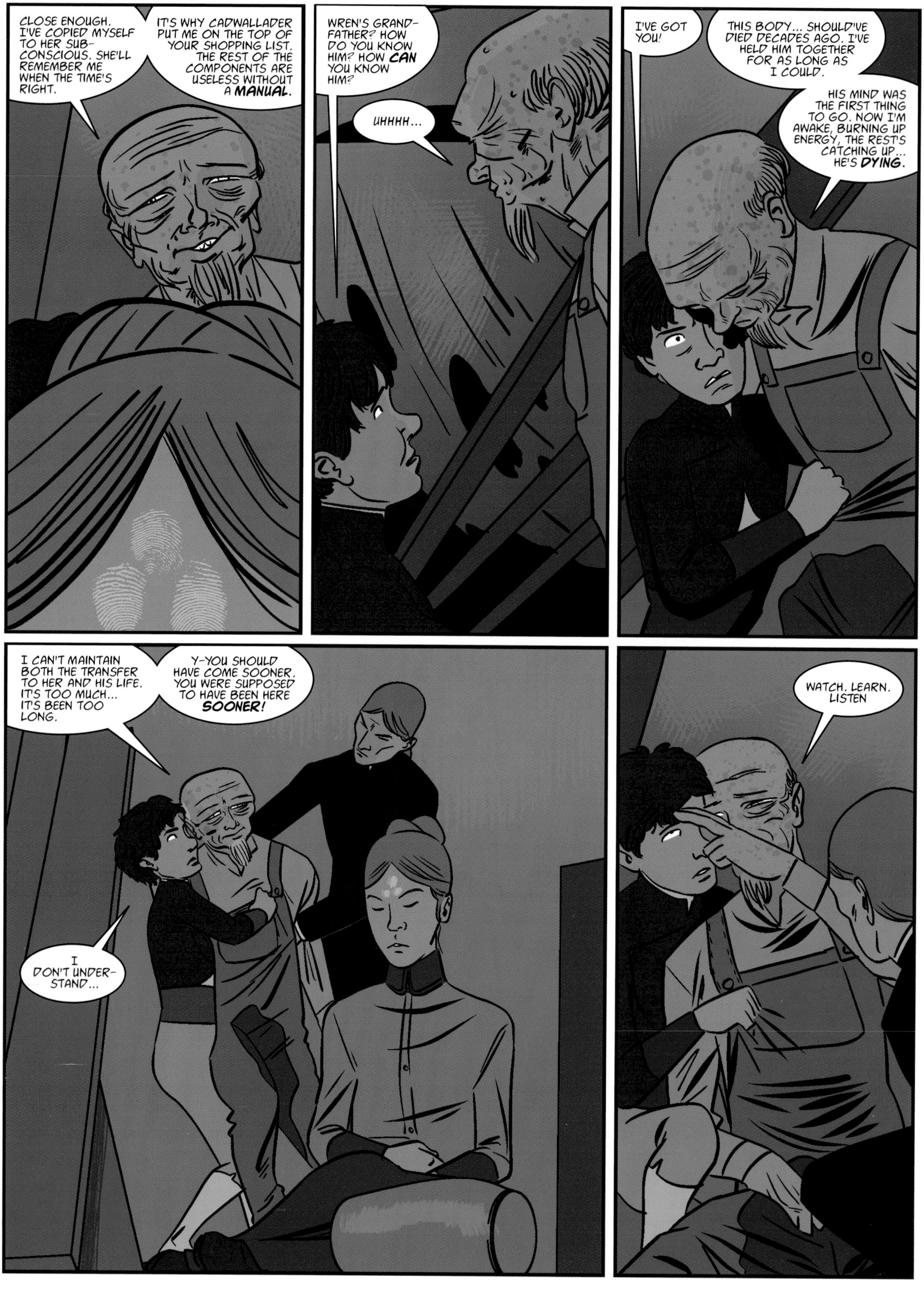
CLOSE ENOUGH. I'VE COPIED MYSELF TO HER SUB-CONSCIOUS. SHE'LL REMEMBER ME WHEN THE TIME'S RIGHT.
IT'S WHY CADWALLADER PUT ME ON THE TOP OF YOUR SHOPPING LIST. THE REST OF THE COMPONENTS ARE USELESS WITHOUT A **MANUAL**.
WREN'S GRAND-FATHER? HOW DO YOU KNOW HIM? HOW **CAN** YOU KNOW HIM?
UHHHH...
I'VE GOT YOU!
THIS BODY... SHOULD'VE DIED DECADES AGO. I'VE HELD HIM TOGETHER FOR AS LONG AS I COULD.
HIS MIND WAS THE FIRST THING TO GO. NOW I'M AWAKE, BURNING UP ENERGY, THE REST'S CATCHING UP... HE'S **DYING**.
I CAN'T MAINTAIN BOTH THE TRANSFER TO HER AND HIS LIFE. IT'S TOO MUCH... IT'S BEEN TOO LONG.
Y-YOU SHOULD HAVE COME SOONER. YOU WERE SUPPOSED TO HAVE BEEN HERE **SOONER!**
I DON'T UNDER-STAND...
WATCH. LEARN. LISTEN

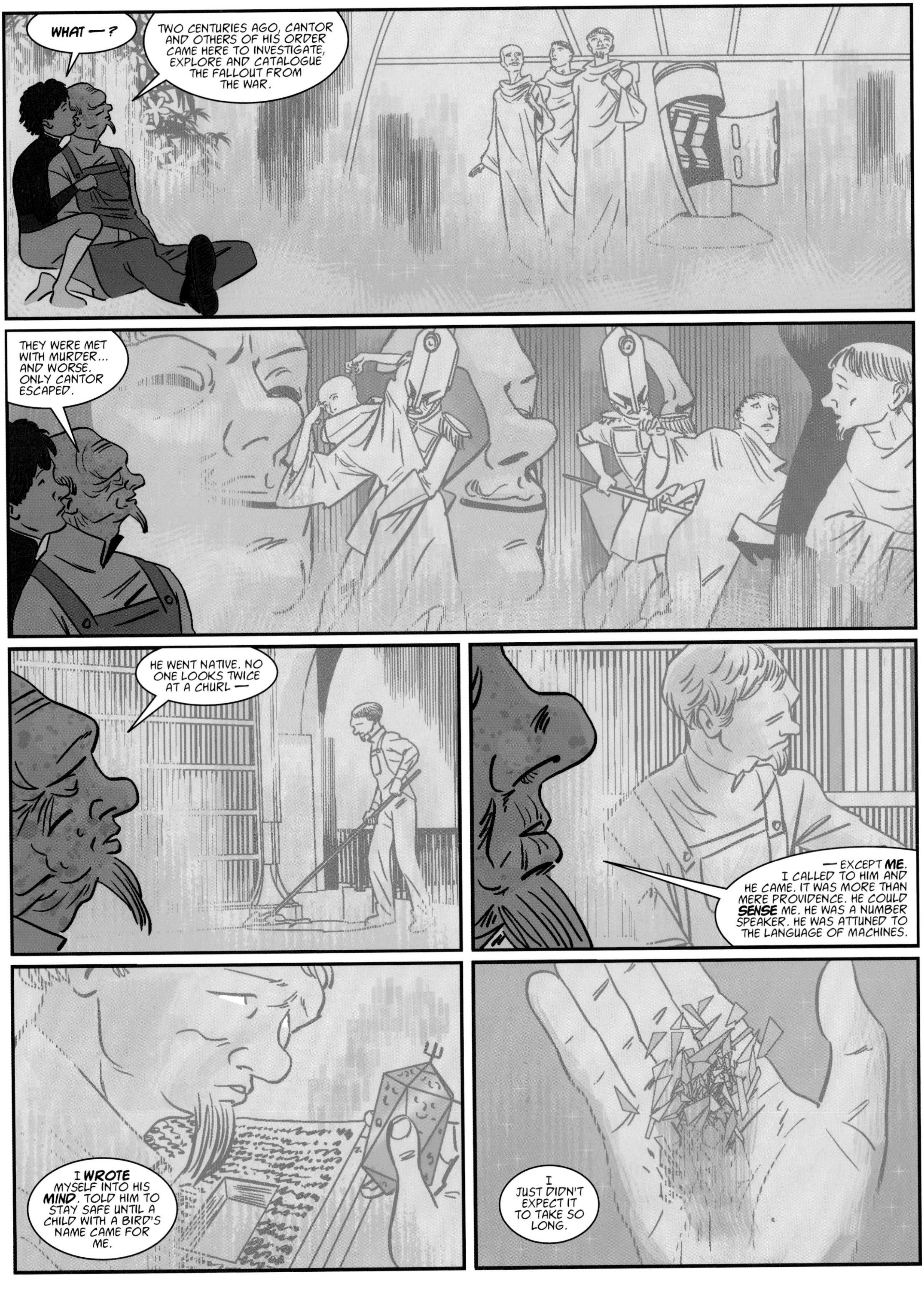
WHAT — ?
TWO CENTURIES AGO, CANTOR AND OTHERS OF HIS ORDER CAME HERE TO INVESTIGATE, EXPLORE AND CATALOGUE THE FALLOUT FROM THE WAR.
THEY WERE MET WITH MURDER... AND WORSE. ONLY CANTOR ESCAPED.
HE WENT NATIVE. NO ONE LOOKS TWICE AT A CHURL —
— EXCEPT ME. I CALLED TO HIM AND HE CAME. IT WAS MORE THAN MERE PROVIDENCE. HE COULD SENSE ME. HE WAS A NUMBER SPEAKER. HE WAS ATTUNED TO THE LANGUAGE OF MACHINES.
I WROTE MYSELF INTO HIS MIND. TOLD HIM TO STAY SAFE UNTIL A CHILD WITH A BIRD'S NAME CAME FOR ME.
I JUST DIDN'T EXPECT IT TO TAKE SO LONG.

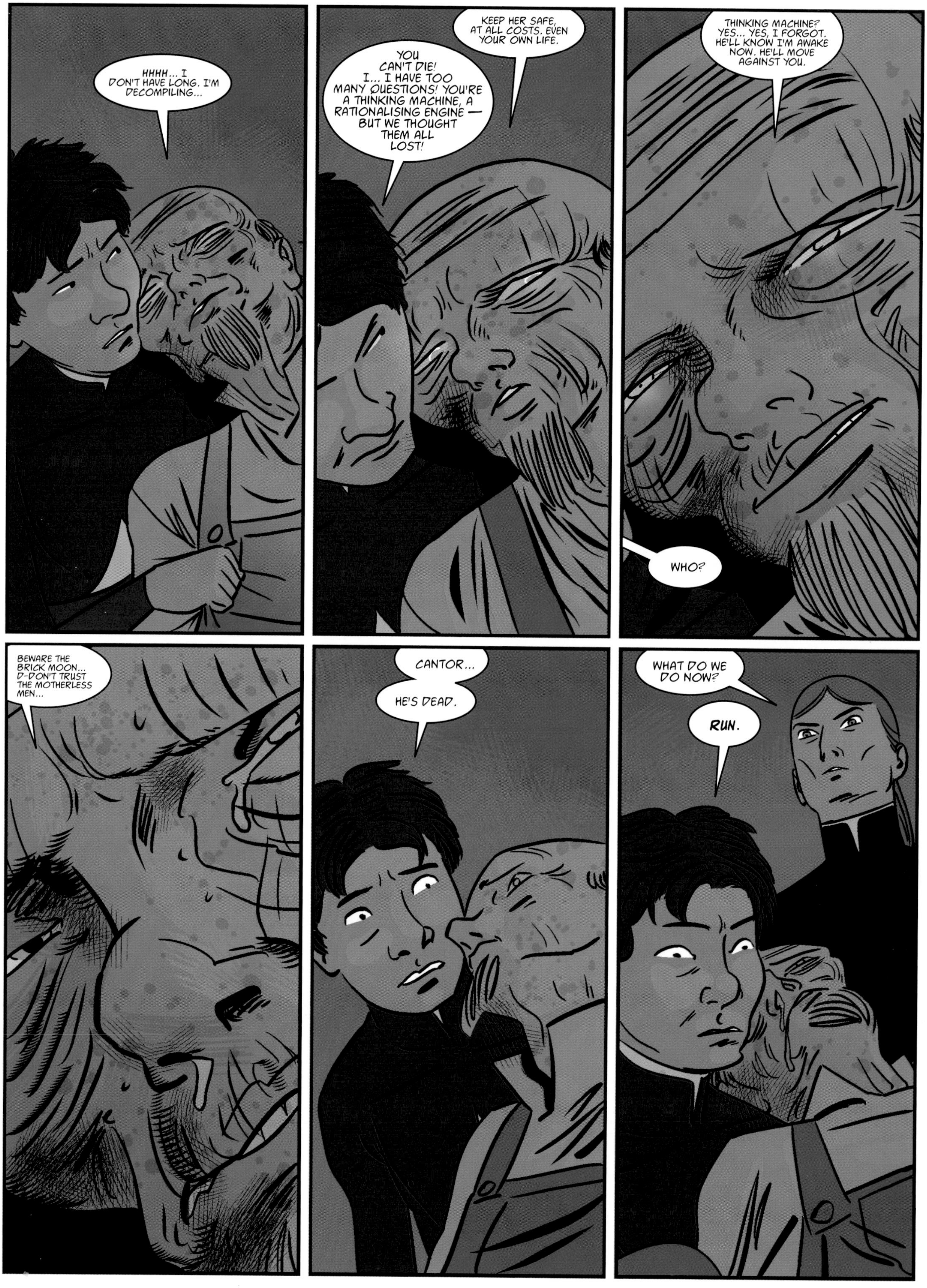
HHHH... I DON'T HAVE LONG. I'M DECOMPILING...
KEEP HER SAFE, AT ALL COSTS. EVEN YOUR OWN LIFE.
YOU CAN'T DIE! I... I HAVE TOO MANY QUESTIONS! YOU'RE A THINKING MACHINE, A RATIONALISING ENGINE — BUT WE THOUGHT THEM ALL LOST!
THINKING MACHINE? YES... YES, I FORGOT. HE'LL KNOW I'M AWAKE NOW. HE'LL MOVE AGAINST YOU.
WHO?
BEWARE THE BRICK MOON... D-DON'T TRUST THE MOTHERLESS MEN...
CANTOR...
HE'S DEAD.
WHAT DO WE DO NOW?
RUN.

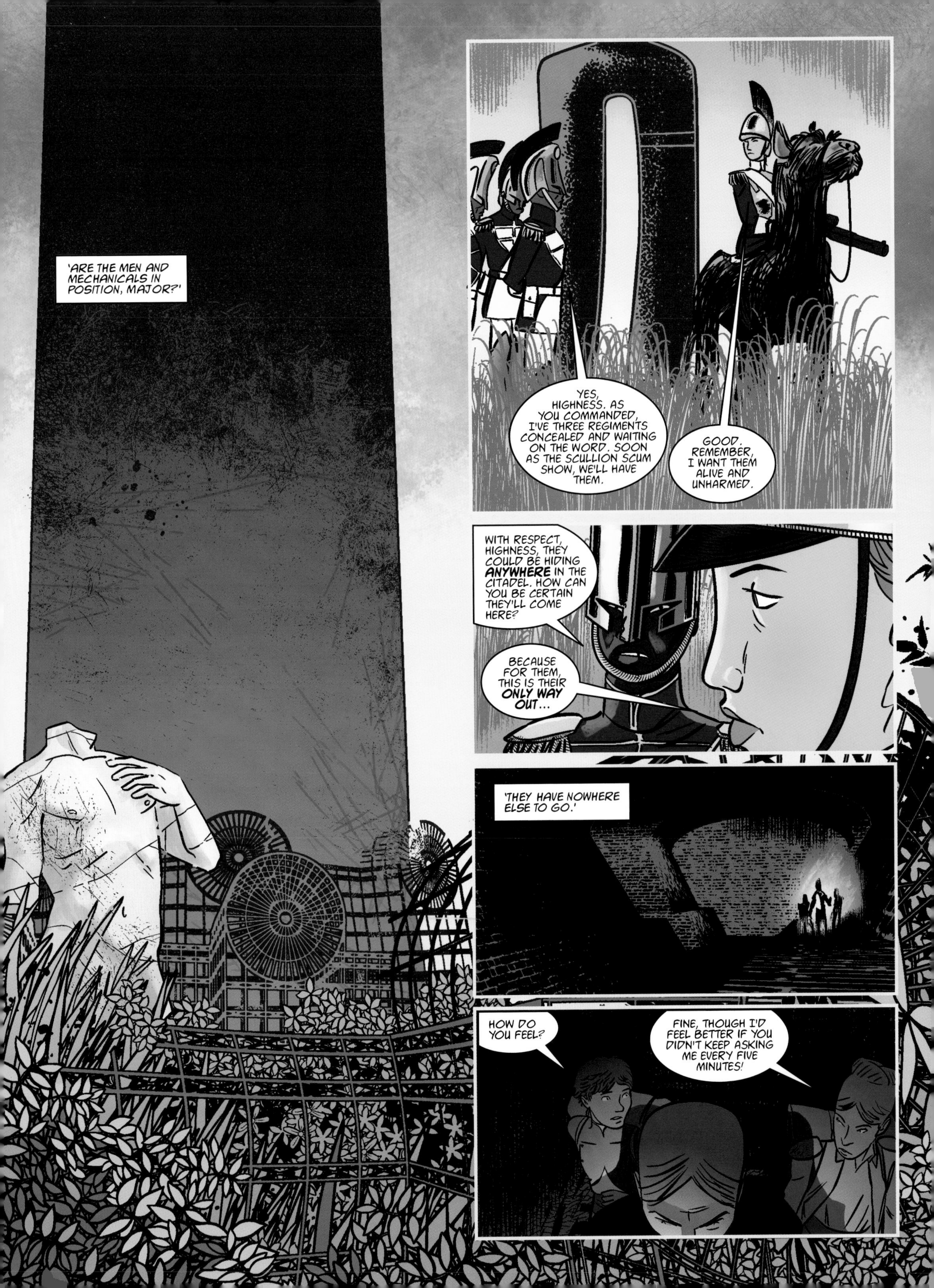
'ARE THE MEN AND MECHANICALS IN POSITION, MAJOR?'
YES, HIGHNESS. AS YOU COMMANDED, I'VE THREE REGIMENTS CONCEALED AND WAITING ON THE WORD. SOON AS THE SCULLION SCUM SHOW, WE'LL HAVE THEM.
GOOD. REMEMBER, I WANT THEM ALIVE AND UNHARMED.
WITH RESPECT, HIGHNESS, THEY COULD BE HIDING ANYWHERE IN THE CITADEL. HOW CAN YOU BE CERTAIN THEY'LL COME HERE?
BECAUSE FOR THEM, THIS IS THEIR ONLY WAY OUT...
'THEY HAVE NOWHERE ELSE TO GO.'
HOW DO YOU FEEL?
FINE, THOUGH I'D FEEL BETTER IF YOU DIDN'T KEEP ASKING ME EVERY FIVE MINUTES!

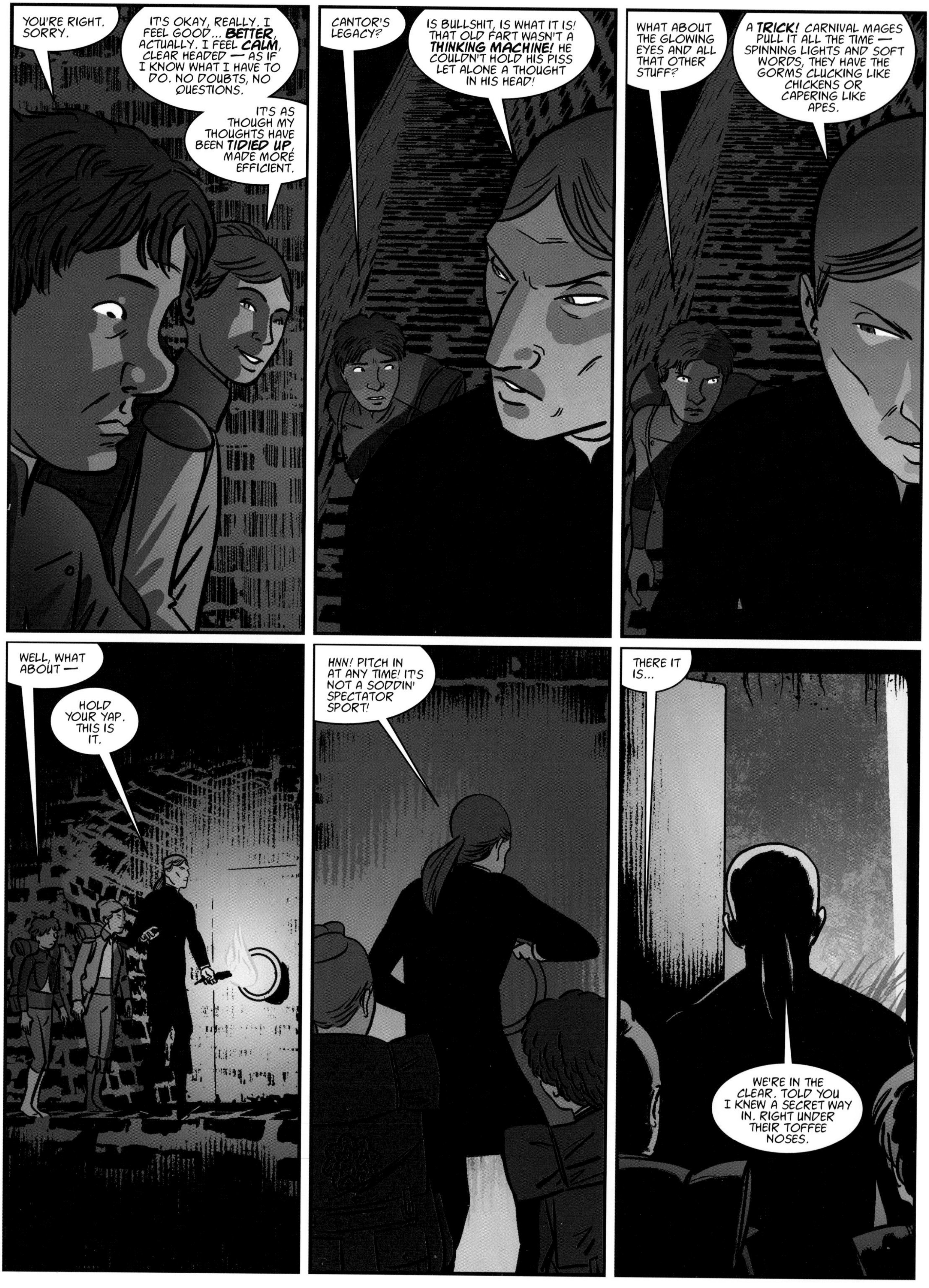
YOU'RE RIGHT. SORRY.
IT'S OKAY, REALLY. I FEEL GOOD... BETTER, ACTUALLY. I FEEL CALM, CLEAR HEADED — AS IF I KNOW WHAT I HAVE TO DO. NO DOUBTS, NO QUESTIONS.
IT'S AS THOUGH MY THOUGHTS HAVE BEEN TIDIED UP, MADE MORE EFFICIENT.
CANTOR'S LEGACY?
IS BULLSHIT, IS WHAT IT IS! THAT OLD FART WASN'T A THINKING MACHINE! HE COULDN'T HOLD HIS PISS LET ALONE A THOUGHT IN HIS HEAD!
WHAT ABOUT THE GLOWING EYES AND ALL THAT OTHER STUFF?
A TRICK! CARNIVAL MAGES PULL IT ALL THE TIME — SPINNING LIGHTS AND SOFT WORDS, THEY HAVE THE GORMS CLUCKING LIKE CHICKENS OR CAPERING LIKE APES.
WELL, WHAT ABOUT —
HOLD YOUR YAP. THIS IS IT.
HNN! PITCH IN AT ANY TIME! IT'S NOT A SODDIN' SPECTATOR SPORT!
THERE IT IS...
WE'RE IN THE CLEAR. TOLD YOU I KNEW A SECRET WAY IN. RIGHT UNDER THEIR TOFFEE NOSES.

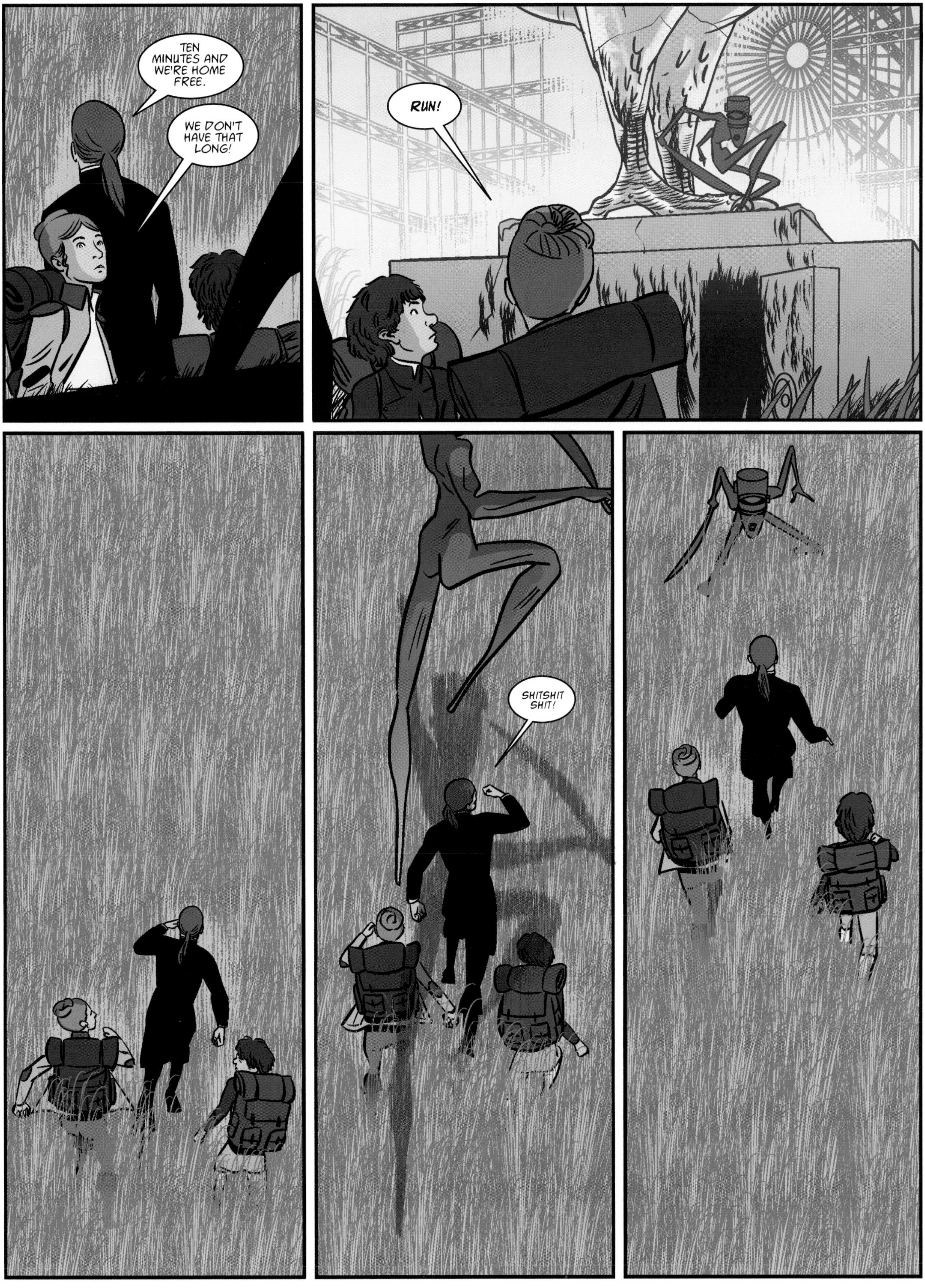
TEN MINUTES AND WE'RE HOME FREE.
WE DON'T HAVE THAT LONG!
RUN!
SHITSHIT SHIT!

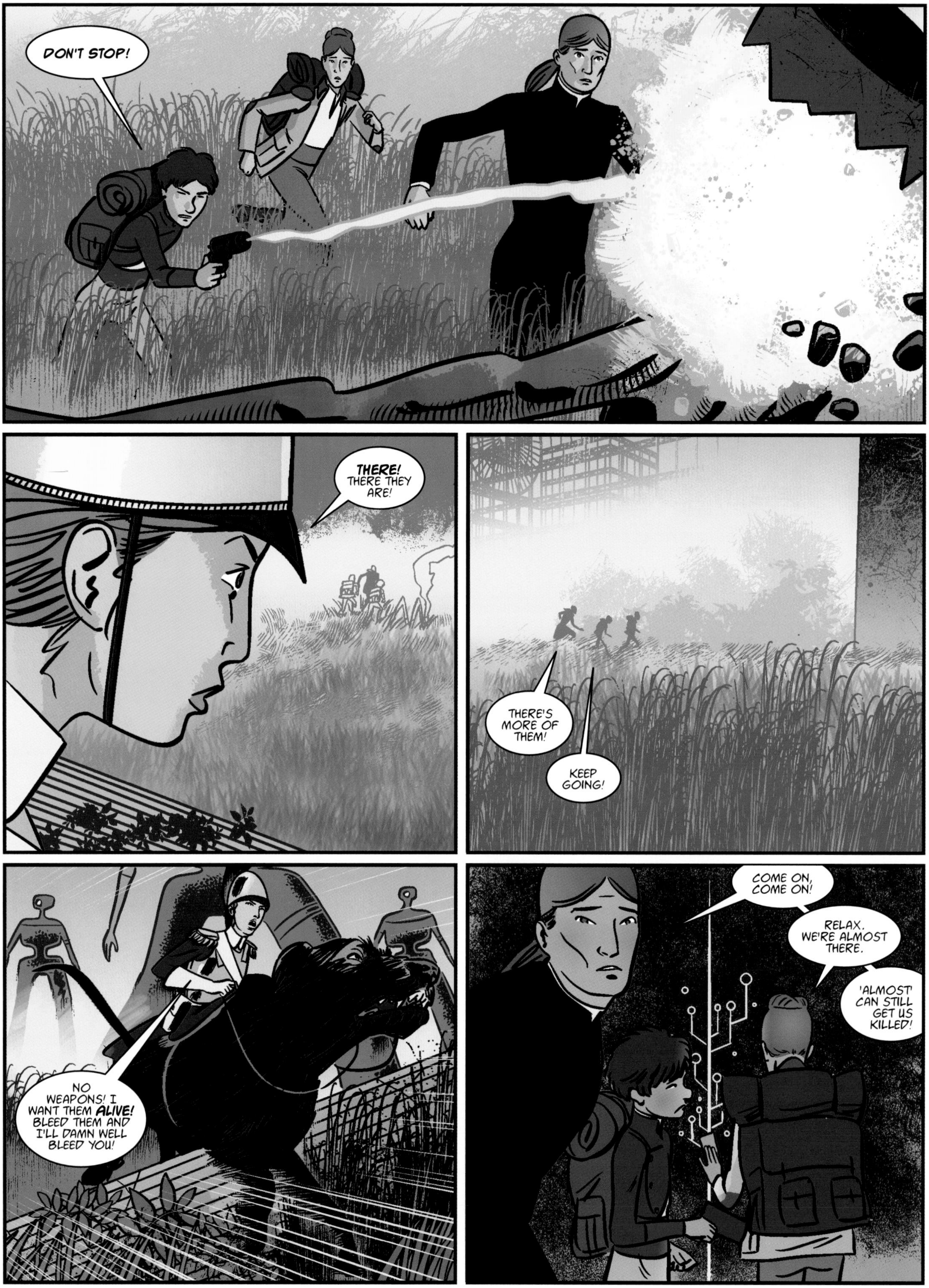
DON'T STOP!
THERE! THERE THEY ARE!
THERE'S MORE OF THEM!
KEEP GOING!
NO WEAPONS! I WANT THEM ALIVE! BLEED THEM AND I'LL DAMN WELL BLEED YOU!
COME ON, COME ON!
RELAX. WE'RE ALMOST THERE.
'ALMOST' CAN STILL GET US KILLED!

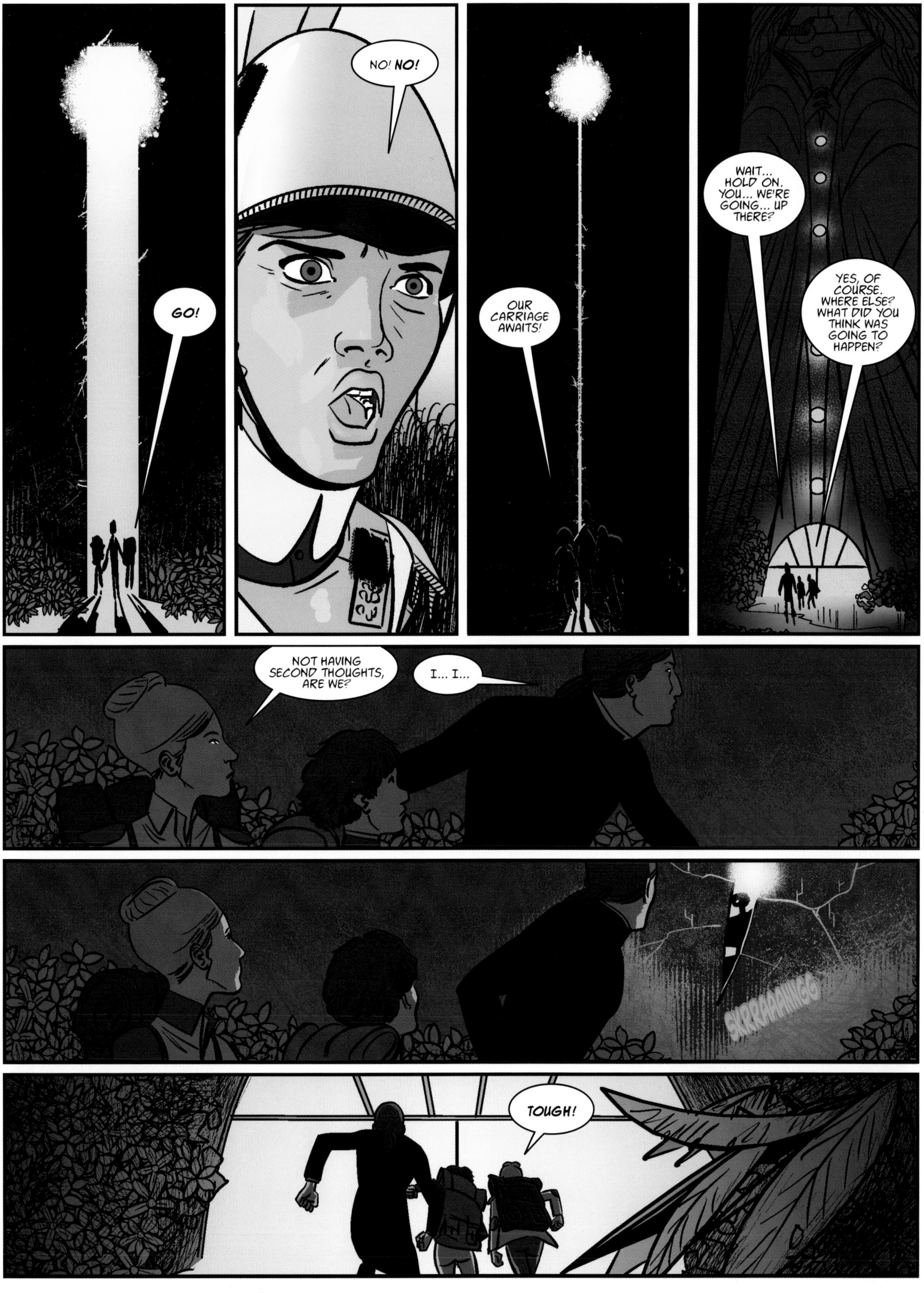
GO!
NO! NO!
OUR CARRIAGE AWAITS!
WAIT... HOLD ON. YOU... WE'RE GOING... UP THERE?
YES, OF COURSE. WHERE ELSE? WHAT DID YOU THINK WAS GOING TO HAPPEN?
NOT HAVING SECOND THOUGHTS, ARE WE?
I... I...
SKRRAAANNGG
TOUGH!

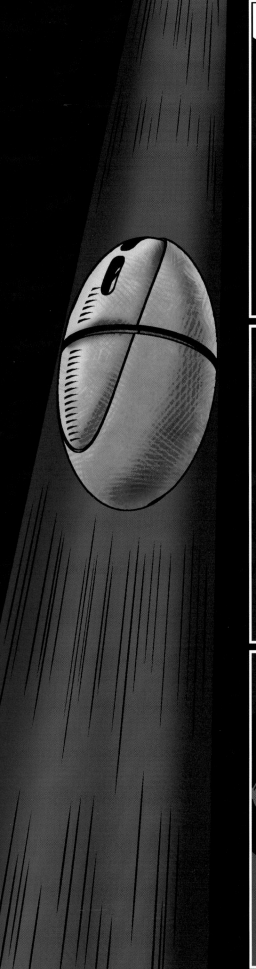

OH GODS!
OH GODS!
OH GODS!

WHAT'S WRONG? IT DIDN'T VIBRATE LIKE THIS BEFORE!

IT WAS A DIFFERENT VEHICLE BEFORE. I'VE NOT DRIVEN ONE LIKE THIS.

MORE IMPORTANTLY, THERE WASN'T TIME TO PLAN AN APPROPRIATE TRAJECTORY. WE DON'T HAVE A LOCKED-IN **END POINT**.

MEANING?

WITHOUT A SET DESTINATION, I NEED TO FIND A WORLD WE CAN BRANCH OFF TO, OR WE'LL CRASH INTO THE **SUN!**

HOLD ON, WE MIGHT HAVE A CHANCE. THERE'S A **JUNCTION BOX** COMING UP...

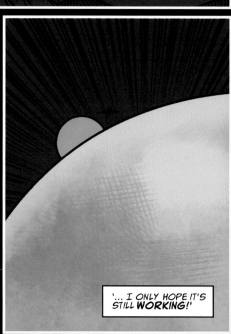

'... I ONLY HOPE IT'S STILL **WORKING!**'

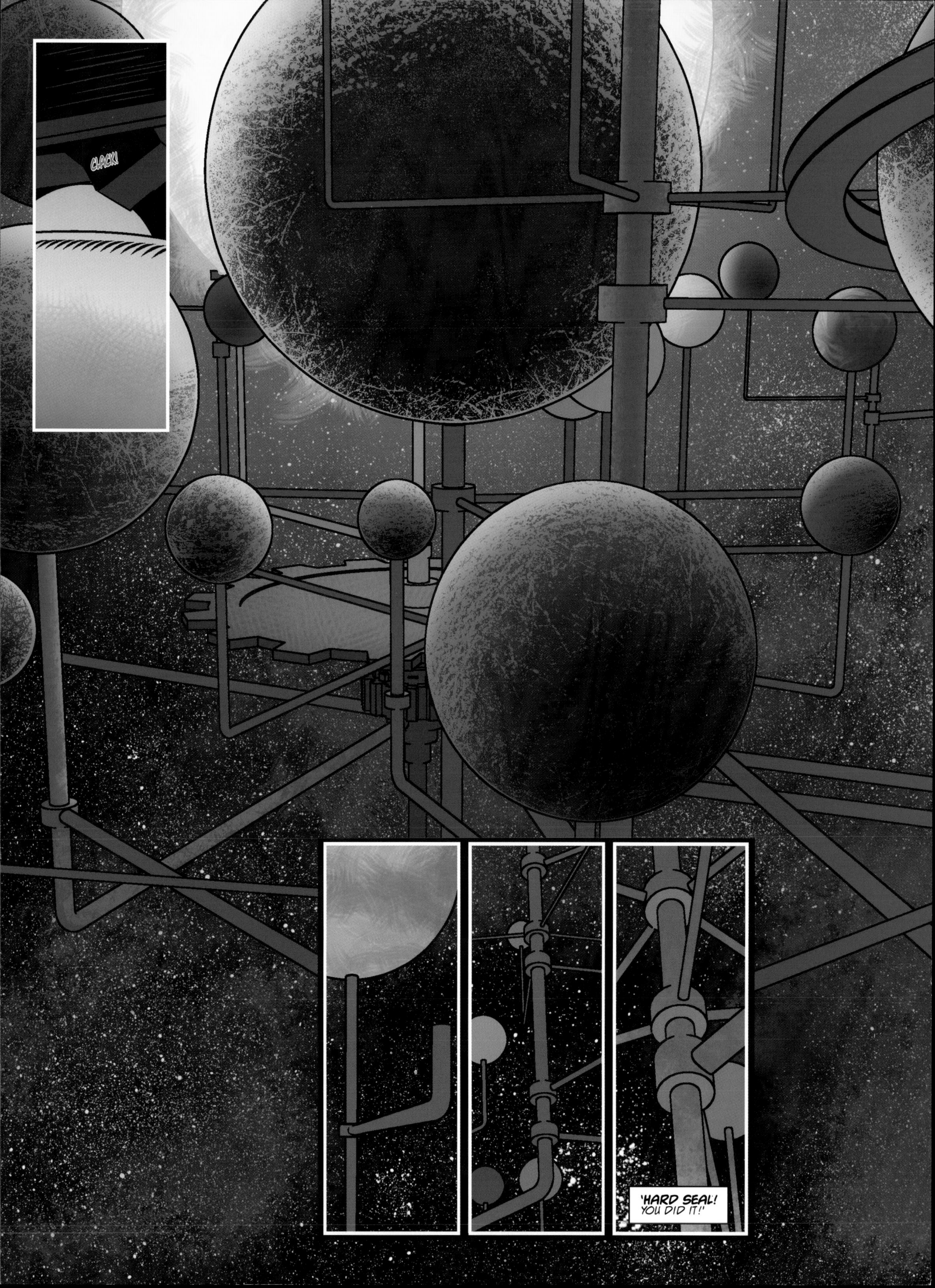
CLACK!
'HARD SEAL!
YOU DID IT!'

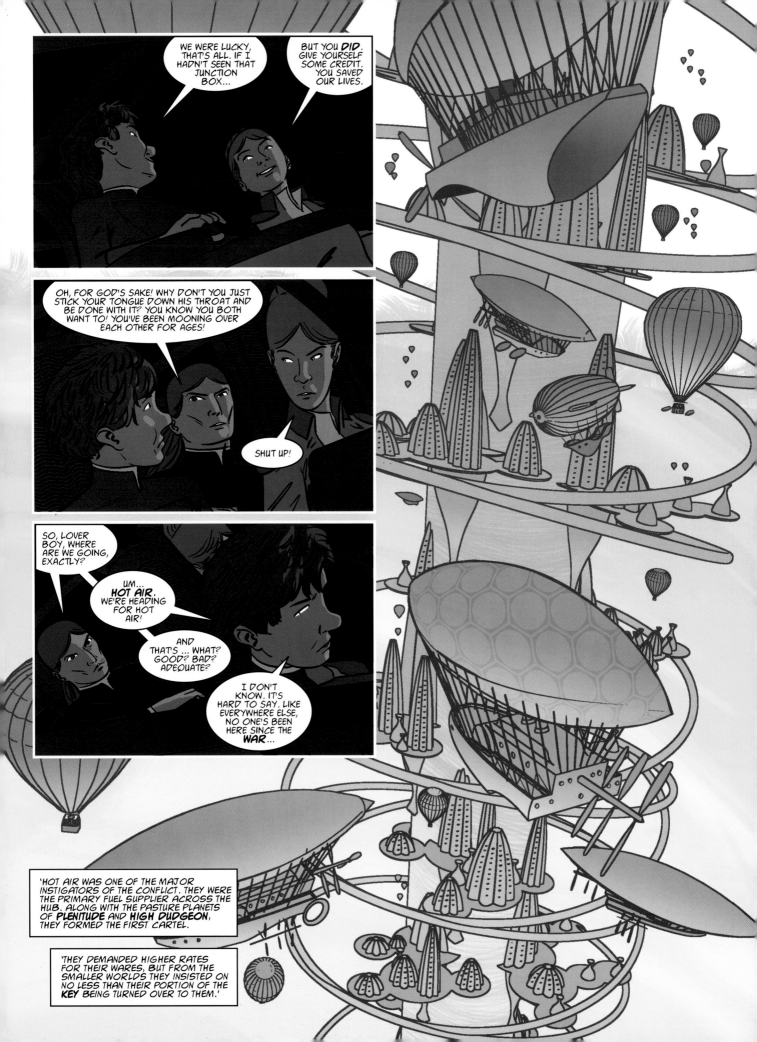

WE WERE LUCKY, THAT'S ALL. IF I HADN'T SEEN THAT JUNCTION BOX...

BUT YOU *DID*. GIVE YOURSELF SOME CREDIT. YOU SAVED OUR LIVES.

OH, FOR GOD'S SAKE! WHY DON'T YOU JUST STICK YOUR TONGUE DOWN HIS THROAT AND BE DONE WITH IT? YOU KNOW YOU BOTH WANT TO! YOU'VE BEEN MOONING OVER EACH OTHER FOR AGES!

SHUT UP!

SO, LOVER BOY, WHERE ARE WE GOING, EXACTLY?

UM... *HOT AIR*. WE'RE HEADING FOR HOT AIR!

AND THAT'S ... WHAT? GOOD? BAD? ADEQUATE?

I DON'T KNOW. IT'S HARD TO SAY. LIKE EVERYWHERE ELSE, NO ONE'S BEEN HERE SINCE THE *WAR*...

'HOT AIR WAS ONE OF THE MAJOR INSTIGATORS OF THE CONFLICT. THEY WERE THE PRIMARY FUEL SUPPLIER ACROSS THE HUB. ALONG WITH THE PASTURE PLANETS OF *PLENITUDE* AND *HIGH DUDGEON*, THEY FORMED THE FIRST CARTEL.

'THEY DEMANDED HIGHER RATES FOR THEIR WARES, BUT FROM THE SMALLER WORLDS THEY INSISTED ON NO LESS THAN THEIR PORTION OF THE *KEY* BEING TURNED OVER TO THEM.'

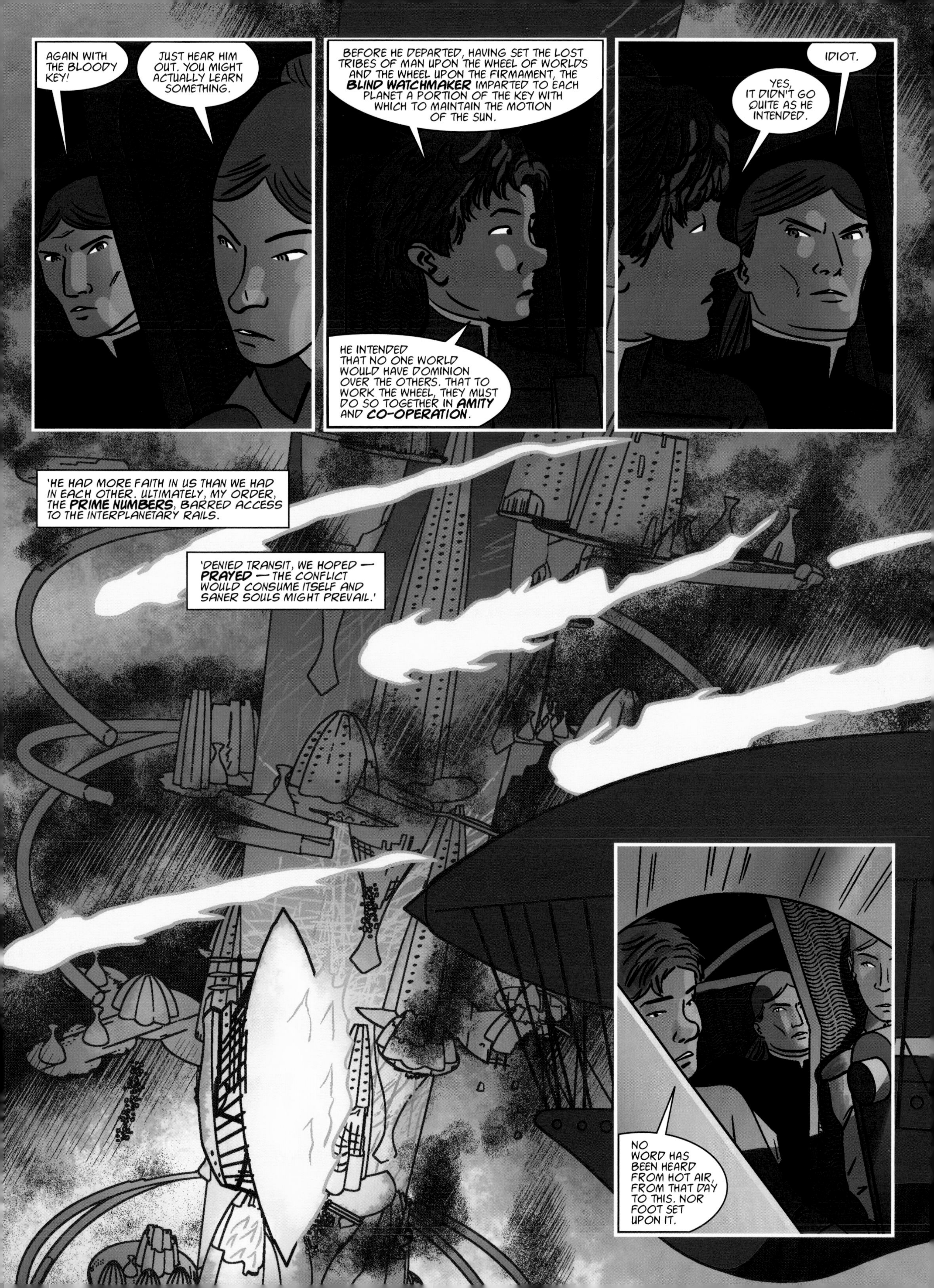

AGAIN WITH THE BLOODY KEY!
JUST HEAR HIM OUT. YOU MIGHT ACTUALLY LEARN SOMETHING.
BEFORE HE DEPARTED, HAVING SET THE LOST TRIBES OF MAN UPON THE WHEEL OF WORLDS AND THE WHEEL UPON THE FIRMAMENT, THE BLIND WATCHMAKER IMPARTED TO EACH PLANET A PORTION OF THE KEY WITH WHICH TO MAINTAIN THE MOTION OF THE SUN.
HE INTENDED THAT NO ONE WORLD WOULD HAVE DOMINION OVER THE OTHERS. THAT TO WORK THE WHEEL, THEY MUST DO SO TOGETHER IN AMITY AND CO-OPERATION.
IDIOT.
YES, IT DIDN'T GO QUITE AS HE INTENDED.
'HE HAD MORE FAITH IN US THAN WE HAD IN EACH OTHER. ULTIMATELY, MY ORDER, THE PRIME NUMBERS, BARRED ACCESS TO THE INTERPLANETARY RAILS.
'DENIED TRANSIT, WE HOPED — PRAYED — THE CONFLICT WOULD CONSUME ITSELF AND SANER SOULS MIGHT PREVAIL.'
NO WORD HAS BEEN HEARD FROM HOT AIR, FROM THAT DAY TO THIS. NOR FOOT SET UPON IT.

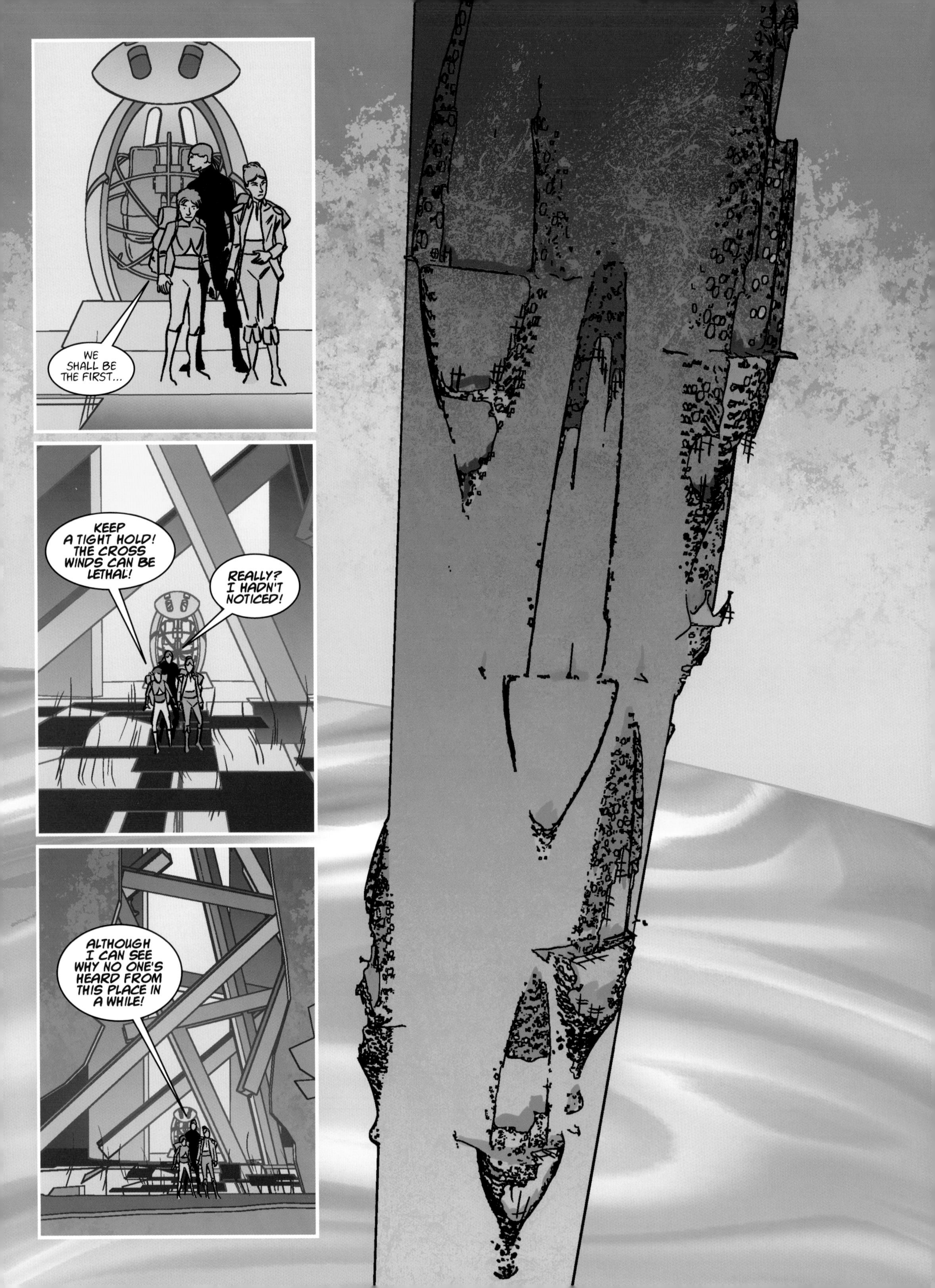
WE SHALL BE THE FIRST...
KEEP A TIGHT HOLD! THE CROSS WINDS CAN BE LETHAL!
REALLY? I HADN'T NOTICED!
ALTHOUGH I CAN SEE WHY NO ONE'S HEARD FROM THIS PLACE IN A WHILE!

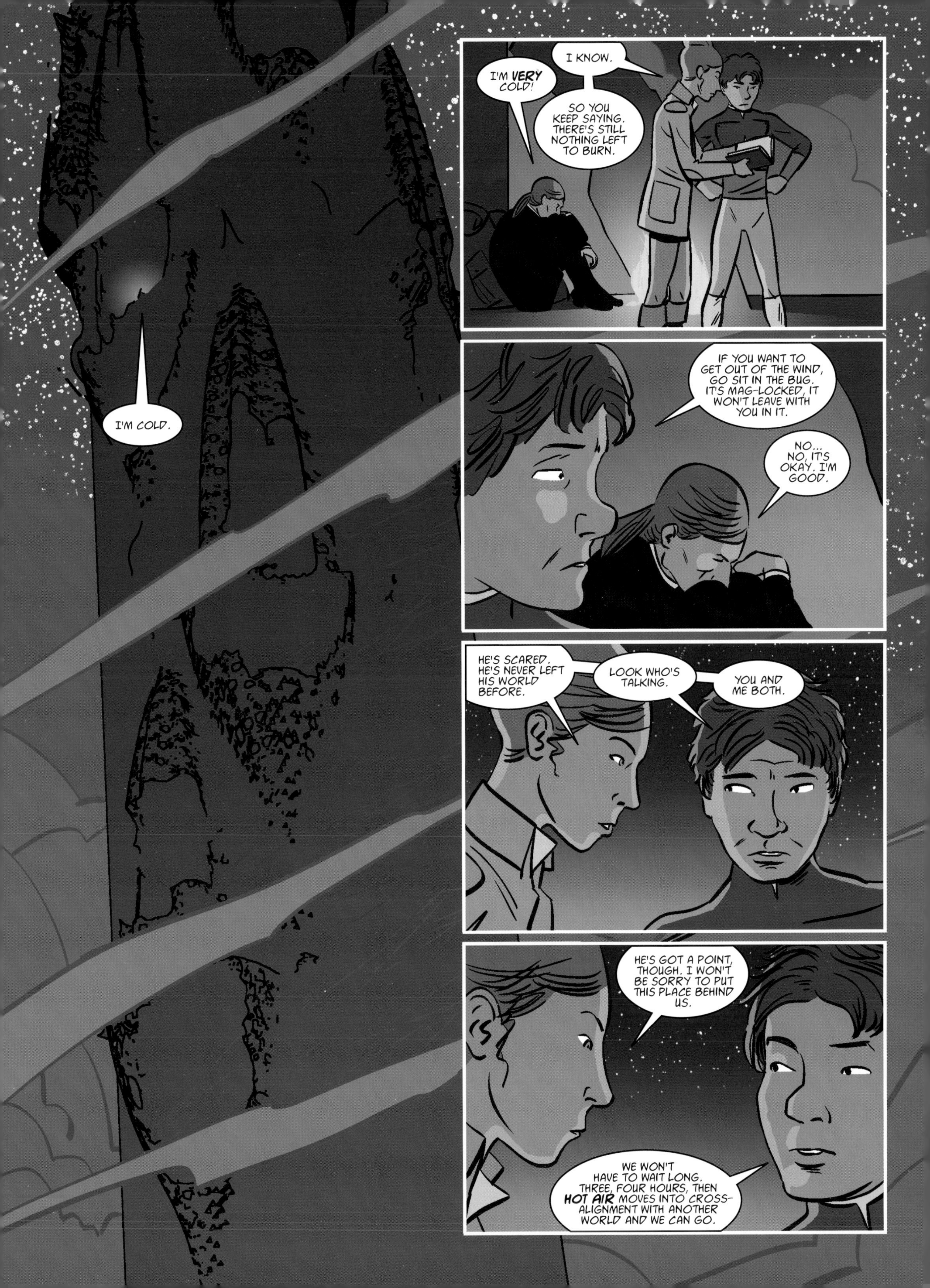
I'M COLD.
I'M VERY COLD!
I KNOW.
SO YOU KEEP SAYING. THERE'S STILL NOTHING LEFT TO BURN.
IF YOU WANT TO GET OUT OF THE WIND, GO SIT IN THE BUG. IT'S MAG-LOCKED, IT WON'T LEAVE WITH YOU IN IT.
NO... NO, IT'S OKAY. I'M GOOD.
HE'S SCARED. HE'S NEVER LEFT HIS WORLD BEFORE.
LOOK WHO'S TALKING.
YOU AND ME BOTH.
HE'S GOT A POINT, THOUGH. I WON'T BE SORRY TO PUT THIS PLACE BEHIND US.
WE WON'T HAVE TO WAIT LONG. THREE, FOUR HOURS, THEN HOT AIR MOVES INTO CROSS-ALIGNMENT WITH ANOTHER WORLD AND WE CAN GO.

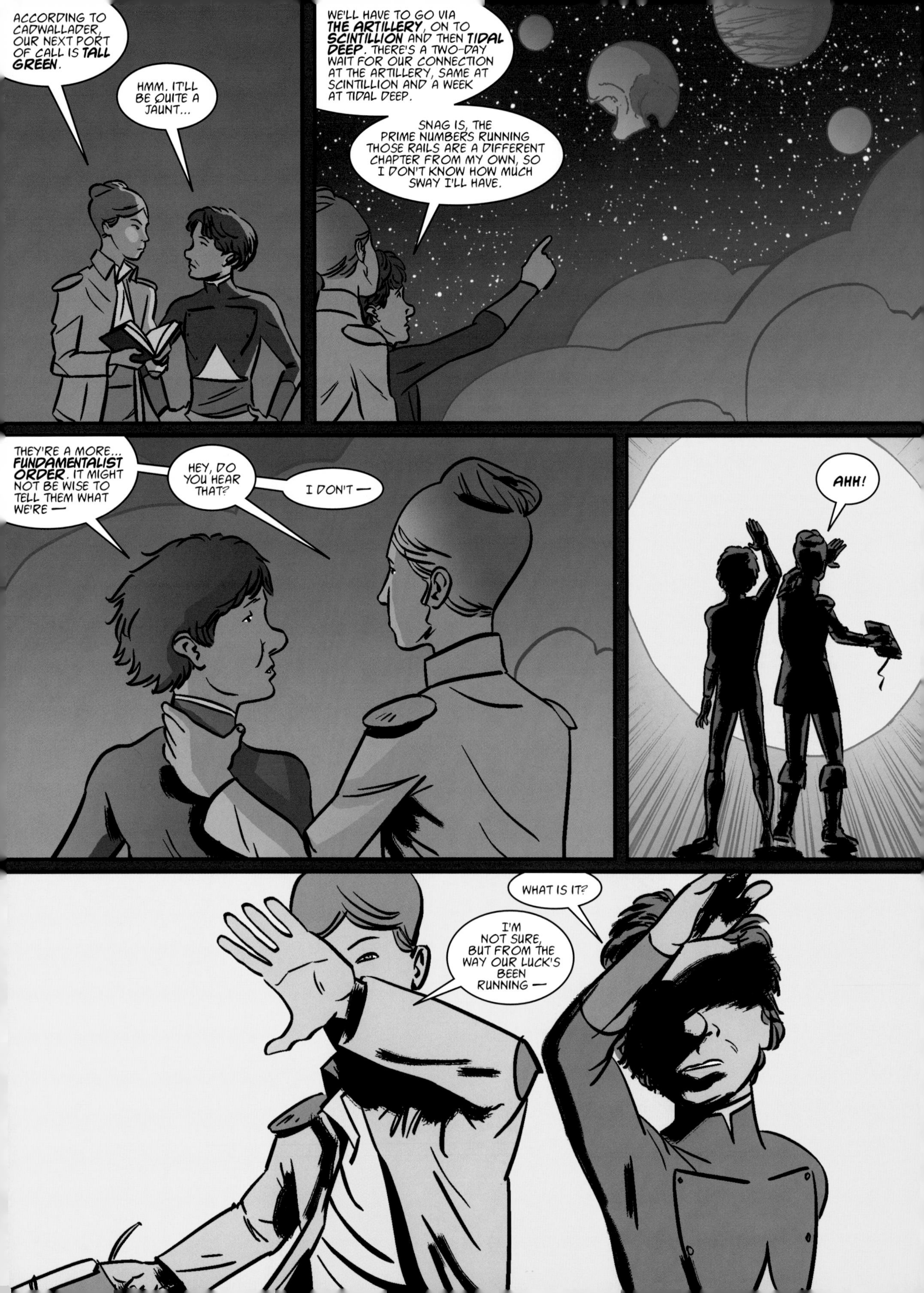

ACCORDING TO CADWALLADER, OUR NEXT PORT OF CALL IS TALL GREEN.
HMM. IT'LL BE QUITE A JAUNT...
WE'LL HAVE TO GO VIA THE ARTILLERY, ON TO SCINTILLION AND THEN TIDAL DEEP. THERE'S A TWO-DAY WAIT FOR OUR CONNECTION AT THE ARTILLERY, SAME AT SCINTILLION AND A WEEK AT TIDAL DEEP.
SNAG IS, THE PRIME NUMBERS RUNNING THOSE RAILS ARE A DIFFERENT CHAPTER FROM MY OWN, SO I DON'T KNOW HOW MUCH SWAY I'LL HAVE.
THEY'RE A MORE... FUNDAMENTALIST ORDER. IT MIGHT NOT BE WISE TO TELL THEM WHAT WE'RE —
HEY, DO YOU HEAR THAT?
I DON'T —
AHH!
WHAT IS IT?
I'M NOT SURE, BUT FROM THE WAY OUR LUCK'S BEEN RUNNING —

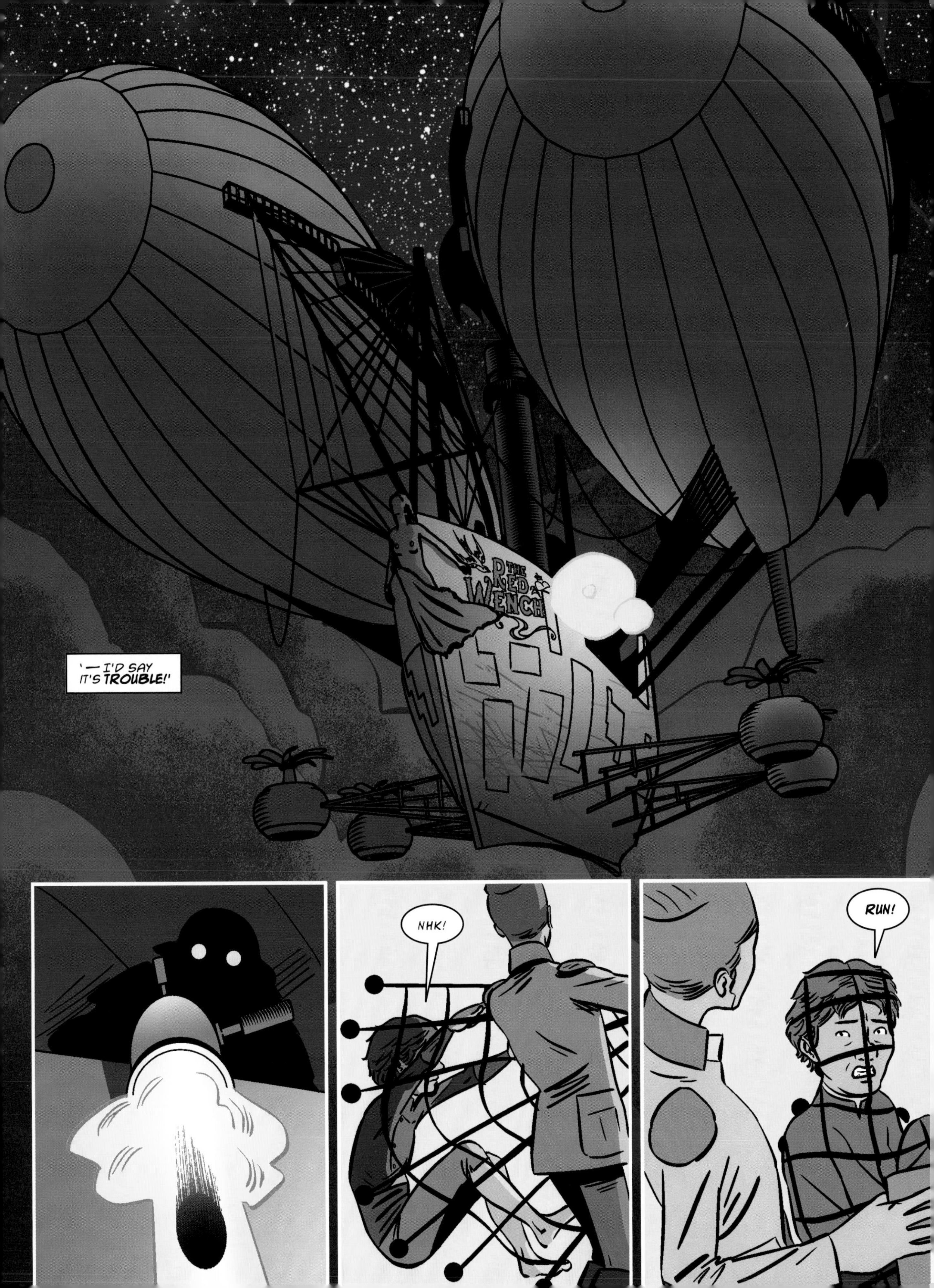
'— I'D SAY IT'S TROUBLE!'
THE RED WENCH
NHK!
RUN!

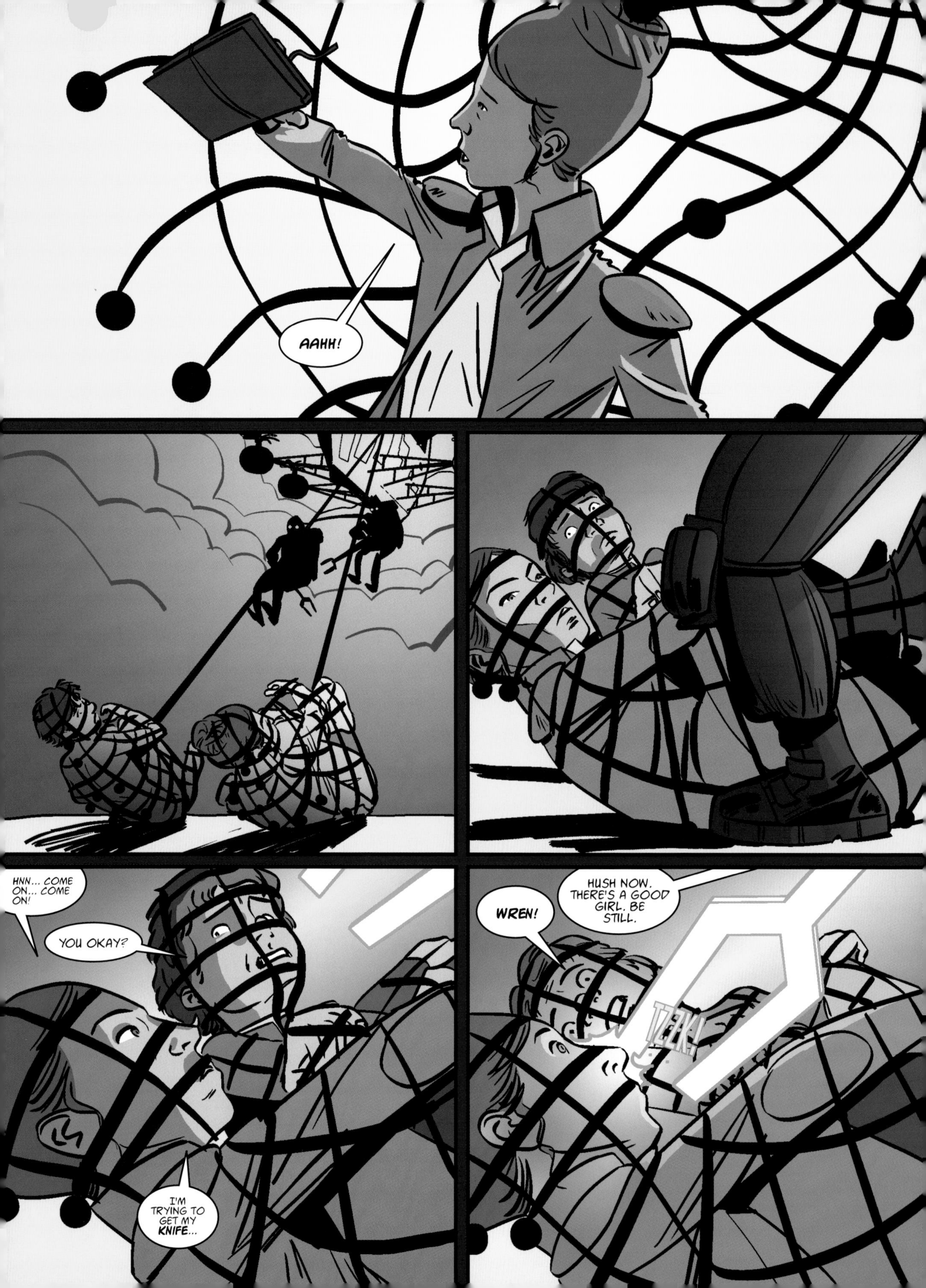
AAHH!
HNN... COME ON... COME ON!
YOU OKAY?
I'M TRYING TO GET MY KNIFE...
WREN!
HUSH NOW. THERE'S A GOOD GIRL. BE STILL.
TZZK!

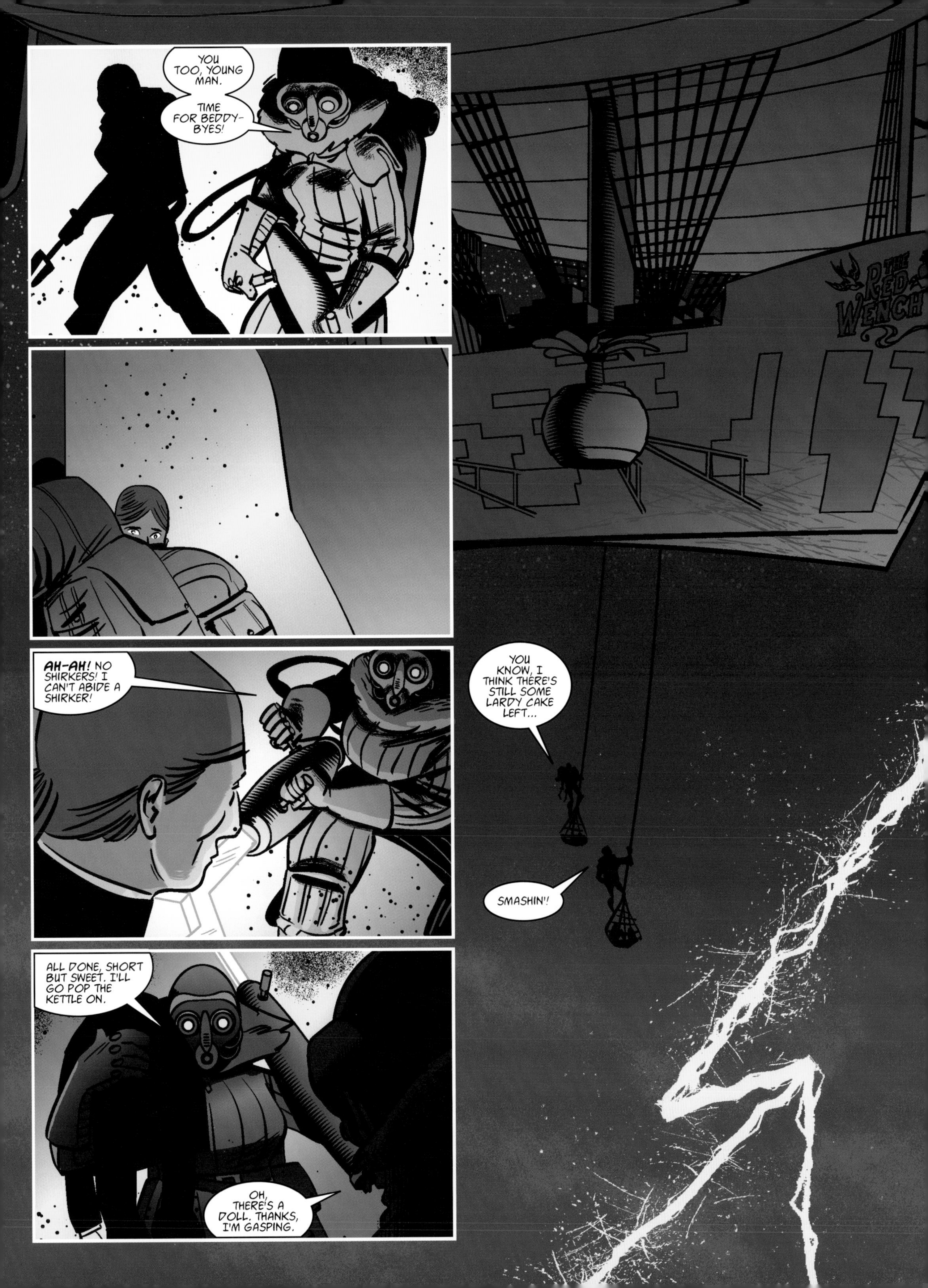
YOU TOO, YOUNG MAN.
TIME FOR BEDDY-BYES!
THE RED WENCH
AH-AH! NO SHIRKERS! I CAN'T ABIDE A SHIRKER!
YOU KNOW, I THINK THERE'S STILL SOME LARDY CAKE LEFT...
SMASHIN'!
ALL DONE, SHORT BUT SWEET. I'LL GO POP THE KETTLE ON.
OH, THERE'S A DOLL. THANKS, I'M GASPING.

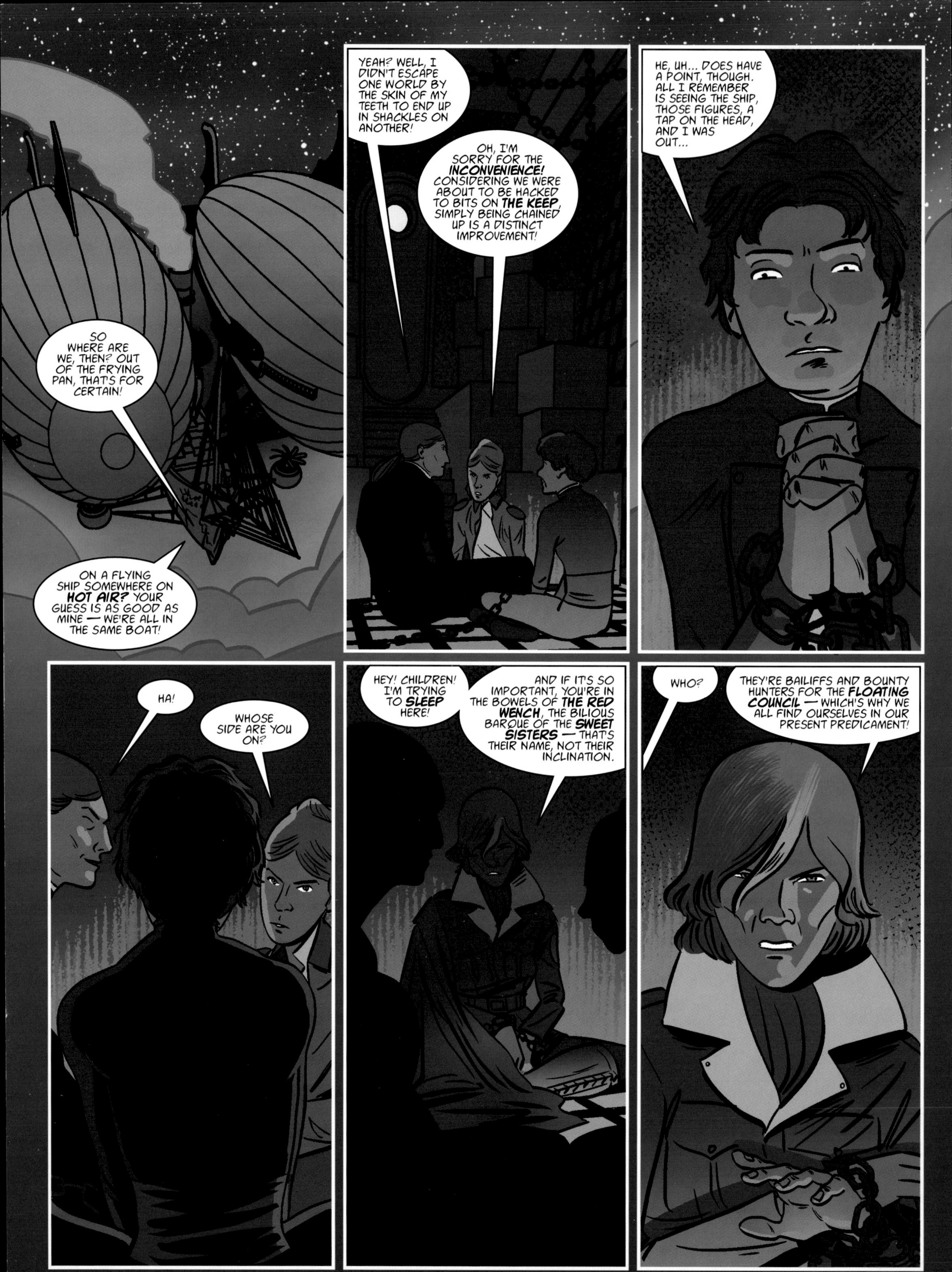
SO WHERE ARE WE, THEN? OUT OF THE FRYING PAN, THAT'S FOR CERTAIN!
ON A FLYING SHIP SOMEWHERE ON HOT AIR? YOUR GUESS IS AS GOOD AS MINE — WE'RE ALL IN THE SAME BOAT!
YEAH? WELL, I DIDN'T ESCAPE ONE WORLD BY THE SKIN OF MY TEETH TO END UP IN SHACKLES ON ANOTHER!
OH, I'M SORRY FOR THE INCONVENIENCE! CONSIDERING WE WERE ABOUT TO BE HACKED TO BITS ON THE KEEP, SIMPLY BEING CHAINED UP IS A DISTINCT IMPROVEMENT!
HE, UH... DOES HAVE A POINT, THOUGH. ALL I REMEMBER IS SEEING THE SHIP, THOSE FIGURES, A TAP ON THE HEAD, AND I WAS OUT...
HA!
WHOSE SIDE ARE YOU ON?
HEY! CHILDREN! I'M TRYING TO SLEEP HERE!
AND IF IT'S SO IMPORTANT, YOU'RE IN THE BOWELS OF THE RED WENCH, THE BILIOUS BARQUE OF THE SWEET SISTERS — THAT'S THEIR NAME, NOT THEIR INCLINATION.
WHO?
THEY'RE BAILIFFS AND BOUNTY HUNTERS FOR THE FLOATING COUNCIL — WHICH'S WHY WE ALL FIND OURSELVES IN OUR PRESENT PREDICAMENT!

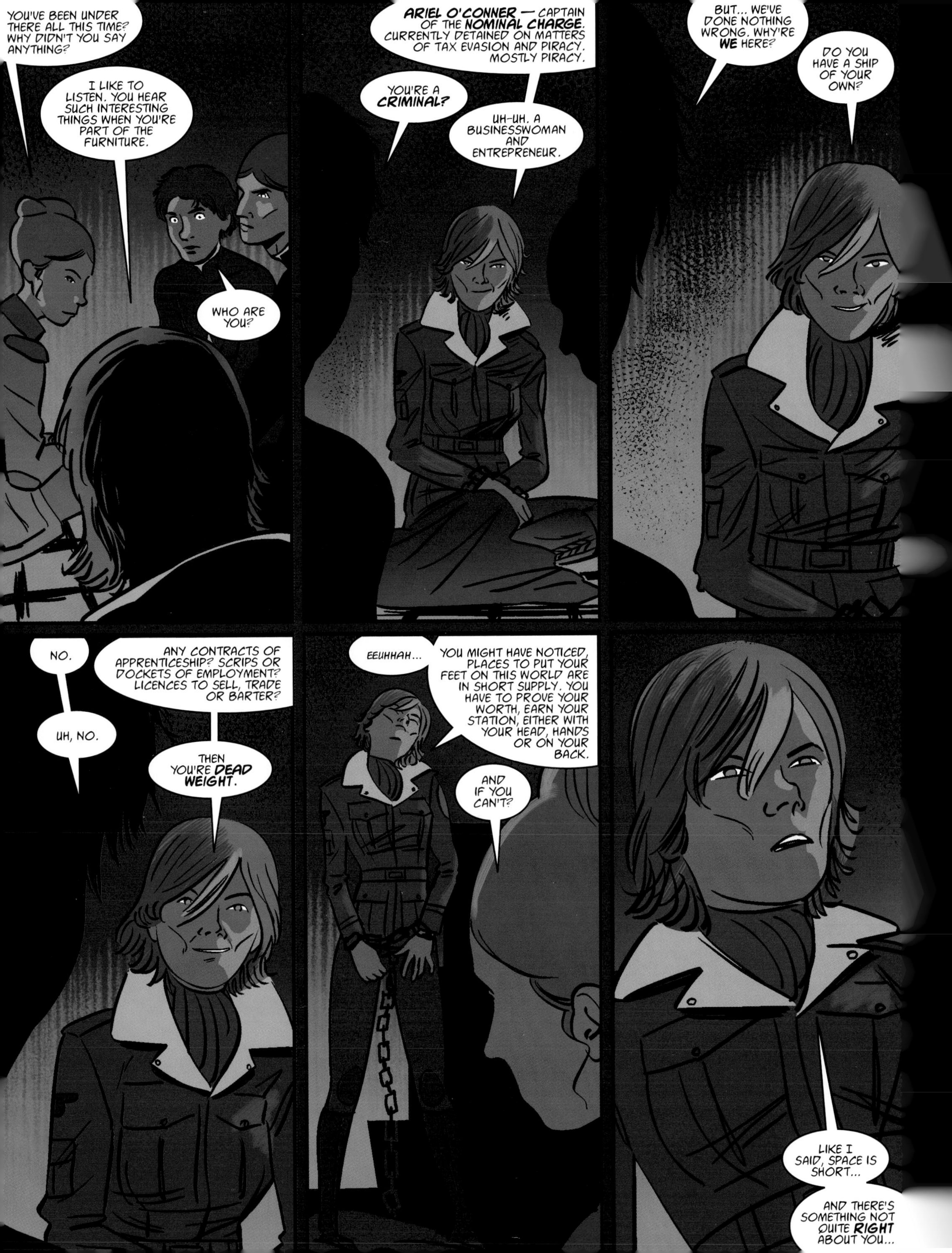
YOU'VE BEEN UNDER THERE ALL THIS TIME? WHY DIDN'T YOU SAY ANYTHING?
I LIKE TO LISTEN. YOU HEAR SUCH INTERESTING THINGS WHEN YOU'RE PART OF THE FURNITURE.
WHO ARE YOU?
ARIEL O'CONNER — CAPTAIN OF THE NOMINAL CHARGE. CURRENTLY DETAINED ON MATTERS OF TAX EVASION AND PIRACY. MOSTLY PIRACY.
YOU'RE A CRIMINAL?
UH-UH. A BUSINESSWOMAN AND ENTREPRENEUR.
BUT... WE'VE DONE NOTHING WRONG. WHY'RE WE HERE?
DO YOU HAVE A SHIP OF YOUR OWN?
NO.
ANY CONTRACTS OF APPRENTICESHIP? SCRIPS OR DOCKETS OF EMPLOYMENT? LICENCES TO SELL, TRADE OR BARTER?
UH, NO.
THEN YOU'RE DEAD WEIGHT.
EEUHHAH...
YOU MIGHT HAVE NOTICED, PLACES TO PUT YOUR FEET ON THIS WORLD ARE IN SHORT SUPPLY. YOU HAVE TO PROVE YOUR WORTH, EARN YOUR STATION, EITHER WITH YOUR HEAD, HANDS OR ON YOUR BACK.
AND IF YOU CAN'T?
LIKE I SAID, SPACE IS SHORT...
AND THERE'S SOMETHING NOT QUITE RIGHT ABOUT YOU...

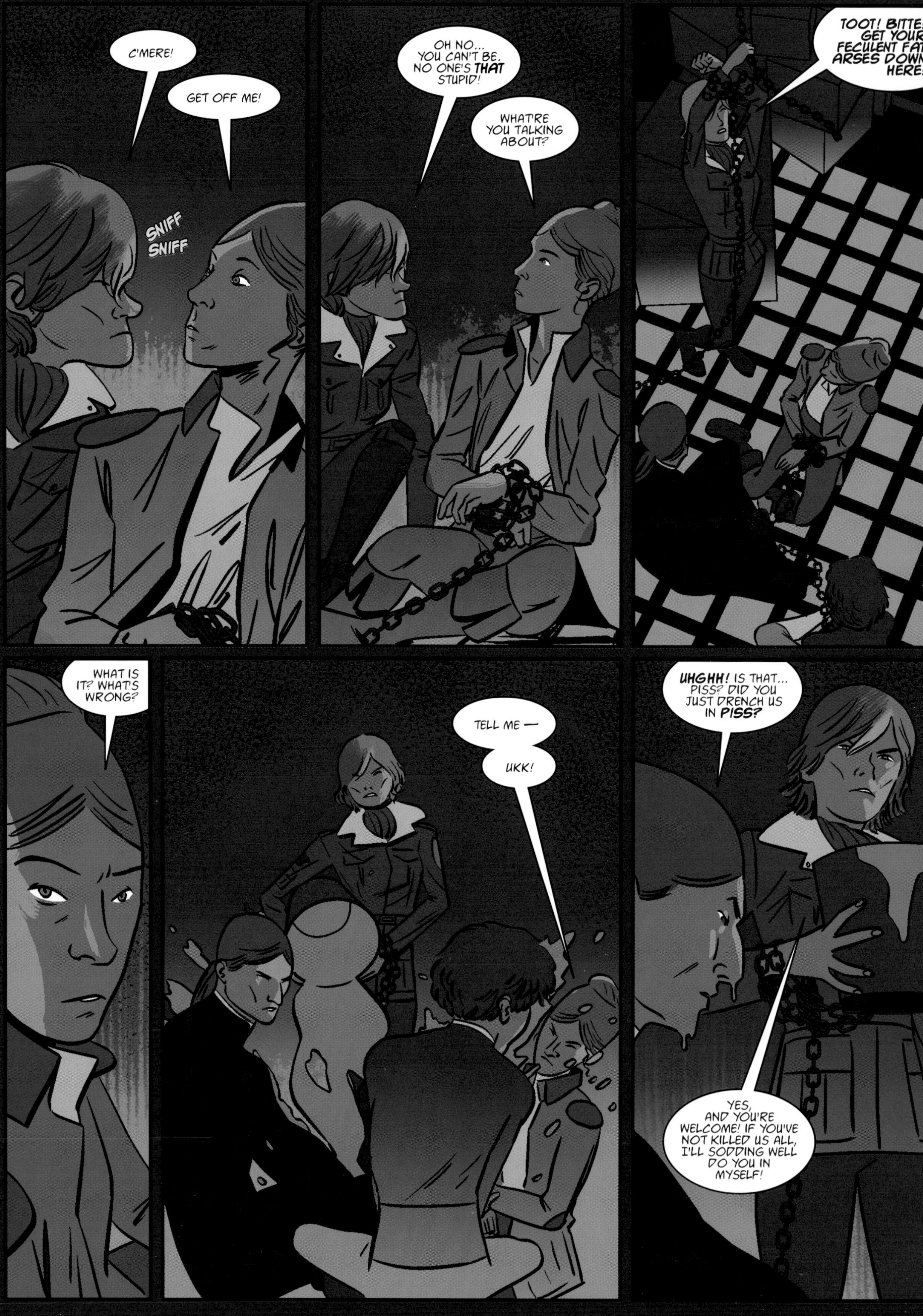
C'MERE!
GET OFF ME!
SNIFF SNIFF
OH NO... YOU CAN'T BE. NO ONE'S THAT STUPID!
WHAT'RE YOU TALKING ABOUT?
TOOT! BITTE! GET YOUR FECULENT FAT ARSES DOWN HERE!
WHAT IS IT? WHAT'S WRONG?
TELL ME —
UKK!
UHGHH! IS THAT... PISS? DID YOU JUST DRENCH US IN PISS?
YES, AND YOU'RE WELCOME! IF YOU'VE NOT KILLED US ALL, I'LL SODDING WELL DO YOU IN MYSELF!

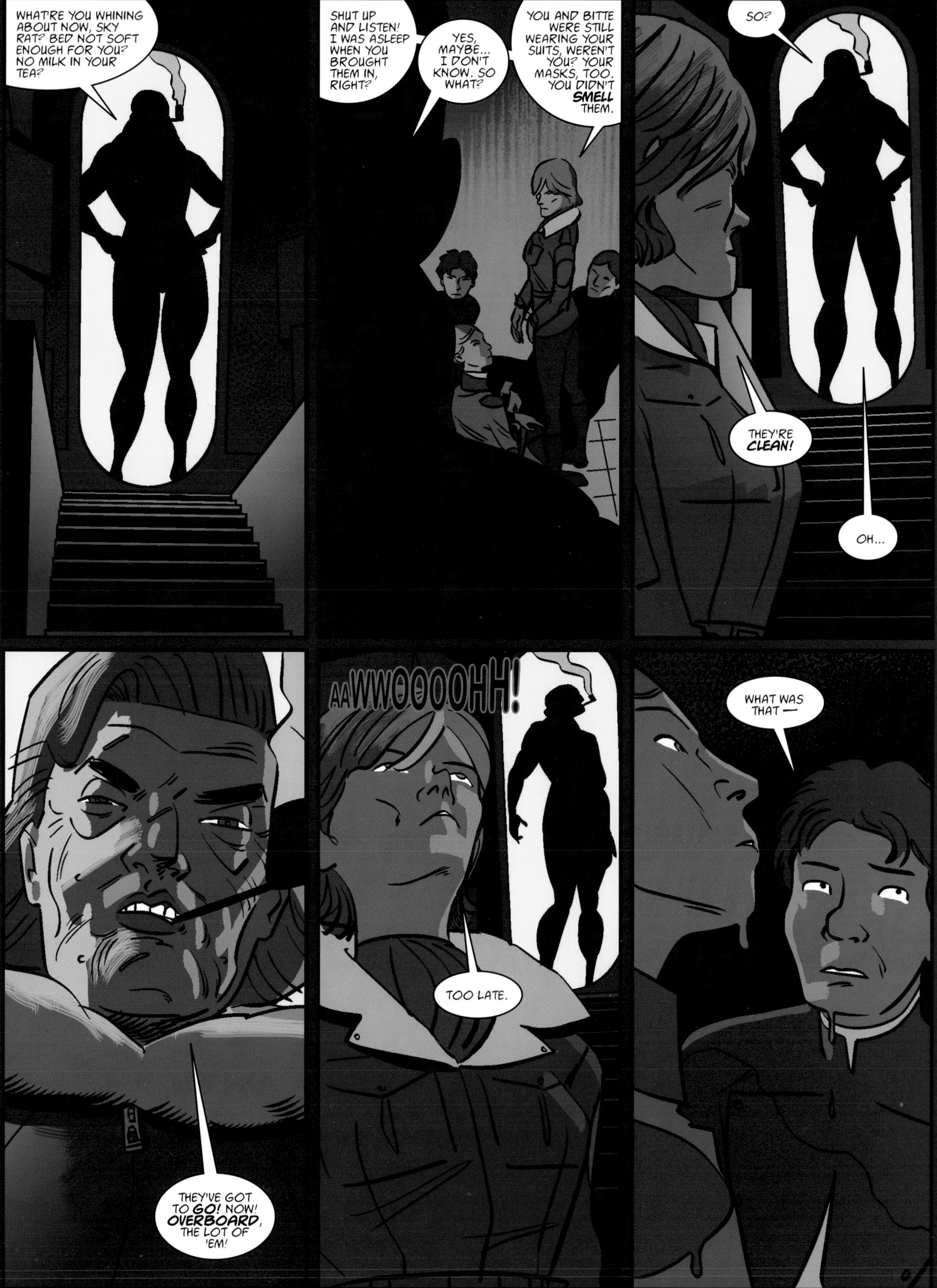
WHAT'RE YOU WHINING ABOUT NOW, SKY RAT? BED NOT SOFT ENOUGH FOR YOU? NO MILK IN YOUR TEA?
SHUT UP AND LISTEN! I WAS ASLEEP WHEN YOU BROUGHT THEM IN, RIGHT?
YES, MAYBE... I DON'T KNOW. SO WHAT?
YOU AND BITTE WERE STILL WEARING YOUR SUITS, WEREN'T YOU? YOUR MASKS, TOO. YOU DIDN'T **SMELL** THEM.
SO?
THEY'RE **CLEAN!**
OH...
THEY'VE GOT TO **GO!** NOW! **OVERBOARD**, THE LOT OF 'EM!
AAWWOOOOHH!
TOO LATE.
WHAT WAS THAT —

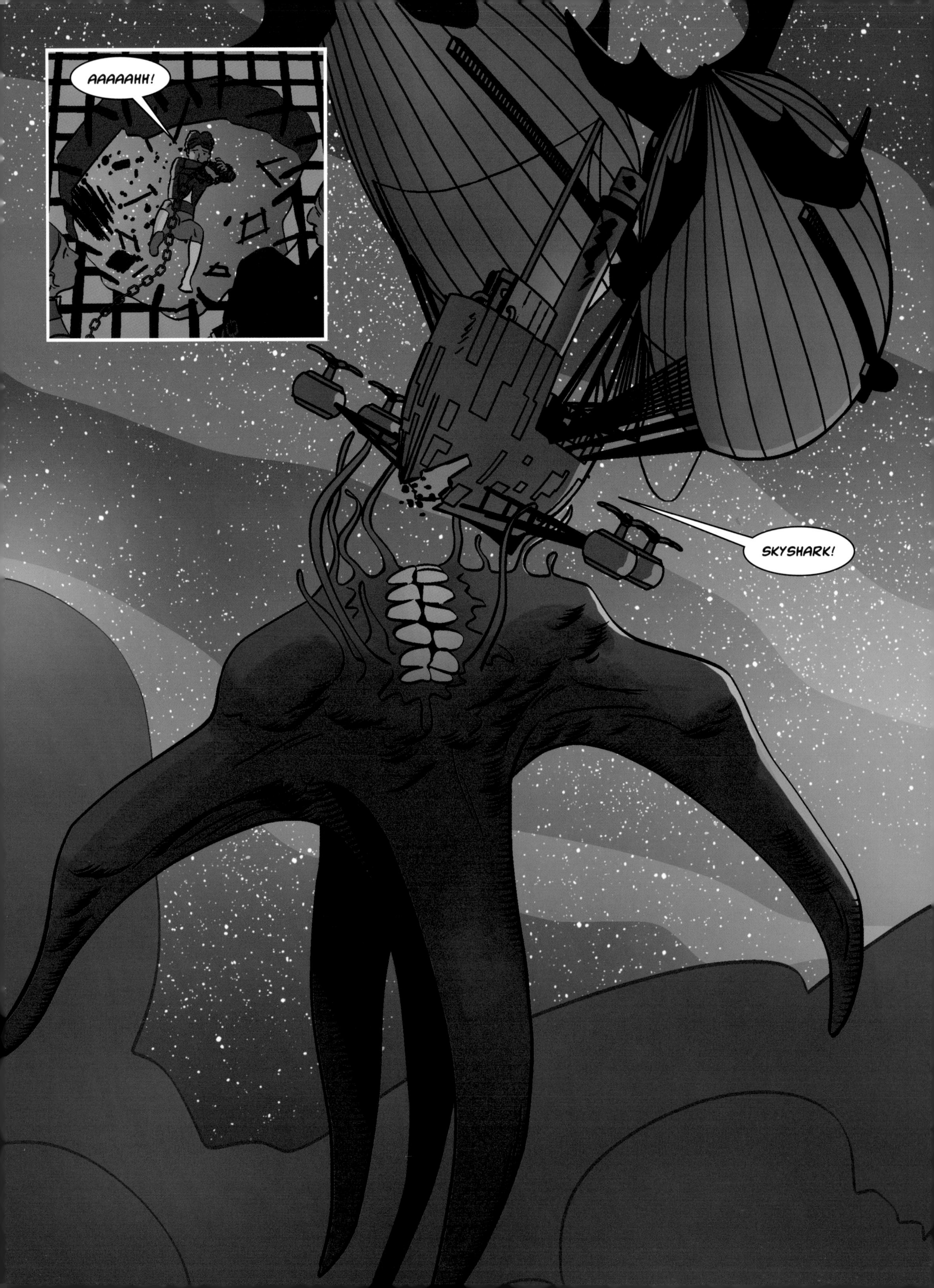
AAAAAHH!
SKYSHARK!

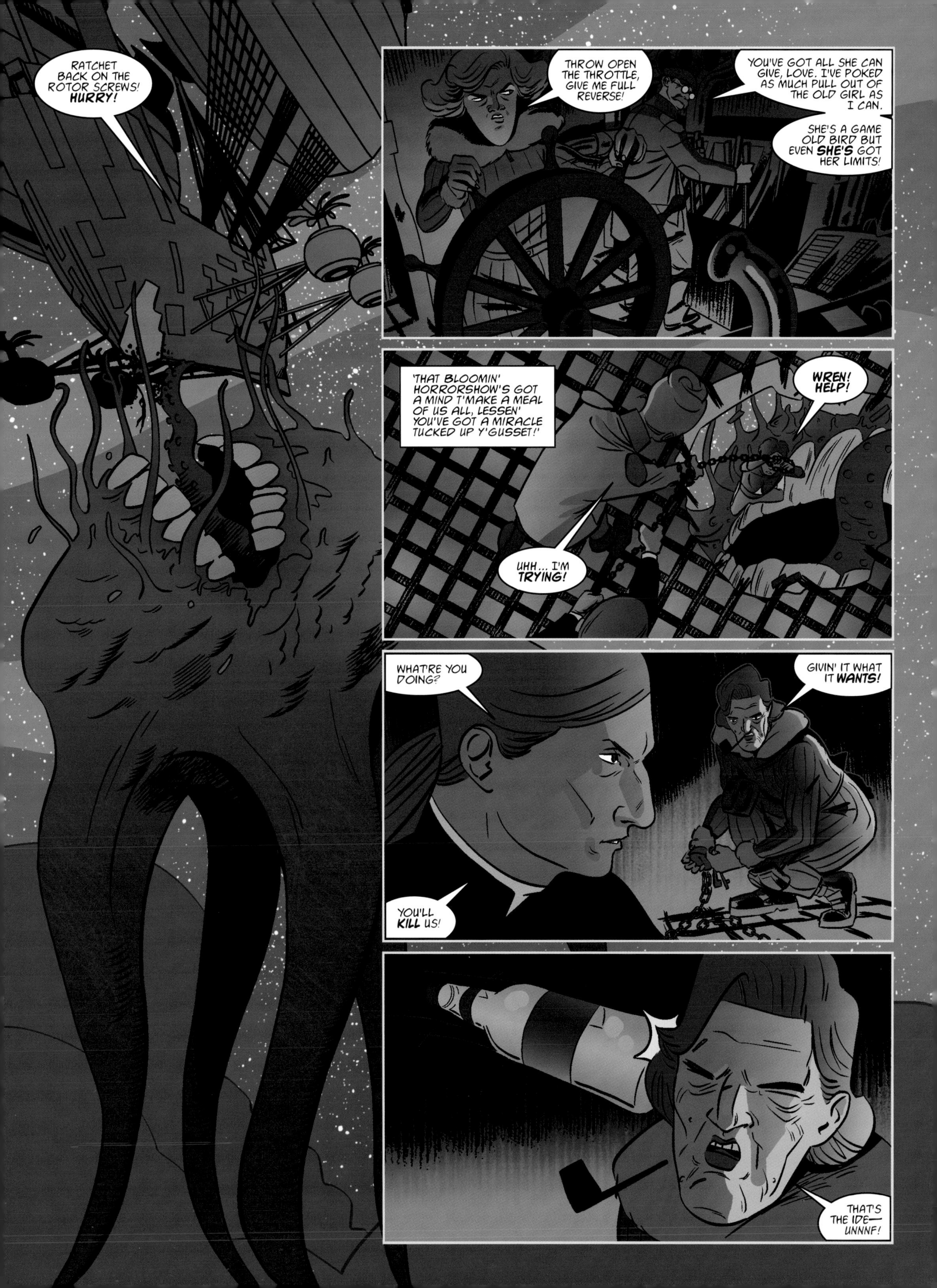

RATCHET BACK ON THE ROTOR SCREWS! HURRY!
THROW OPEN THE THROTTLE, GIVE ME FULL REVERSE!
YOU'VE GOT ALL SHE CAN GIVE, LOVE. I'VE POKED AS MUCH PULL OUT OF THE OLD GIRL AS I CAN.
SHE'S A GAME OLD BIRD BUT EVEN SHE'S GOT HER LIMITS!
'THAT BLOOMIN' HORRORSHOW'S GOT A MIND T'MAKE A MEAL OF US ALL, LESSEN' YOU'VE GOT A MIRACLE TUCKED UP Y'GUSSET!'
WREN! HELP!
UHH... I'M TRYING!
WHAT'RE YOU DOING?
GIVIN' IT WHAT IT WANTS!
YOU'LL KILL US!
THAT'S THE IDE— UNNNF!

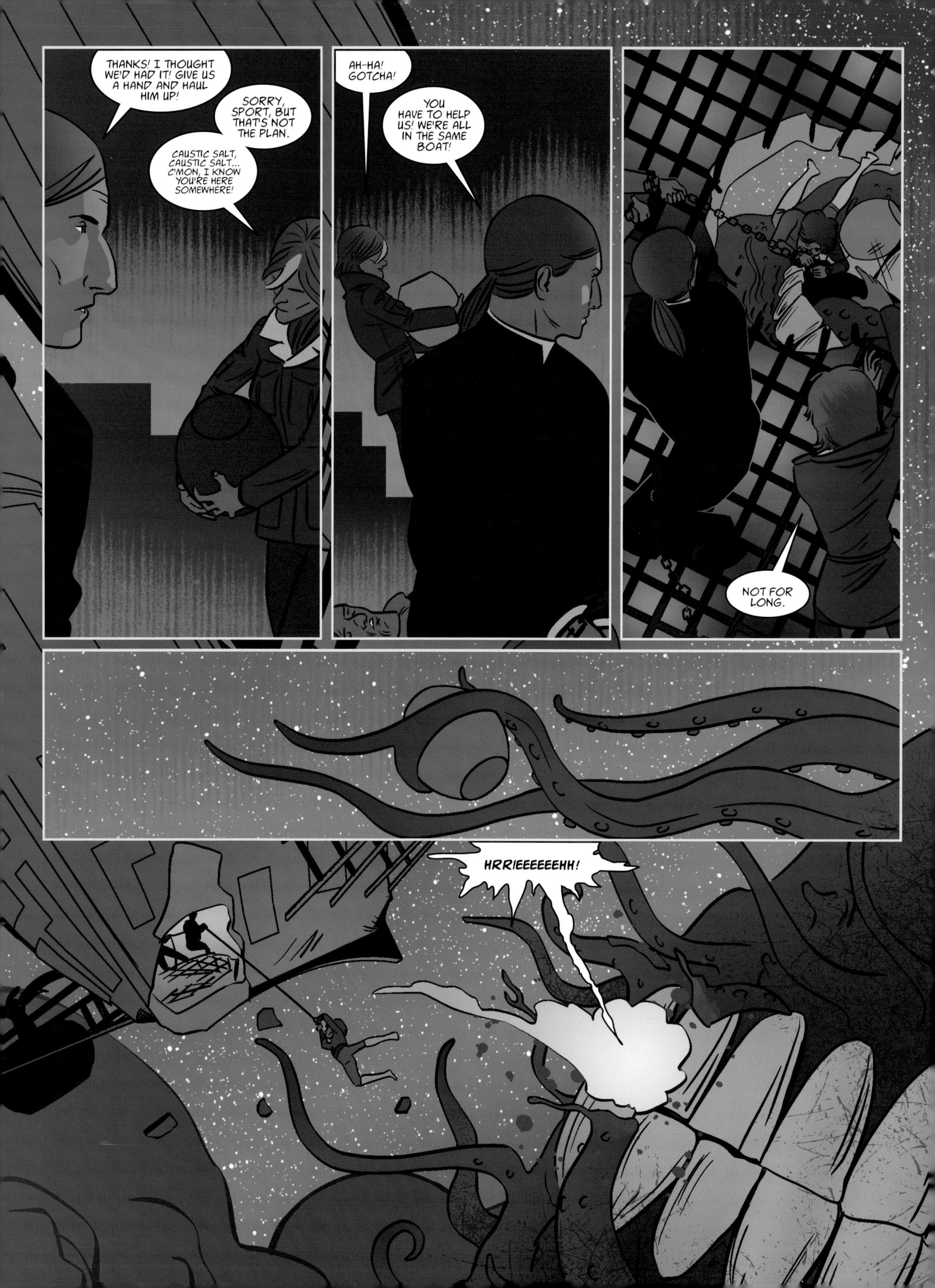
THANKS! I THOUGHT WE'D HAD IT! GIVE US A HAND AND HAUL HIM UP!
SORRY, SPORT, BUT THAT'S NOT THE PLAN.
CAUSTIC SALT, CAUSTIC SALT... C'MON, I KNOW YOU'RE HERE SOMEWHERE!
AH-HA! GOTCHA!
YOU HAVE TO HELP US! WE'RE ALL IN THE SAME BOAT!
NOT FOR LONG.
HRRIEEEEEEHH!

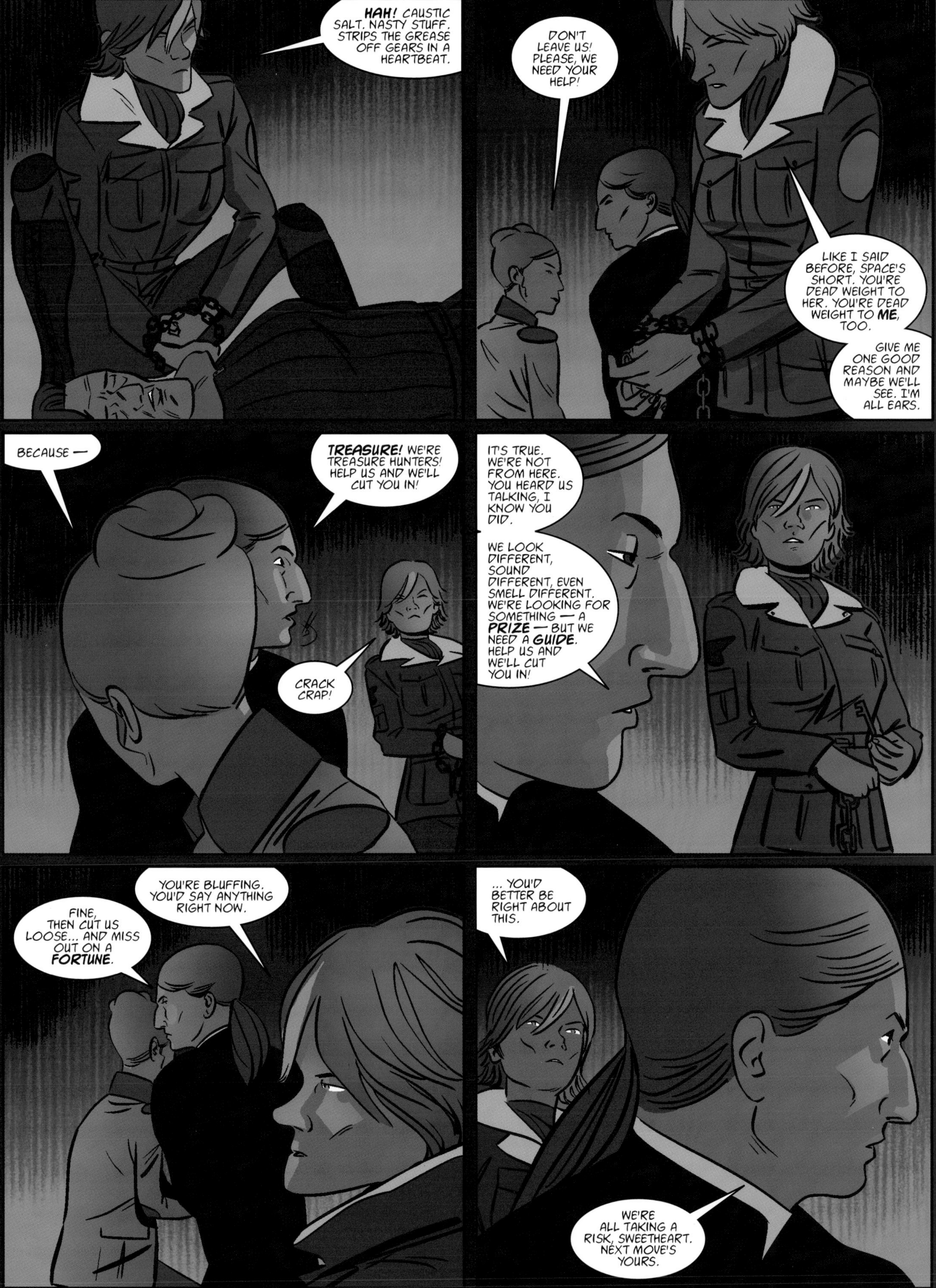
HAH! CAUSTIC SALT. NASTY STUFF. STRIPS THE GREASE OFF GEARS IN A HEARTBEAT.
DON'T LEAVE US! PLEASE, WE NEED YOUR HELP!
LIKE I SAID BEFORE, SPACE'S SHORT. YOU'RE DEAD WEIGHT TO HER. YOU'RE DEAD WEIGHT TO ME, TOO.
GIVE ME ONE GOOD REASON AND MAYBE WE'LL SEE. I'M ALL EARS.
BECAUSE —
TREASURE! WE'RE TREASURE HUNTERS! HELP US AND WE'LL CUT YOU IN!
CRACK CRAP!
IT'S TRUE. WE'RE NOT FROM HERE. YOU HEARD US TALKING, I KNOW YOU DID.
WE LOOK DIFFERENT, SOUND DIFFERENT, EVEN SMELL DIFFERENT. WE'RE LOOKING FOR SOMETHING — A PRIZE — BUT WE NEED A GUIDE. HELP US AND WE'LL CUT YOU IN!
YOU'RE BLUFFING. YOU'D SAY ANYTHING RIGHT NOW.
FINE, THEN CUT US LOOSE... AND MISS OUT ON A FORTUNE.
... YOU'D BETTER BE RIGHT ABOUT THIS.
WE'RE ALL TAKING A RISK, SWEETHEART. NEXT MOVE'S YOURS.

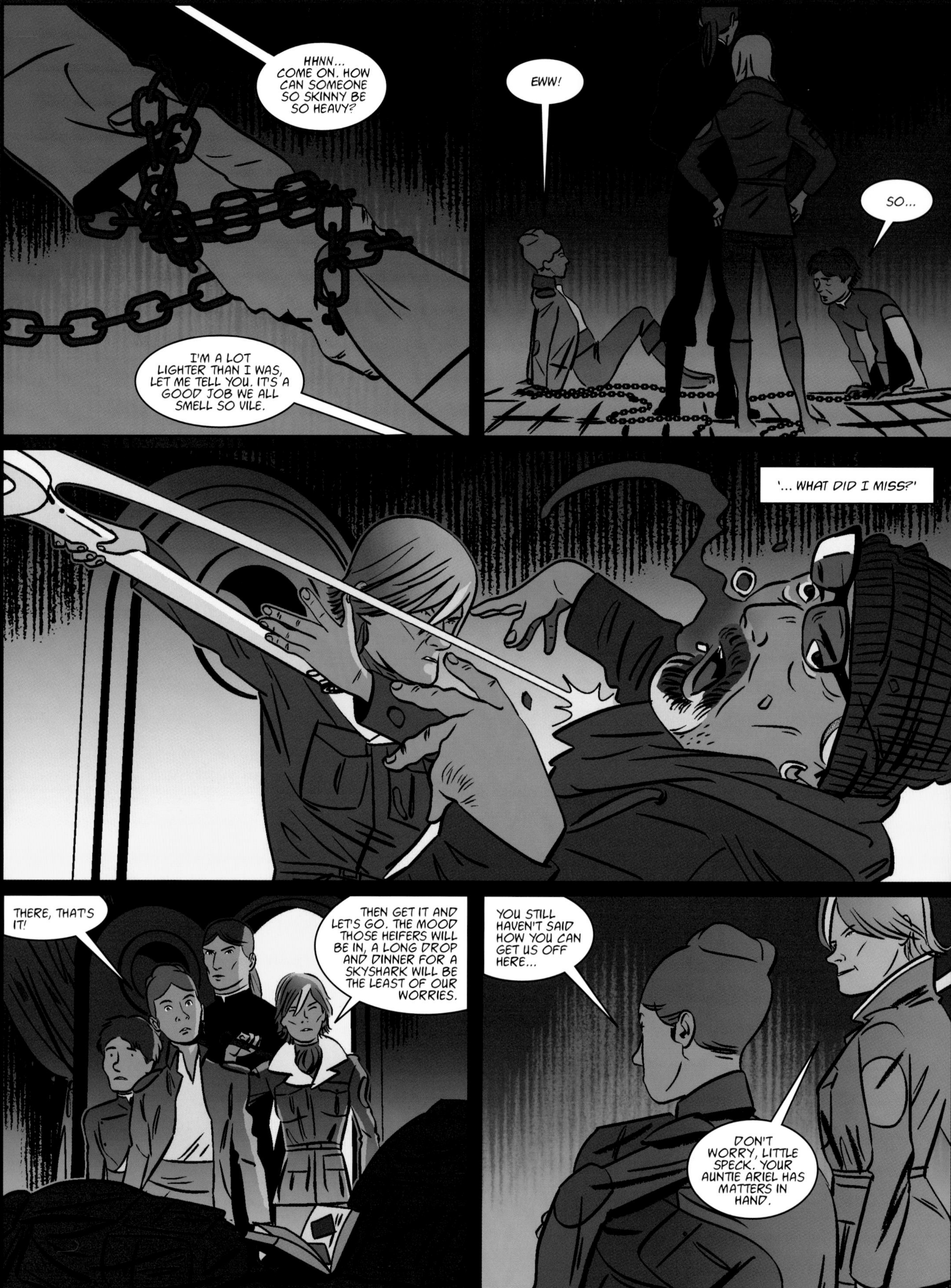

HHNN... COME ON. HOW CAN SOMEONE SO SKINNY BE SO HEAVY?
I'M A LOT LIGHTER THAN I WAS, LET ME TELL YOU. IT'S A GOOD JOB WE ALL SMELL SO VILE.
EWW!
SO...
'... WHAT DID I MISS?'
THERE, THAT'S IT!
THEN GET IT AND LET'S GO. THE MOOD THOSE HEIFERS WILL BE IN, A LONG DROP AND DINNER FOR A SKYSHARK WILL BE THE LEAST OF OUR WORRIES.
YOU STILL HAVEN'T SAID HOW YOU CAN GET US OFF HERE...
DON'T WORRY, LITTLE SPECK. YOUR AUNTIE ARIEL HAS MATTERS IN HAND.

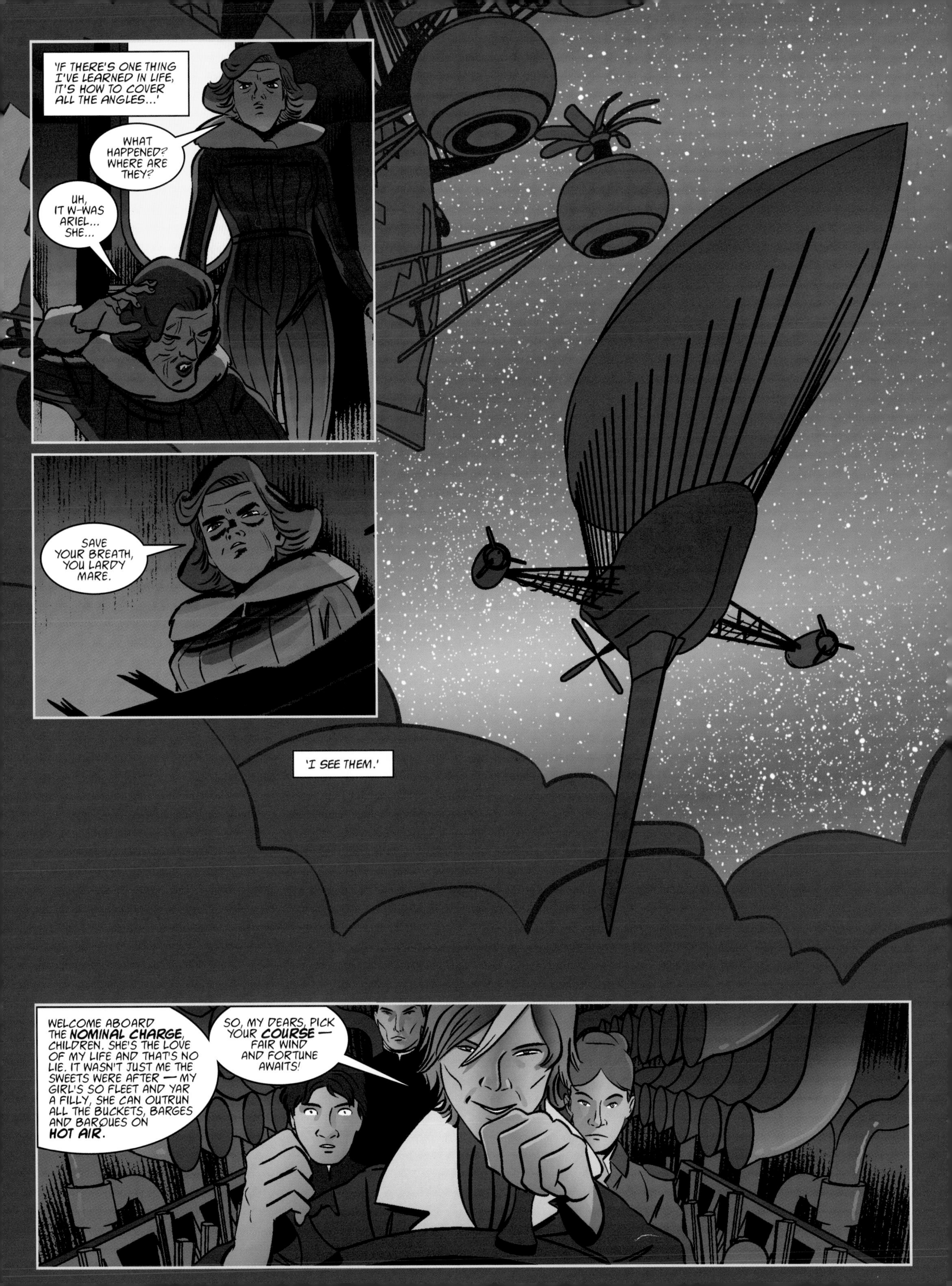
'IF THERE'S ONE THING I'VE LEARNED IN LIFE, IT'S HOW TO COVER ALL THE ANGLES...'
WHAT HAPPENED? WHERE ARE THEY?
UH, IT W-WAS ARIEL... SHE...
SAVE YOUR BREATH, YOU LARDY MARE.
'I SEE THEM.'
WELCOME ABOARD THE NOMINAL CHARGE, CHILDREN. SHE'S THE LOVE OF MY LIFE AND THAT'S NO LIE. IT WASN'T JUST ME THE SWEETS WERE AFTER — MY GIRL'S SO FLEET AND YAR A FILLY, SHE CAN OUTRUN ALL THE BUCKETS, BARGES AND BARQUES ON HOT AIR.
SO, MY DEARS, PICK YOUR COURSE — FAIR WIND AND FORTUNE AWAITS!

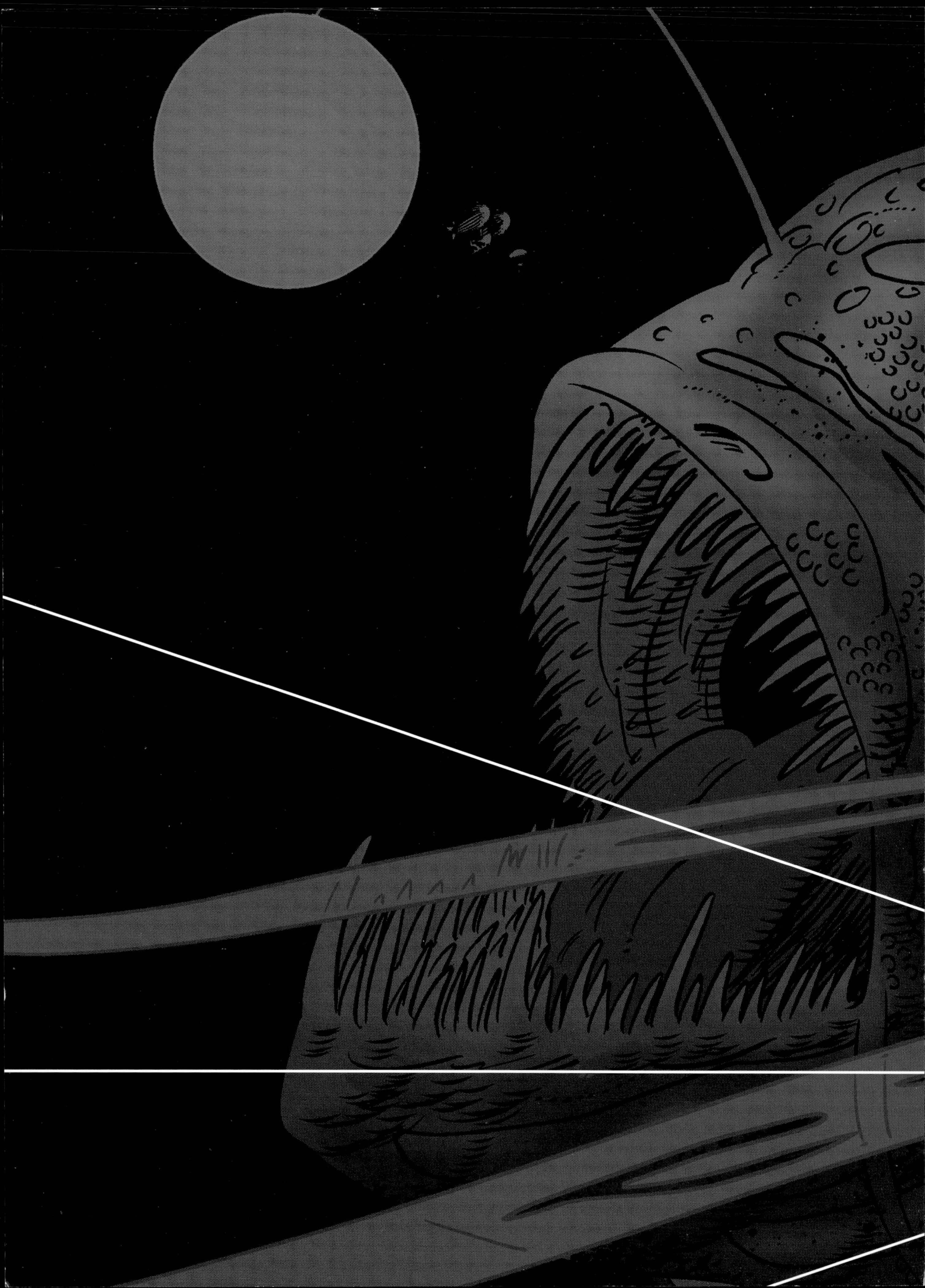

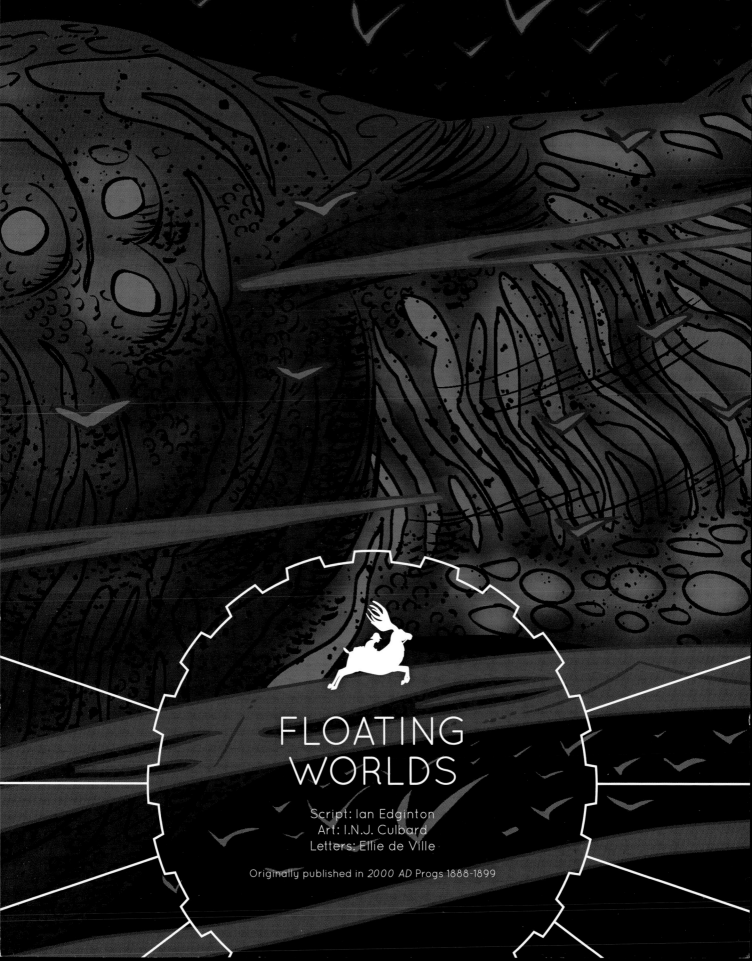

FLOATING WORLDS

Script: Ian Edginton
Art: I.N.J. Culbard
Letters: Ellie de Ville

Originally published in *2000 AD* Progs 1888-1899

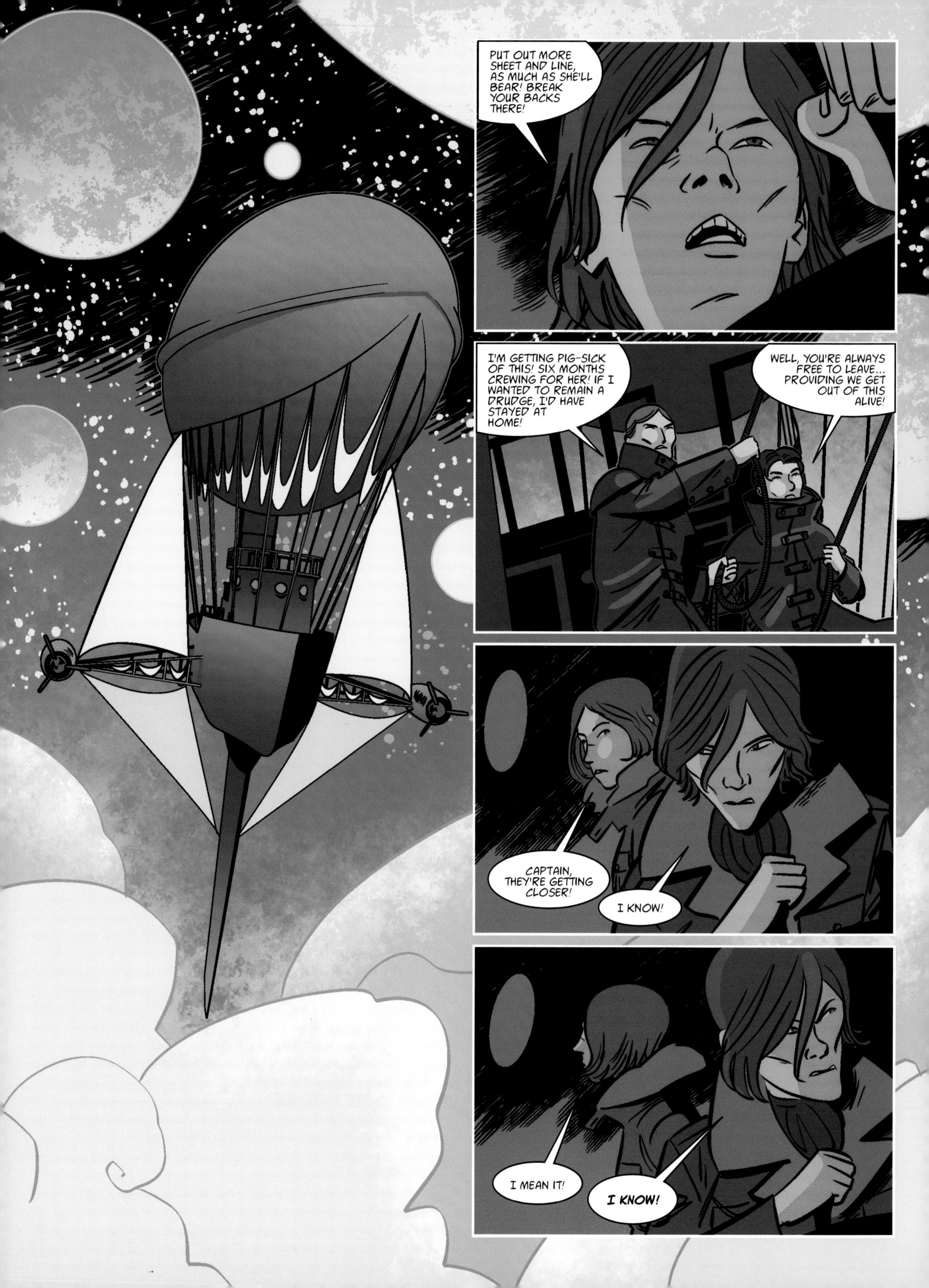
PUT OUT MORE SHEET AND LINE, AS MUCH AS SHE'LL BEAR! BREAK YOUR BACKS THERE!
I'M GETTING PIG-SICK OF THIS! SIX MONTHS CREWING FOR HER! IF I WANTED TO REMAIN A DRUDGE, I'D HAVE STAYED AT HOME!
WELL, YOU'RE ALWAYS FREE TO LEAVE... PROVIDING WE GET OUT OF THIS ALIVE!
CAPTAIN, THEY'RE GETTING CLOSER!
I KNOW!
I MEAN IT!
I KNOW!

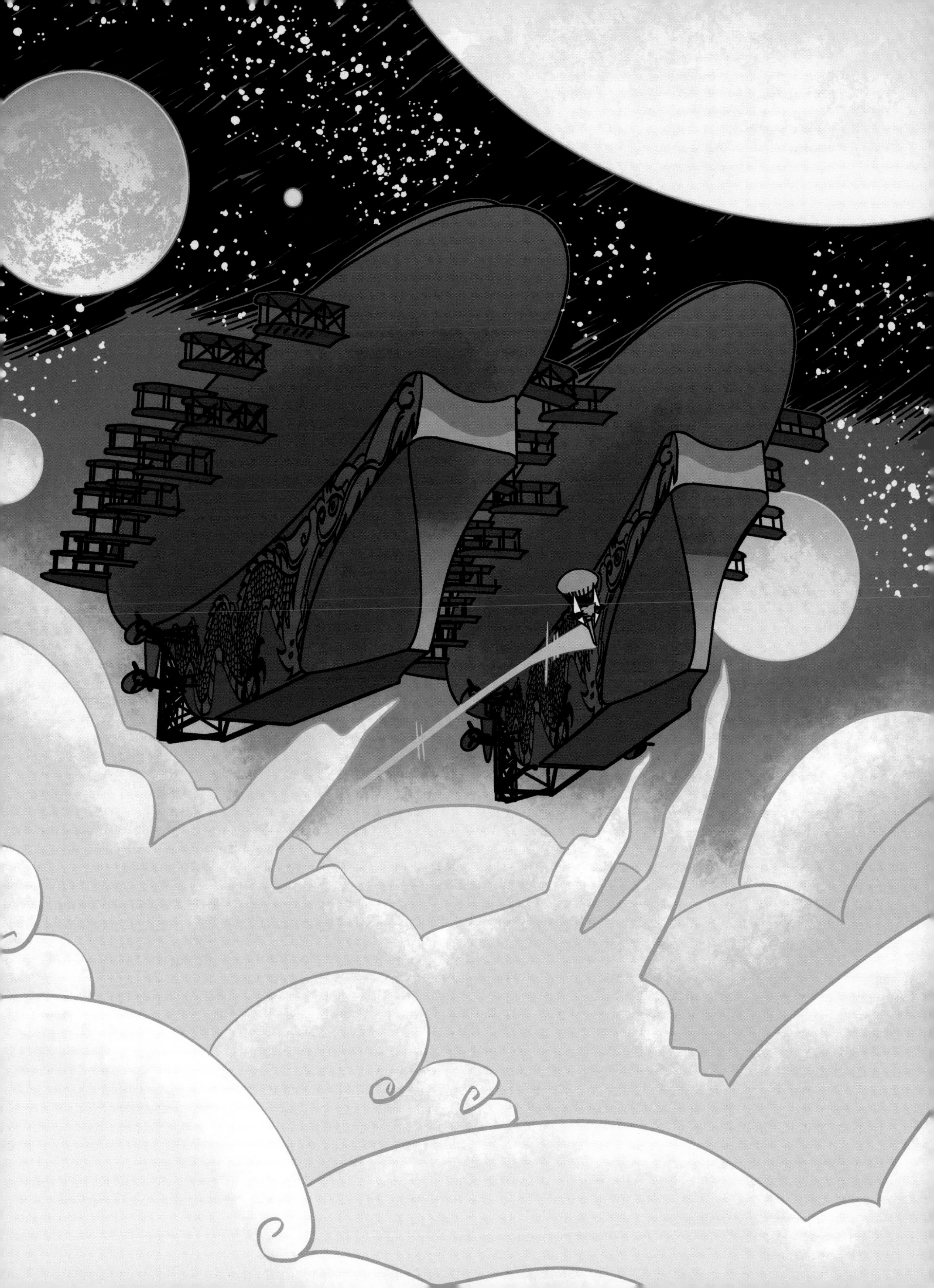

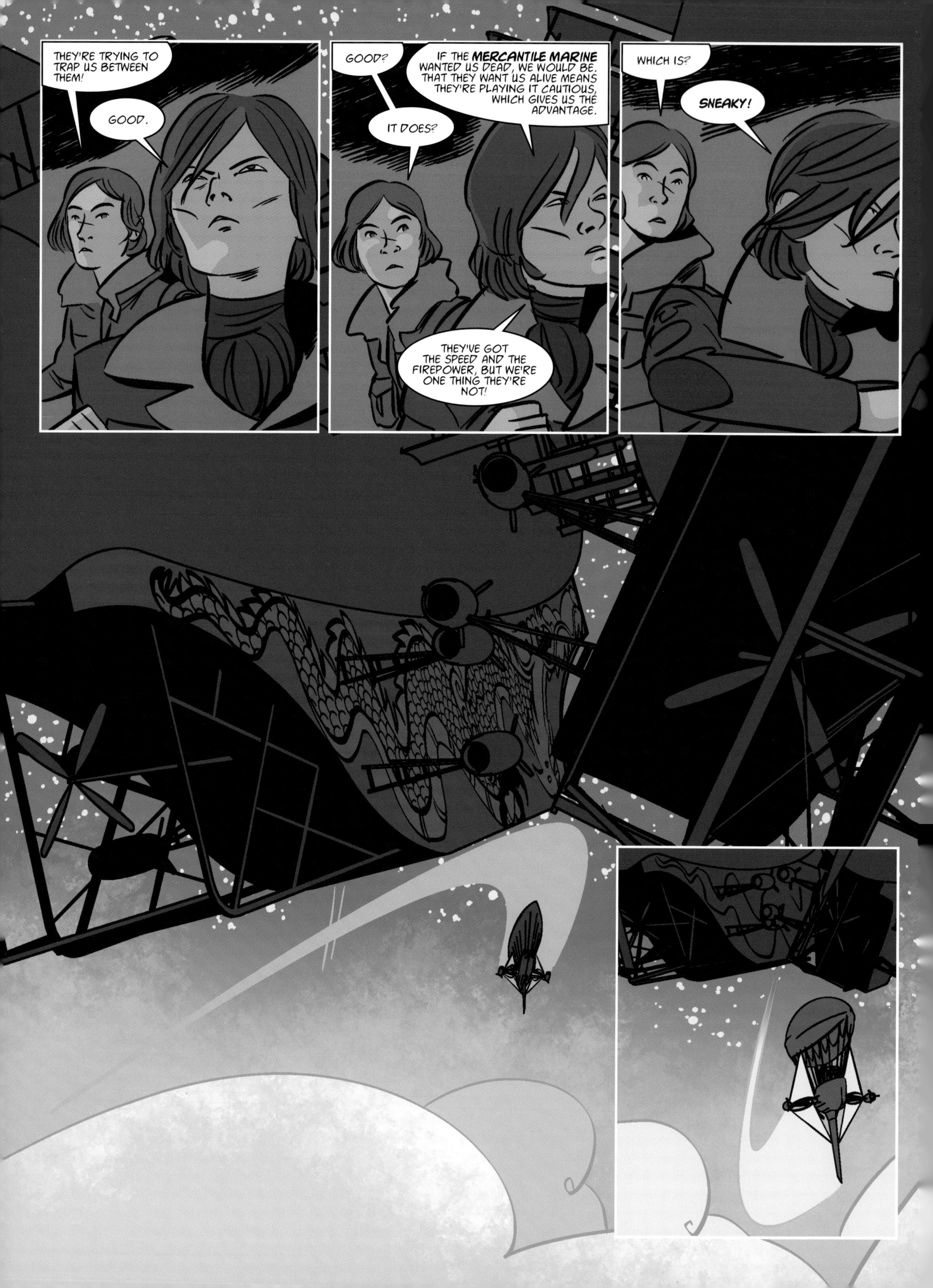

THEY'RE TRYING TO TRAP US BETWEEN THEM!
GOOD.
GOOD?
IF THE MERCANTILE MARINE WANTED US DEAD, WE WOULD BE. THAT THEY WANT US ALIVE MEANS THEY'RE PLAYING IT CAUTIOUS, WHICH GIVES US THE ADVANTAGE.
IT DOES?
THEY'VE GOT THE SPEED AND THE FIREPOWER, BUT WE'RE ONE THING THEY'RE NOT!
WHICH IS?
SNEAKY!

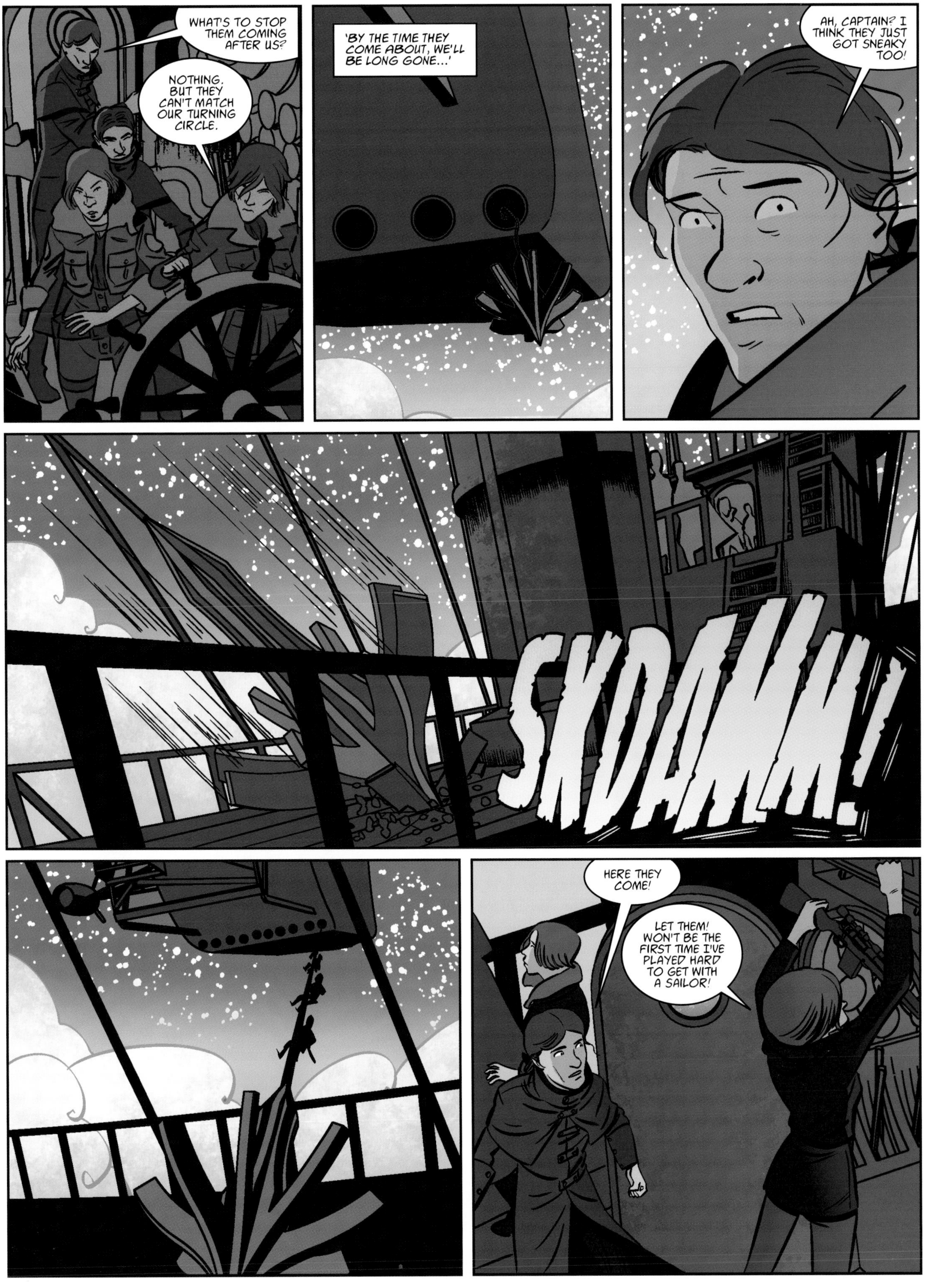
WHAT'S TO STOP THEM COMING AFTER US?
NOTHING. BUT THEY CAN'T MATCH OUR TURNING CIRCLE.
'BY THE TIME THEY COME ABOUT, WE'LL BE LONG GONE...'
AH, CAPTAIN? I THINK THEY JUST GOT SNEAKY TOO!
SKDAMM!
HERE THEY COME!
LET THEM! WON'T BE THE FIRST TIME I'VE PLAYED HARD TO GET WITH A SAILOR!

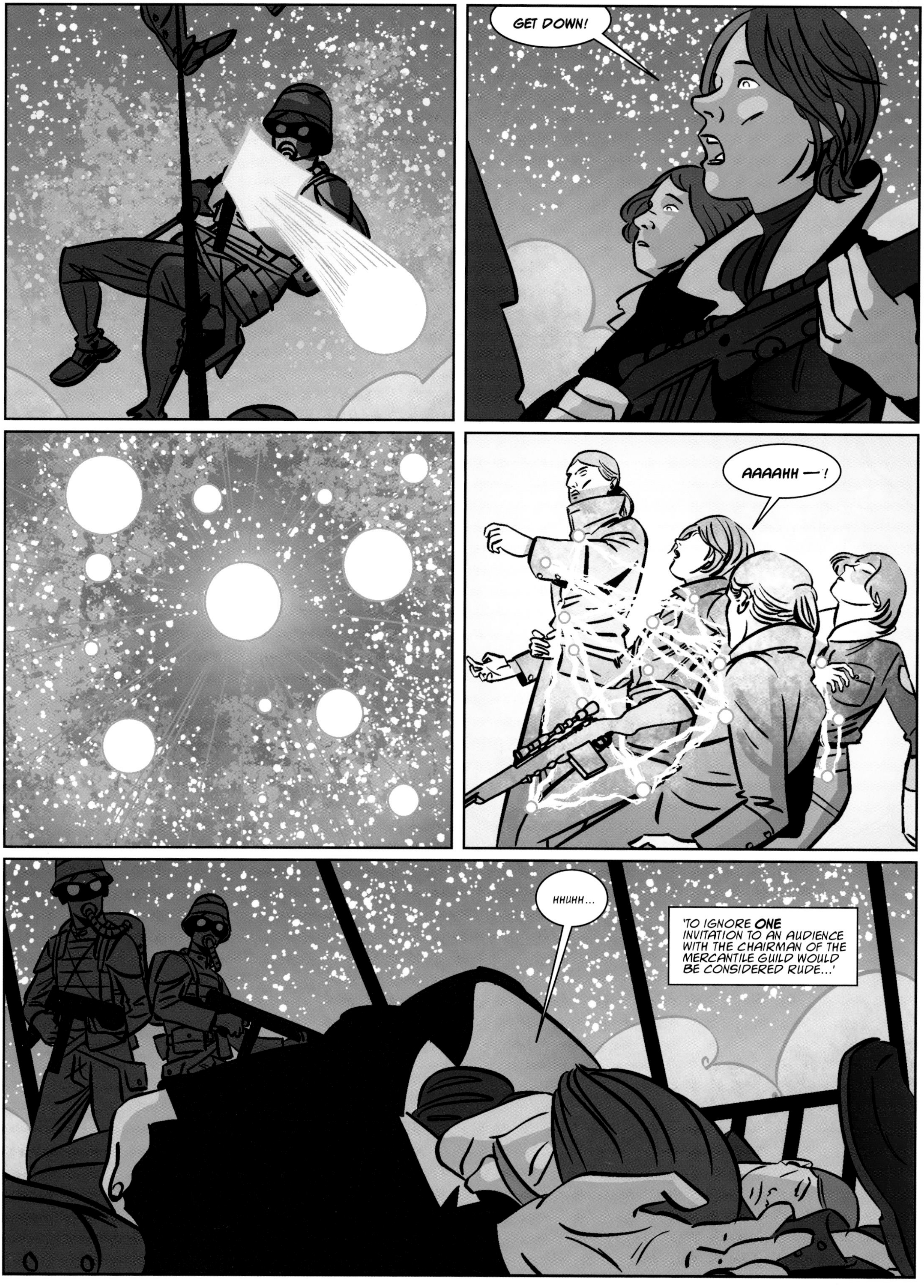
GET DOWN!
AAAAHH —!
HHUHH...
'TO IGNORE ONE INVITATION TO AN AUDIENCE WITH THE CHAIRMAN OF THE MERCANTILE GUILD WOULD BE CONSIDERED RUDE...'

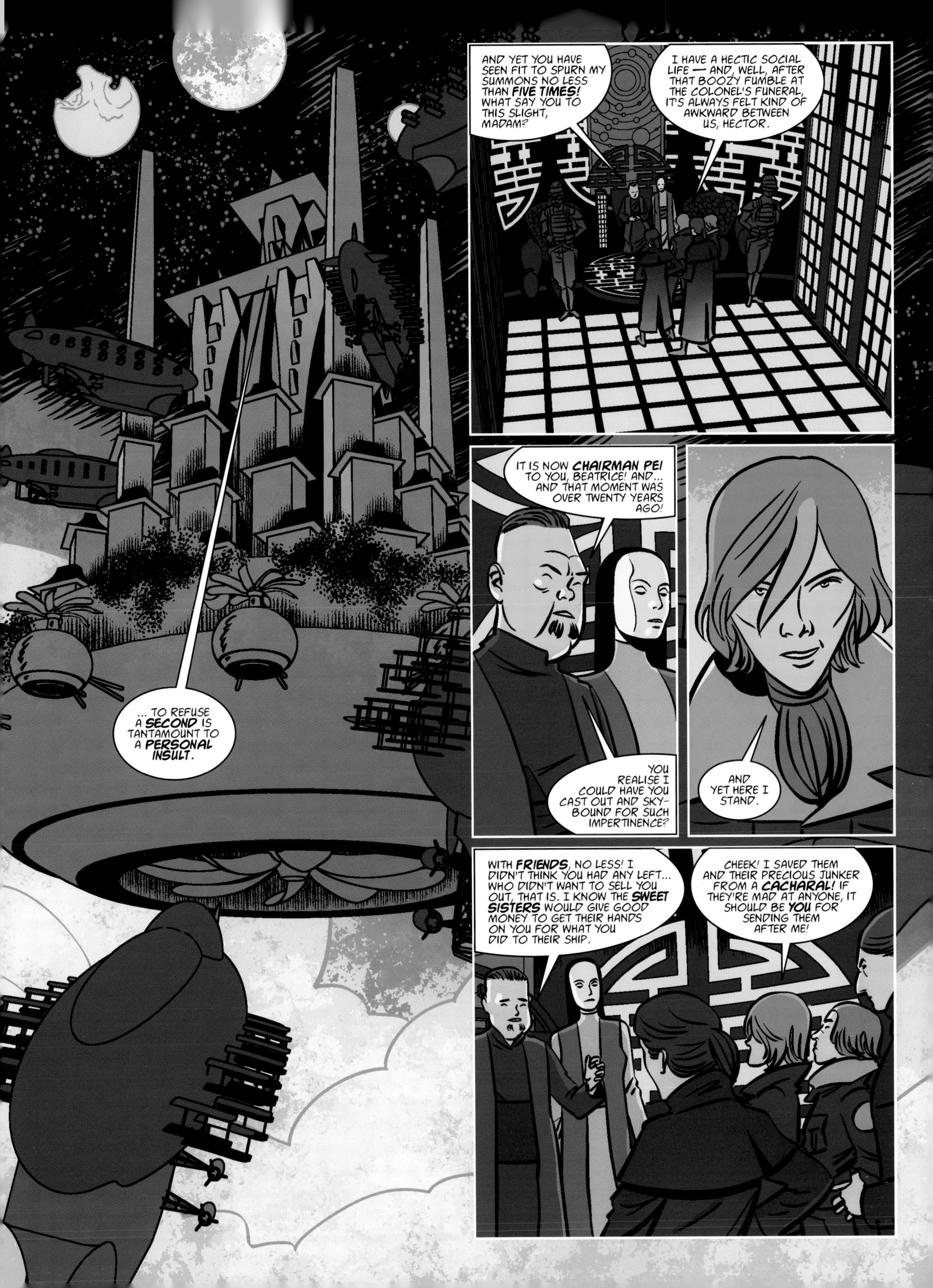
AND YET YOU HAVE SEEN FIT TO SPURN MY SUMMONS NO LESS THAN **FIVE TIMES!** WHAT SAY YOU TO THIS SLIGHT, MADAM?
I HAVE A HECTIC SOCIAL LIFE — AND, WELL, AFTER THAT BOOZY FUMBLE AT THE COLONEL'S FUNERAL, IT'S ALWAYS FELT KIND OF AWKWARD BETWEEN US, HECTOR.
... TO REFUSE A **SECOND** IS TANTAMOUNT TO A **PERSONAL INSULT**.
IT IS NOW **CHAIRMAN PEI** TO YOU, BEATRICE! AND... AND THAT MOMENT WAS OVER TWENTY YEARS AGO!
YOU REALISE I COULD HAVE YOU CAST OUT AND SKY-BOUND FOR SUCH IMPERTINENCE?
AND YET HERE I STAND.
WITH **FRIENDS**, NO LESS! I DIDN'T THINK YOU HAD ANY LEFT... WHO DIDN'T WANT TO SELL YOU OUT, THAT IS. I KNOW THE **SWEET SISTERS** WOULD GIVE GOOD MONEY TO GET THEIR HANDS ON YOU FOR WHAT YOU DID TO THEIR SHIP.
CHEEK! I SAVED THEM AND THEIR PRECIOUS JUNKER FROM A **CACHARAL!** IF THEY'RE MAD AT ANYONE, IT SHOULD BE **YOU** FOR SENDING THEM AFTER ME!

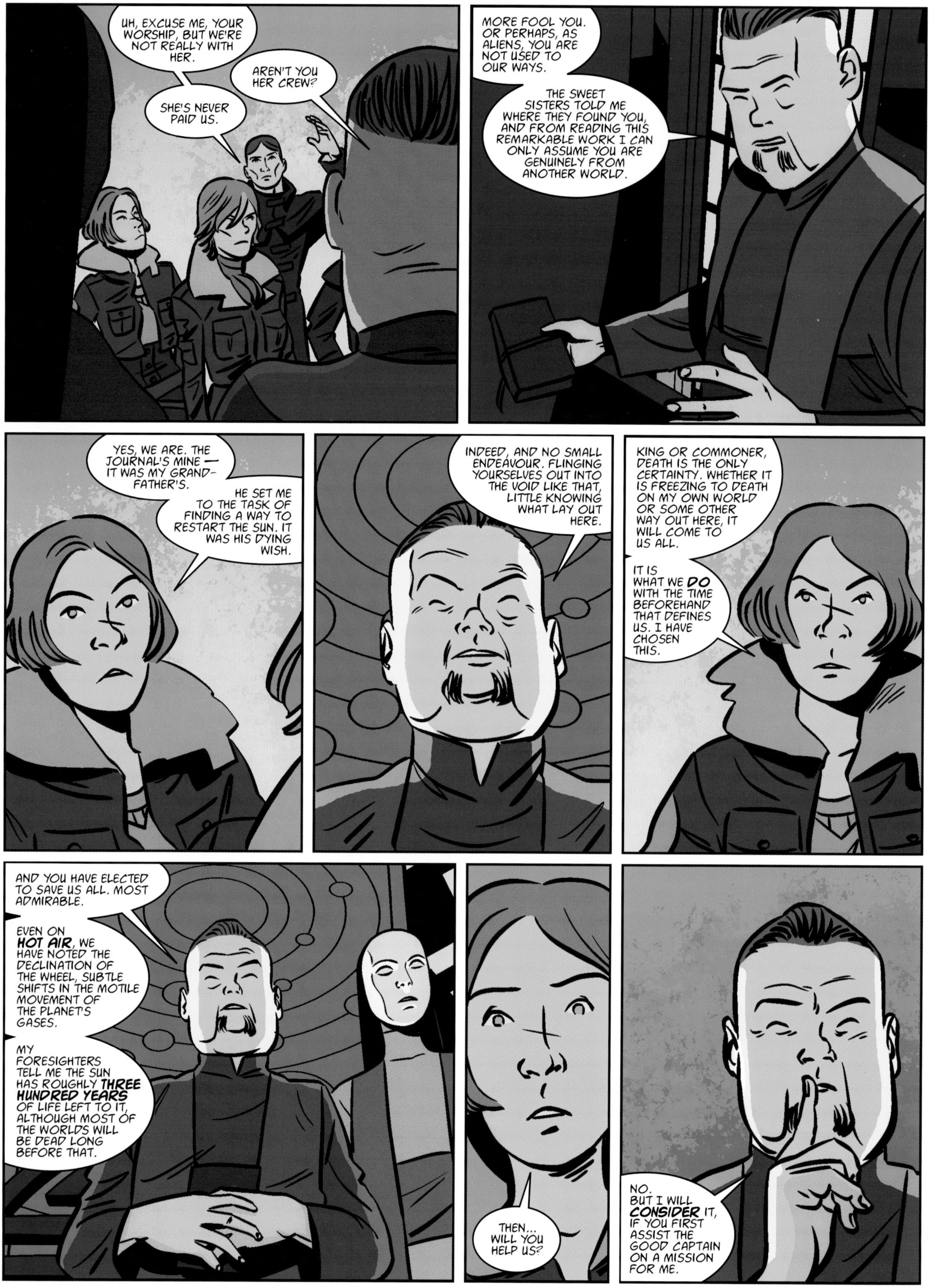
UH, EXCUSE ME, YOUR WORSHIP, BUT WE'RE NOT REALLY WITH HER.
AREN'T YOU HER CREW?
SHE'S NEVER PAID US.
MORE FOOL YOU. OR PERHAPS, AS ALIENS, YOU ARE NOT USED TO OUR WAYS.
THE SWEET SISTERS TOLD ME WHERE THEY FOUND YOU, AND FROM READING THIS REMARKABLE WORK I CAN ONLY ASSUME YOU ARE GENUINELY FROM ANOTHER WORLD.
YES, WE ARE. THE JOURNAL'S MINE — IT WAS MY GRAND-FATHER'S.
HE SET ME TO THE TASK OF FINDING A WAY TO RESTART THE SUN. IT WAS HIS DYING WISH.
INDEED, AND NO SMALL ENDEAVOUR. FLINGING YOURSELVES OUT INTO THE VOID LIKE THAT, LITTLE KNOWING WHAT LAY OUT HERE.
KING OR COMMONER, DEATH IS THE ONLY CERTAINTY. WHETHER IT IS FREEZING TO DEATH ON MY OWN WORLD OR SOME OTHER WAY OUT HERE, IT WILL COME TO US ALL.
IT IS WHAT WE **DO** WITH THE TIME BEFOREHAND THAT DEFINES US. I HAVE CHOSEN THIS.
AND YOU HAVE ELECTED TO SAVE US ALL. MOST ADMIRABLE.
EVEN ON **HOT AIR**, WE HAVE NOTED THE DECLINATION OF THE WHEEL, SUBTLE SHIFTS IN THE MOTILE MOVEMENT OF THE PLANET'S GASES.
MY FORESIGHTERS TELL ME THE SUN HAS ROUGHLY **THREE HUNDRED YEARS** OF LIFE LEFT TO IT, ALTHOUGH MOST OF THE WORLDS WILL BE DEAD LONG BEFORE THAT.
THEN... WILL YOU HELP US?
NO. BUT I WILL **CONSIDER** IT, IF YOU FIRST ASSIST THE GOOD CAPTAIN ON A MISSION FOR ME.

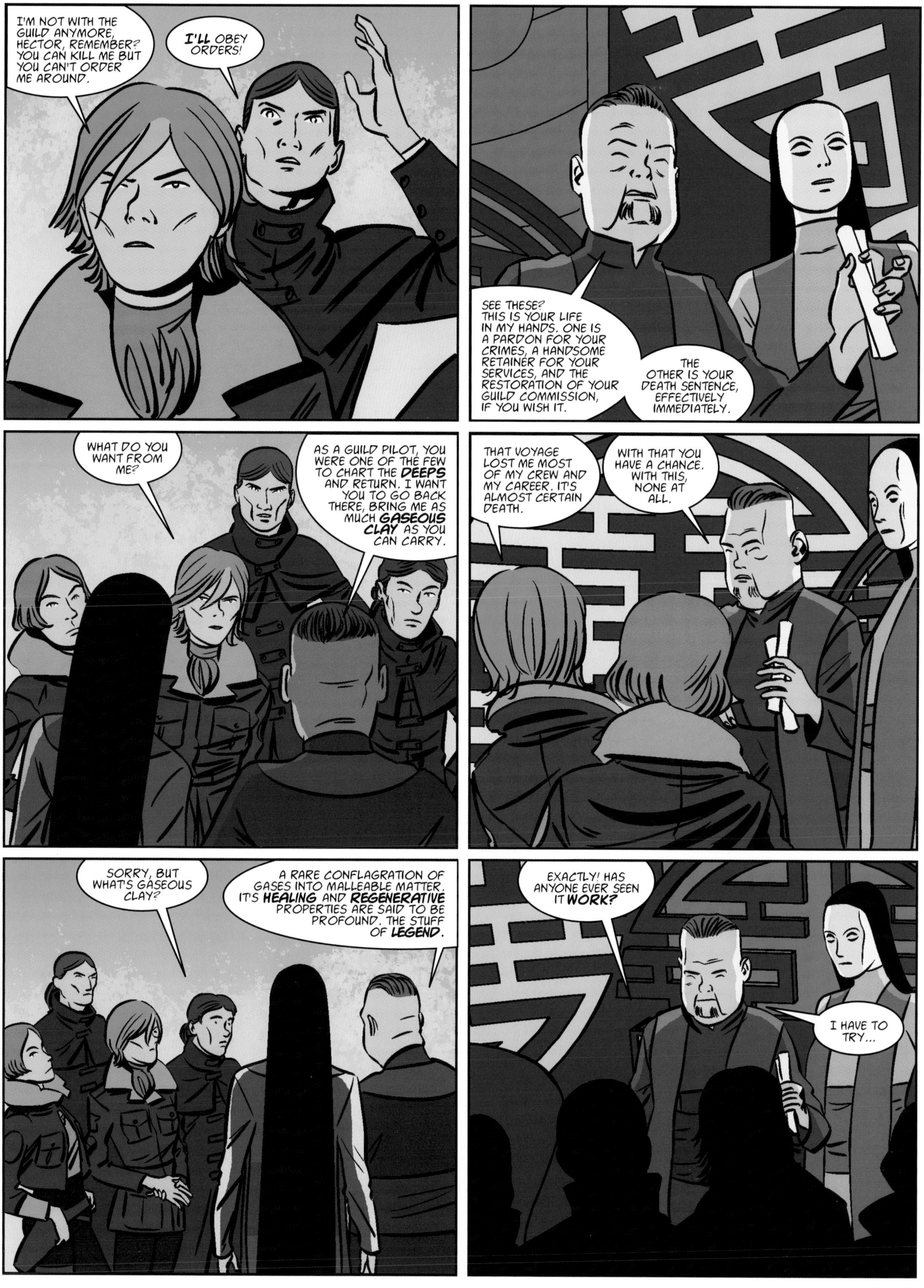
I'M NOT WITH THE GUILD ANYMORE, HECTOR, REMEMBER? YOU CAN KILL ME BUT YOU CAN'T ORDER ME AROUND.
I'LL OBEY ORDERS!
SEE THESE? THIS IS YOUR LIFE IN MY HANDS. ONE IS A PARDON FOR YOUR CRIMES, A HANDSOME RETAINER FOR YOUR SERVICES, AND THE RESTORATION OF YOUR GUILD COMMISSION, IF YOU WISH IT.
THE OTHER IS YOUR DEATH SENTENCE, EFFECTIVELY IMMEDIATELY.
WHAT DO YOU WANT FROM ME?
AS A GUILD PILOT, YOU WERE ONE OF THE FEW TO CHART THE DEEPS AND RETURN. I WANT YOU TO GO BACK THERE, BRING ME AS MUCH GASEOUS CLAY AS YOU CAN CARRY.
THAT VOYAGE LOST ME MOST OF MY CREW AND MY CAREER. IT'S ALMOST CERTAIN DEATH.
WITH THAT YOU HAVE A CHANCE. WITH THIS, NONE AT ALL.
SORRY, BUT WHAT'S GASEOUS CLAY?
A RARE CONFLAGRATION OF GASES INTO MALLEABLE MATTER. IT'S HEALING AND REGENERATIVE PROPERTIES ARE SAID TO BE PROFOUND. THE STUFF OF LEGEND.
EXACTLY! HAS ANYONE EVER SEEN IT WORK?
I HAVE TO TRY...

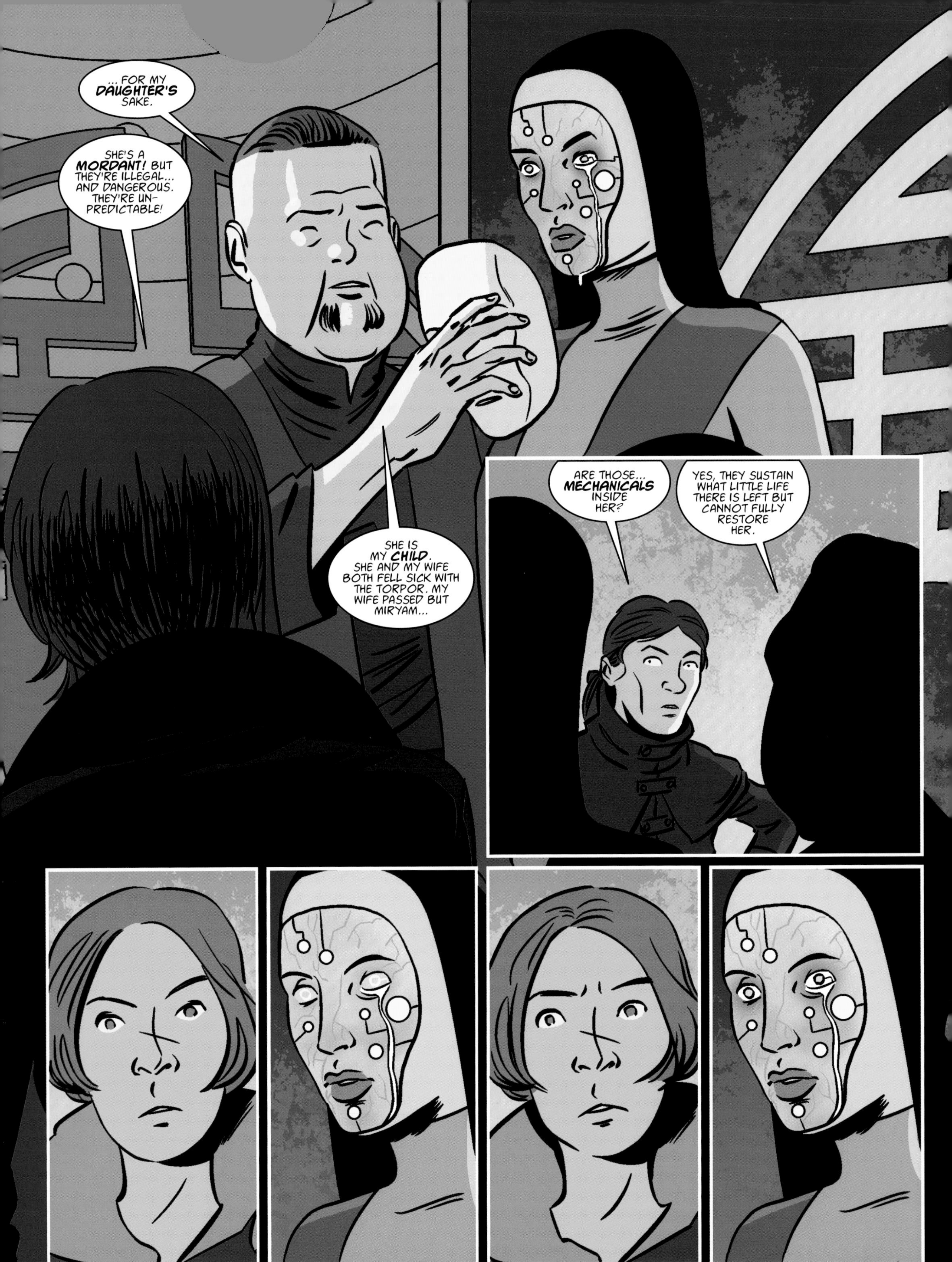

...FOR MY DAUGHTER'S SAKE.
SHE'S A MORDANT! BUT THEY'RE ILLEGAL... AND DANGEROUS. THEY'RE UN-PREDICTABLE!
SHE IS MY CHILD. SHE AND MY WIFE BOTH FELL SICK WITH THE TORPOR. MY WIFE PASSED BUT MIRYAM...
ARE THOSE... MECHANICALS INSIDE HER?
YES, THEY SUSTAIN WHAT LITTLE LIFE THERE IS LEFT BUT CANNOT FULLY RESTORE HER.

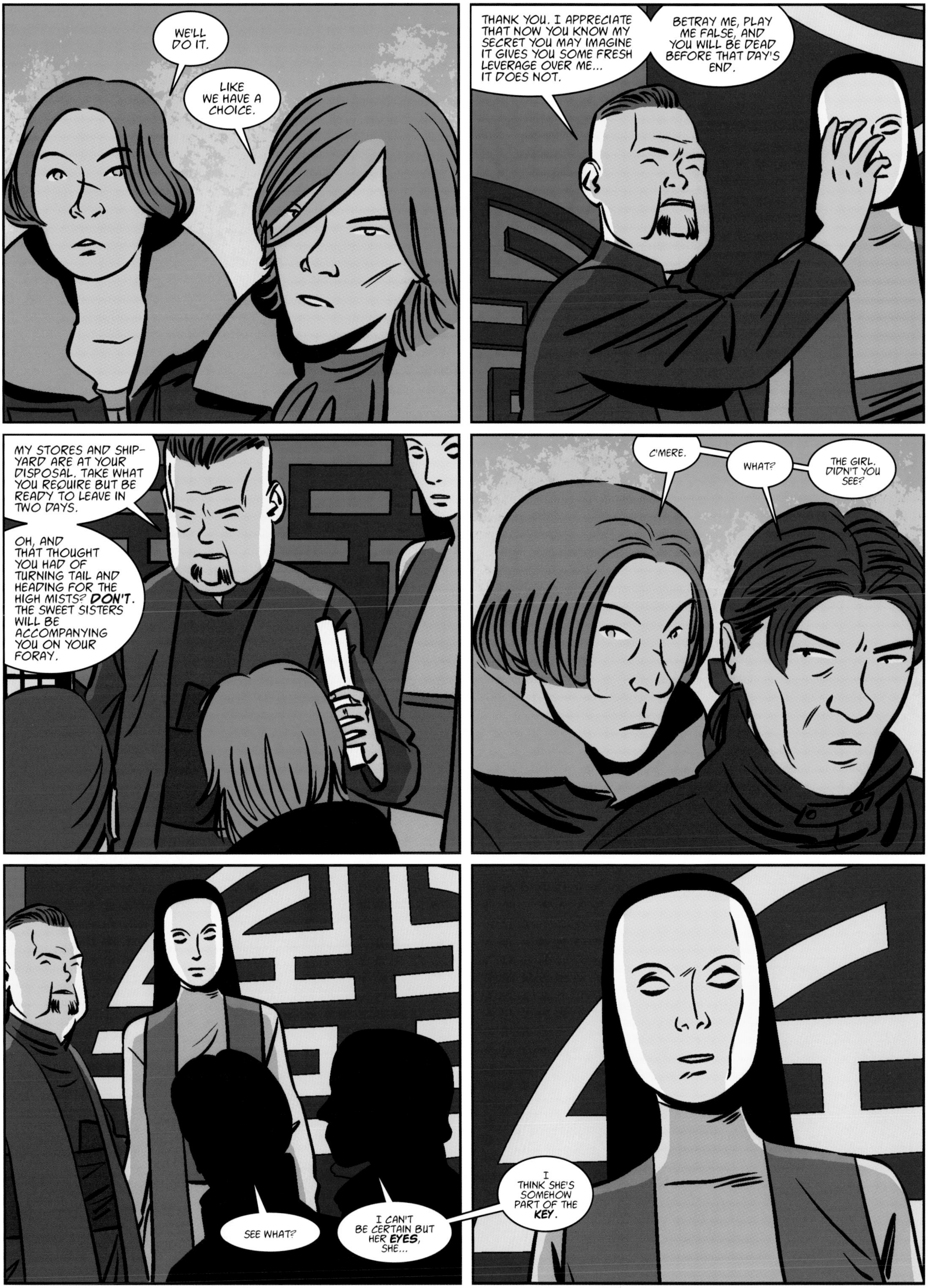
WE'LL DO IT.
LIKE WE HAVE A CHOICE.
THANK YOU. I APPRECIATE THAT NOW YOU KNOW MY SECRET YOU MAY IMAGINE IT GIVES YOU SOME FRESH LEVERAGE OVER ME... IT DOES NOT.
BETRAY ME, PLAY ME FALSE, AND YOU WILL BE DEAD BEFORE THAT DAY'S END.
MY STORES AND SHIPYARD ARE AT YOUR DISPOSAL. TAKE WHAT YOU REQUIRE BUT BE READY TO LEAVE IN TWO DAYS.
OH, AND THAT THOUGHT YOU HAD OF TURNING TAIL AND HEADING FOR THE HIGH MISTS? **DON'T**. THE SWEET SISTERS WILL BE ACCOMPANYING YOU ON YOUR FORAY.
C'MERE.
WHAT?
THE GIRL. DIDN'T YOU SEE?
SEE WHAT?
I CAN'T BE CERTAIN BUT HER **EYES**, SHE...
I THINK SHE'S SOMEHOW PART OF THE **KEY**.

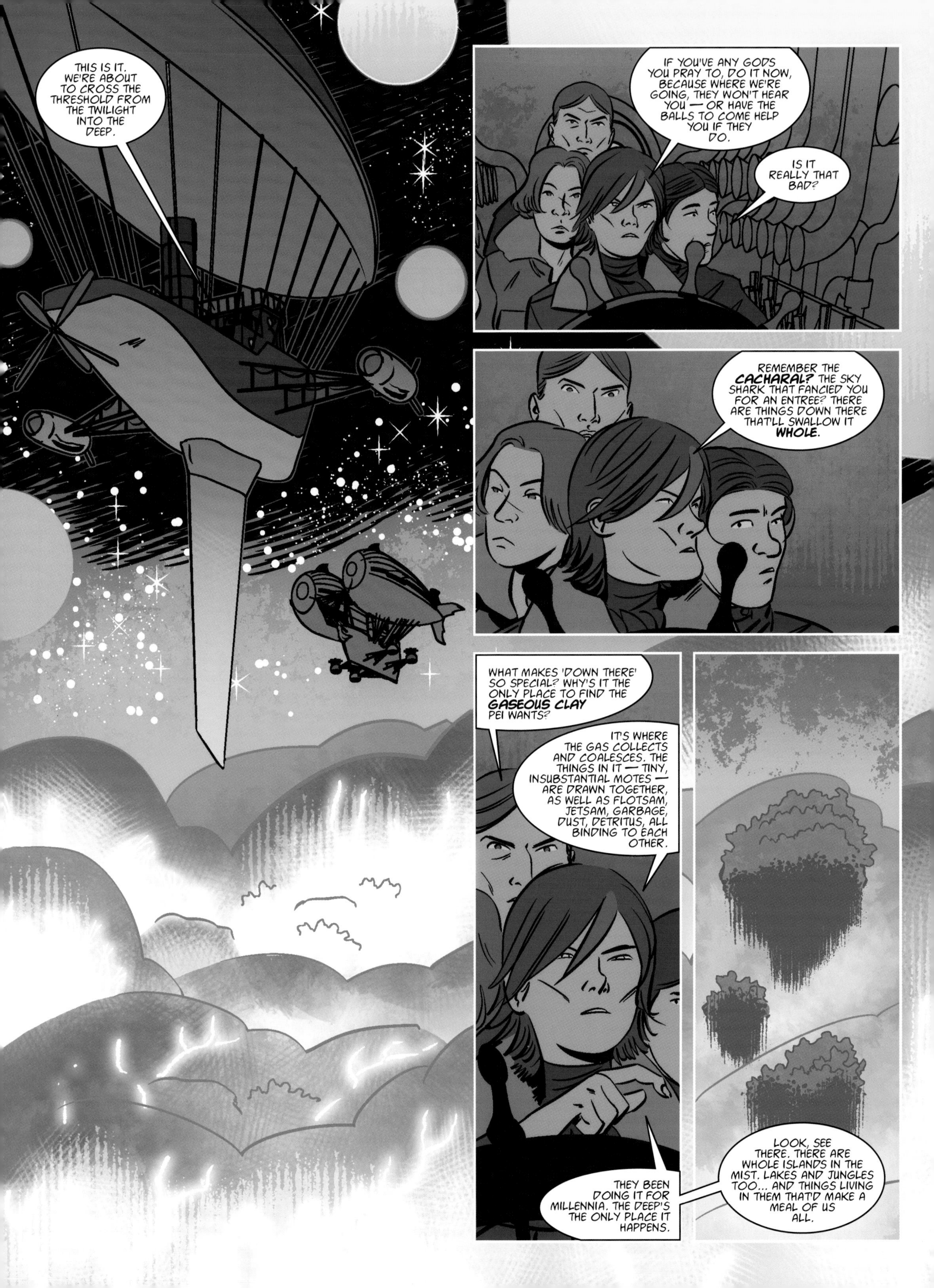
THIS IS IT. WE'RE ABOUT TO CROSS THE THRESHOLD FROM THE TWILIGHT INTO THE DEEP.
IF YOU'VE ANY GODS YOU PRAY TO, DO IT NOW, BECAUSE WHERE WE'RE GOING, THEY WON'T HEAR YOU — OR HAVE THE BALLS TO COME HELP YOU IF THEY DO.
IS IT REALLY THAT BAD?
REMEMBER THE **CACHARAL?** THE SKY SHARK THAT FANCIED YOU FOR AN ENTREE? THERE ARE THINGS DOWN THERE THAT'LL SWALLOW IT **WHOLE.**
WHAT MAKES 'DOWN THERE' SO SPECIAL? WHY'S IT THE ONLY PLACE TO FIND THE **GASEOUS CLAY** PEI WANTS?
IT'S WHERE THE GAS COLLECTS AND COALESCES. THE THINGS IN IT — TINY, INSUBSTANTIAL MOTES — ARE DRAWN TOGETHER, AS WELL AS FLOTSAM, JETSAM, GARBAGE, DUST, DETRITUS, ALL BINDING TO EACH OTHER.
THEY BEEN DOING IT FOR MILLENNIA. THE DEEP'S THE ONLY PLACE IT HAPPENS.
LOOK, SEE THERE. THERE ARE WHOLE ISLANDS IN THE MIST. LAKES AND JUNGLES TOO... AND THINGS LIVING IN THEM THAT'D MAKE A MEAL OF US ALL.

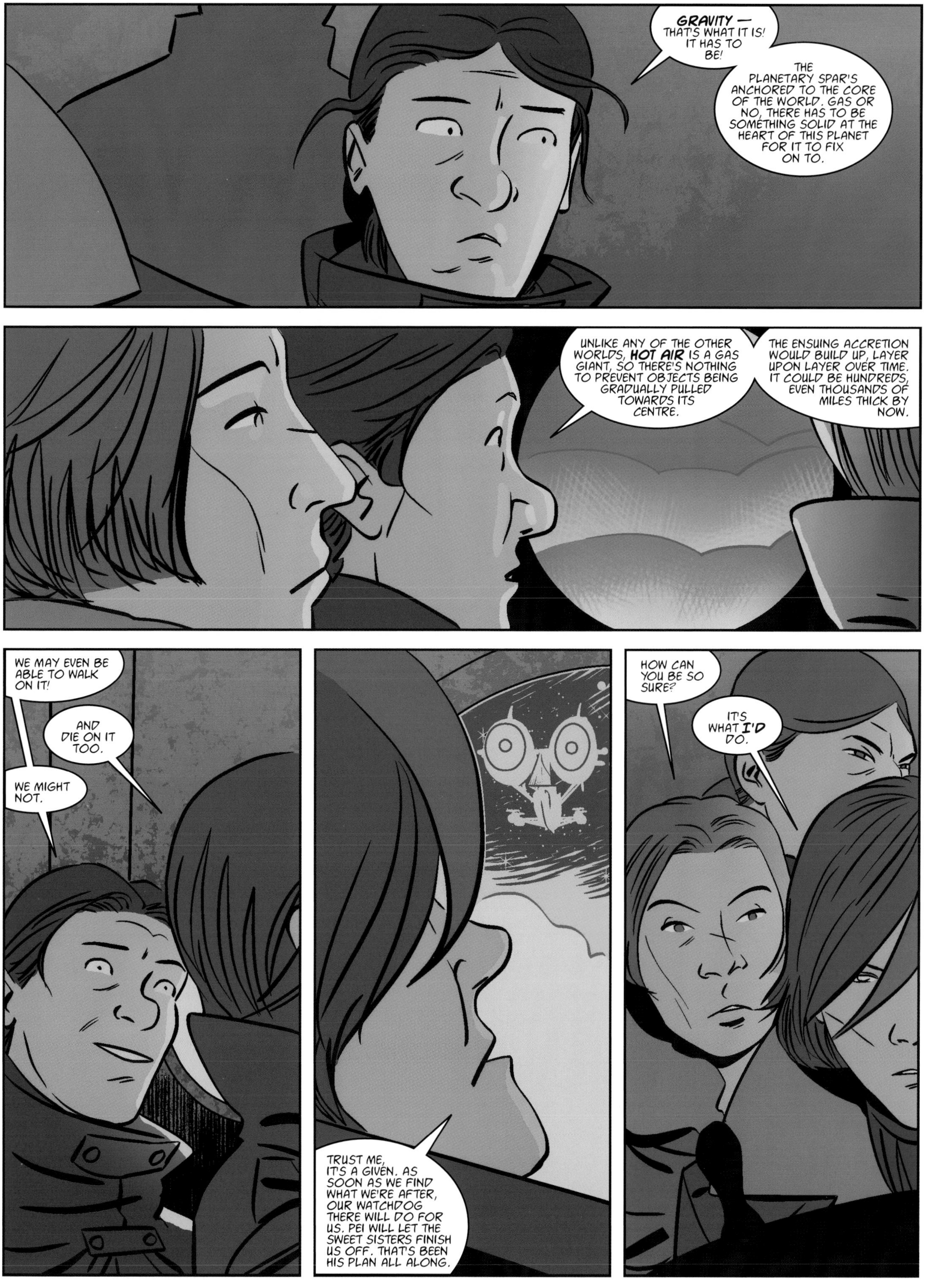
GRAVITY — THAT'S WHAT IT IS! IT HAS TO BE!
THE PLANETARY SPAR'S ANCHORED TO THE CORE OF THE WORLD. GAS OR NO, THERE HAS TO BE SOMETHING SOLID AT THE HEART OF THIS PLANET FOR IT TO FIX ON TO.
UNLIKE ANY OF THE OTHER WORLDS, HOT AIR IS A GAS GIANT, SO THERE'S NOTHING TO PREVENT OBJECTS BEING GRADUALLY PULLED TOWARDS ITS CENTRE.
THE ENSUING ACCRETION WOULD BUILD UP, LAYER UPON LAYER OVER TIME. IT COULD BE HUNDREDS, EVEN THOUSANDS OF MILES THICK BY NOW.
WE MAY EVEN BE ABLE TO WALK ON IT!
AND DIE ON IT TOO.
WE MIGHT NOT.
TRUST ME, IT'S A GIVEN. AS SOON AS WE FIND WHAT WE'RE AFTER, OUR WATCHDOG THERE WILL DO FOR US. PEI WILL LET THE SWEET SISTERS FINISH US OFF. THAT'S BEEN HIS PLAN ALL ALONG.
HOW CAN YOU BE SO SURE?
IT'S WHAT I'D DO.

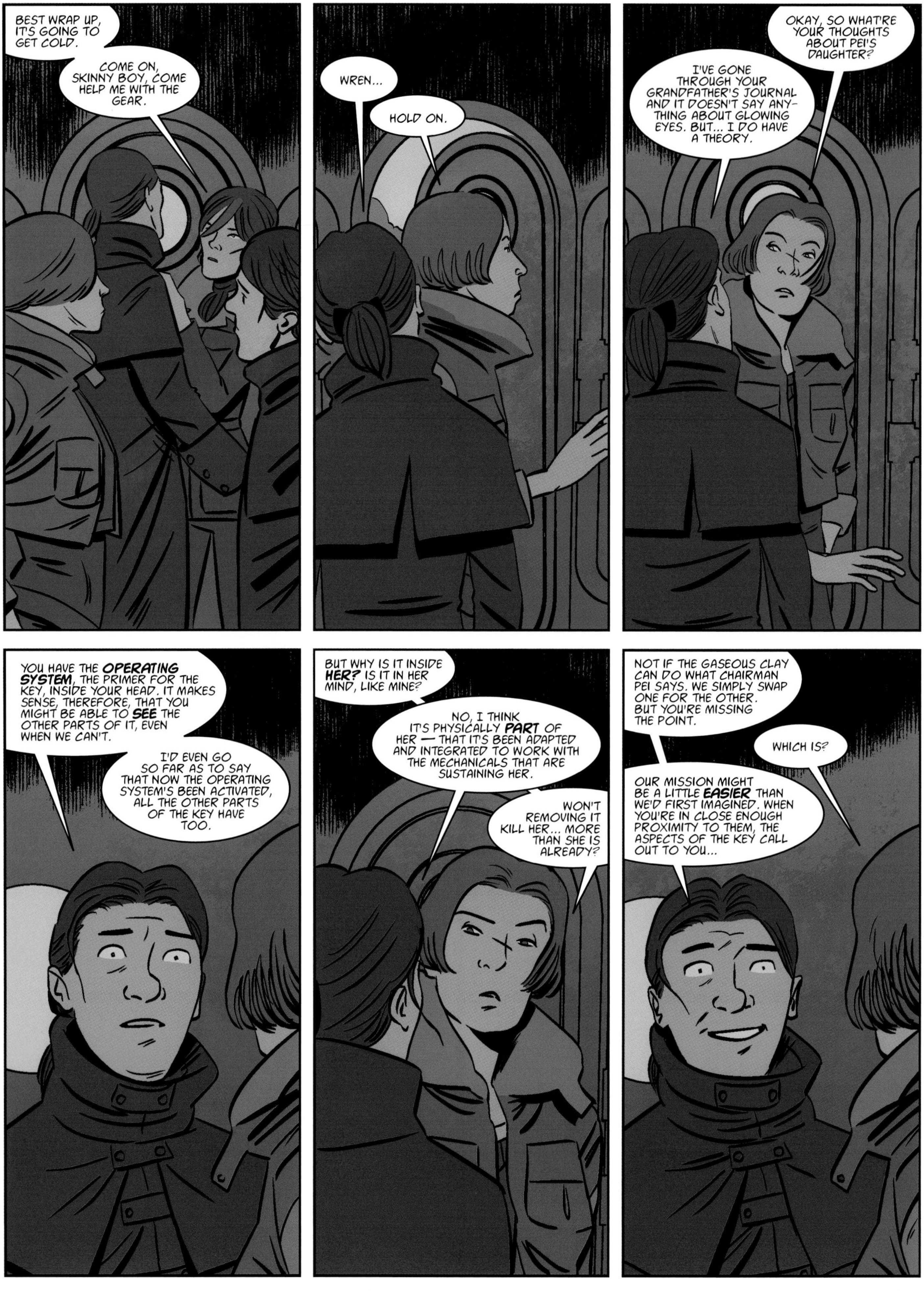

BEST WRAP UP, IT'S GOING TO GET COLD.
COME ON, SKINNY BOY, COME HELP ME WITH THE GEAR.
WREN...
HOLD ON.
OKAY, SO WHAT'RE YOUR THOUGHTS ABOUT PEI'S DAUGHTER?
I'VE GONE THROUGH YOUR GRANDFATHER'S JOURNAL AND IT DOESN'T SAY ANY-THING ABOUT GLOWING EYES. BUT... I DO HAVE A THEORY.
YOU HAVE THE **OPERATING SYSTEM**, THE PRIMER FOR THE KEY, INSIDE YOUR HEAD. IT MAKES SENSE, THEREFORE, THAT YOU MIGHT BE ABLE TO **SEE** THE OTHER PARTS OF IT, EVEN WHEN WE CAN'T.
I'D EVEN GO SO FAR AS TO SAY THAT NOW THE OPERATING SYSTEM'S BEEN ACTIVATED, ALL THE OTHER PARTS OF THE KEY HAVE TOO.
BUT WHY IS IT INSIDE **HER?** IS IT IN HER MIND, LIKE MINE?
NO, I THINK IT'S PHYSICALLY **PART** OF HER — THAT IT'S BEEN ADAPTED AND INTEGRATED TO WORK WITH THE MECHANICALS THAT ARE SUSTAINING HER.
WON'T REMOVING IT KILL HER... MORE THAN SHE IS ALREADY?
NOT IF THE GASEOUS CLAY CAN DO WHAT CHAIRMAN PEI SAYS. WE SIMPLY SWAP ONE FOR THE OTHER. BUT YOU'RE MISSING THE POINT.
WHICH IS?
OUR MISSION MIGHT BE A LITTLE **EASIER** THAN WE'D FIRST IMAGINED. WHEN YOU'RE IN CLOSE ENOUGH PROXIMITY TO THEM, THE ASPECTS OF THE KEY CALL OUT TO YOU...

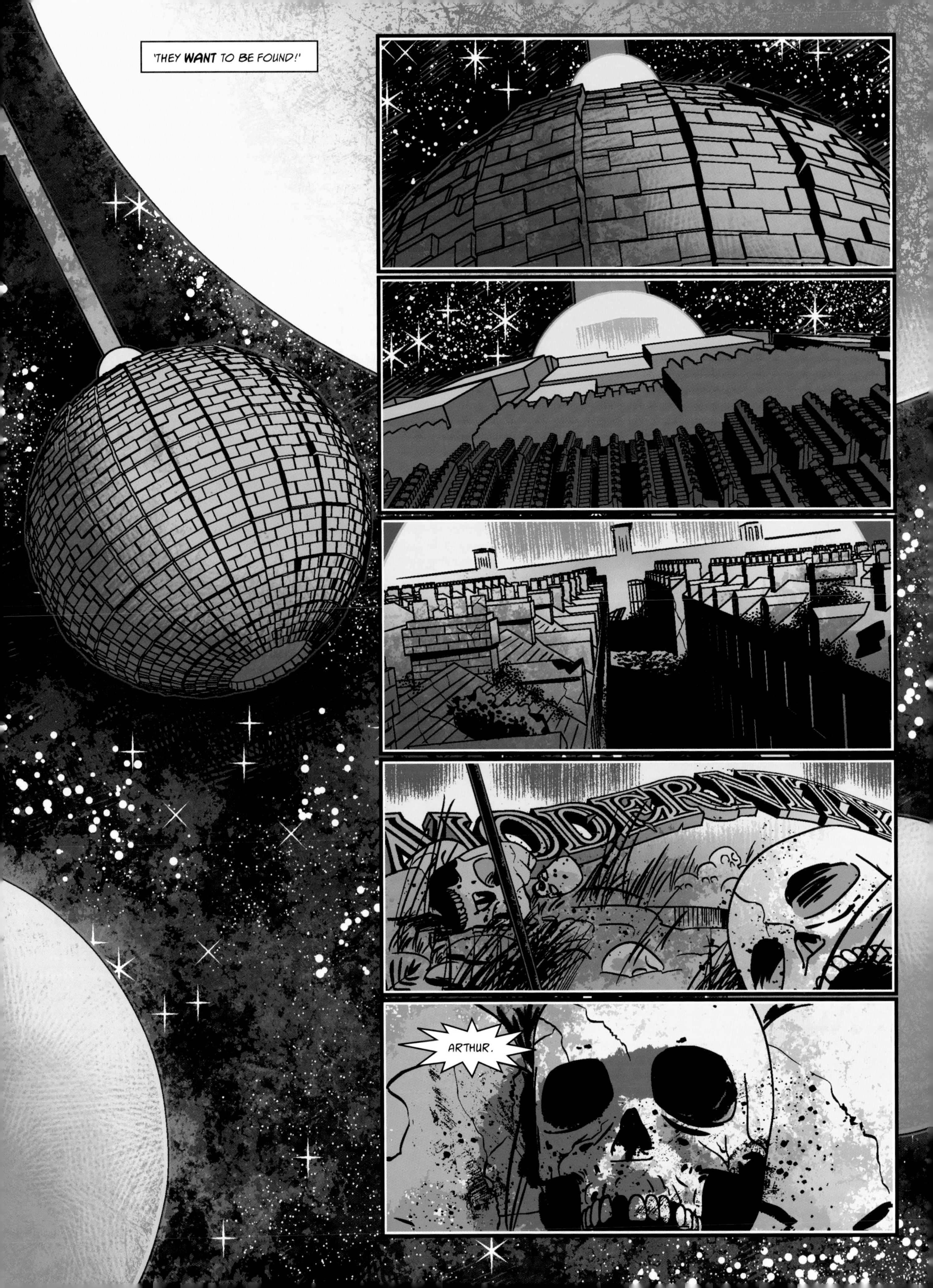
'THEY WANT TO BE FOUND!'
ARTHUR.

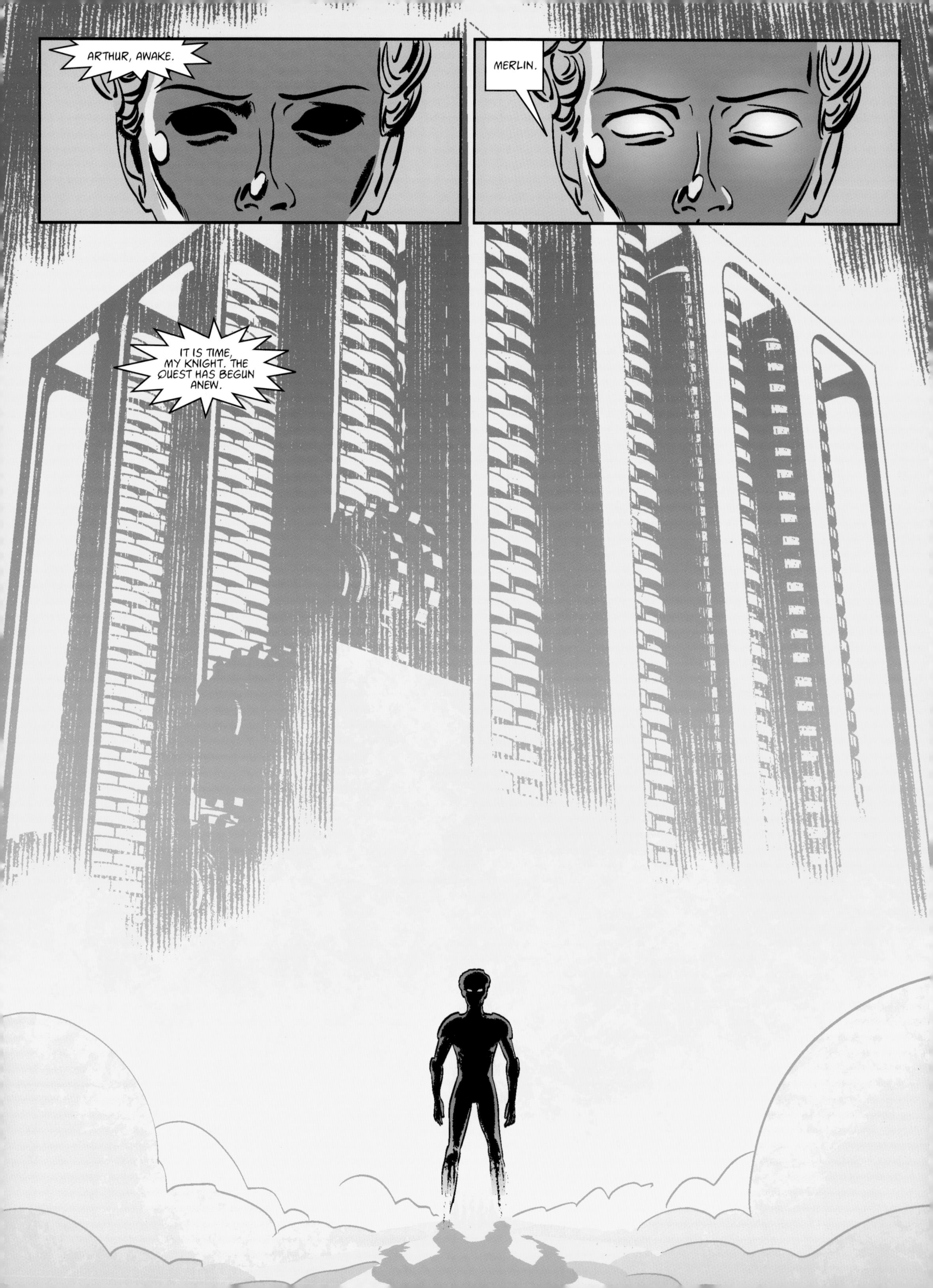
ARTHUR, AWAKE.
MERLIN.
IT IS TIME, MY KNIGHT. THE QUEST HAS BEGUN ANEW.

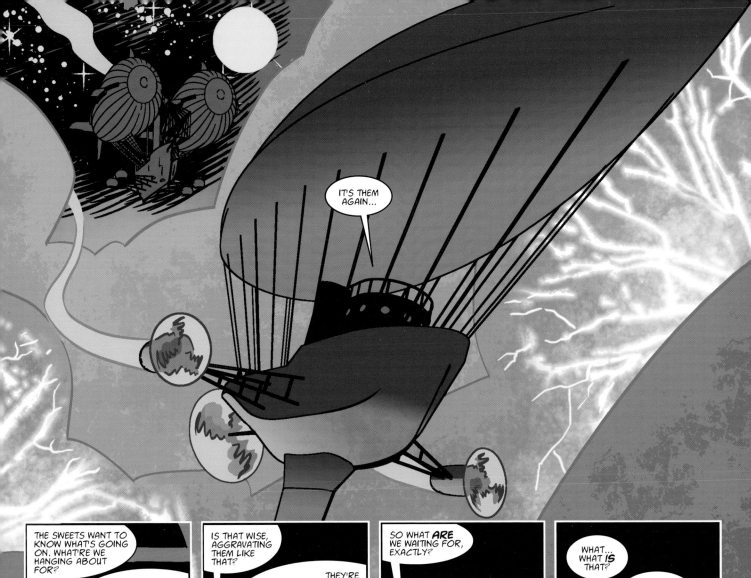

IT'S THEM AGAIN...

THE SWEETS WANT TO KNOW WHAT'S GOING ON. WHAT'RE WE HANGING ABOUT FOR?

TELL THEM WE MOVE WHEN I SAY SO. **I'M** IN COMMAND OF THIS EXPEDITION, SO THEY'LL BLOODY WELL FOLLOW MY LEAD. UNDERSTAND ME, PRETTY BOY?

Y-YES, UH, CAPTAIN.

IS THAT WISE, AGGRAVATING THEM LIKE THAT?

THEY'RE PLANNING ON KILLING US ANYWAY BUT ONLY AFTER WE'VE GOT WHAT PEI WANTS. UNTIL THEN, THEY'RE OBLIGED TO PLAY NICE, WHETHER THEY LIKE IT OR NOT.

SO WHAT **ARE** WE WAITING FOR, EXACTLY?

AH... THERE. COME AND SEE.

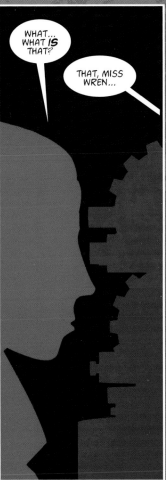

WHAT... WHAT **IS** THAT?

THAT, MISS WREN...

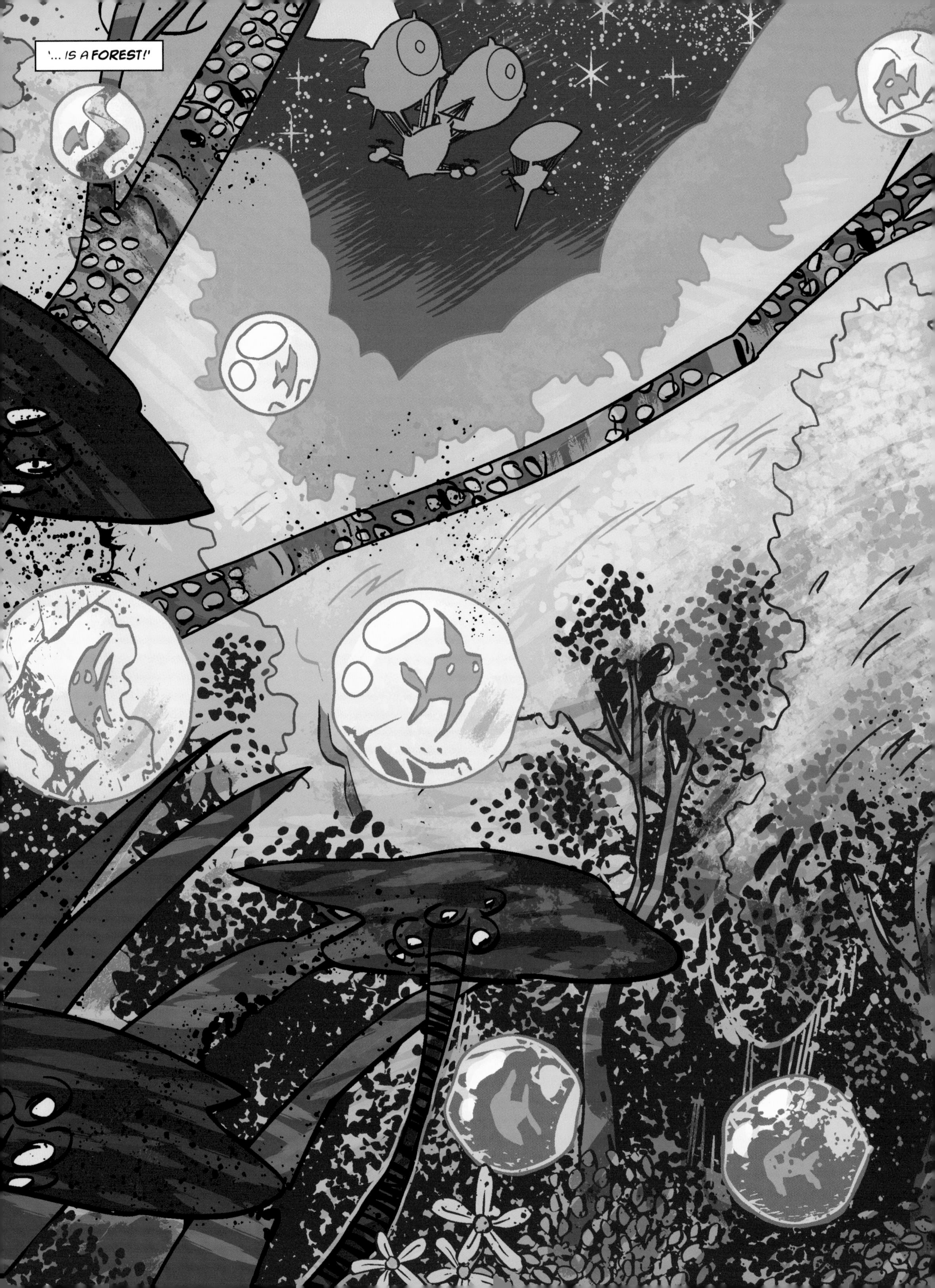
'... IS A FOREST!'

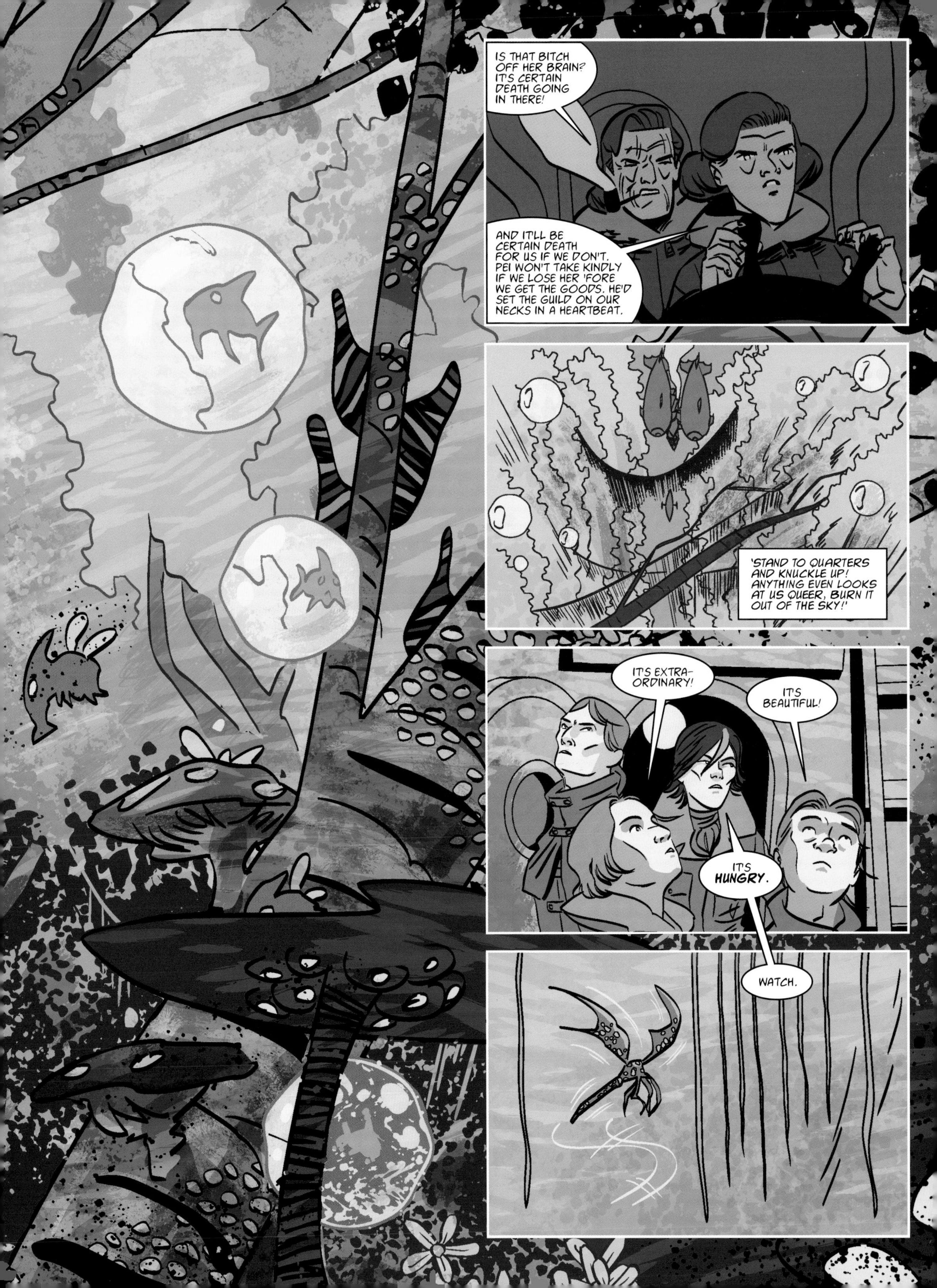

IS THAT BITCH OFF HER BRAIN? IT'S CERTAIN DEATH GOING IN THERE!
AND IT'LL BE CERTAIN DEATH FOR US IF WE DON'T. PEI WON'T TAKE KINDLY IF WE LOSE HER 'FORE WE GET THE GOODS. HE'D SET THE GUILD ON OUR NECKS IN A HEARTBEAT.
'STAND TO QUARTERS AND KNUCKLE UP! ANYTHING EVEN LOOKS AT US QUEER, BURN IT OUT OF THE SKY!'
IT'S EXTRA-ORDINARY!
IT'S BEAUTIFUL!
IT'S **HUNGRY**.
WATCH.

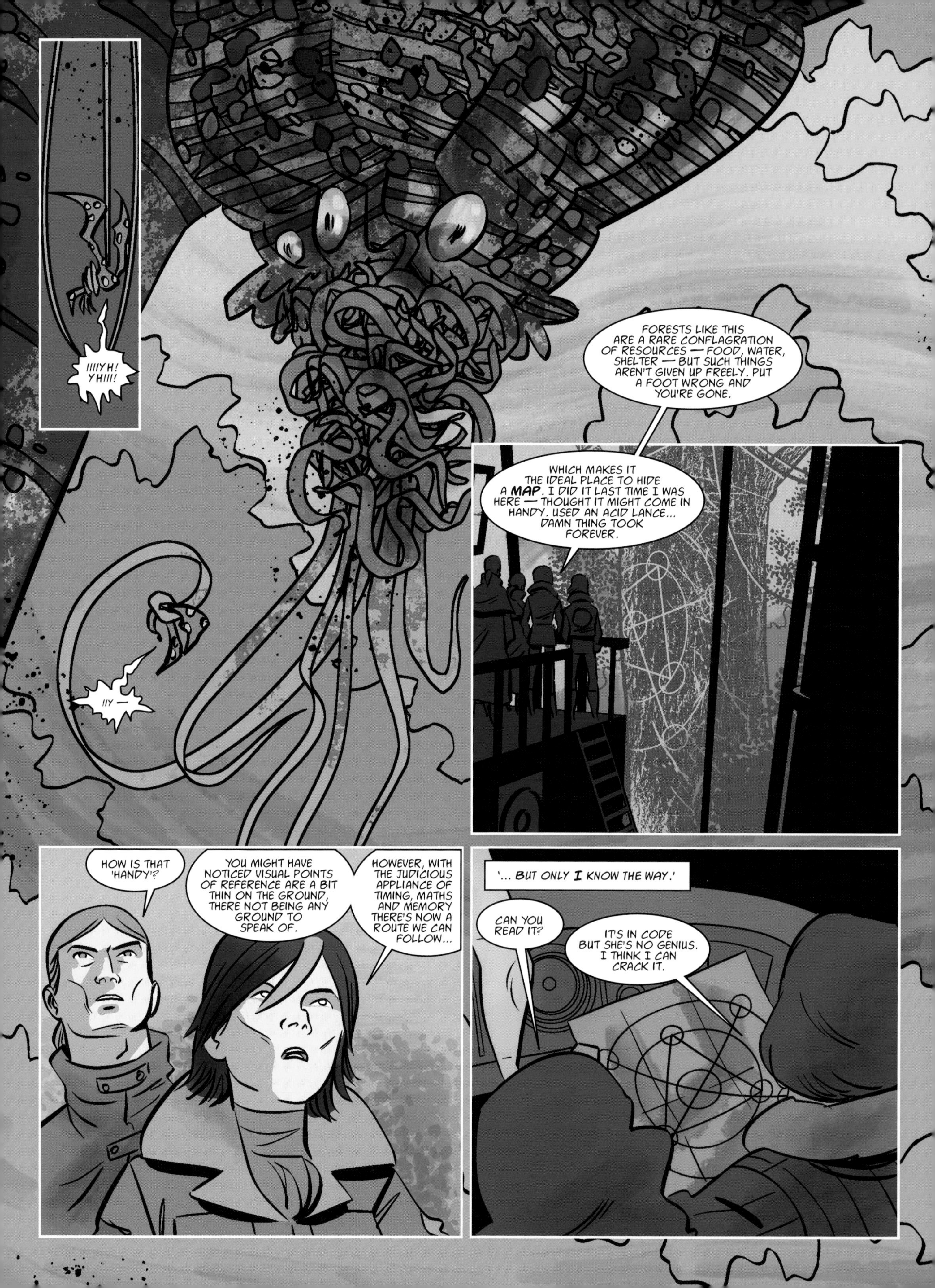

!!!!YH! YH!!!!
IIY —
FORESTS LIKE THIS ARE A RARE CONFLAGRATION OF RESOURCES — FOOD, WATER, SHELTER — BUT SUCH THINGS AREN'T GIVEN UP FREELY. PUT A FOOT WRONG AND YOU'RE GONE.
WHICH MAKES IT THE IDEAL PLACE TO HIDE A MAP. I DID IT LAST TIME I WAS HERE — THOUGHT IT MIGHT COME IN HANDY. USED AN ACID LANCE... DAMN THING TOOK FOREVER.
HOW IS THAT 'HANDY'?
YOU MIGHT HAVE NOTICED VISUAL POINTS OF REFERENCE ARE A BIT THIN ON THE GROUND, THERE NOT BEING ANY GROUND TO SPEAK OF.
HOWEVER, WITH THE JUDICIOUS APPLIANCE OF TIMING, MATHS AND MEMORY THERE'S NOW A ROUTE WE CAN FOLLOW...
'... BUT ONLY I KNOW THE WAY.'
CAN YOU READ IT?
IT'S IN CODE BUT SHE'S NO GENIUS. I THINK I CAN CRACK IT.

'WHICH MEANS THE GOOD CAPTAIN ARIEL IS NOT QUITE SO **INDISPENSABLE** AS SHE IMAGINES.'

CAPTAIN, THAT TREE, OVER THERE... I COULD'VE SWORN I SAW ITS SURFACE MOVE. IT RIPPLED LIKE WATER.

WHERE?

THERE, SEE!

OH NO... IT'S A WHOLE DAMN ROOST! THEY MUST HAVE MIGRATED HERE!

WHO DID? WHAT ARE THEY?

'JACKANAPES — IT LOOKS LIKE THEY'VE ALREADY EATEN AND ARE SLEEPING IT OFF. IF WE'RE QUICK AND QUIET MAYBE WE CAN SLIP BY WITHOUT WAKING THEM...'

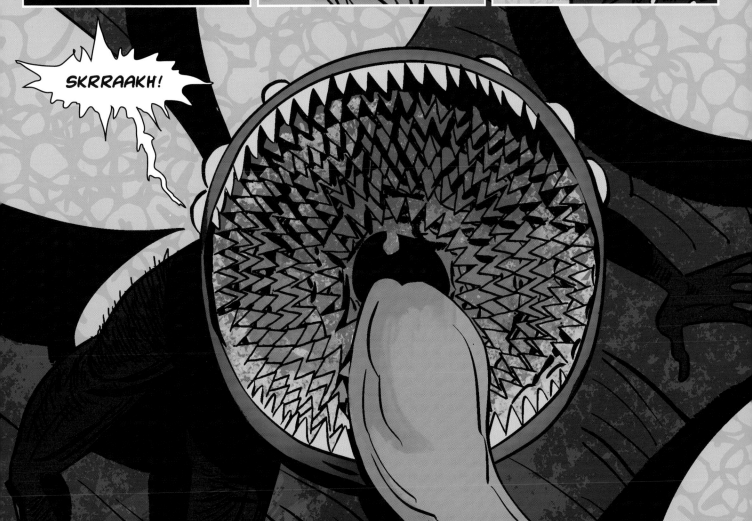

SKRRAAKH!

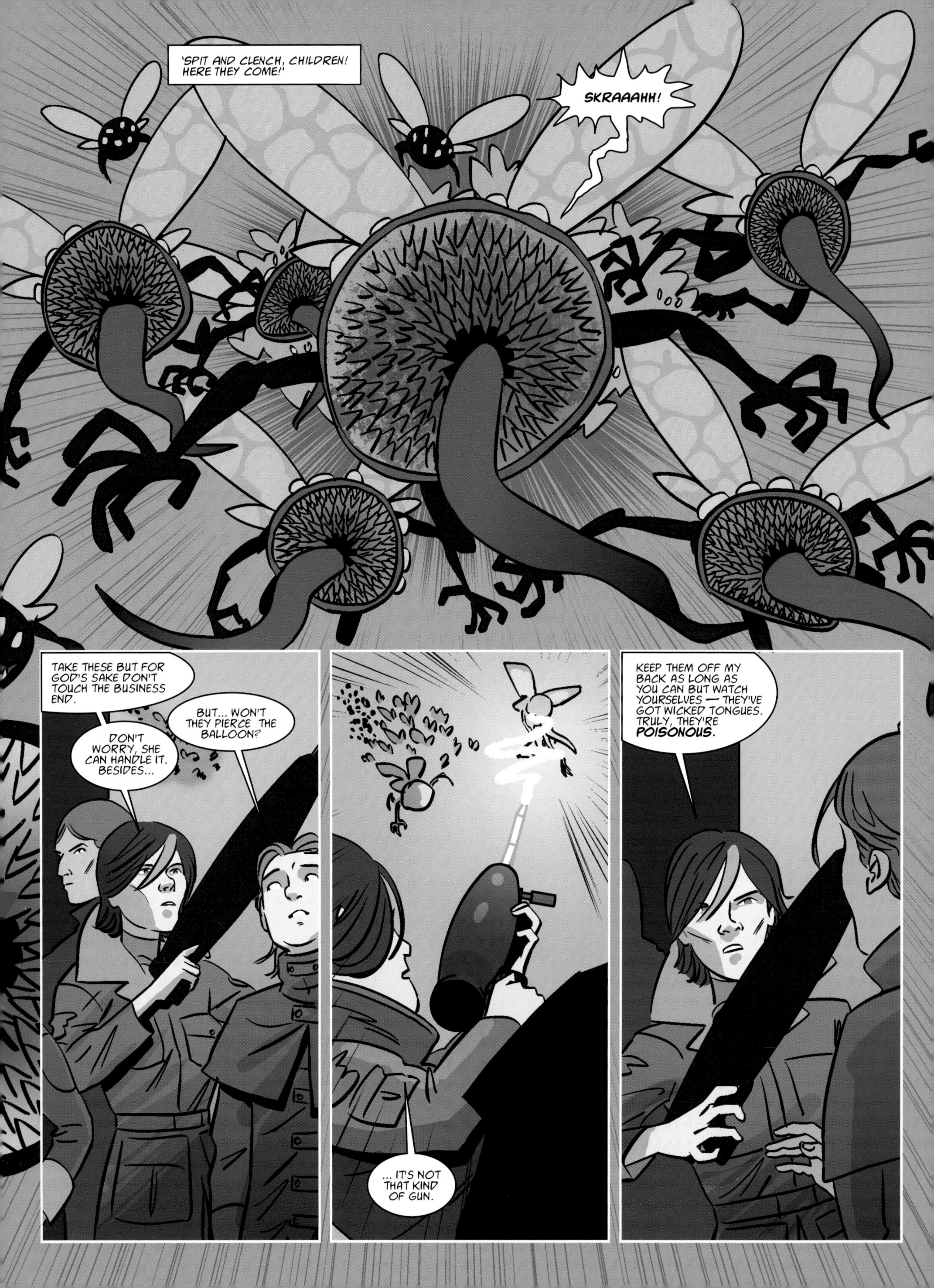
'SPIT AND CLENCH, CHILDREN! HERE THEY COME!'
SKRAAAHH!
TAKE THESE BUT FOR GOD'S SAKE DON'T TOUCH THE BUSINESS END.
DON'T WORRY, SHE CAN HANDLE IT. BESIDES...
BUT... WON'T THEY PIERCE THE BALLOON?
... IT'S NOT THAT KIND OF GUN.
KEEP THEM OFF MY BACK AS LONG AS YOU CAN BUT WATCH YOURSELVES — THEY'VE GOT WICKED TONGUES. TRULY, THEY'RE POISONOUS.

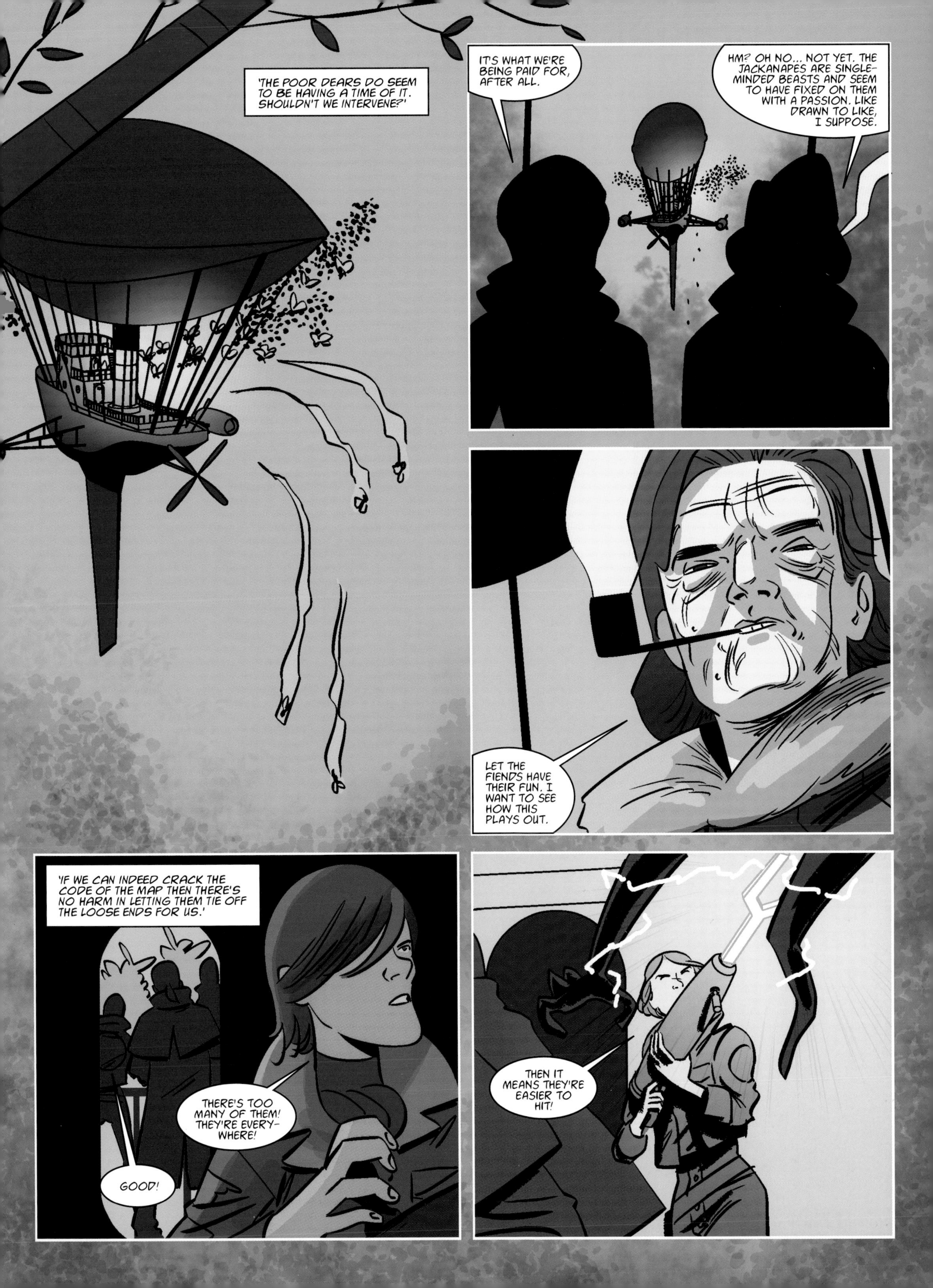
'THE POOR DEARS DO SEEM TO BE HAVING A TIME OF IT. SHOULDN'T WE INTERVENE?'
IT'S WHAT WE'RE BEING PAID FOR, AFTER ALL.
HM? OH NO... NOT YET. THE JACKANAPES ARE SINGLE-MINDED BEASTS AND SEEM TO HAVE FIXED ON THEM WITH A PASSION. LIKE DRAWN TO LIKE, I SUPPOSE.
LET THE FIENDS HAVE THEIR FUN. I WANT TO SEE HOW THIS PLAYS OUT.
'IF WE CAN INDEED CRACK THE CODE OF THE MAP THEN THERE'S NO HARM IN LETTING THEM TIE OFF THE LOOSE ENDS FOR US.'
THERE'S TOO MANY OF THEM! THEY'RE EVERY-WHERE!
GOOD!
THEN IT MEANS THEY'RE EASIER TO HIT!

KHHAAGH!
AHHH!
DUCK!
IF YOU WANT ME TO SAVE OUR NECKS, SODDING WELL KEEP THEM OFF MINE!
GET BACK TO IT!
COME ON, COME ON! THE LAST ONE WAS A BABY. THERE'S GOT TO BE A BIG MOMMA SOMEWHERE...
GOTCHA!

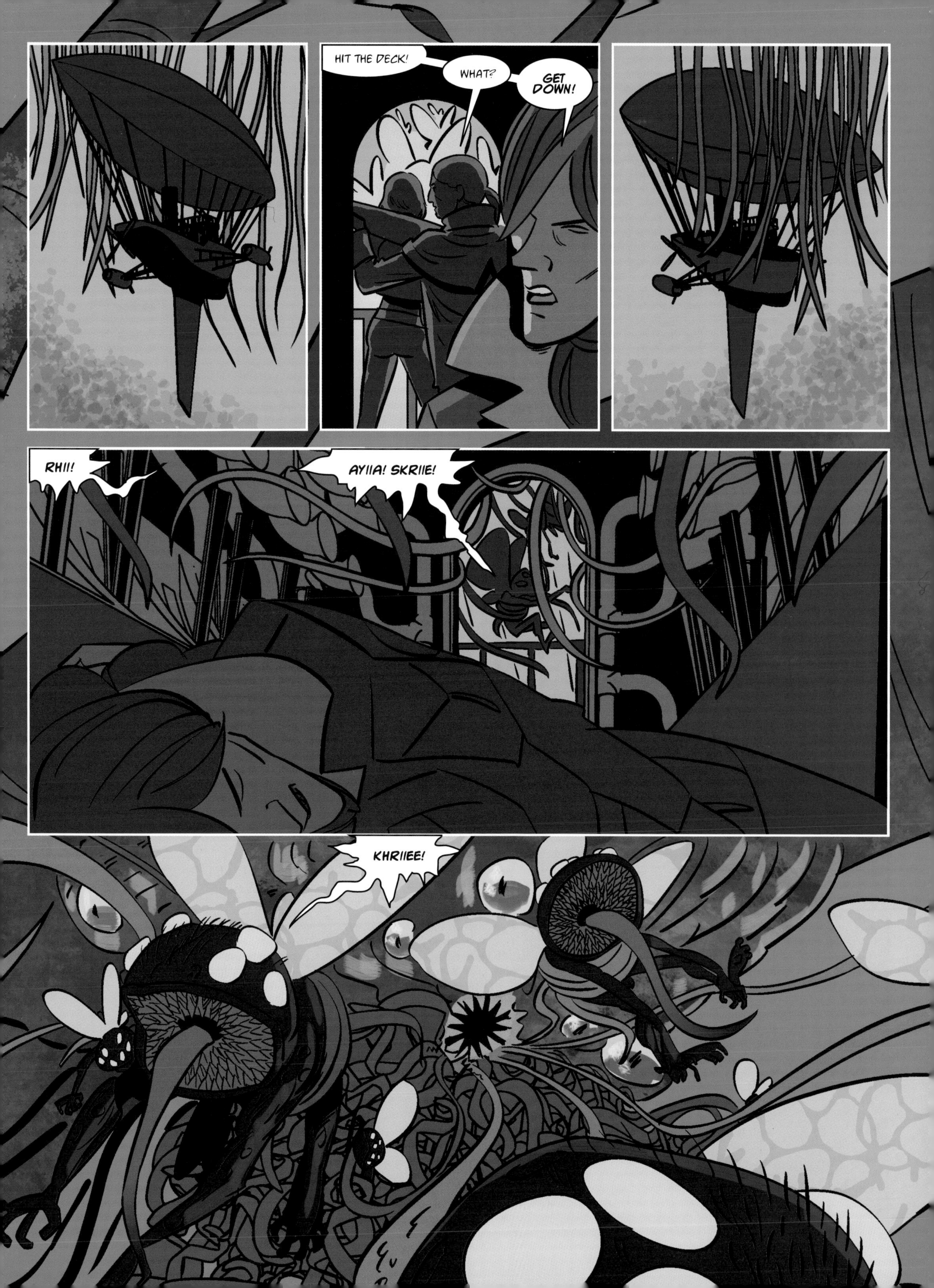
HIT THE DECK!
WHAT?
GET DOWN!
RHII!
AYIIA! SKRIIE!
KHRIIEE!

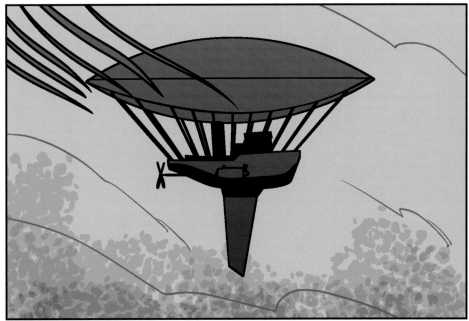

WE'RE GOOD. WE'RE OKAY. THE COAST'S CLEAR.

YOU DID IT! THAT WAS INCREDIBLE —

AAKK!

WREN!

SKRRREEEE!

WREN!

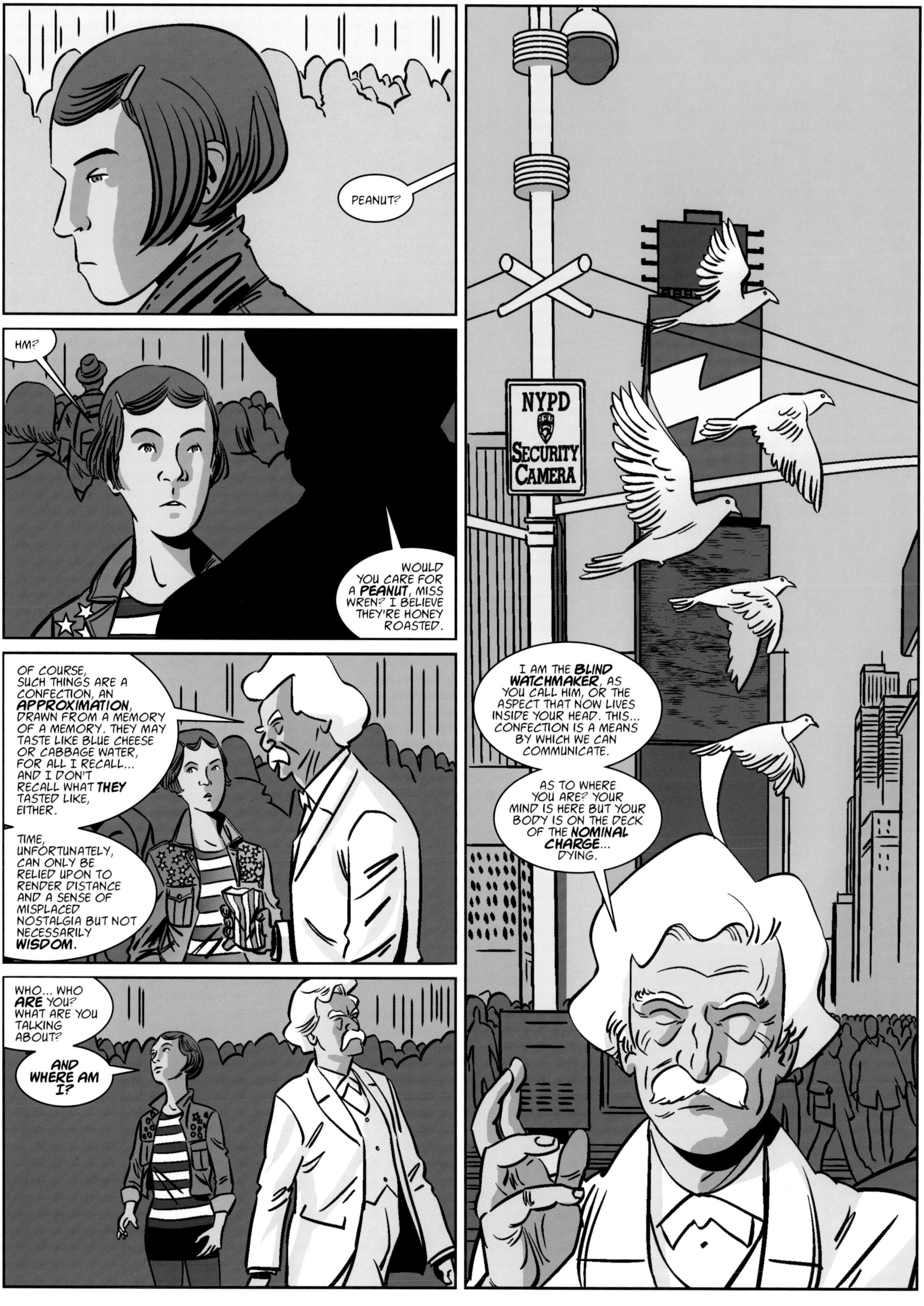
PEANUT?
HM?
WOULD YOU CARE FOR A **PEANUT**, MISS WREN? I BELIEVE THEY'RE HONEY ROASTED.
OF COURSE, SUCH THINGS ARE A CONFECTION, AN **APPROXIMATION**, DRAWN FROM A MEMORY OF A MEMORY. THEY MAY TASTE LIKE BLUE CHEESE OR CABBAGE WATER, FOR ALL I RECALL... AND I DON'T RECALL WHAT **THEY** TASTED LIKE, EITHER.
TIME, UNFORTUNATELY, CAN ONLY BE RELIED UPON TO RENDER DISTANCE AND A SENSE OF MISPLACED NOSTALGIA BUT NOT NECESSARILY **WISDOM**.
WHO... WHO **ARE** YOU? WHAT ARE YOU TALKING ABOUT?
AND WHERE AM I?
NYPD
SECURITY CAMERA
I AM THE **BLIND WATCHMAKER**, AS YOU CALL HIM, OR THE ASPECT THAT NOW LIVES INSIDE YOUR HEAD. THIS... CONFECTION IS A MEANS BY WHICH WE CAN COMMUNICATE.
AS TO WHERE YOU ARE? YOUR MIND IS HERE BUT YOUR BODY IS ON THE DECK OF THE **NOMINAL CHARGE**... DYING.

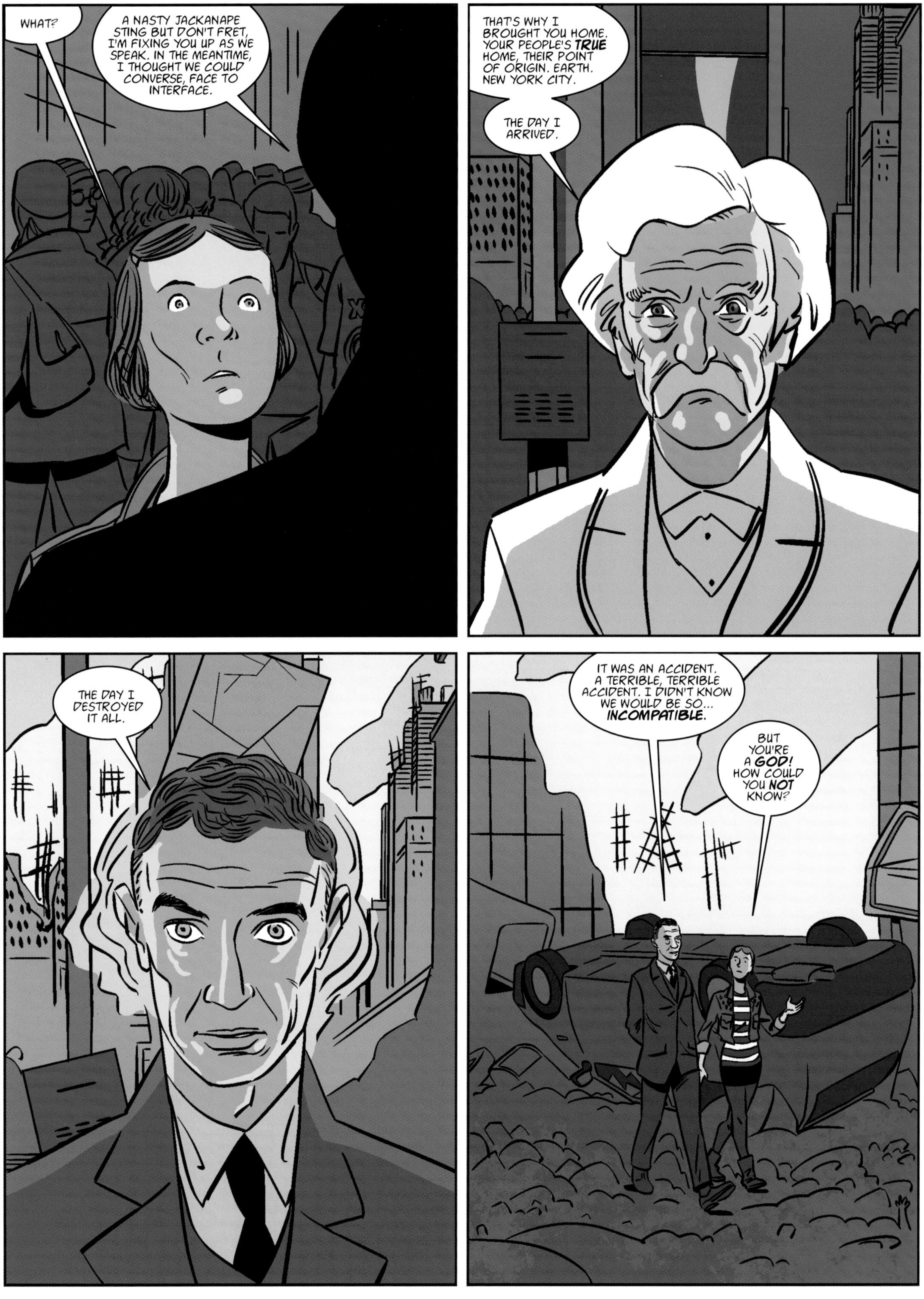
WHAT?
A NASTY JACKANAPE STING BUT DON'T FRET, I'M FIXING YOU UP AS WE SPEAK. IN THE MEANTIME, I THOUGHT WE COULD CONVERSE, FACE TO INTERFACE.
THAT'S WHY I BROUGHT YOU HOME. YOUR PEOPLE'S **TRUE** HOME, THEIR POINT OF ORIGIN. EARTH. NEW YORK CITY.
THE DAY I ARRIVED.
THE DAY I DESTROYED IT ALL.
IT WAS AN ACCIDENT. A TERRIBLE, TERRIBLE ACCIDENT. I DIDN'T KNOW WE WOULD BE SO... **INCOMPATIBLE**.
BUT YOU'RE A **GOD!** HOW COULD YOU **NOT** KNOW?

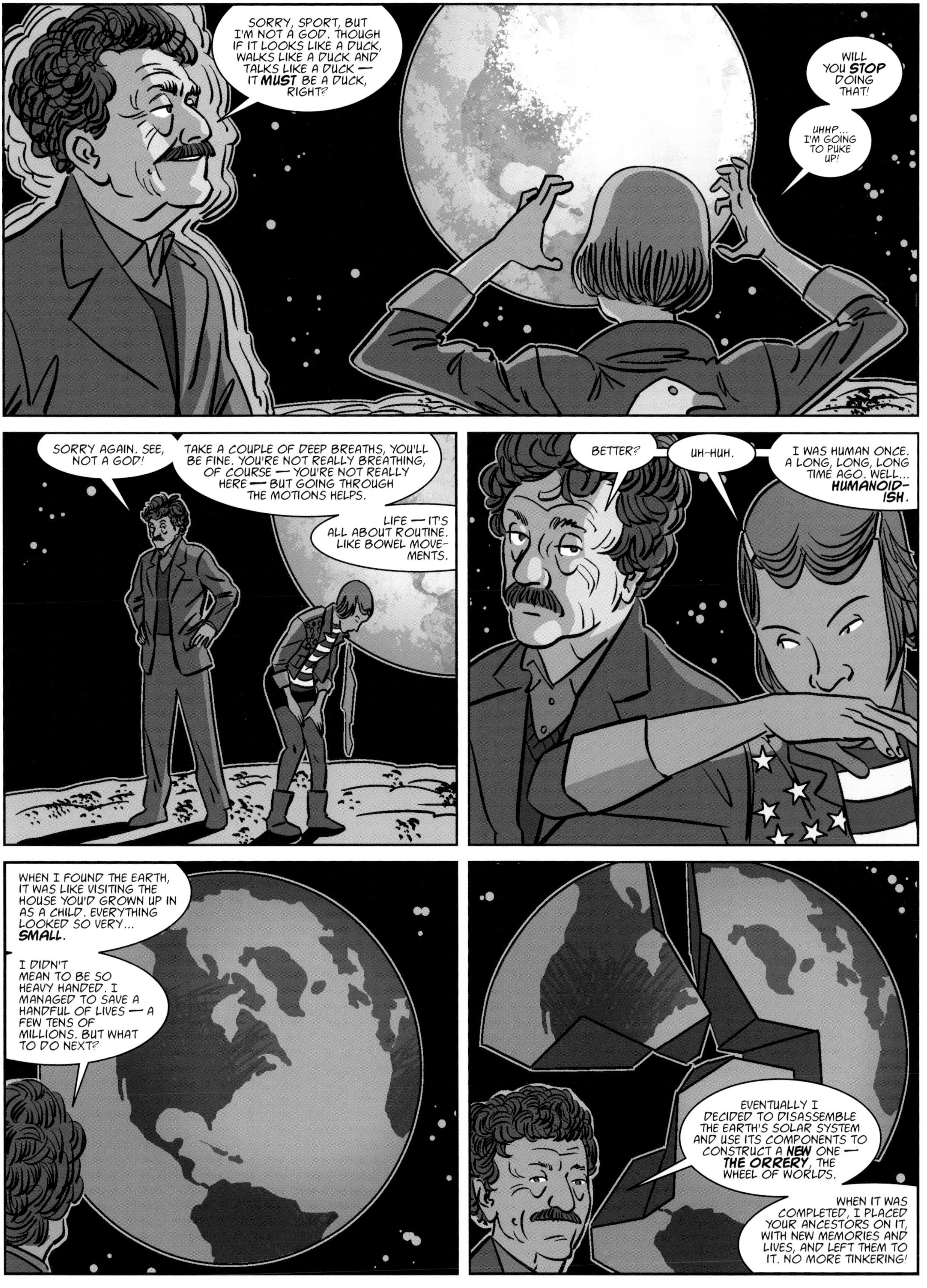
SORRY, SPORT, BUT I'M NOT A GOD. THOUGH IF IT LOOKS LIKE A DUCK, WALKS LIKE A DUCK AND TALKS LIKE A DUCK — IT MUST BE A DUCK, RIGHT?
WILL YOU STOP DOING THAT!
UHHP... I'M GOING TO PUKE UP!
SORRY AGAIN. SEE, NOT A GOD!
TAKE A COUPLE OF DEEP BREATHS, YOU'LL BE FINE. YOU'RE NOT REALLY BREATHING, OF COURSE — YOU'RE NOT REALLY HERE — BUT GOING THROUGH THE MOTIONS HELPS.
LIFE — IT'S ALL ABOUT ROUTINE. LIKE BOWEL MOVEMENTS.
BETTER?
UH-HUH.
I WAS HUMAN ONCE. A LONG, LONG, LONG TIME AGO. WELL... HUMANOID-ISH.
WHEN I FOUND THE EARTH, IT WAS LIKE VISITING THE HOUSE YOU'D GROWN UP IN AS A CHILD. EVERYTHING LOOKED SO VERY... SMALL.
I DIDN'T MEAN TO BE SO HEAVY HANDED. I MANAGED TO SAVE A HANDFUL OF LIVES — A FEW TENS OF MILLIONS. BUT WHAT TO DO NEXT?
EVENTUALLY I DECIDED TO DISASSEMBLE THE EARTH'S SOLAR SYSTEM AND USE ITS COMPONENTS TO CONSTRUCT A NEW ONE — THE ORRERY, THE WHEEL OF WORLDS.
WHEN IT WAS COMPLETED, I PLACED YOUR ANCESTORS ON IT, WITH NEW MEMORIES AND LIVES, AND LEFT THEM TO IT. NO MORE TINKERING!

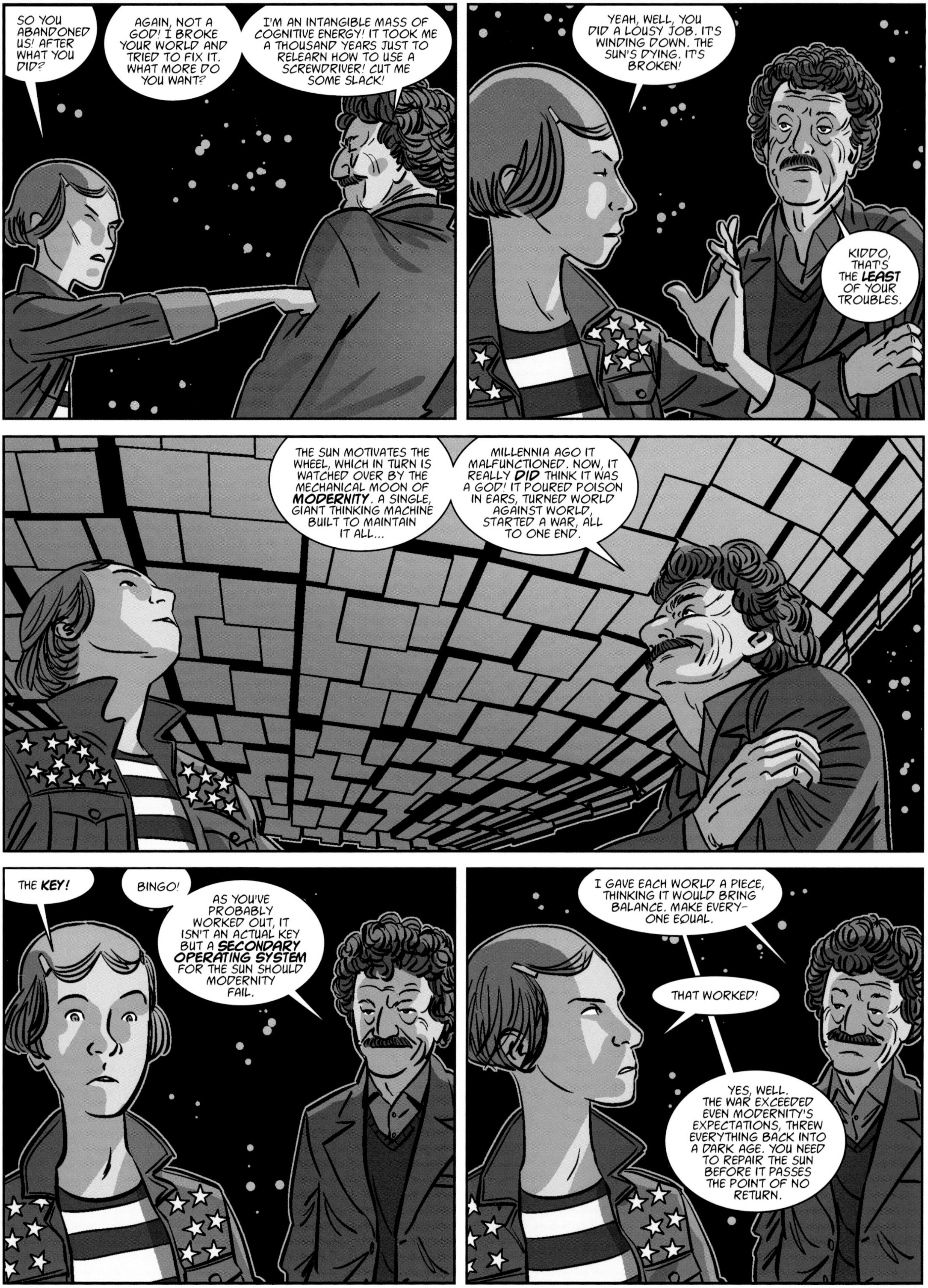
SO YOU ABANDONED US! AFTER WHAT YOU DID?
AGAIN, NOT A GOD! I BROKE YOUR WORLD AND TRIED TO FIX IT. WHAT MORE DO YOU WANT?
I'M AN INTANGIBLE MASS OF COGNITIVE ENERGY! IT TOOK ME A THOUSAND YEARS JUST TO RELEARN HOW TO USE A SCREWDRIVER! CUT ME SOME SLACK!
YEAH, WELL, YOU DID A LOUSY JOB. IT'S WINDING DOWN. THE SUN'S DYING. IT'S BROKEN!
KIDDO, THAT'S THE LEAST OF YOUR TROUBLES.
THE SUN MOTIVATES THE WHEEL, WHICH IN TURN IS WATCHED OVER BY THE MECHANICAL MOON OF MODERNITY. A SINGLE, GIANT THINKING MACHINE BUILT TO MAINTAIN IT ALL...
MILLENNIA AGO IT MALFUNCTIONED. NOW, IT REALLY DID THINK IT WAS A GOD! IT POURED POISON IN EARS, TURNED WORLD AGAINST WORLD, STARTED A WAR, ALL TO ONE END.
THE KEY!
BINGO!
AS YOU'VE PROBABLY WORKED OUT, IT ISN'T AN ACTUAL KEY BUT A SECONDARY OPERATING SYSTEM FOR THE SUN SHOULD MODERNITY FAIL.
I GAVE EACH WORLD A PIECE, THINKING IT WOULD BRING BALANCE. MAKE EVERY-ONE EQUAL.
THAT WORKED!
YES, WELL. THE WAR EXCEEDED EVEN MODERNITY'S EXPECTATIONS, THREW EVERYTHING BACK INTO A DARK AGE. YOU NEED TO REPAIR THE SUN BEFORE IT PASSES THE POINT OF NO RETURN.

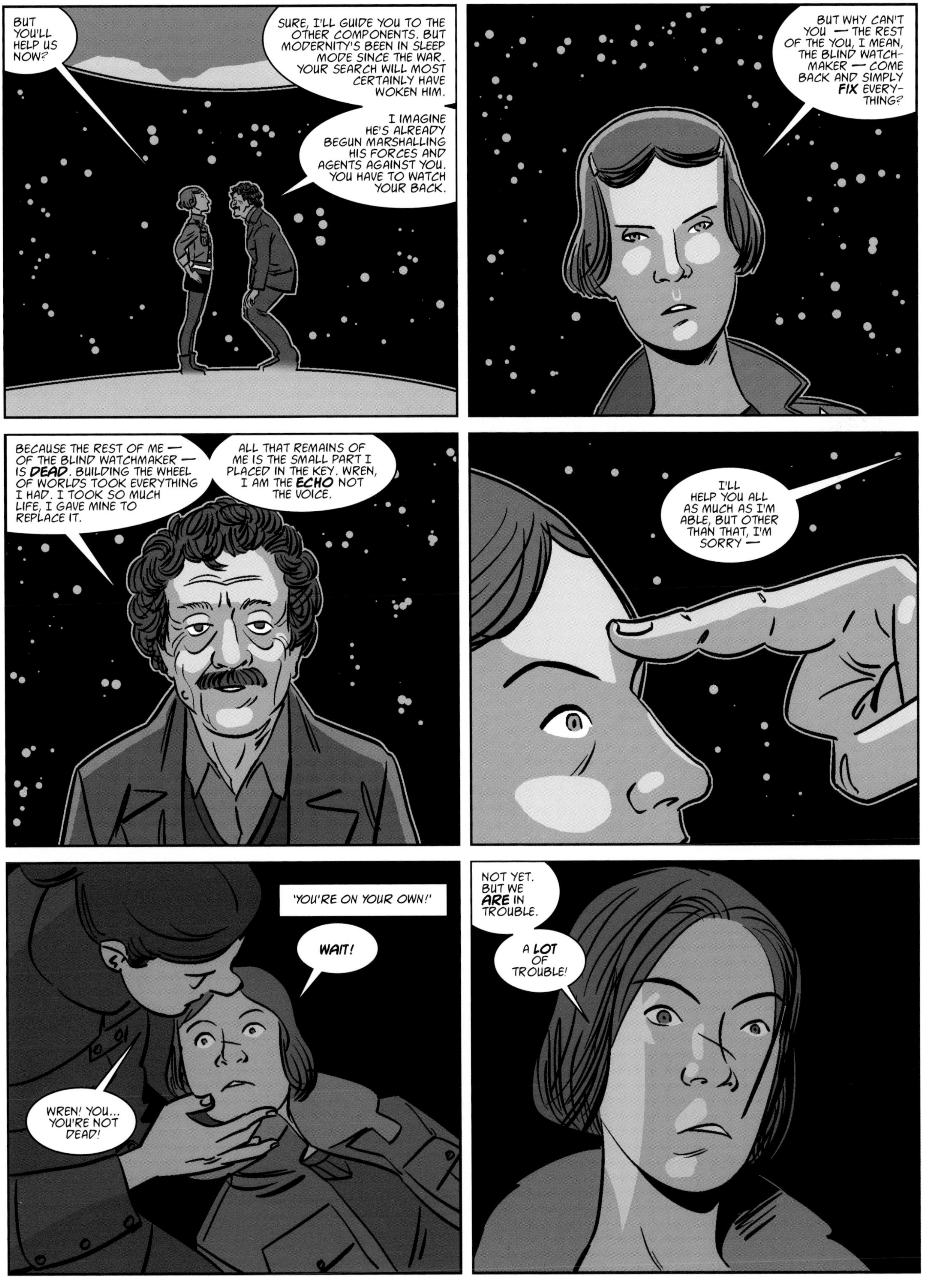
BUT YOU'LL HELP US NOW?
SURE, I'LL GUIDE YOU TO THE OTHER COMPONENTS. BUT MODERNITY'S BEEN IN SLEEP MODE SINCE THE WAR. YOUR SEARCH WILL MOST CERTAINLY HAVE WOKEN HIM.
I IMAGINE HE'S ALREADY BEGUN MARSHALLING HIS FORCES AND AGENTS AGAINST YOU. YOU HAVE TO WATCH YOUR BACK.
BUT WHY CAN'T YOU — THE REST OF THE YOU, I MEAN, THE BLIND WATCH-MAKER — COME BACK AND SIMPLY FIX EVERY-THING?
BECAUSE THE REST OF ME — OF THE BLIND WATCHMAKER — IS DEAD. BUILDING THE WHEEL OF WORLDS TOOK EVERYTHING I HAD. I TOOK SO MUCH LIFE, I GAVE MINE TO REPLACE IT.
ALL THAT REMAINS OF ME IS THE SMALL PART I PLACED IN THE KEY. WREN, I AM THE ECHO NOT THE VOICE.
I'LL HELP YOU ALL AS MUCH AS I'M ABLE, BUT OTHER THAN THAT, I'M SORRY —
'YOU'RE ON YOUR OWN!'
WAIT!
WREN! YOU... YOU'RE NOT DEAD!
NOT YET. BUT WE ARE IN TROUBLE.
A LOT OF TROUBLE!

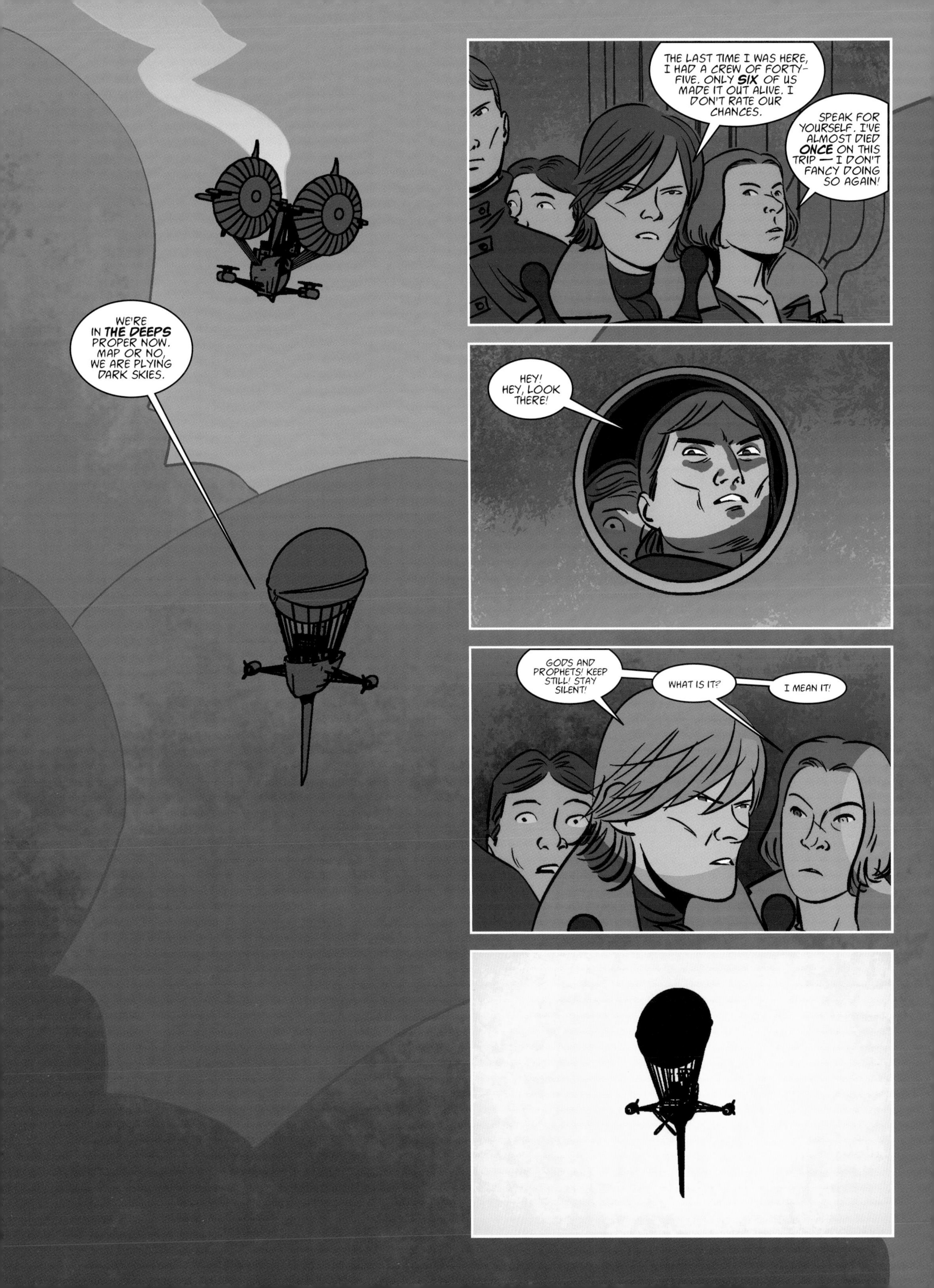
WE'RE IN THE DEEPS PROPER NOW. MAP OR NO, WE ARE PLYING DARK SKIES.
THE LAST TIME I WAS HERE, I HAD A CREW OF FORTY-FIVE. ONLY SIX OF US MADE IT OUT ALIVE. I DON'T RATE OUR CHANCES.
SPEAK FOR YOURSELF. I'VE ALMOST DIED ONCE ON THIS TRIP — I DON'T FANCY DOING SO AGAIN!
HEY! HEY, LOOK THERE!
GODS AND PROPHETS! KEEP STILL! STAY SILENT!
WHAT IS IT?
I MEAN IT!

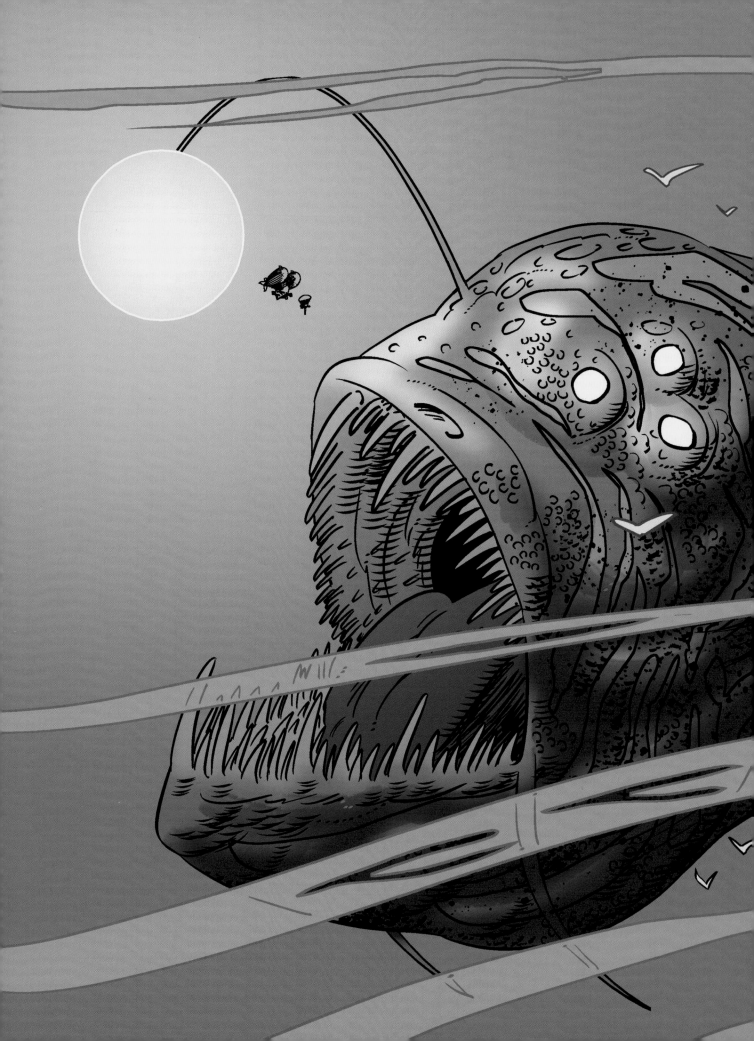

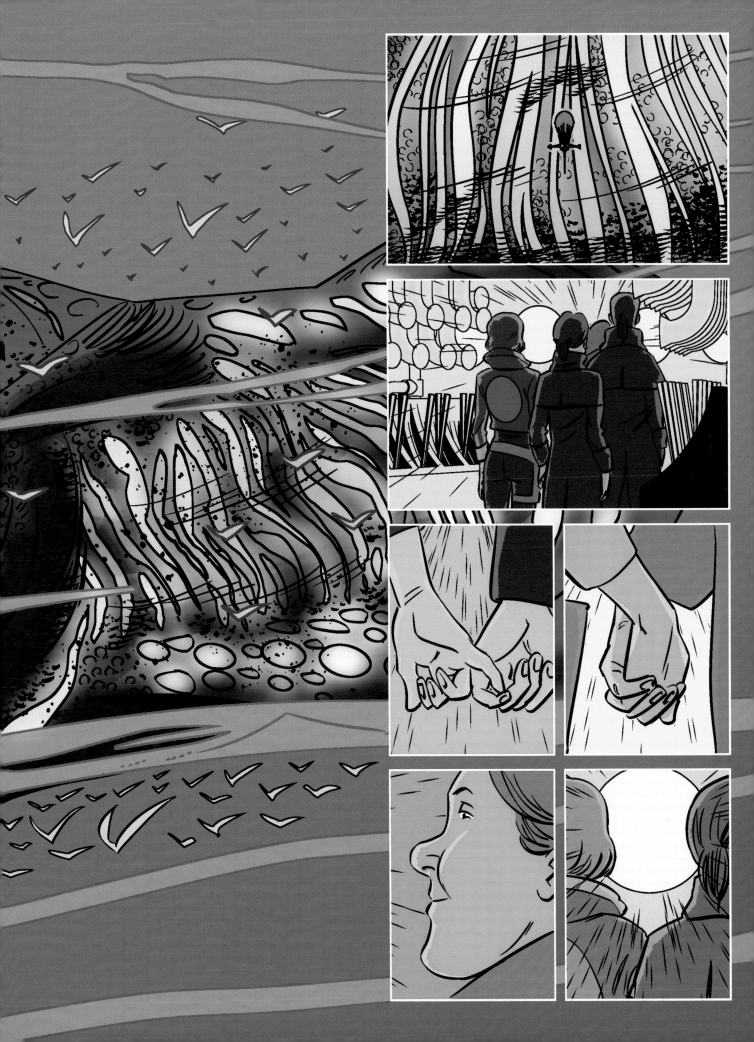

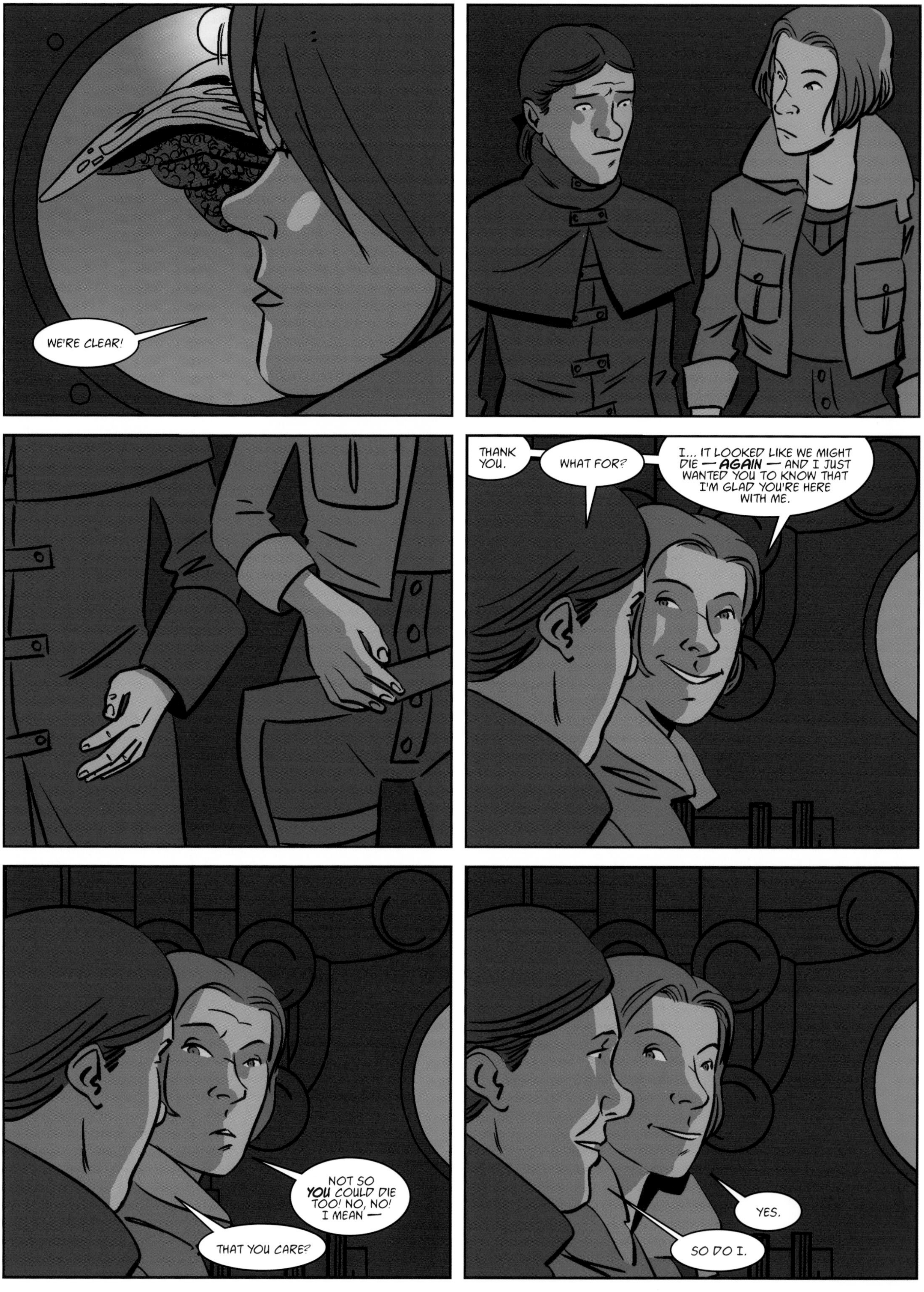
WE'RE CLEAR!
THANK YOU.
WHAT FOR?
I... IT LOOKED LIKE WE MIGHT DIE — AGAIN — AND I JUST WANTED YOU TO KNOW THAT I'M GLAD YOU'RE HERE WITH ME.
NOT SO YOU COULD DIE TOO! NO, NO! I MEAN —
THAT YOU CARE?
YES.
SO DO I.

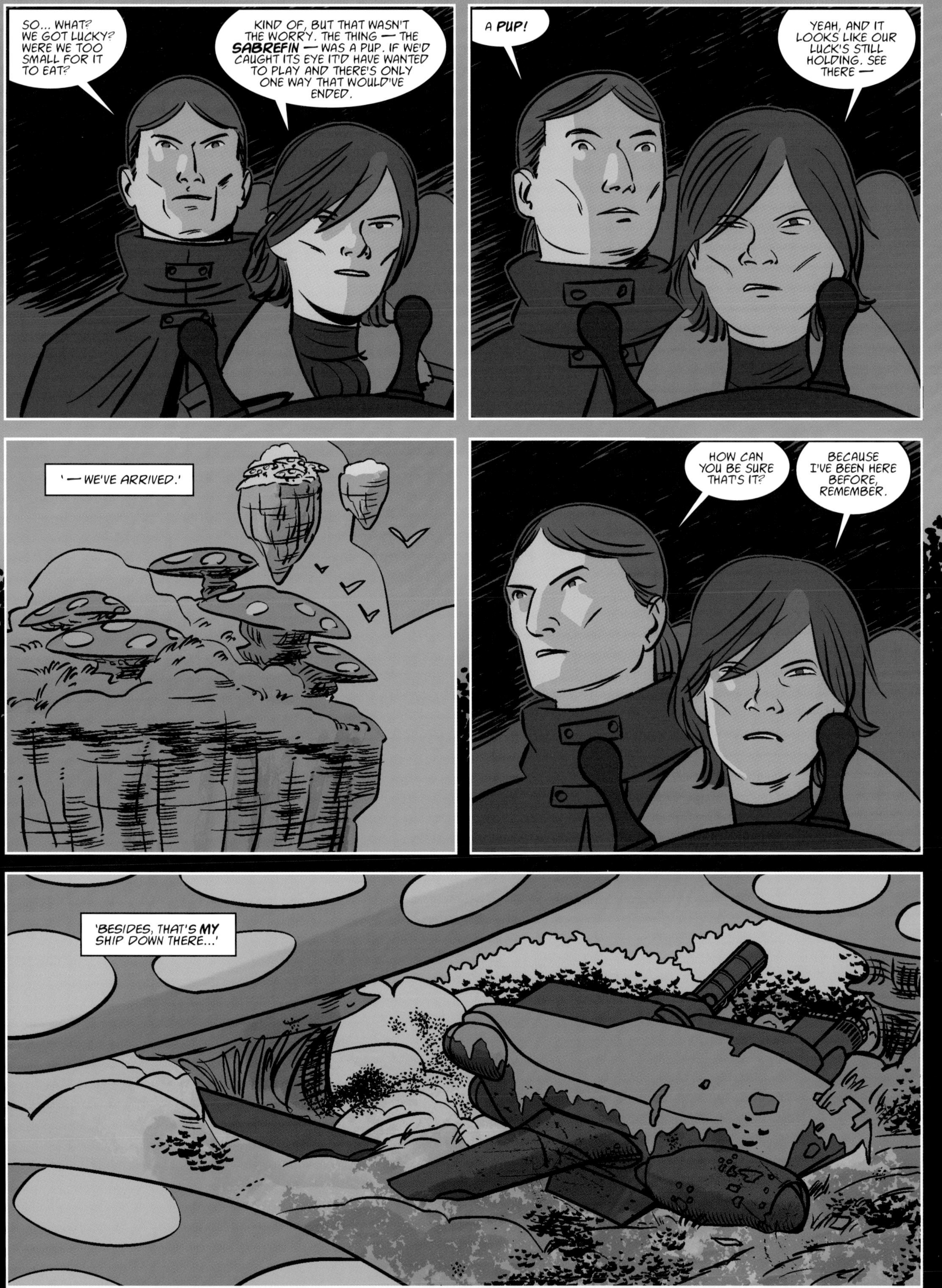
SO... WHAT? WE GOT LUCKY? WERE WE TOO SMALL FOR IT TO EAT?
KIND OF, BUT THAT WASN'T THE WORRY. THE THING — THE SABREFIN — WAS A PUP. IF WE'D CAUGHT ITS EYE IT'D HAVE WANTED TO PLAY AND THERE'S ONLY ONE WAY THAT WOULD'VE ENDED.
A PUP!
YEAH, AND IT LOOKS LIKE OUR LUCK'S STILL HOLDING. SEE THERE —
'— WE'VE ARRIVED.'
HOW CAN YOU BE SURE THAT'S IT?
BECAUSE I'VE BEEN HERE BEFORE, REMEMBER.
'BESIDES, THAT'S MY SHIP DOWN THERE...'

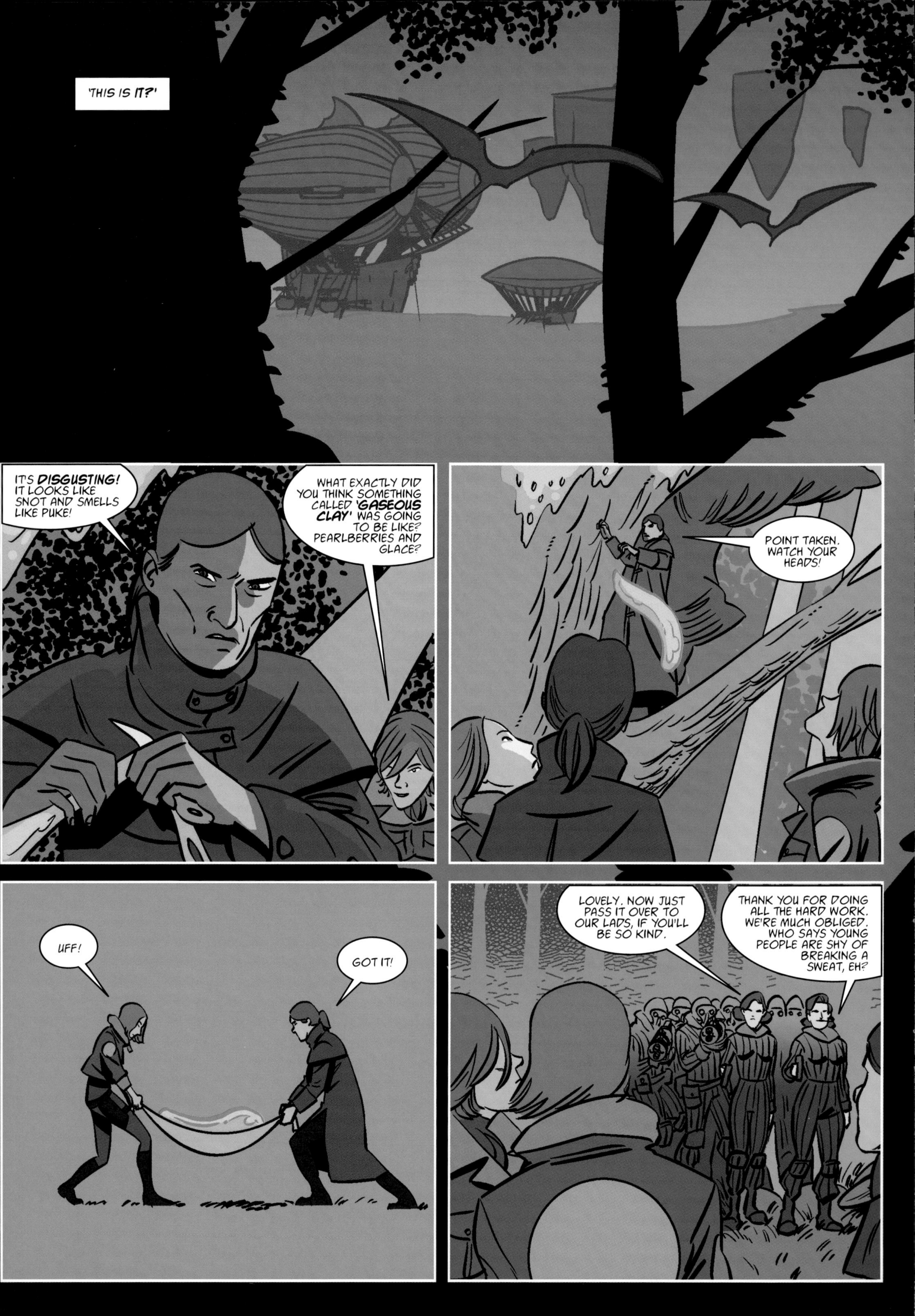
'THIS IS IT?'
IT'S DISGUSTING! IT LOOKS LIKE SNOT AND SMELLS LIKE PUKE!
WHAT EXACTLY DID YOU THINK SOMETHING CALLED 'GASEOUS CLAY' WAS GOING TO BE LIKE? PEARLBERRIES AND GLACE?
POINT TAKEN. WATCH YOUR HEADS!
UFF!
GOT IT!
LOVELY. NOW JUST PASS IT OVER TO OUR LADS, IF YOU'LL BE SO KIND.
THANK YOU FOR DOING ALL THE HARD WORK. WE'RE MUCH OBLIGED. WHO SAYS YOUNG PEOPLE ARE SHY OF BREAKING A SWEAT, EH?

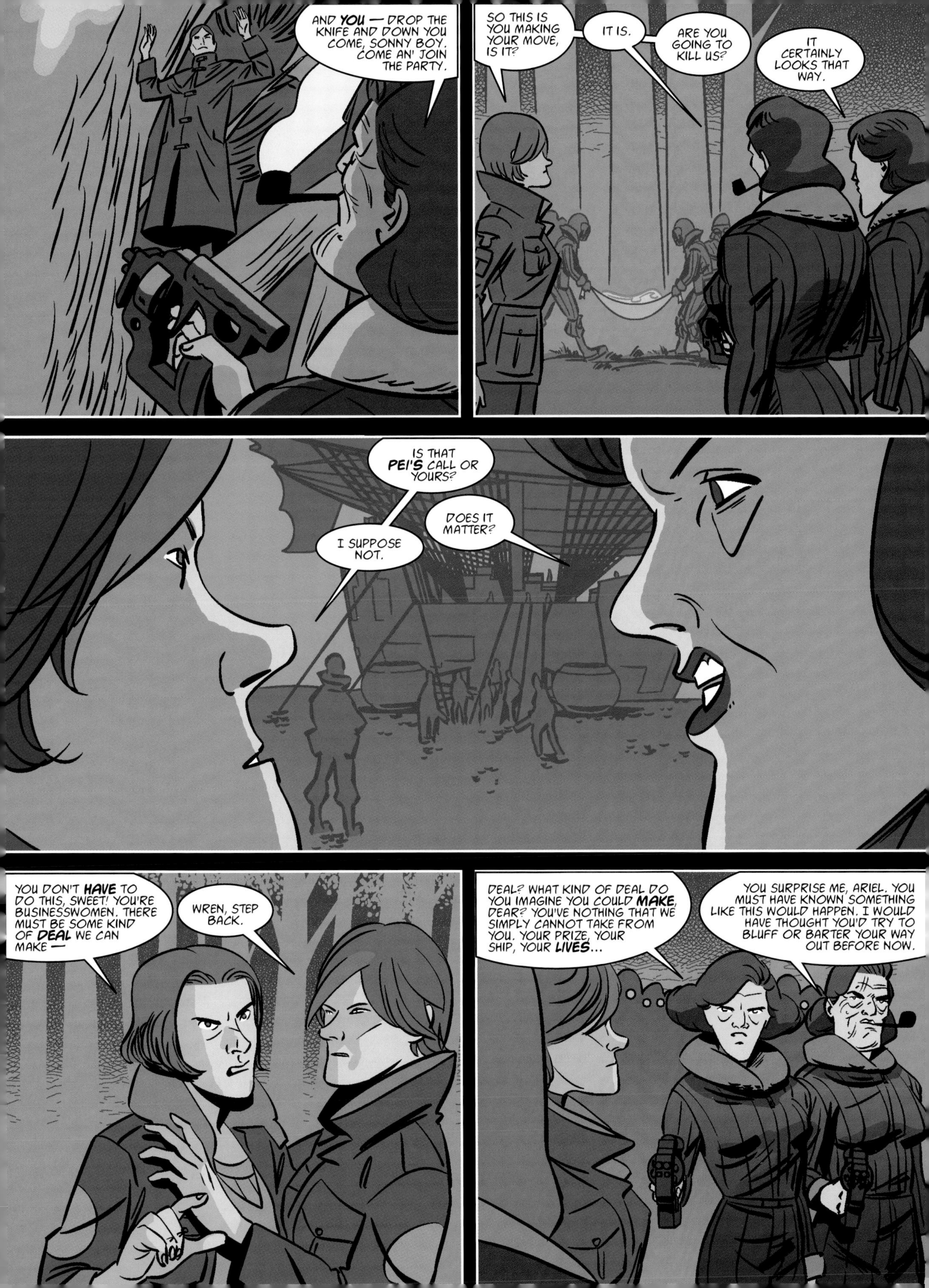
AND YOU — DROP THE KNIFE AND DOWN YOU COME, SONNY BOY. COME AN' JOIN THE PARTY.
SO THIS IS YOU MAKING YOUR MOVE, IS IT?
IT IS.
ARE YOU GOING TO KILL US?
IT CERTAINLY LOOKS THAT WAY.
IS THAT PEI'S CALL OR YOURS?
DOES IT MATTER?
I SUPPOSE NOT.
YOU DON'T HAVE TO DO THIS, SWEET! YOU'RE BUSINESSWOMEN. THERE MUST BE SOME KIND OF DEAL WE CAN MAKE —
WREN, STEP BACK.
DEAL? WHAT KIND OF DEAL DO YOU IMAGINE YOU COULD MAKE, DEAR? YOU'VE NOTHING THAT WE SIMPLY CANNOT TAKE FROM YOU. YOUR PRIZE, YOUR SHIP, YOUR LIVES...
YOU SURPRISE ME, ARIEL. YOU MUST HAVE KNOWN SOMETHING LIKE THIS WOULD HAPPEN. I WOULD HAVE THOUGHT YOU'D TRY TO BLUFF OR BARTER YOUR WAY OUT BEFORE NOW.

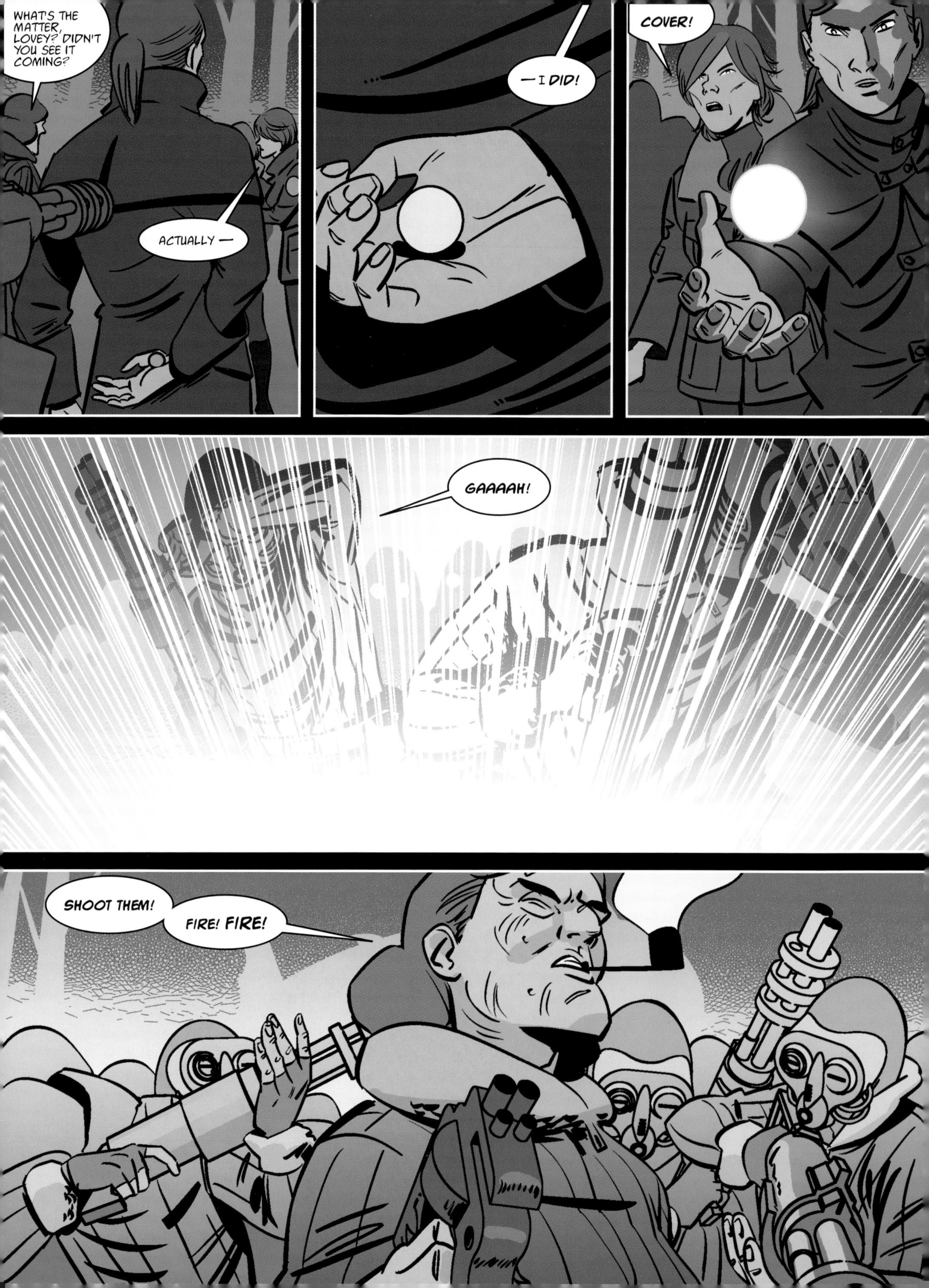
WHAT'S THE MATTER, LOVEY? DIDN'T YOU SEE IT COMING?
ACTUALLY —
— I DID!
COVER!
GAAAAH!
SHOOT THEM!
FIRE! FIRE!

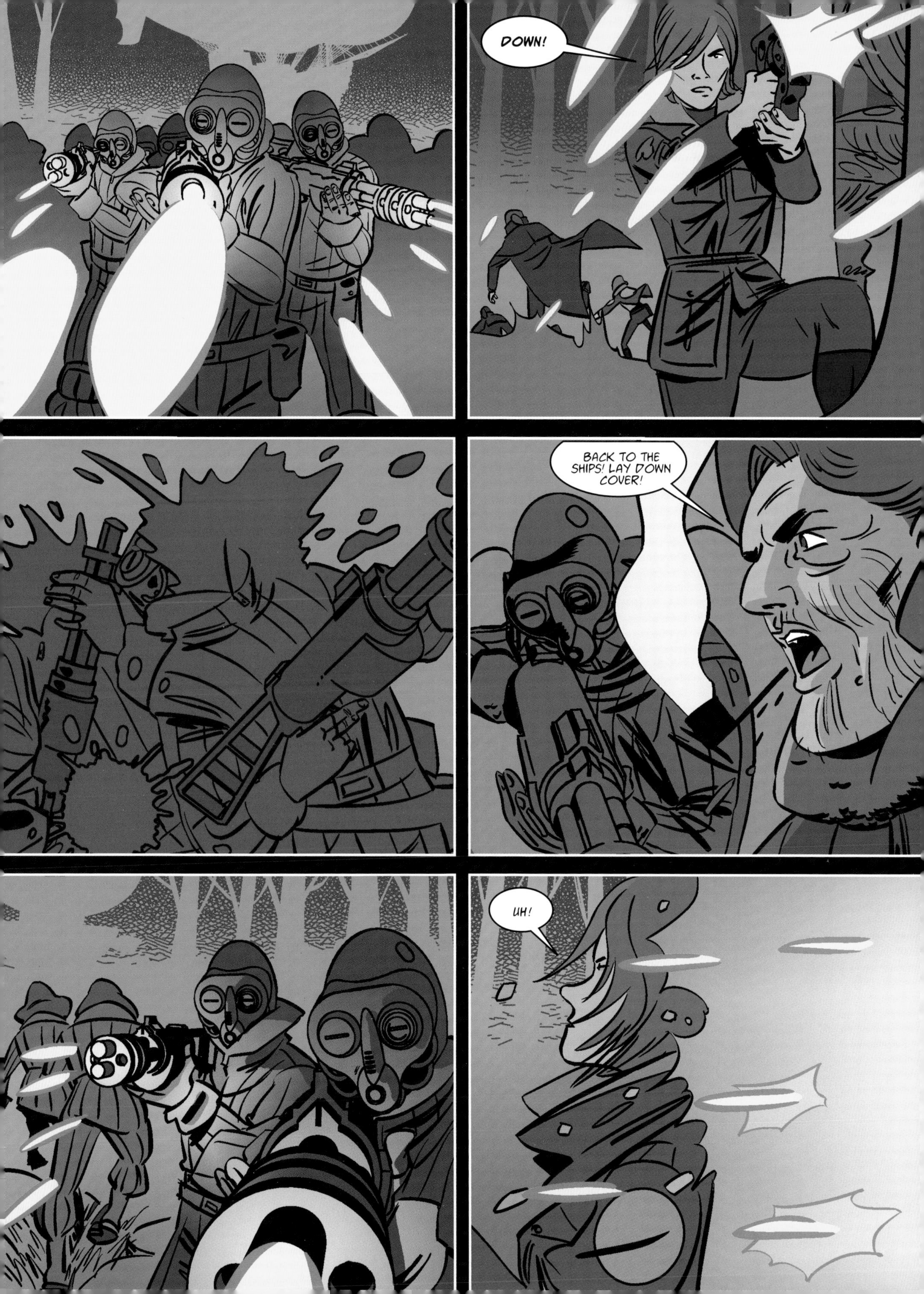
DOWN!
BACK TO THE SHIPS! LAY DOWN COVER!
UH!

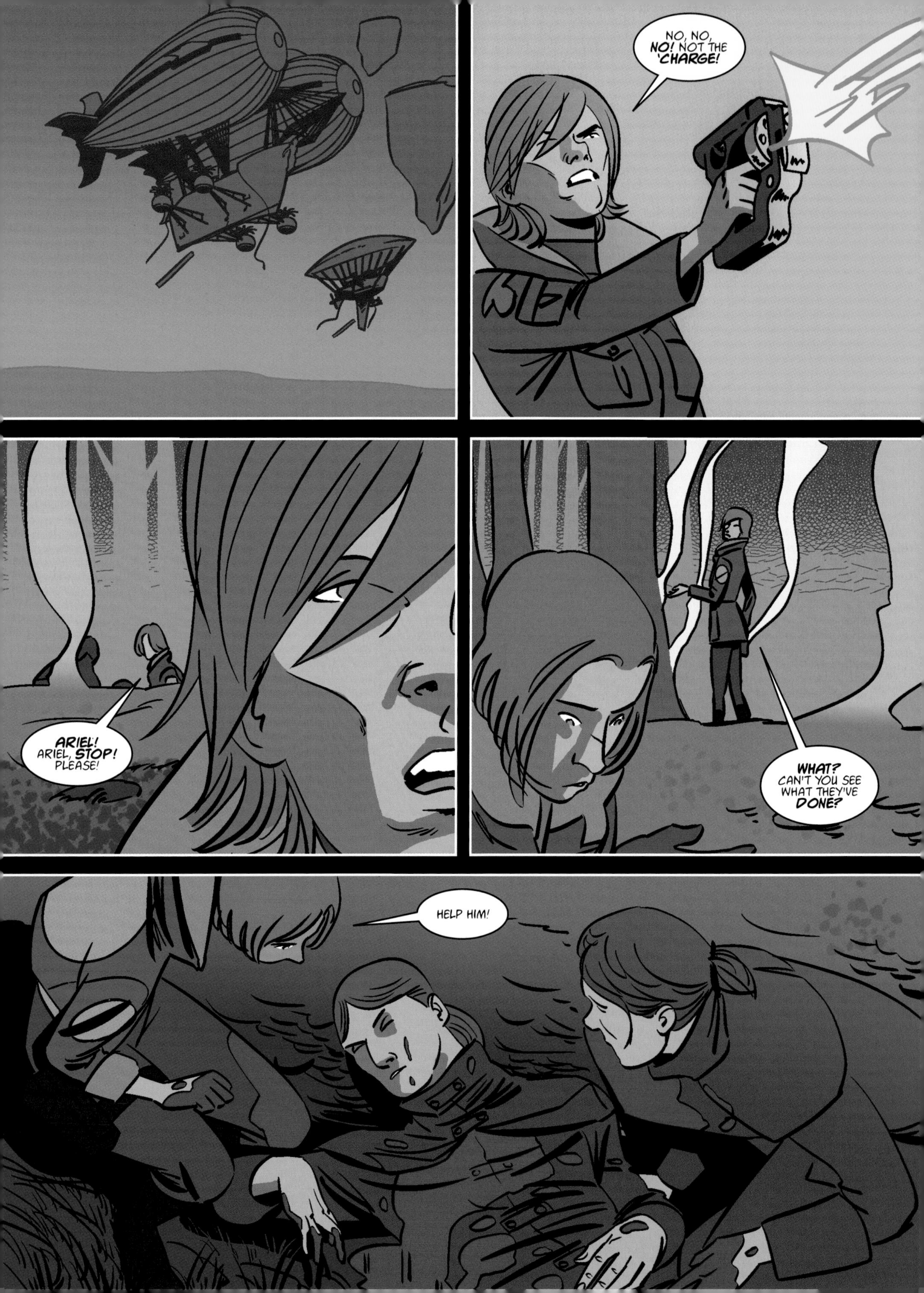
NO, NO, NO! NOT THE 'CHARGE!
ARIEL! ARIEL, STOP! PLEASE!
WHAT? CAN'T YOU SEE WHAT THEY'VE DONE?
HELP HIM!

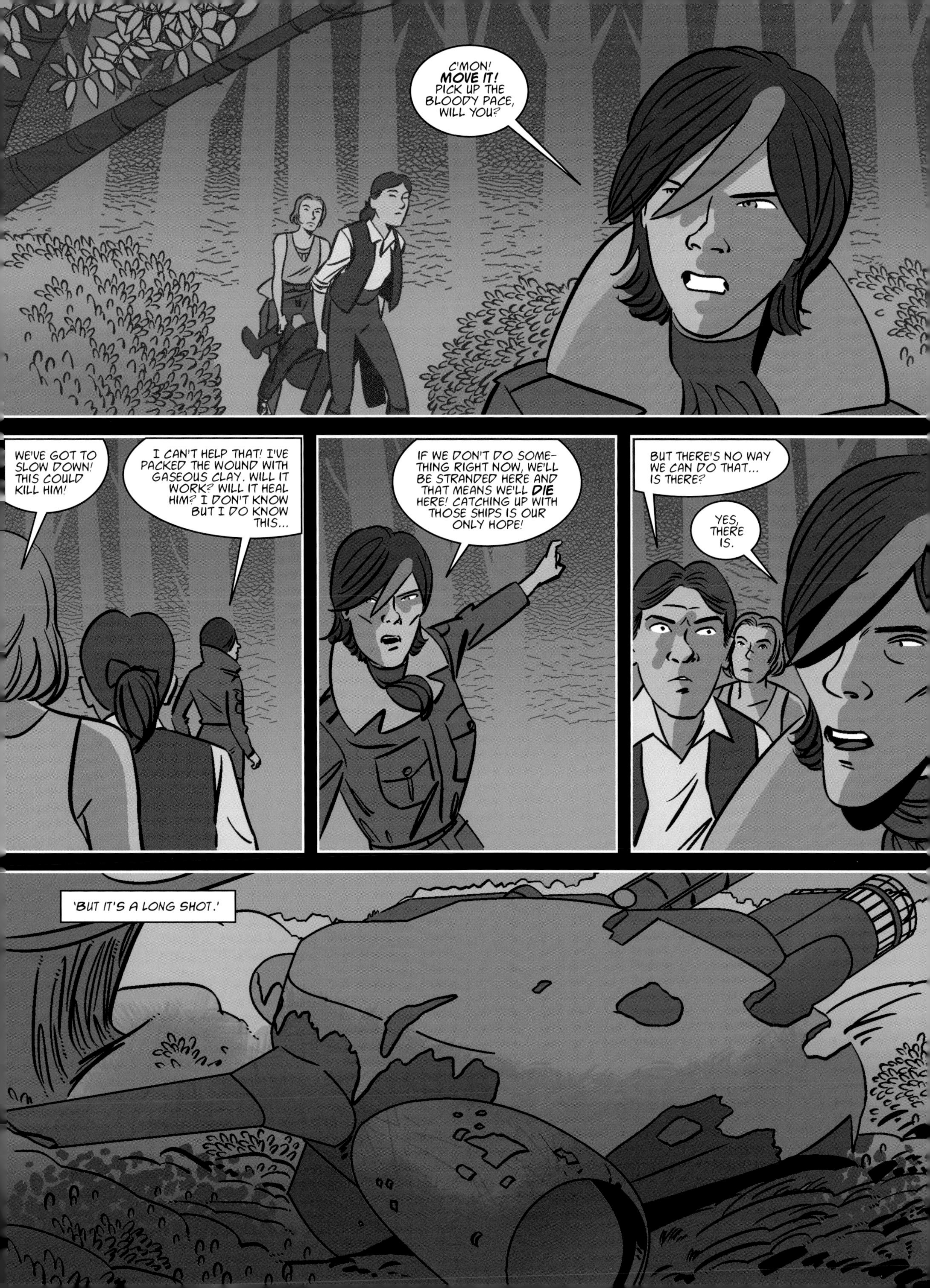
C'MON! MOVE IT! PICK UP THE BLOODY PACE, WILL YOU?
WE'VE GOT TO SLOW DOWN! THIS COULD KILL HIM!
I CAN'T HELP THAT! I'VE PACKED THE WOUND WITH GASEOUS CLAY. WILL IT WORK? WILL IT HEAL HIM? I DON'T KNOW BUT I DO KNOW THIS...
IF WE DON'T DO SOME-THING RIGHT NOW, WE'LL BE STRANDED HERE AND THAT MEANS WE'LL DIE HERE! CATCHING UP WITH THOSE SHIPS IS OUR ONLY HOPE!
BUT THERE'S NO WAY WE CAN DO THAT... IS THERE?
YES, THERE IS.
'BUT IT'S A LONG SHOT.'

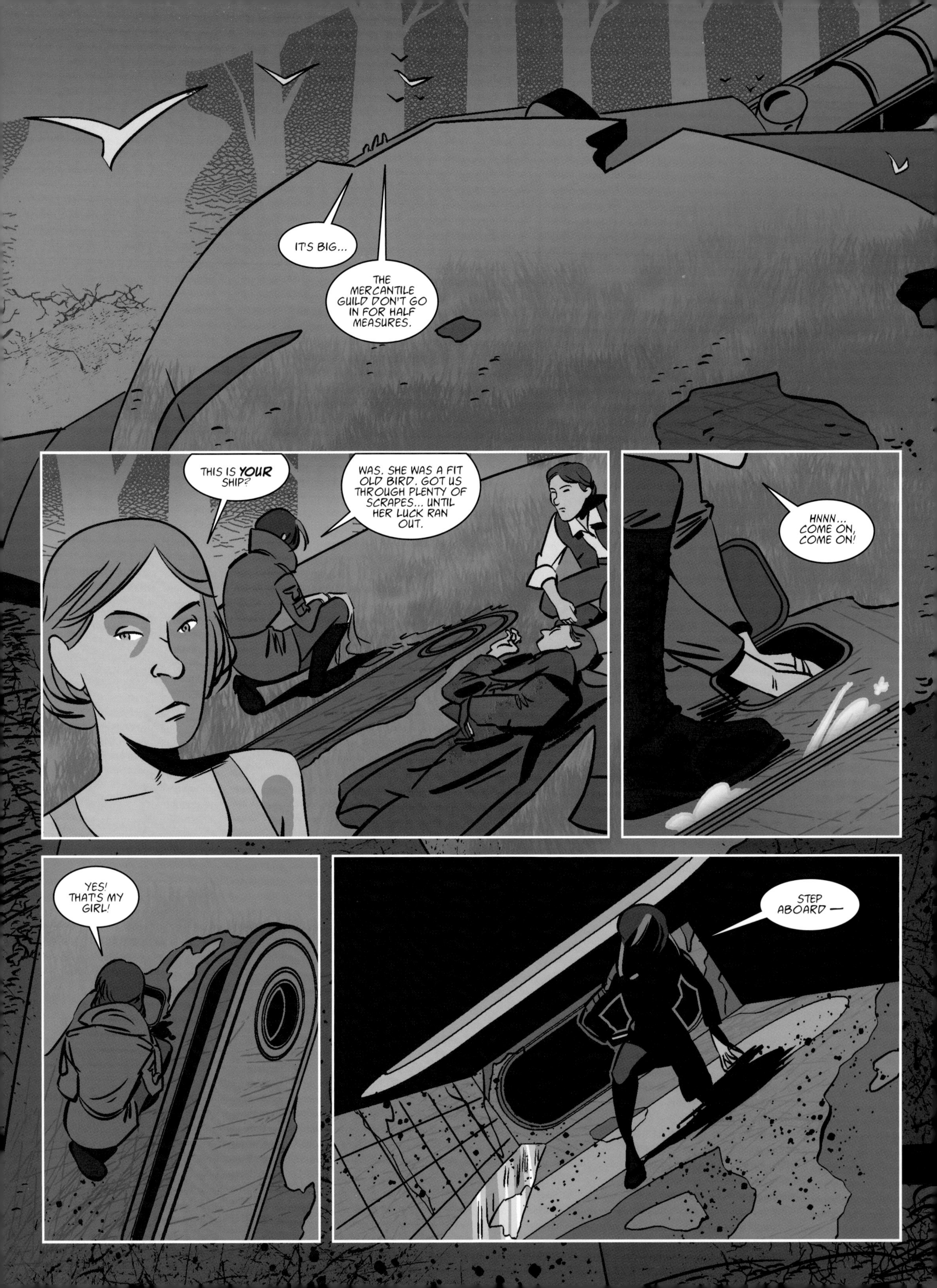
IT'S BIG...
THE MERCANTILE GUILD DON'T GO IN FOR HALF MEASURES.
THIS IS **YOUR** SHIP?
WAS. SHE WAS A FIT OLD BIRD. GOT US THROUGH PLENTY OF SCRAPES... UNTIL HER LUCK RAN OUT.
HNNN... COME ON, COME ON!
YES! THAT'S MY GIRL!
STEP ABOARD —

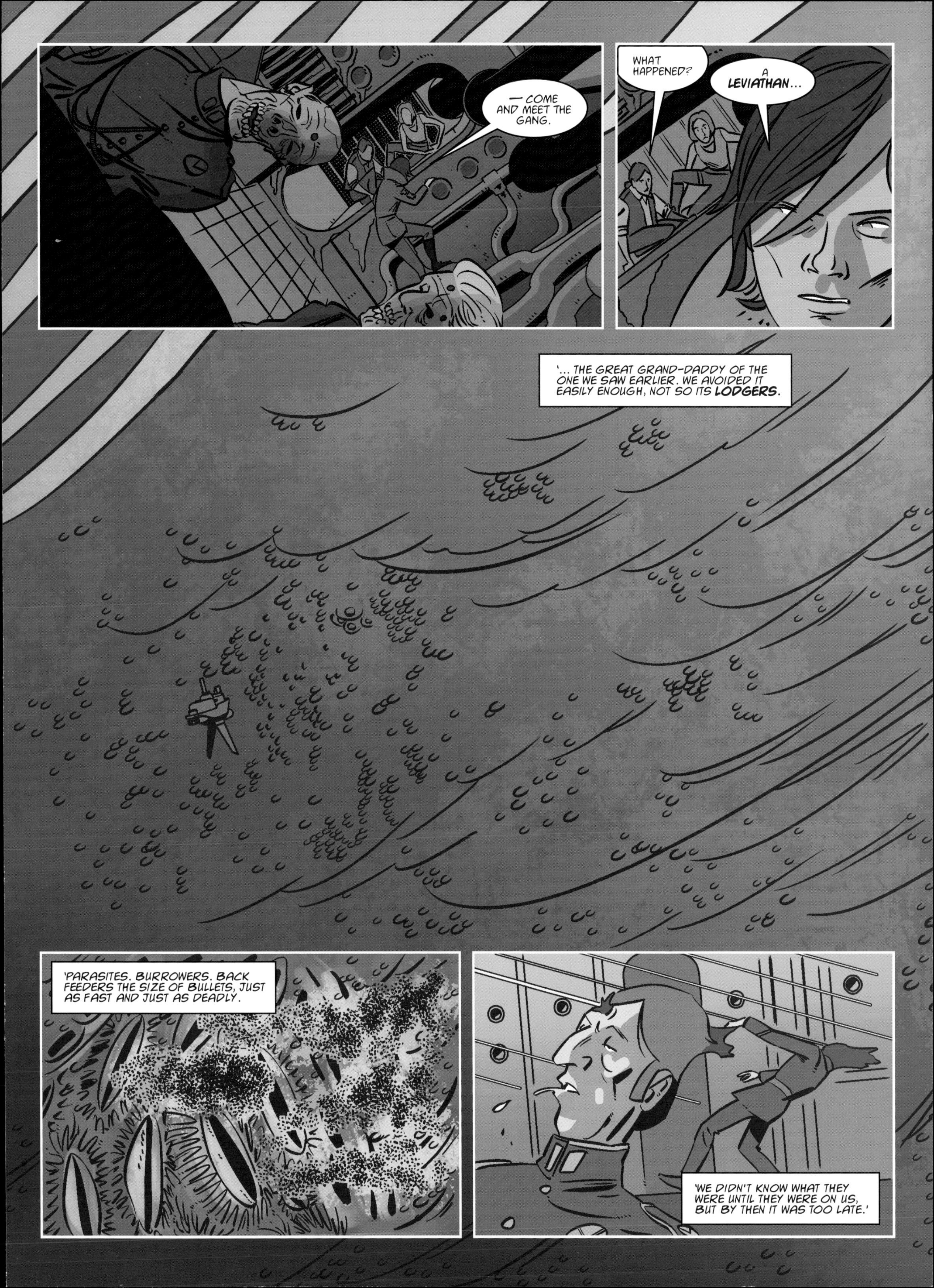
— COME AND MEET THE GANG.
WHAT HAPPENED?
A LEVIATHAN...
'... THE GREAT GRAND-DADDY OF THE ONE WE SAW EARLIER. WE AVOIDED IT EASILY ENOUGH, NOT SO ITS LODGERS.
'PARASITES. BURROWERS. BACK FEEDERS THE SIZE OF BULLETS, JUST AS FAST AND JUST AS DEADLY.
'WE DIDN'T KNOW WHAT THEY WERE UNTIL THEY WERE ON US, BUT BY THEN IT WAS TOO LATE.'

THE BULK OF THE CREW DIED IN UNDER FIVE MINUTES. I SEALED THE VENTS AND MADE AN EMERGENCY LANDING — MORE BY LUCK THAN JUDGEMENT.

WHEN WE GOT BACK HOME I WAS COURT-MARSHALLED FOR WILFUL ABANDONMENT OF GUILD PROPERTY. I WAS CLUED UP, THOUGH — HAD SOME DIRT ON MY SUPERIORS SQUIRRELED AWAY FOR A RAINY DAY.

I WAS CONVENIENTLY ACQUITTED. NO COMMAND, NO CAREER, NO PENSION, BUT I WAS FREE BECAUSE I HAD SOMETHING THEY WANTED.

HOW TO FIND YOUR WAY BACK HERE?

GOT IT IN ONE.

I DON'T UNDERSTAND.

THE **CLAY!** THE REASON I FIRST GOT SENT OUT HERE. HOW MUCH IS A UNIVERSAL PANACEA WORTH? MORE THAN THE LIVES OF MY MEN OR THE DOZENS OF OTHER DEAD SHIPS AND CREWS THAT I BET ARE MOULDERING OUT THERE RIGHT NOW.

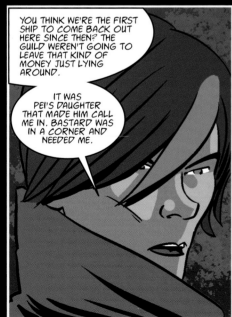

YOU THINK WE'RE THE FIRST SHIP TO COME BACK OUT HERE SINCE THEN? THE GUILD WEREN'T GOING TO LEAVE THAT KIND OF MONEY JUST LYING AROUND.

IT WAS PEI'S DAUGHTER THAT MADE HIM CALL ME IN. BASTARD WAS IN A CORNER AND NEEDED ME.

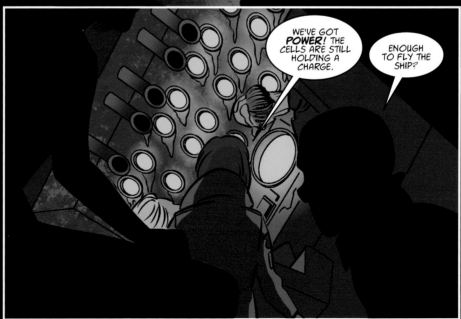

WE'VE GOT **POWER!** THE CELLS ARE STILL HOLDING A CHARGE.

ENOUGH TO FLY THE SHIP?

NOT **THIS** ONE. SHE'S PAST HOPE.

'THE **AUXILIARY ESCAPE SHUTTLE'S** ANOTHER MATTER.'

WILL IT WORK?

ONLY ONE WAY TO FIND OUT!

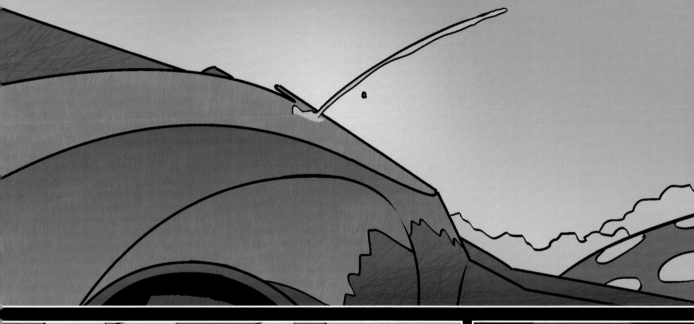

LOOKS LIKE WE'RE BACK IN BUSINESS!

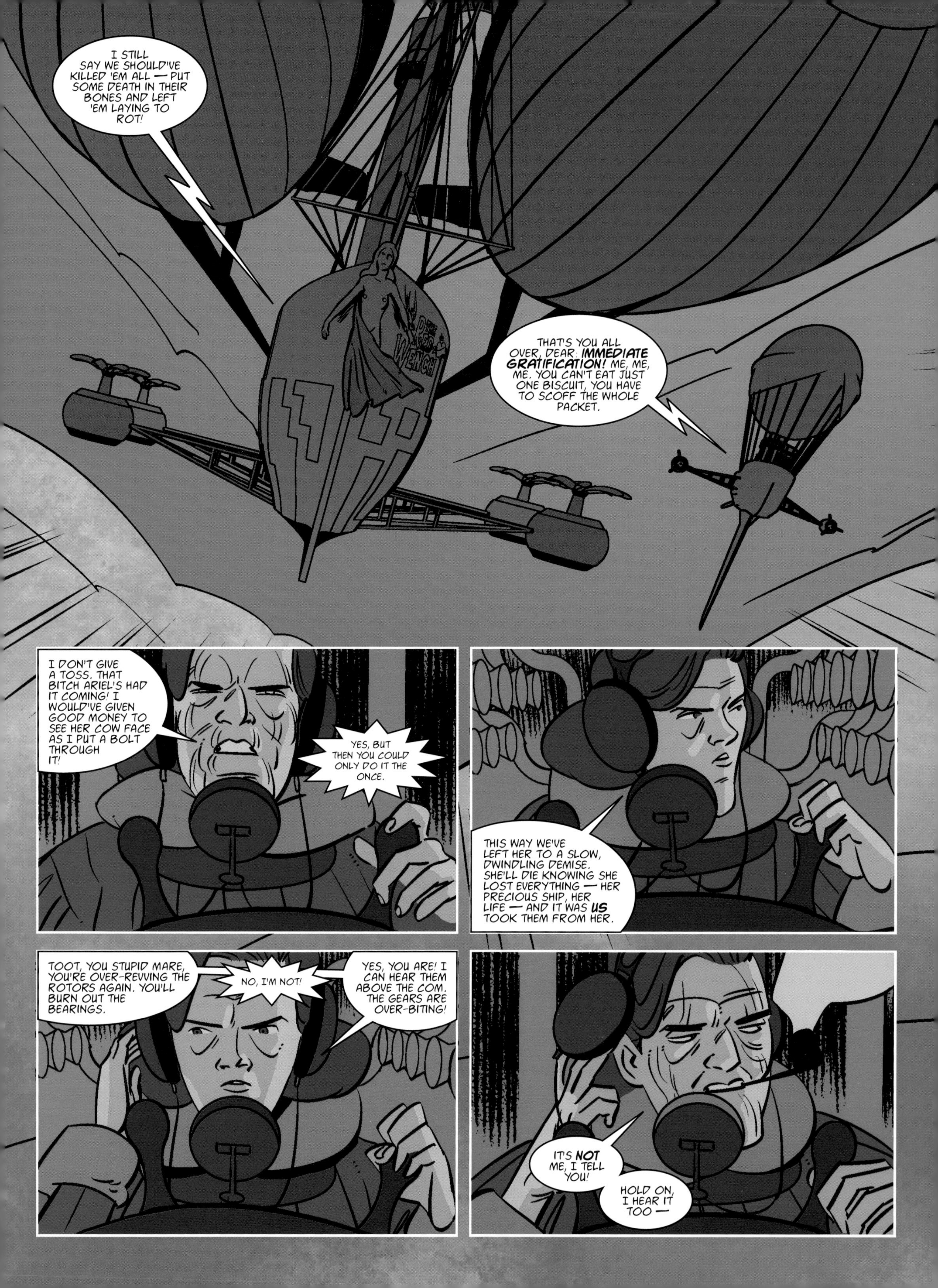
I STILL SAY WE SHOULD'VE KILLED 'EM ALL — PUT SOME DEATH IN THEIR BONES AND LEFT 'EM LAYING TO ROT!
THAT'S YOU ALL OVER, DEAR: **IMMEDIATE GRATIFICATION!** ME, ME, ME. YOU CAN'T EAT JUST ONE BISCUIT, YOU HAVE TO SCOFF THE WHOLE PACKET.
I DON'T GIVE A TOSS. THAT BITCH ARIEL'S HAD IT COMING! I WOULD'VE GIVEN GOOD MONEY TO SEE HER COW FACE AS I PUT A BOLT THROUGH IT!
YES, BUT THEN YOU COULD ONLY DO IT THE ONCE.
THIS WAY WE'VE LEFT HER TO A SLOW, DWINDLING DEMISE. SHE'LL DIE KNOWING SHE LOST EVERYTHING — HER PRECIOUS SHIP, HER LIFE — AND IT WAS **US** TOOK THEM FROM HER.
TOOT, YOU STUPID MARE, YOU'RE OVER-REVVING THE ROTORS AGAIN. YOU'LL BURN OUT THE BEARINGS.
NO, I'M NOT!
YES, YOU ARE! I CAN HEAR THEM ABOVE THE COM. THE GEARS ARE OVER-BITING!
IT'S **NOT** ME, I TELL YOU!
HOLD ON, I HEAR IT TOO —

'IT'S COMING FROM **OUTSIDE!**'

WAKEY-WAKEY!

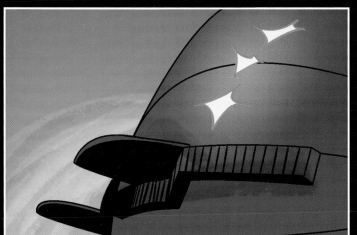

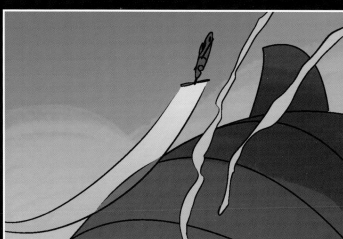

HHHURHHP!

SORRY —

NOTHING'S HAPPENED! IS THE BALLOON **ARMOURED** OR SOMETHING?

WE'LL SEE.

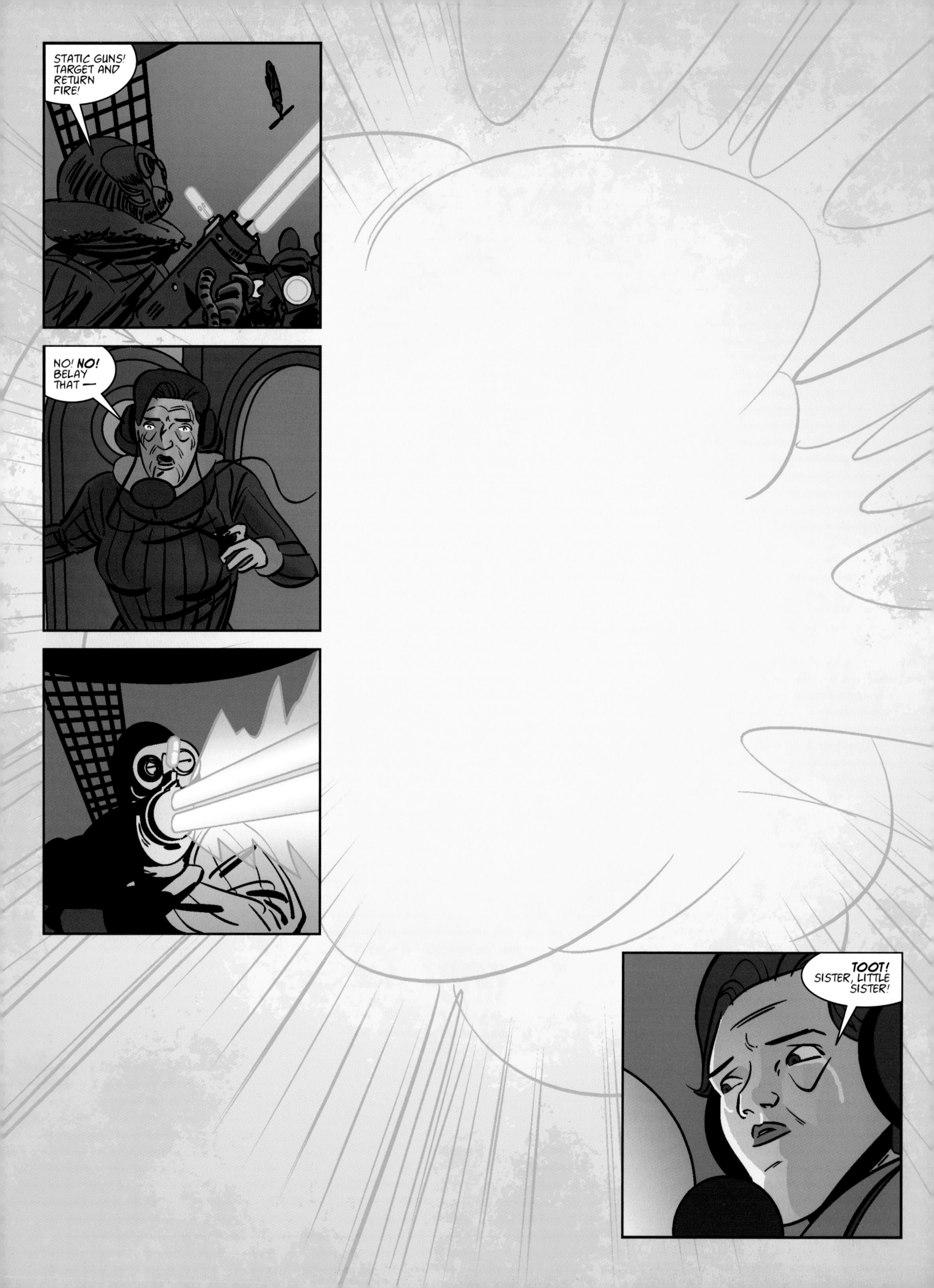
STATIC GUNS! TARGET AND RETURN FIRE!
NO! **NO!** BELAY THAT —
TOOT! SISTER, LITTLE SISTER!

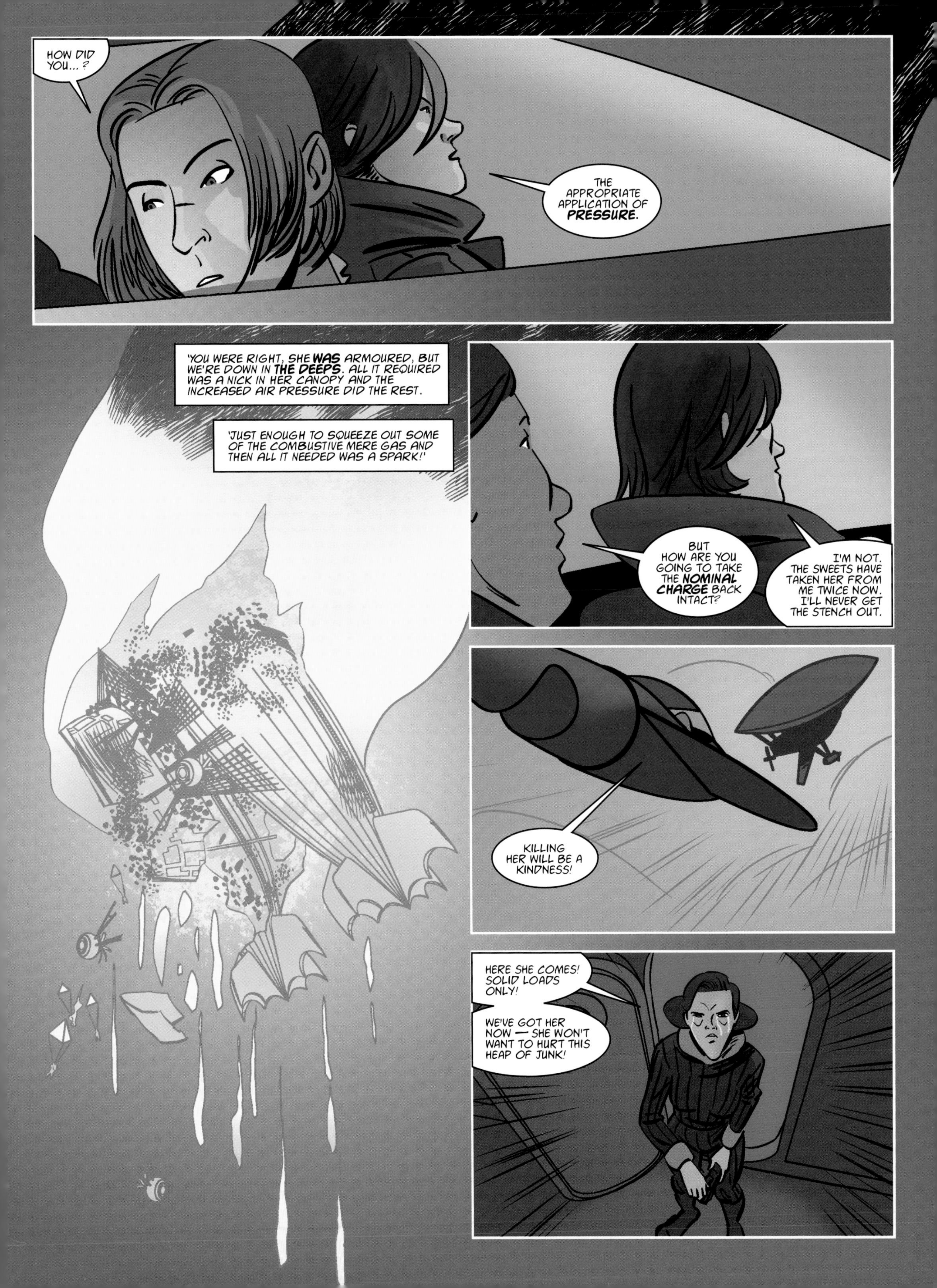
HOW DID YOU...?
THE APPROPRIATE APPLICATION OF PRESSURE.
'YOU WERE RIGHT, SHE WAS ARMOURED, BUT WE'RE DOWN IN THE DEEPS. ALL IT REQUIRED WAS A NICK IN HER CANOPY AND THE INCREASED AIR PRESSURE DID THE REST.
'JUST ENOUGH TO SQUEEZE OUT SOME OF THE COMBUSTIVE MERE GAS AND THEN ALL IT NEEDED WAS A SPARK!'
BUT HOW ARE YOU GOING TO TAKE THE NOMINAL CHARGE BACK INTACT?
I'M NOT. THE SWEETS HAVE TAKEN HER FROM ME TWICE NOW. I'LL NEVER GET THE STENCH OUT.
KILLING HER WILL BE A KINDNESS!
HERE SHE COMES! SOLID LOADS ONLY!
WE'VE GOT HER NOW — SHE WON'T WANT TO HURT THIS HEAP OF JUNK!

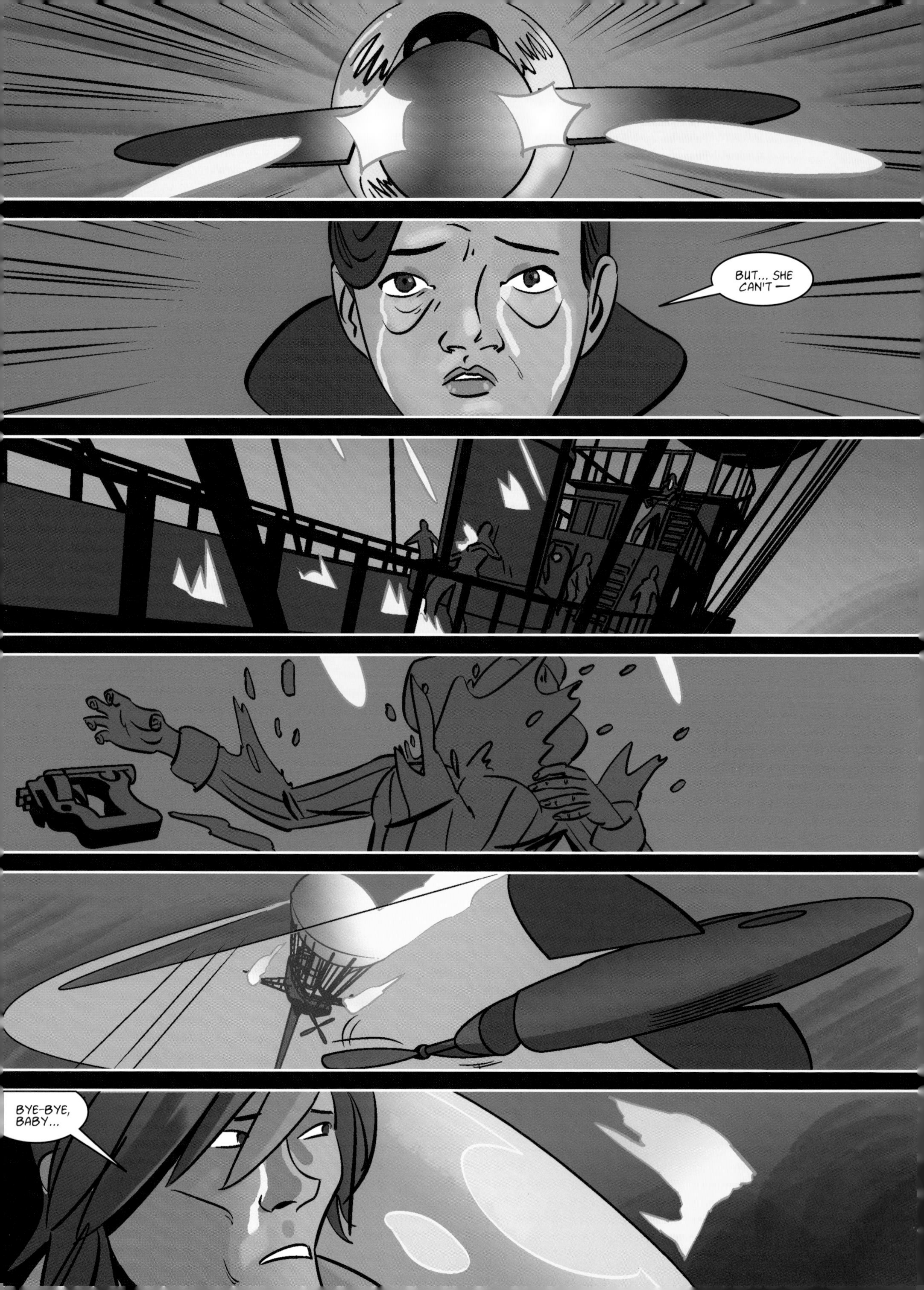
BUT... SHE CAN'T —
BYE-BYE, BABY...

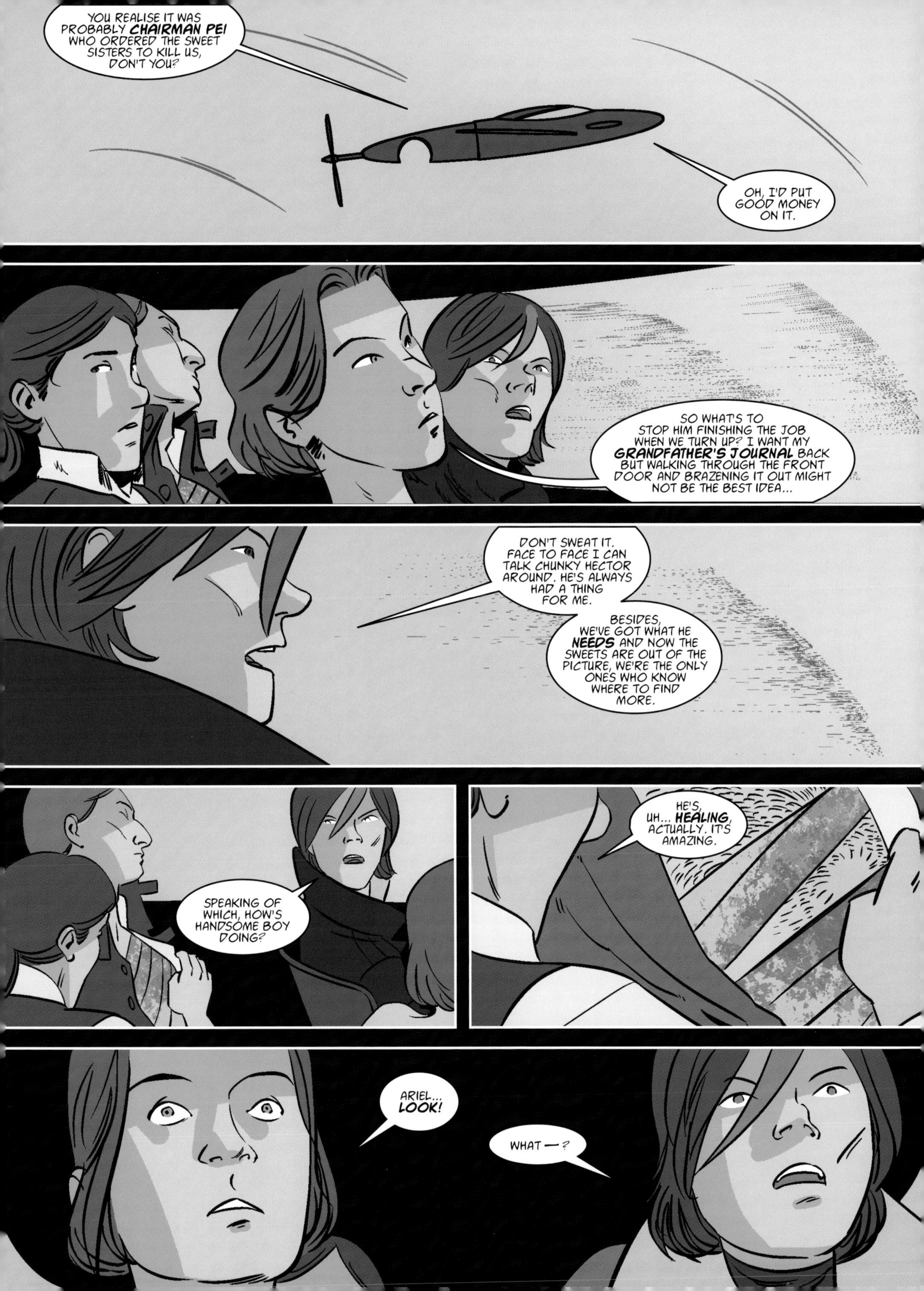
YOU REALISE IT WAS PROBABLY **CHAIRMAN PEI** WHO ORDERED THE SWEET SISTERS TO KILL US, DON'T YOU?
OH, I'D PUT GOOD MONEY ON IT.
SO WHAT'S TO STOP HIM FINISHING THE JOB WHEN WE TURN UP? I WANT MY **GRANDFATHER'S JOURNAL** BACK BUT WALKING THROUGH THE FRONT DOOR AND BRAZENING IT OUT MIGHT NOT BE THE BEST IDEA...
DON'T SWEAT IT. FACE TO FACE I CAN TALK CHUNKY HECTOR AROUND. HE'S ALWAYS HAD A THING FOR ME.
BESIDES, WE'VE GOT WHAT HE **NEEDS** AND NOW THE SWEETS ARE OUT OF THE PICTURE, WE'RE THE ONLY ONES WHO KNOW WHERE TO FIND MORE.
SPEAKING OF WHICH, HOW'S HANDSOME BOY DOING?
HE'S, UH... **HEALING**, ACTUALLY. IT'S AMAZING.
ARIEL... **LOOK!**
WHAT—?

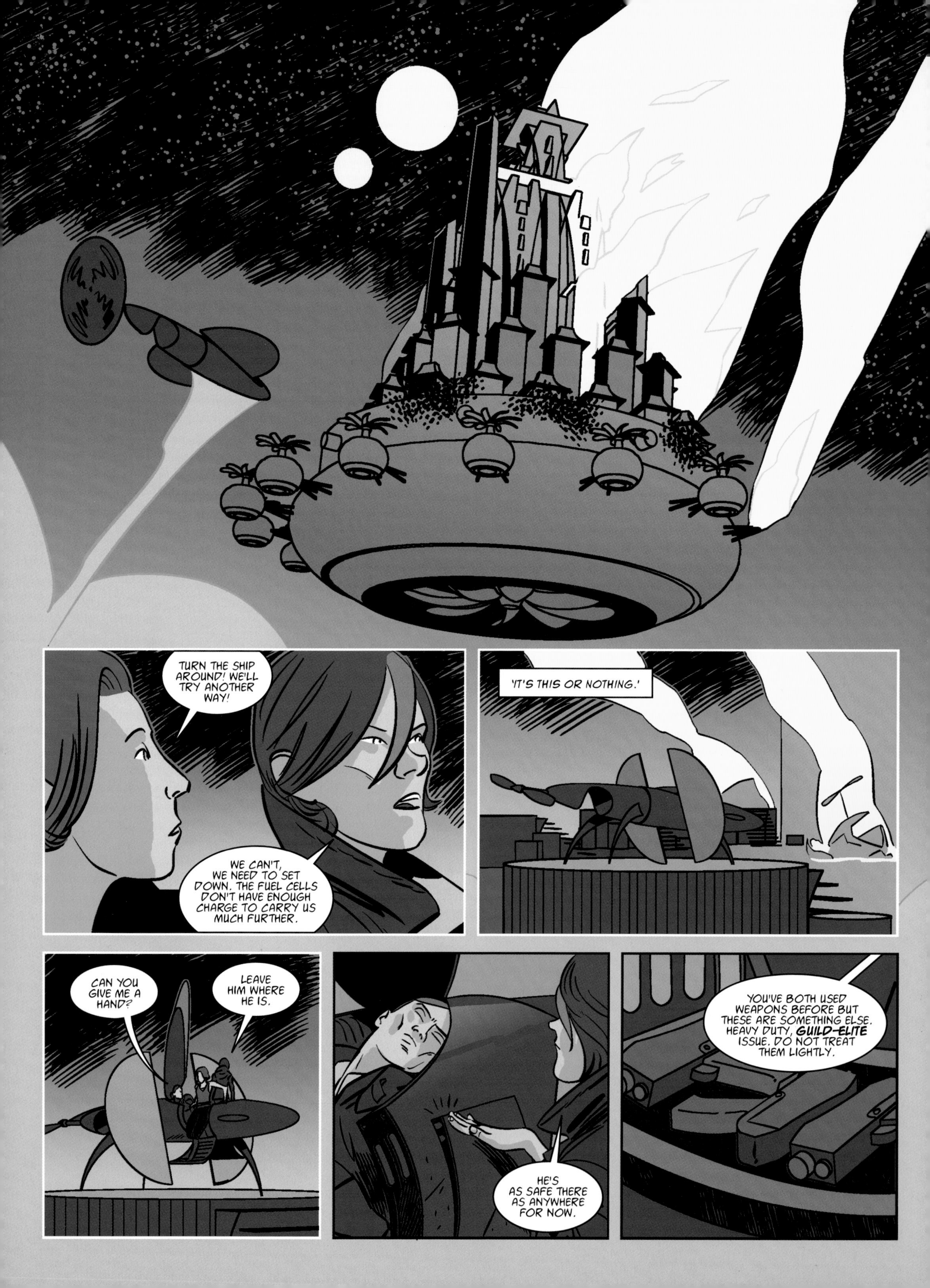
TURN THE SHIP AROUND! WE'LL TRY ANOTHER WAY!
WE CAN'T, WE NEED TO SET DOWN. THE FUEL CELLS DON'T HAVE ENOUGH CHARGE TO CARRY US MUCH FURTHER.
'IT'S THIS OR NOTHING.'
CAN YOU GIVE ME A HAND?
LEAVE HIM WHERE HE IS.
HE'S AS SAFE THERE AS ANYWHERE FOR NOW.
YOU'VE BOTH USED WEAPONS BEFORE BUT THESE ARE SOMETHING ELSE. HEAVY DUTY, GUILD-ELITE ISSUE. DO NOT TREAT THEM LIGHTLY.

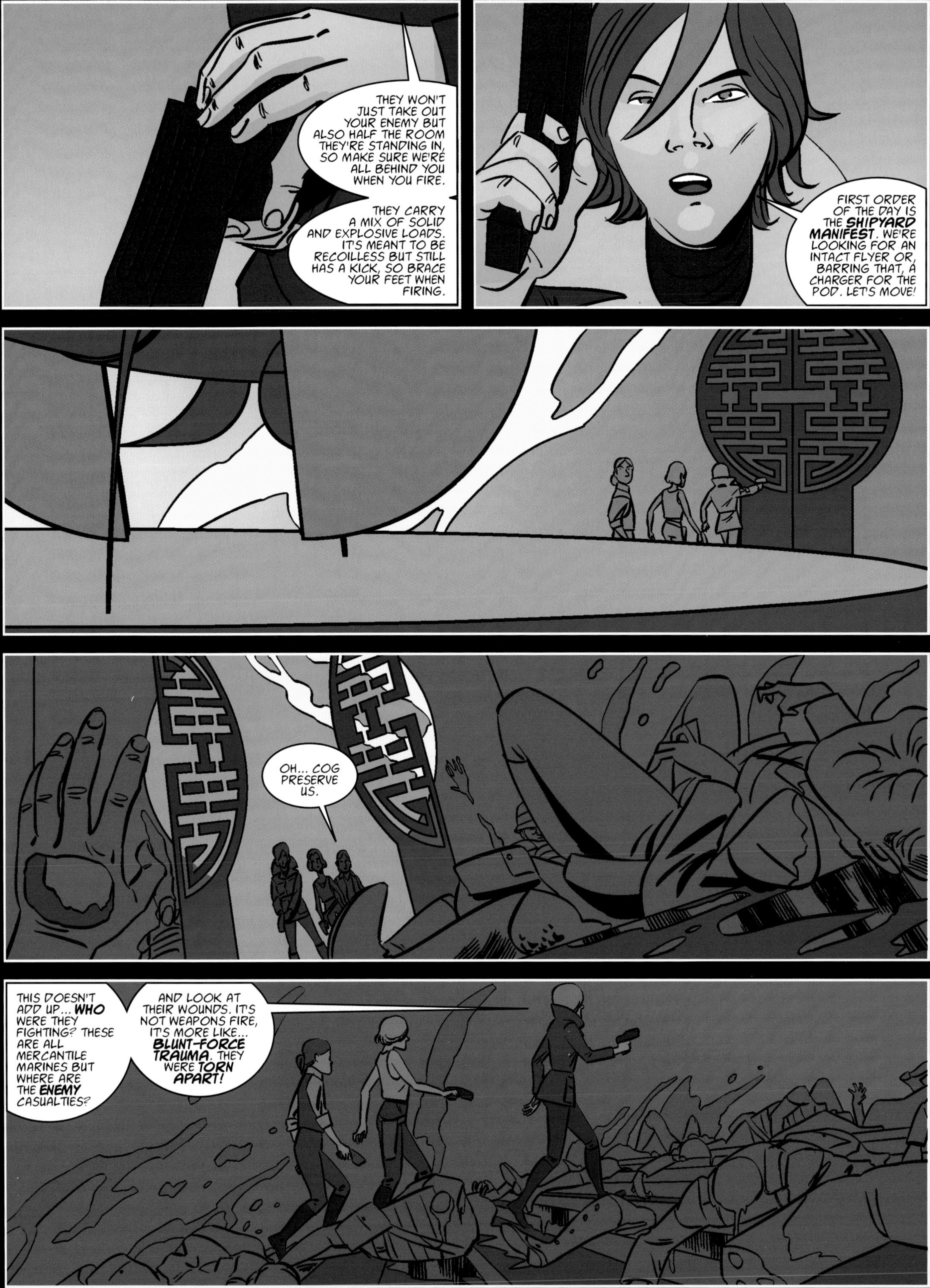
THEY WON'T JUST TAKE OUT YOUR ENEMY BUT ALSO HALF THE ROOM THEY'RE STANDING IN, SO MAKE SURE WE'RE ALL BEHIND YOU WHEN YOU FIRE.
THEY CARRY A MIX OF SOLID AND EXPLOSIVE LOADS. IT'S MEANT TO BE RECOILLESS BUT STILL HAS A KICK, SO BRACE YOUR FEET WHEN FIRING.
FIRST ORDER OF THE DAY IS THE **SHIPYARD MANIFEST**. WE'RE LOOKING FOR AN INTACT FLYER OR, BARRING THAT, A CHARGER FOR THE POD. LET'S MOVE!
OH... COG PRESERVE US.
THIS DOESN'T ADD UP... **WHO** WERE THEY FIGHTING? THESE ARE ALL MERCANTILE MARINES BUT WHERE ARE THE **ENEMY** CASUALTIES?
AND LOOK AT THEIR WOUNDS. IT'S NOT WEAPONS FIRE, IT'S MORE LIKE... **BLUNT-FORCE TRAUMA**. THEY WERE **TORN APART!**

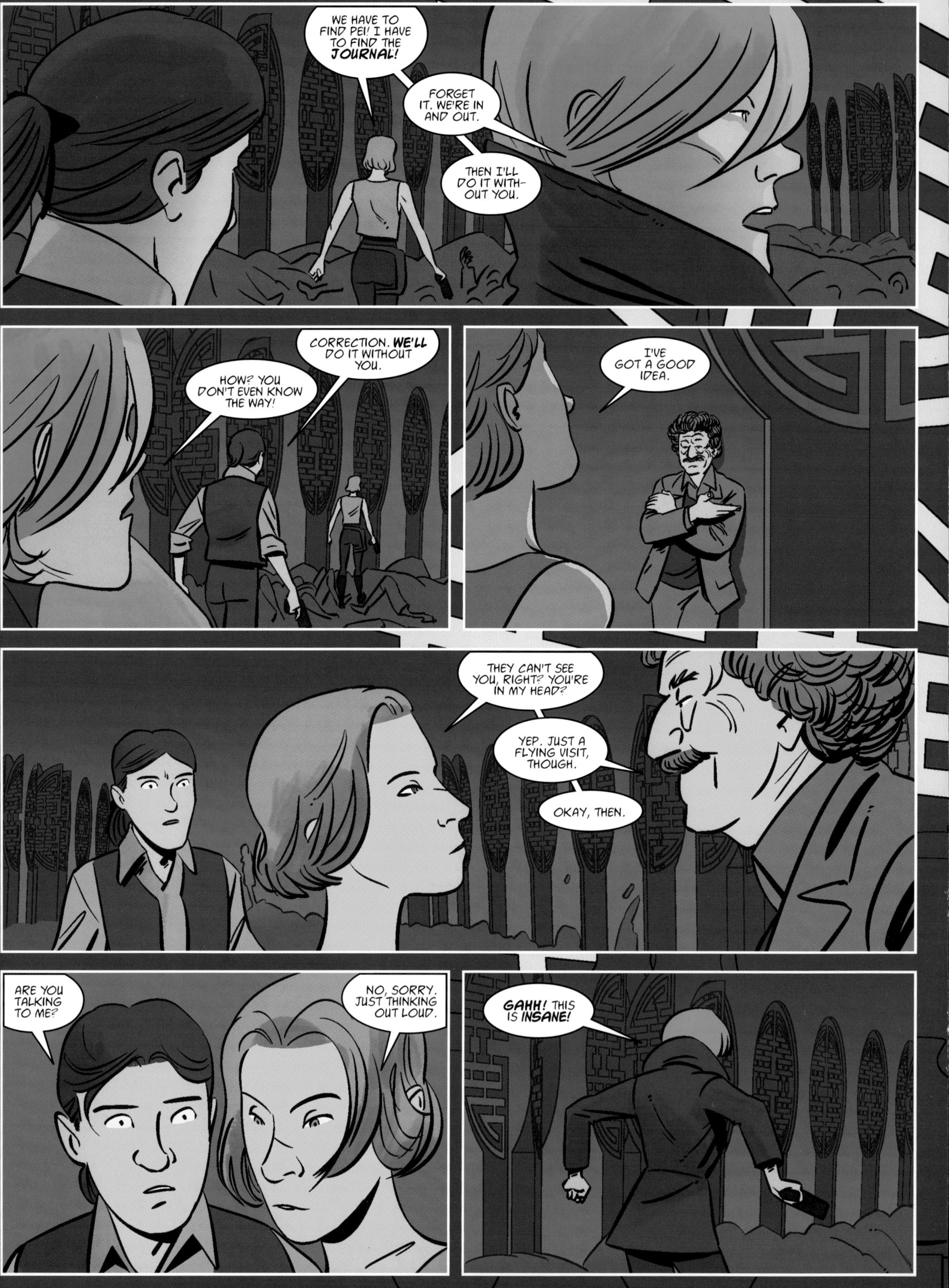
WE HAVE TO FIND PEI! I HAVE TO FIND THE **JOURNAL!**
FORGET IT. WE'RE IN AND OUT.
THEN I'LL DO IT WITH-OUT YOU.
HOW? YOU DON'T EVEN KNOW THE WAY!
CORRECTION. **WE'LL** DO IT WITHOUT YOU.
I'VE GOT A GOOD IDEA.
THEY CAN'T SEE YOU, RIGHT? YOU'RE IN MY HEAD?
YEP. JUST A FLYING VISIT, THOUGH.
OKAY, THEN.
ARE YOU TALKING TO ME?
NO, SORRY. JUST THINKING OUT LOUD.
GAHH! THIS IS **INSANE!**

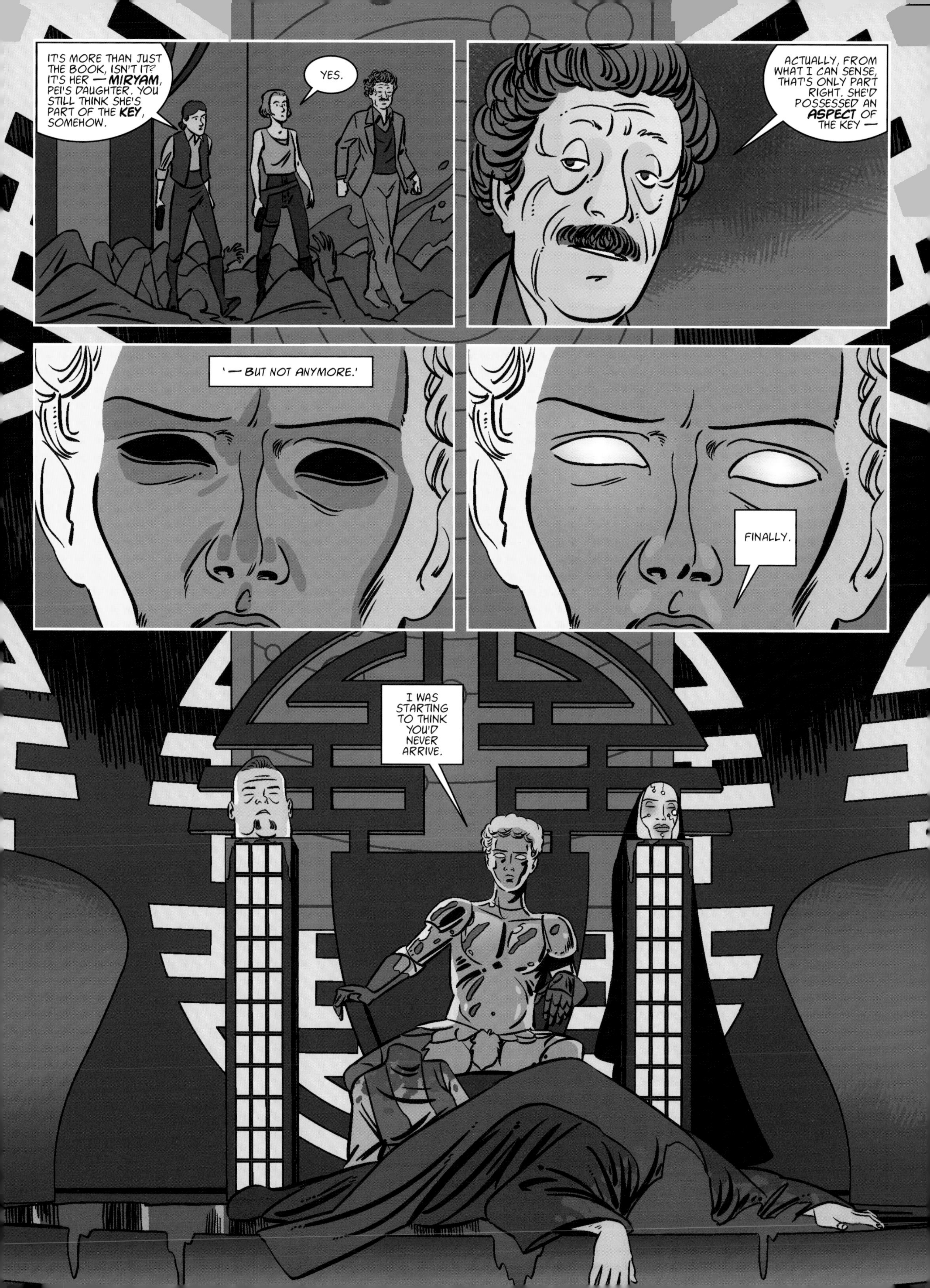
IT'S MORE THAN JUST THE BOOK, ISN'T IT? IT'S HER — MIRYAM, PEI'S DAUGHTER. YOU STILL THINK SHE'S PART OF THE KEY, SOMEHOW.
YES.
ACTUALLY, FROM WHAT I CAN SENSE, THAT'S ONLY PART RIGHT. SHE'D POSSESSED AN ASPECT OF THE KEY —
'— BUT NOT ANYMORE.'
FINALLY.
I WAS STARTING TO THINK YOU'D NEVER ARRIVE.

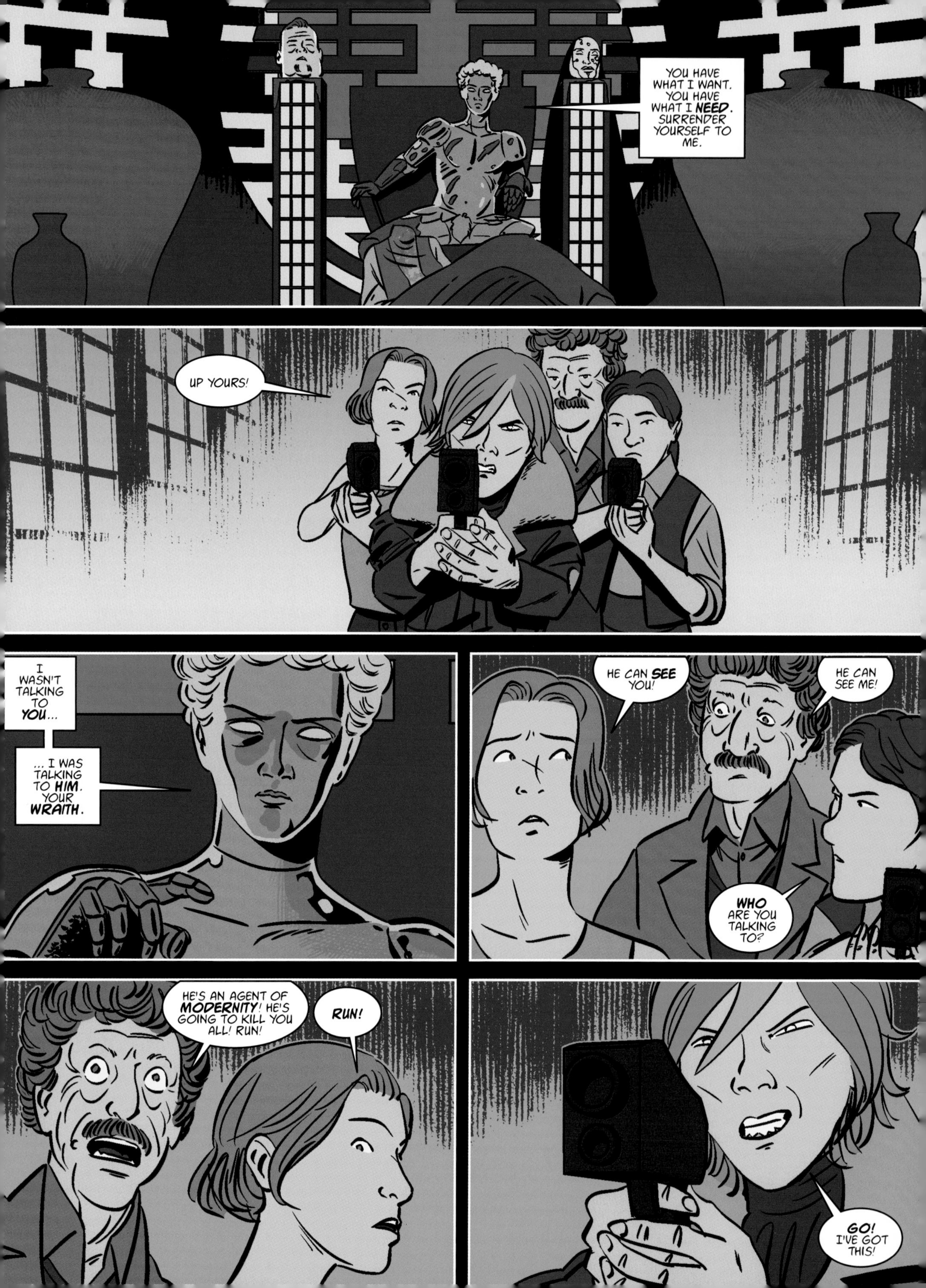
YOU HAVE WHAT I WANT. YOU HAVE WHAT I NEED. SURRENDER YOURSELF TO ME.
UP YOURS!
I WASN'T TALKING TO YOU...
... I WAS TALKING TO HIM. YOUR WRAITH.
HE CAN SEE YOU!
HE CAN SEE ME!
WHO ARE YOU TALKING TO?
HE'S AN AGENT OF MODERNITY! HE'S GOING TO KILL YOU ALL! RUN!
RUN!
GO! I'VE GOT THIS!

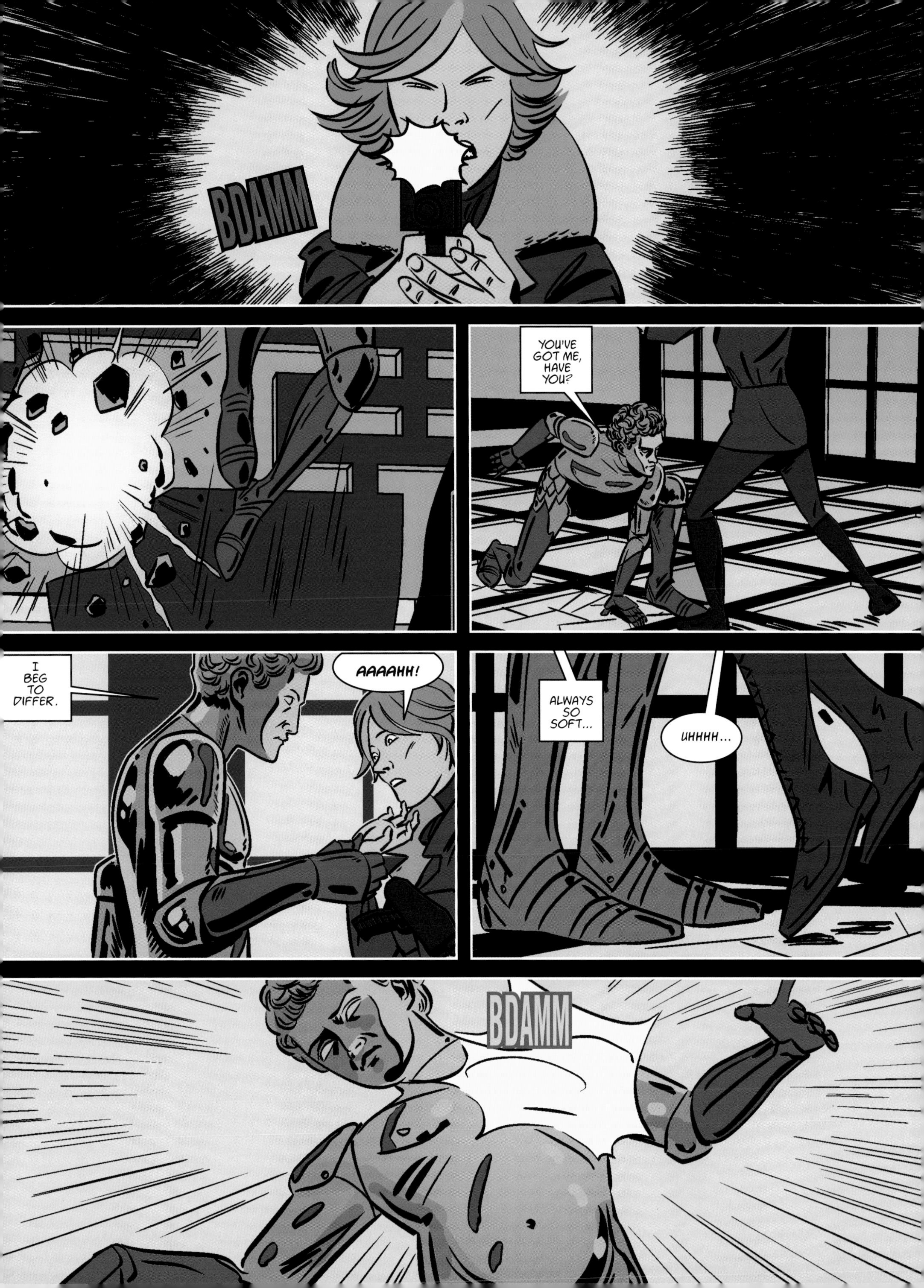
BDAMM
YOU'VE GOT ME, HAVE YOU?
I BEG TO DIFFER.
AAAAHH!
ALWAYS SO SOFT...
UHHHH...
BDAMM

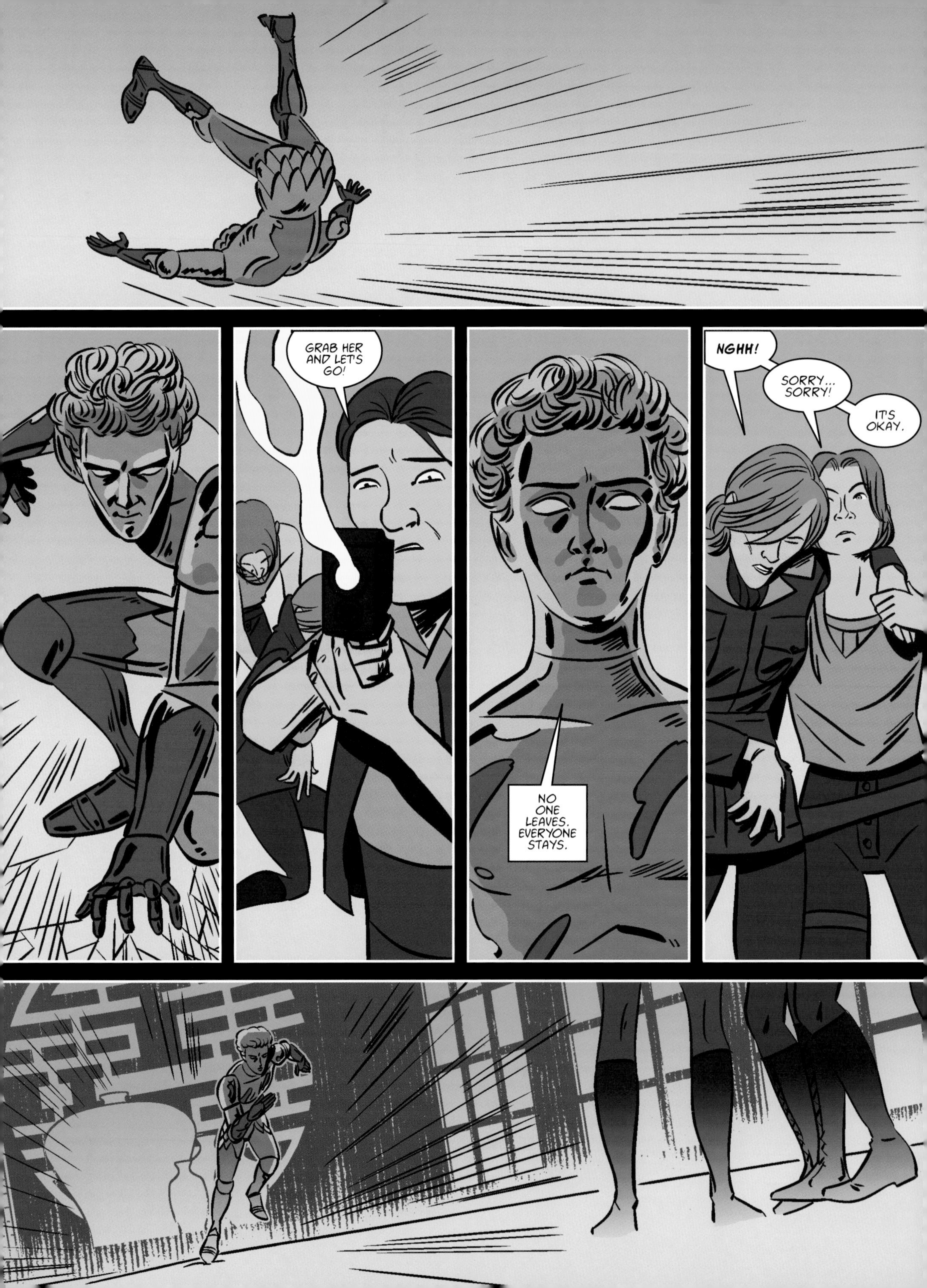
GRAB HER AND LET'S GO!
NO ONE LEAVES. EVERYONE STAYS.
NGHH!
SORRY... SORRY!
IT'S OKAY.

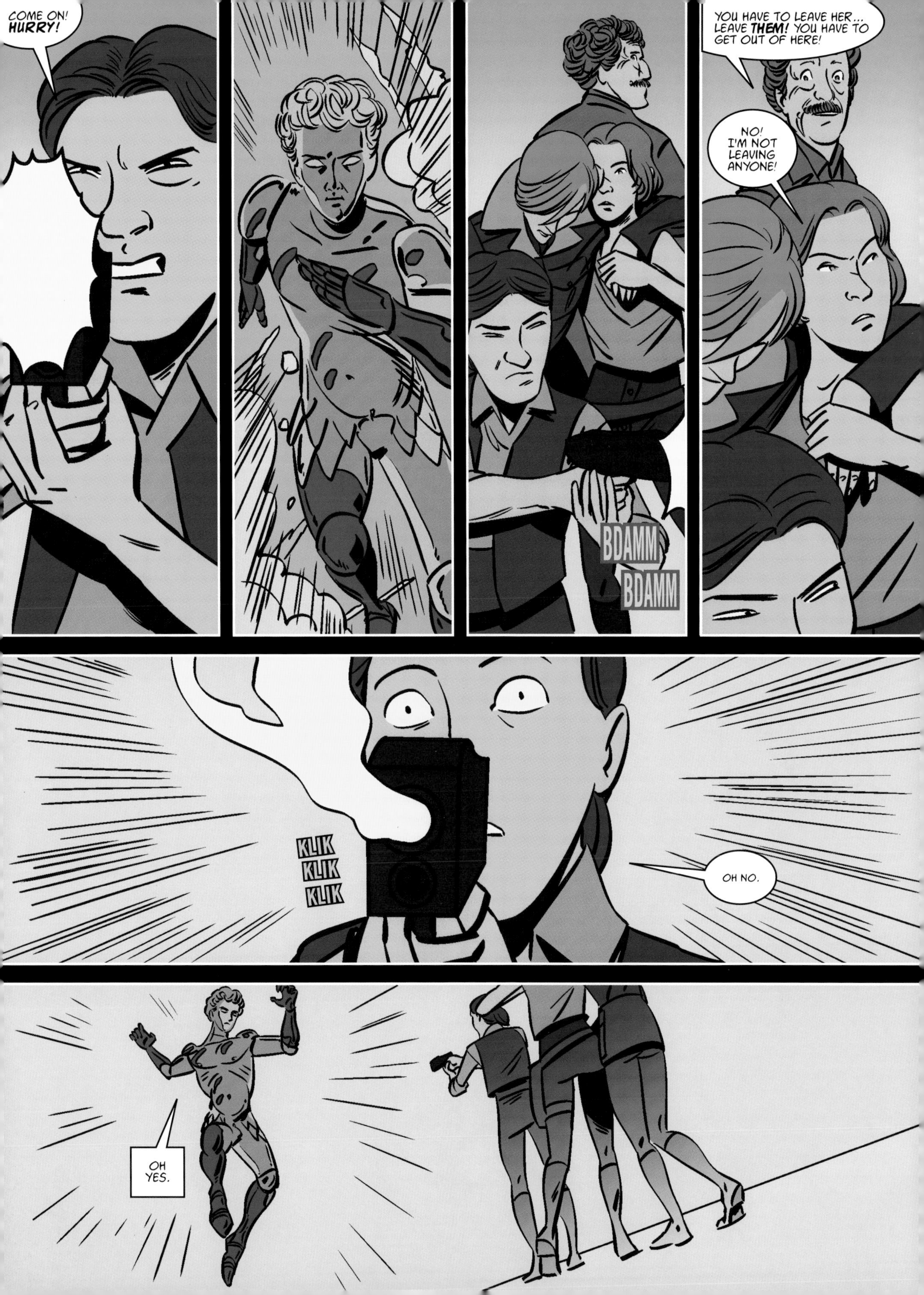
COME ON! HURRY!
BDAMM
BDAMM
YOU HAVE TO LEAVE HER... LEAVE THEM! YOU HAVE TO GET OUT OF HERE!
NO! I'M NOT LEAVING ANYONE!
KLIK
KLIK
KLIK
OH NO.
OH YES.

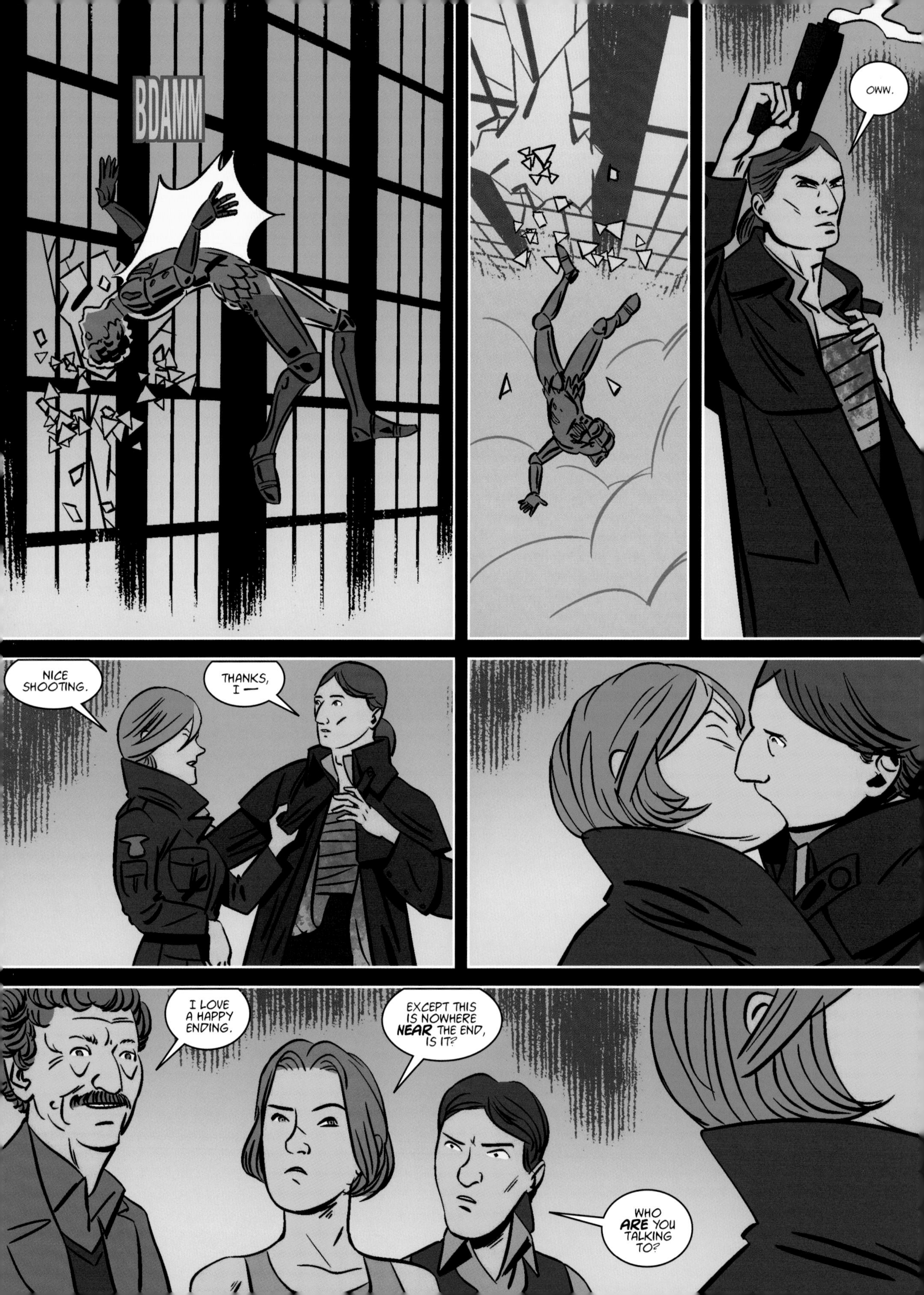
BDAMM
OWW.
NICE SHOOTING.
THANKS, I —
I LOVE A HAPPY ENDING.
EXCEPT THIS IS NOWHERE NEAR THE END, IS IT?
WHO ARE YOU TALKING TO?

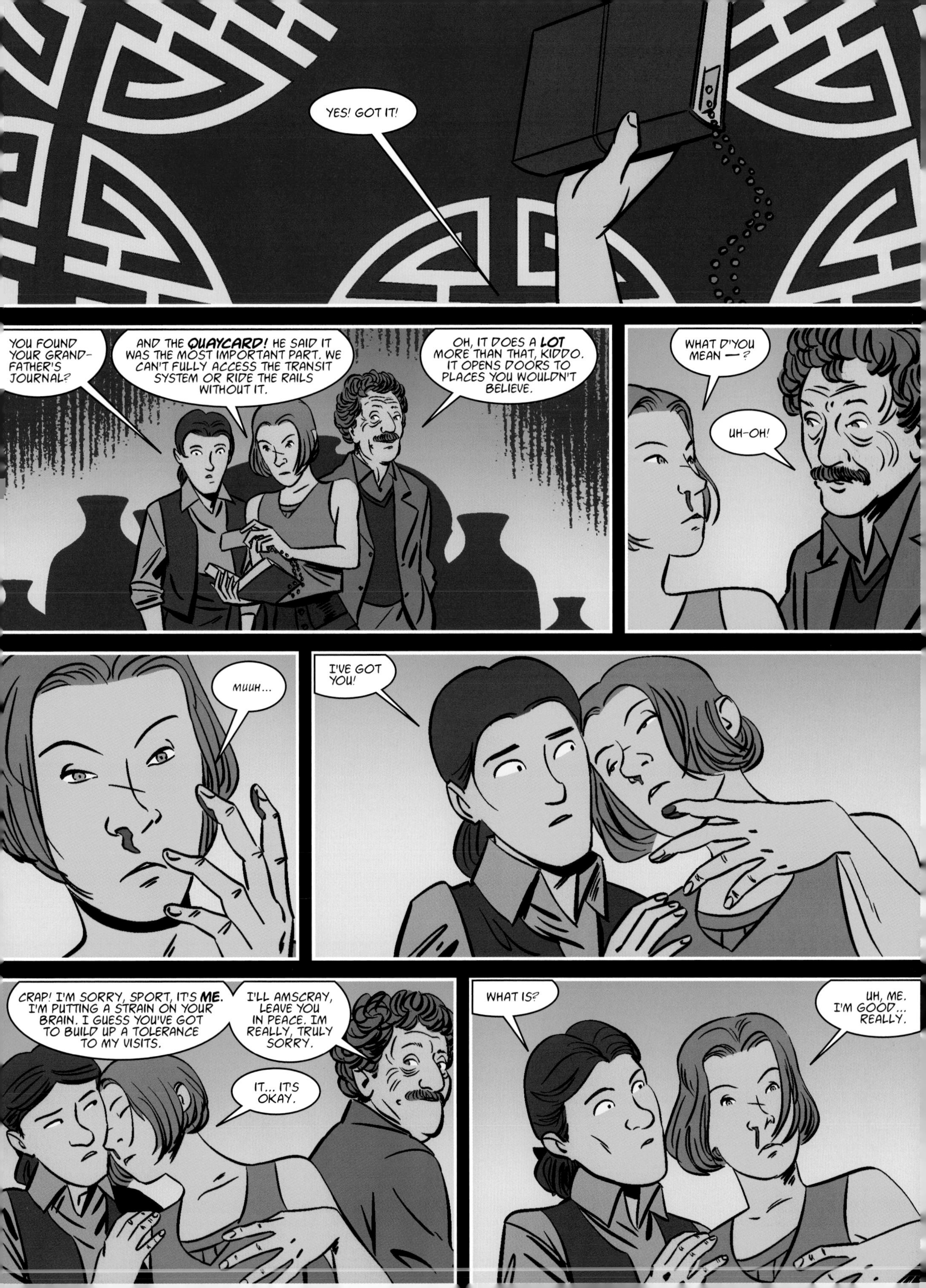
YES! GOT IT!
YOU FOUND YOUR GRAND-FATHER'S JOURNAL?
AND THE **QUAYCARD!** HE SAID IT WAS THE MOST IMPORTANT PART. WE CAN'T FULLY ACCESS THE TRANSIT SYSTEM OR RIDE THE RAILS WITHOUT IT.
OH, IT DOES A **LOT** MORE THAN THAT, KIDDO. IT OPENS DOORS TO PLACES YOU WOULDN'T BELIEVE.
WHAT D'YOU MEAN —?
UH-OH!
MUUH...
I'VE GOT YOU!
CRAP! I'M SORRY, SPORT, IT'S **ME.** I'M PUTTING A STRAIN ON YOUR BRAIN. I GUESS YOU'VE GOT TO BUILD UP A TOLERANCE TO MY VISITS.
I'LL AMSCRAY, LEAVE YOU IN PEACE. IM REALLY, TRULY SORRY.
IT... IT'S OKAY.
WHAT IS?
UH, ME. I'M GOOD... REALLY.

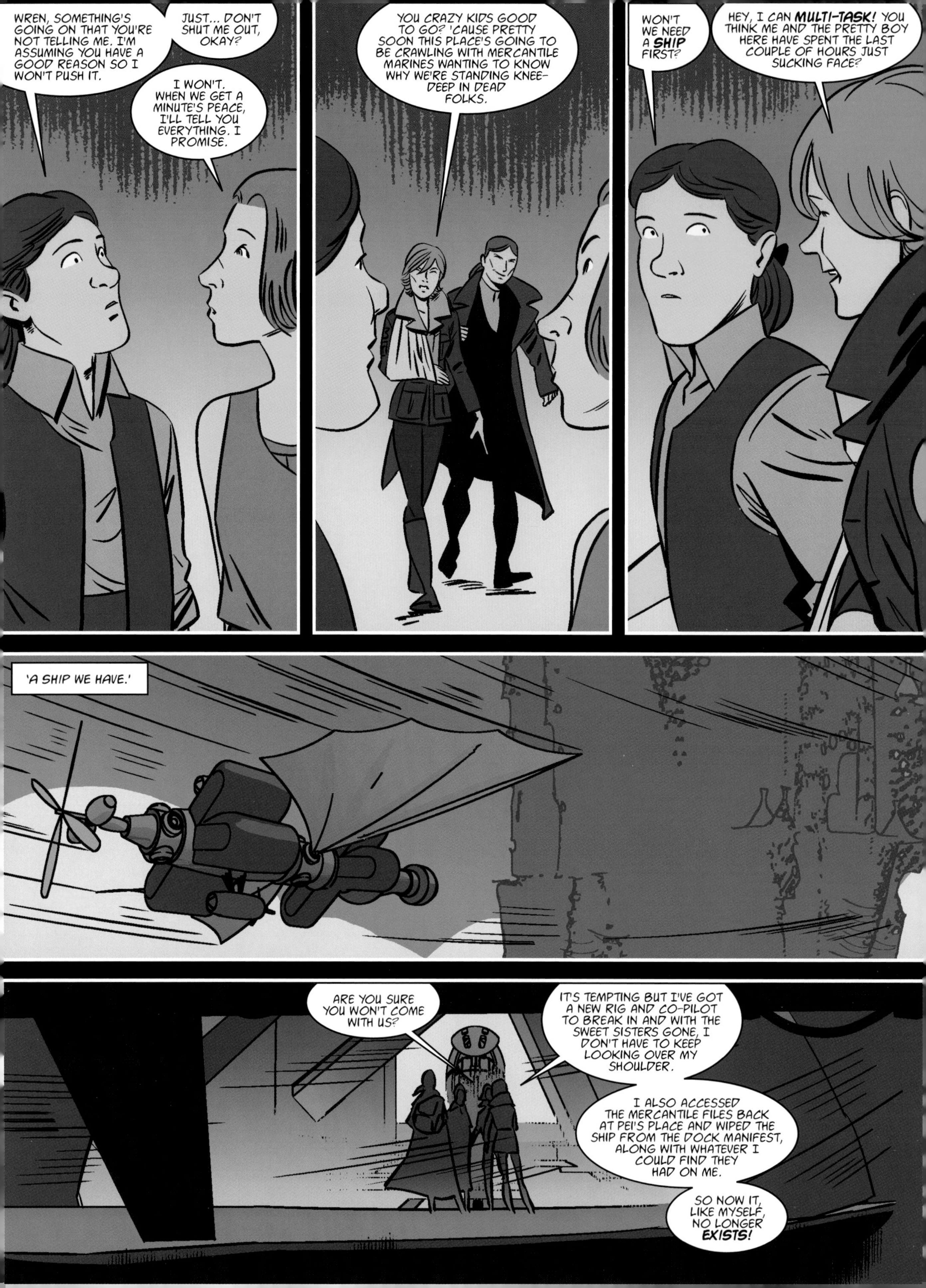
WREN, SOMETHING'S GOING ON THAT YOU'RE NOT TELLING ME. I'M ASSUMING YOU HAVE A GOOD REASON SO I WON'T PUSH IT.
JUST... DON'T SHUT ME OUT, OKAY?
I WON'T. WHEN WE GET A MINUTE'S PEACE, I'LL TELL YOU EVERYTHING. I PROMISE.
YOU CRAZY KIDS GOOD TO GO? 'CAUSE PRETTY SOON THIS PLACE'S GOING TO BE CRAWLING WITH MERCANTILE MARINES WANTING TO KNOW WHY WE'RE STANDING KNEE-DEEP IN DEAD FOLKS.
WON'T WE NEED A **SHIP** FIRST?
HEY, I CAN **MULTI-TASK!** YOU THINK ME AND THE PRETTY BOY HERE HAVE SPENT THE LAST COUPLE OF HOURS JUST SUCKING FACE?
'A SHIP WE HAVE.'
ARE YOU SURE YOU WON'T COME WITH US?
IT'S TEMPTING BUT I'VE GOT A NEW RIG AND CO-PILOT TO BREAK IN AND WITH THE SWEET SISTERS GONE, I DON'T HAVE TO KEEP LOOKING OVER MY SHOULDER.
I ALSO ACCESSED THE MERCANTILE FILES BACK AT PEI'S PLACE AND WIPED THE SHIP FROM THE DOCK MANIFEST, ALONG WITH WHATEVER I COULD FIND THEY HAD ON ME.
SO NOW IT, LIKE MYSELF, NO LONGER **EXISTS!**

TAKE CARE OF EACH OTHER, OKAY?

YOU TOO.

HERE, SOME THINGS I THOUGHT YOU MIGHT NEED.

PISTOLS...

PLUS AMMUNITION AND GASEOUS CLAY — JUST IN CASE. I KNOW YOU DON'T GO LOOKING FOR TROUBLE BUT SOMEHOW IT ALWAYS SEEMS TO FIND YOU OUT.

AND THIS IS FROM ME. THANK YOU FOR GIVING ME A CHANCE OF A BETTER LIFE. I HAVEN'T ALWAYS BEEN GRATEFUL —

OR TRUST-WORTHY.

OR TRUSTWORTHY. BUT YOU STUCK BY ME, AND FOR THAT I OWE YOU.

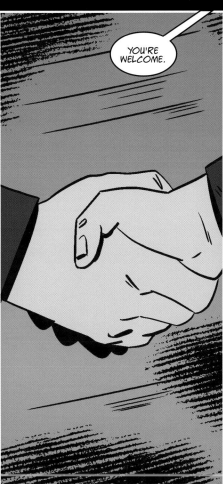

YOU'RE WELCOME.

Y'KNOW, I RECKON THEY'RE EITHER GOING TO KISS OR CRY!

'YOU'D BETTER GO BEFORE IT GETS UGLY!'

ARE WE STILL BOUND FOR **TALL GREEN**?

CADWALLADER'S JOURNAL SAYS IT'S THE NEXT LOCATION WE HAVE TO LOOK FOR THE KEY.

WELL, IT'S A LONG HAUL. WE'VE GOT TO MAKE JUNCTION CHANGES AT **THE ARTILLERY**, **SCINTILLION** AND **TIDAL DEEP** ALONG THE WAY.

SO THERE'S PLENTY OF TIME FOR YOU TO TELL ME WHAT'S GOING ON AND WHO THIS **WRAITH'** IS YOU'VE BEEN TALKING TO...

AH, YOU NOTICED THAT, THEN.

WHAT DO **YOU** THINK? I WAS WORRIED YOU WERE LOSING YOUR MIND.

ME TOO. I STILL MIGHT BE.

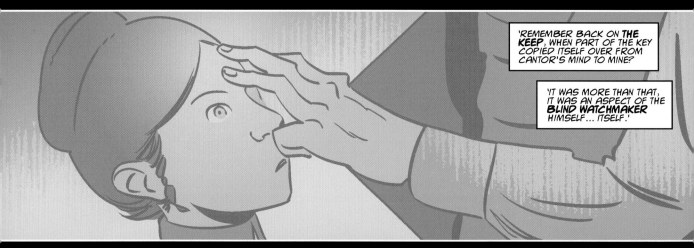

'REMEMBER BACK ON **THE KEEP**, WHEN PART OF THE KEY COPIED ITSELF OVER FROM CANTOR'S MIND TO MINE?

'IT WAS MORE THAN THAT, IT WAS AN ASPECT OF THE **BLIND WATCHMAKER** HIMSELF... ITSELF.'

AND HE VISITS YOU? **TALKS** TO YOU? THAT'S FANTASTIC!

REALLY? TRY IT SOMETIME. PLUS — AND PLEASE DON'T TAKE THIS AS BEING BLASPHEMOUS OR ANYTHING — BUT HE'S NOT QUITE AS OMNIPOTENT AS YOU IMAGINE.

FRANKLY, I THINK HE'S BEEN **WINGING** IT FOR A VERY LONG TIME.

THING IS, CANTOR SAID HE'D BEEN WAITING ALL THOSE YEARS TO PASS THE KEY ON TO A GIRL WITH A BIRD'S NAME — MEANING ME — BUT HOW'S THAT **POSSIBLE**...?

I DON'T RIGHTLY KNOW —

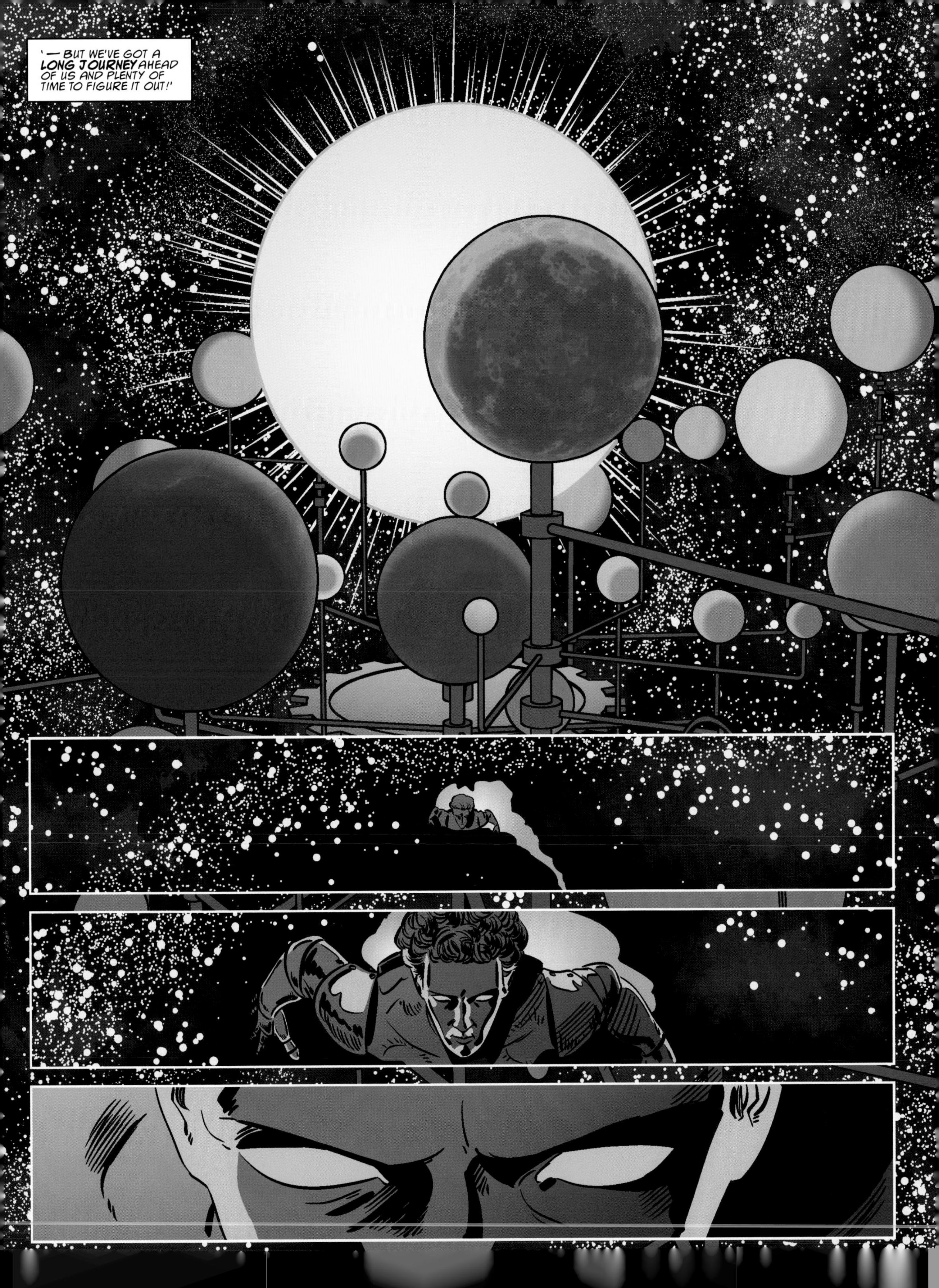
'— BUT WE'VE GOT A **LONG JOURNEY** AHEAD OF US AND PLENTY OF TIME TO FIGURE IT OUT!'

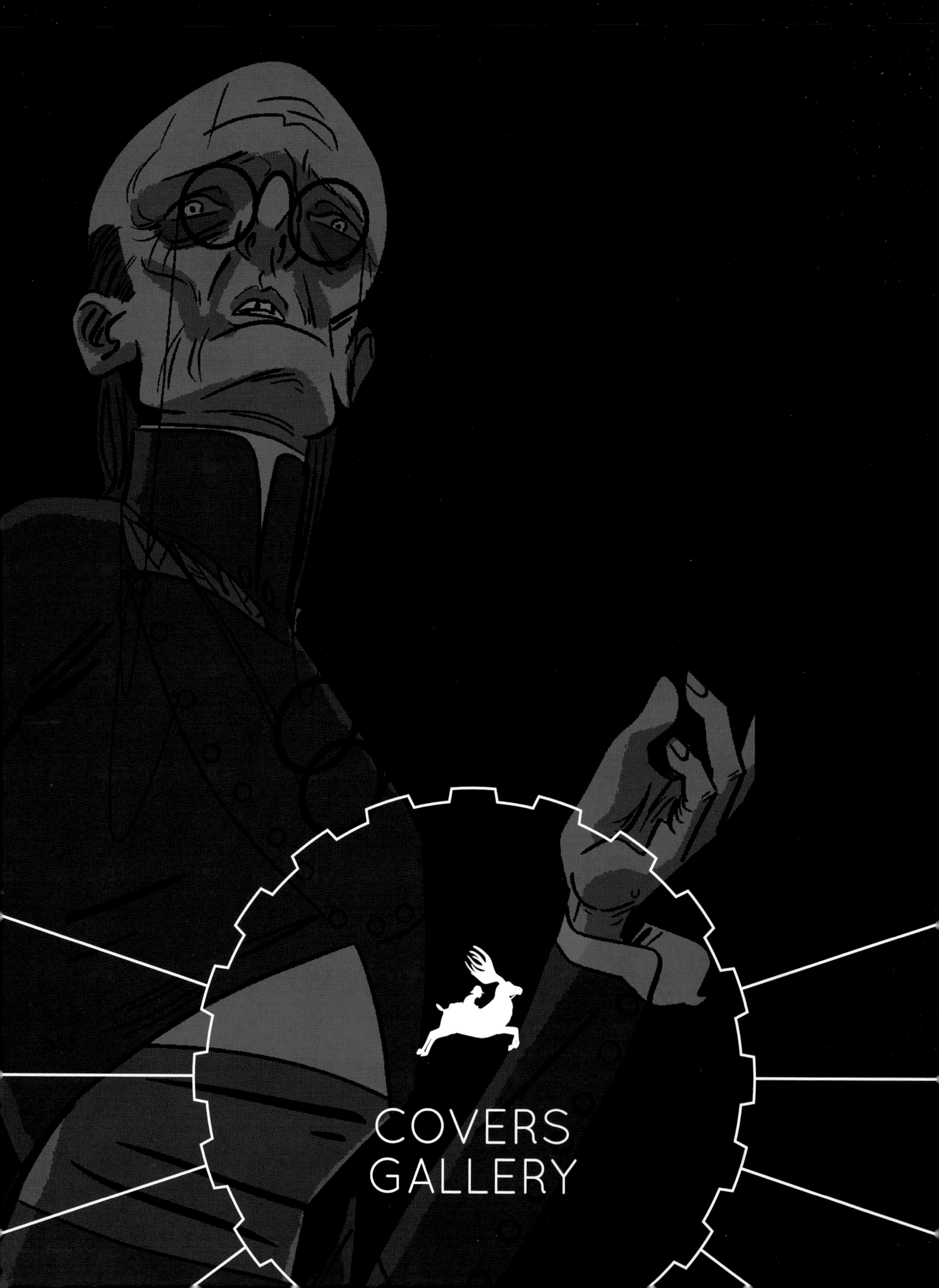

COVERS GALLERY

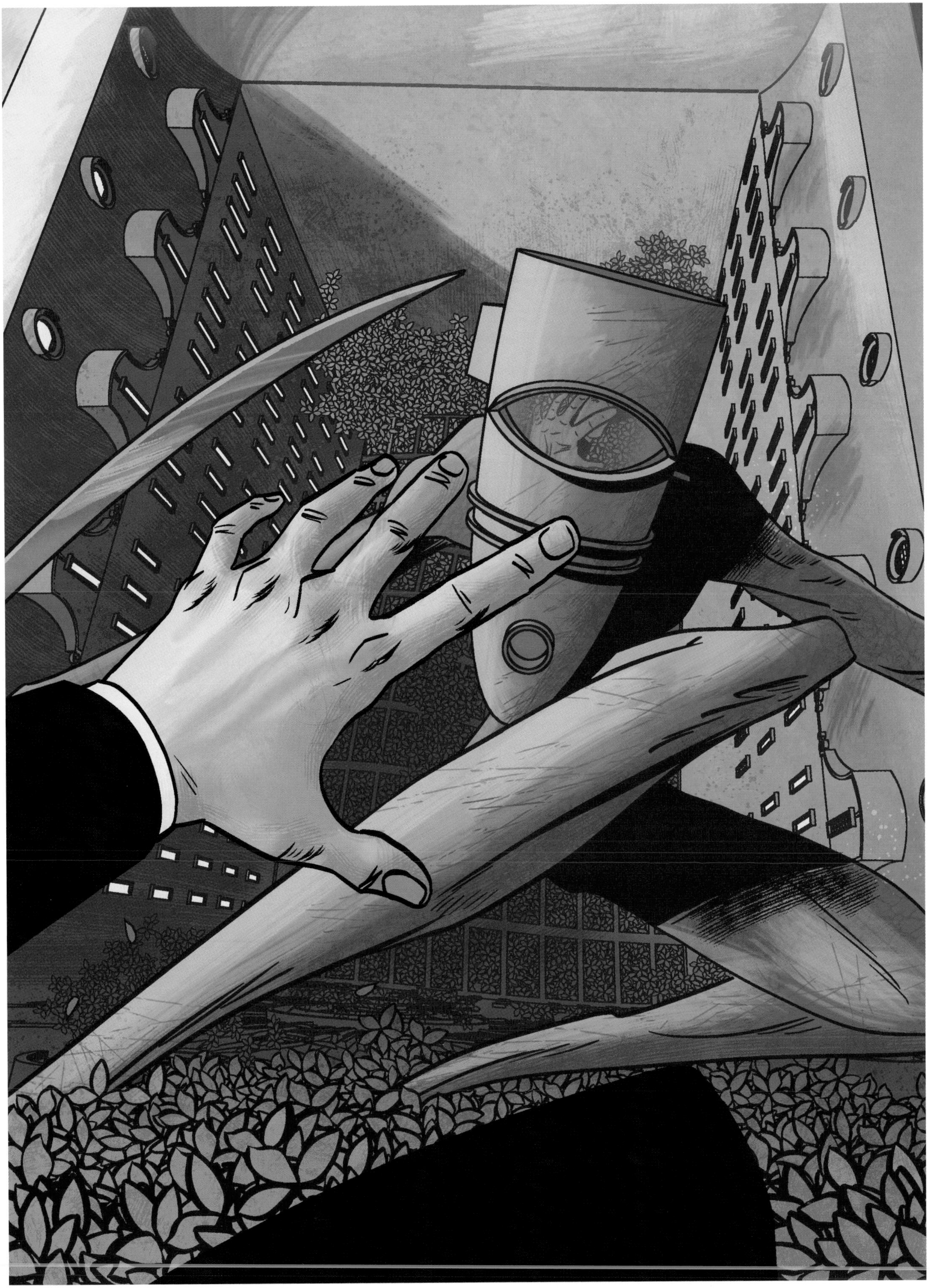

2000 AD Prog 1852: Cover by **I.N.J. Culbard**

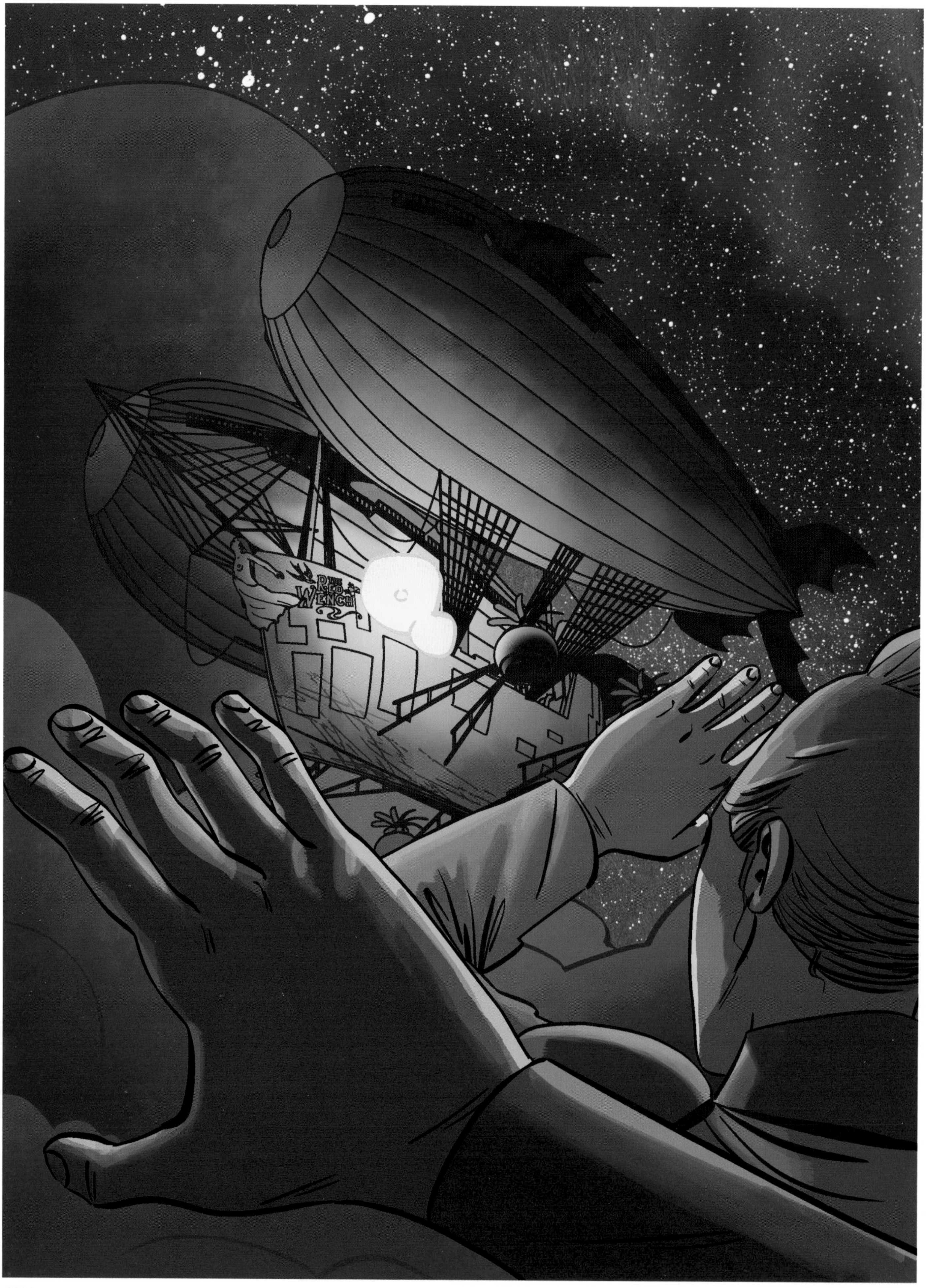
THE RED WENCH
2000 AD Prog 1859: Cover by **I.N.J. Culbard**

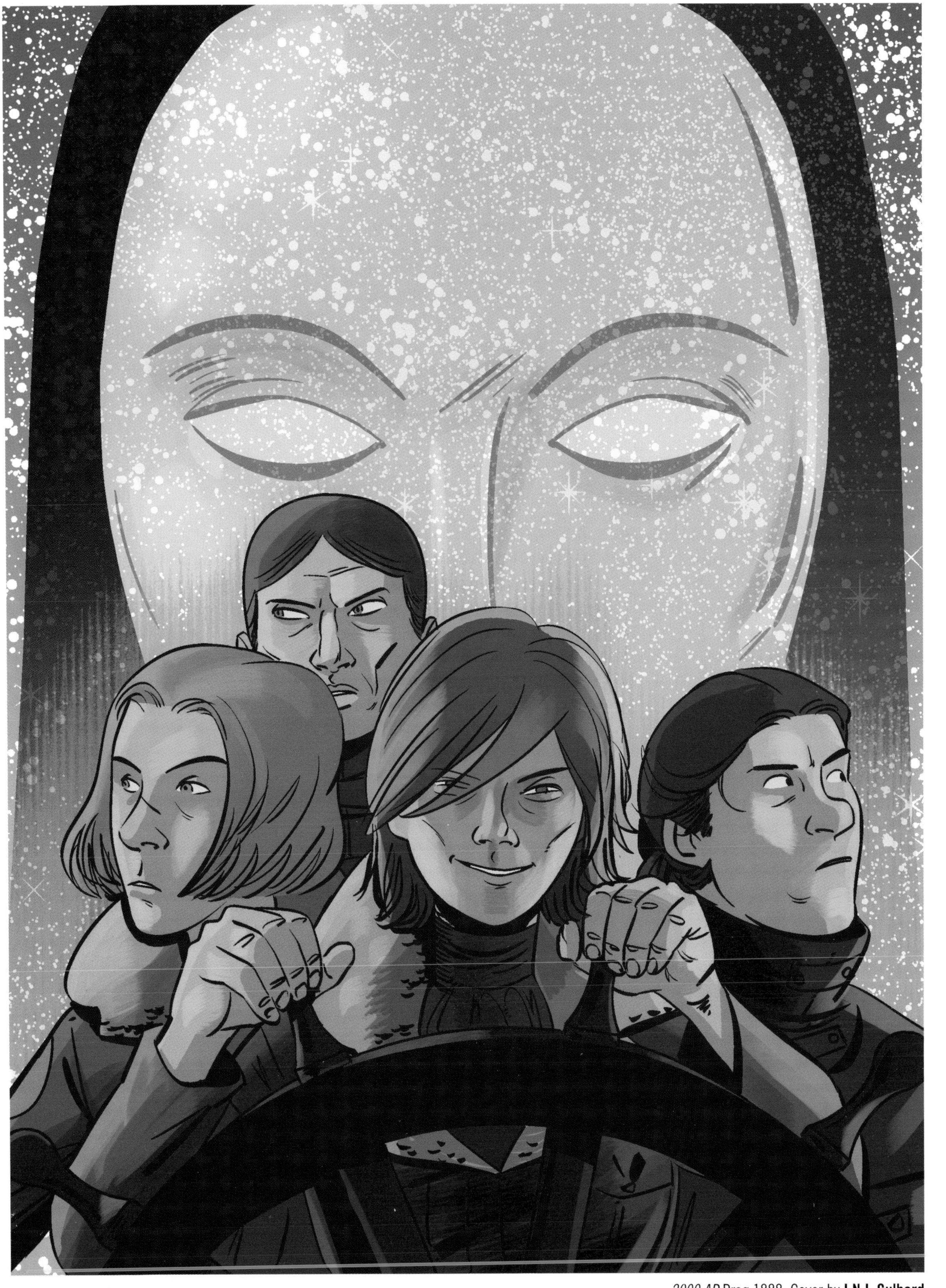

2000 AD Prog 1888: Cover by **I.N.J. Culbard**

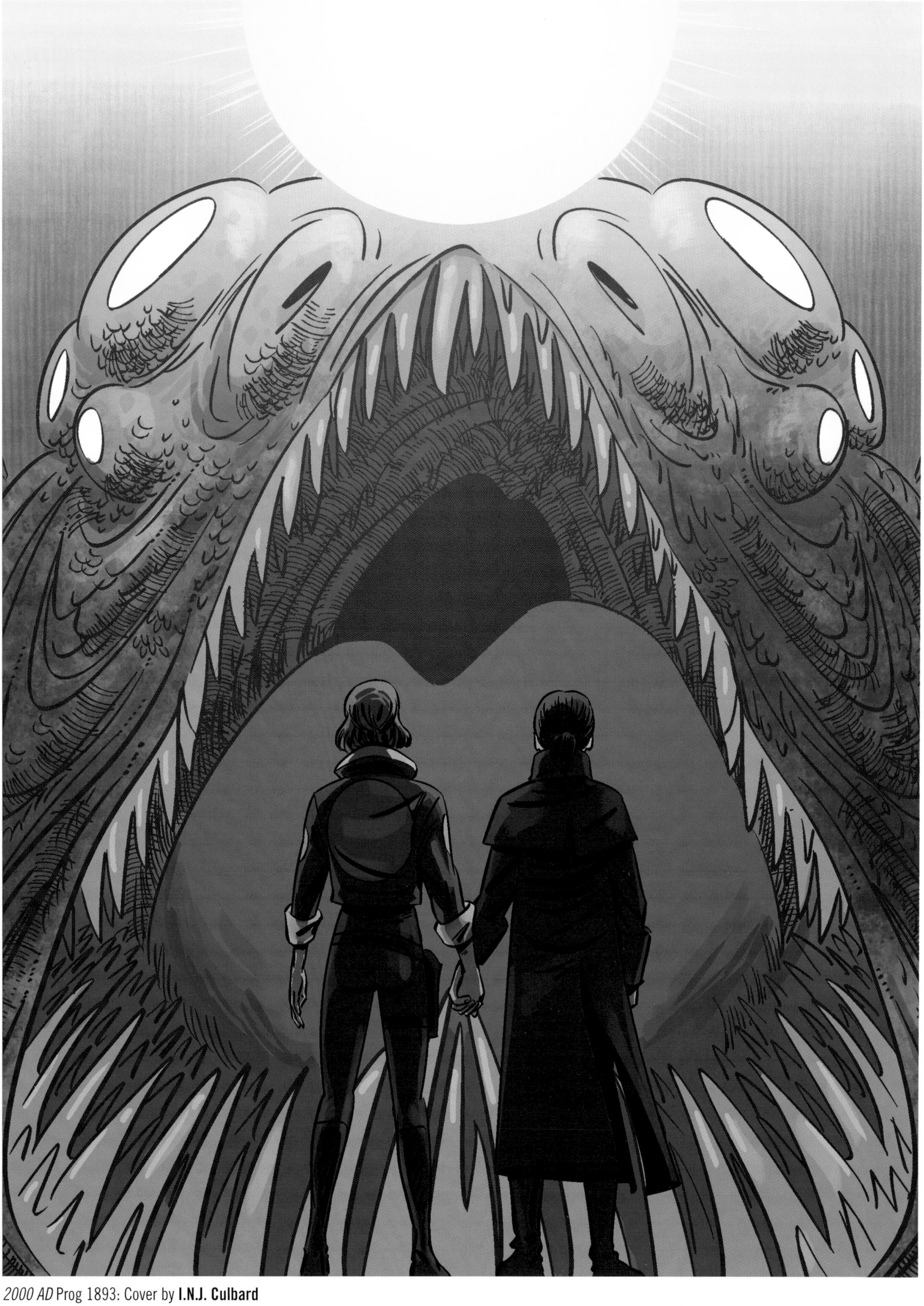

2000 AD Prog 1893: Cover by **I.N.J. Culbard**

IAN EDGINTON

Ian Edginton is a *New York Times* bestselling author and multiple Eisner Award nominee.

His recent titles include the green apocalypse saga *Hinterkind* for DC Vertigo, *Steed and Mrs Peel* for BOOM, the steam- and clock-punk series *Stickleback*, *Ampney Crucis Investigates* and *Brass Sun* for *2000 AD*, game properties *Dead Space: Liberation* and *The Evil Within* for Titan Books, and the audio adventure *Torchwood: Army of One* for the BBC.

He has adapted books by bestselling novelists Robert Muchamore *(CHERUBS)* and Children's Laureate, Malorie Blackman *(NOUGHTS & CROSSES)*. In addition he has adapted the complete canon of Sherlock Holmes novels into a series of graphic novels for SelfMadeHero, as well writing several volumes of Holmes apocrypha entitled *The Victorian Undead*. He has also adapted H.G. Wells, *The War of the Worlds* as well the critically acclaimed sequels *Scarlet Traces* and *Scarlet Traces: The Great Game*.

He lives and works in England.

I.N.J. CULBARD

I.N.J. Culbard is an award-winning artist and writer. He has had work published by SelfMadeHero, Dark Horse comics, Vertigo and BOOM! Studios. He first started working with Ian Edginton on adaptations for SelfMadeHero of *The Picture of Dorian Gray*, *The Hound of the Baskervilles*, *A Study in Scarlet*, *The Sign of the Four*, and *The Valley of Fear*. He has also worked with Dan Abnett on original series such as *The New Deadwardians* (Vertigo), *Dark Ages* (Dark Horse Comics), and *Wild's End* (BOOM! Studios). And lastly he has worked with Chris Lackey and Chad Fifer on the original graphic novel, *Deadbeats* (SelfMadeHero)

He has produced a number of his own adaptations for SelfMadeHero. *The Case of Charles Dexter Ward*, *The Shadow Out of Time*, *The Dream-Quest of Unknown Kadath*, and *At the Mountains of Madness*, for which he won the British Fantasy Award in 2011. Earlier this year he had his first solo original graphic novel published by SelfMadeHero, *Celeste*.

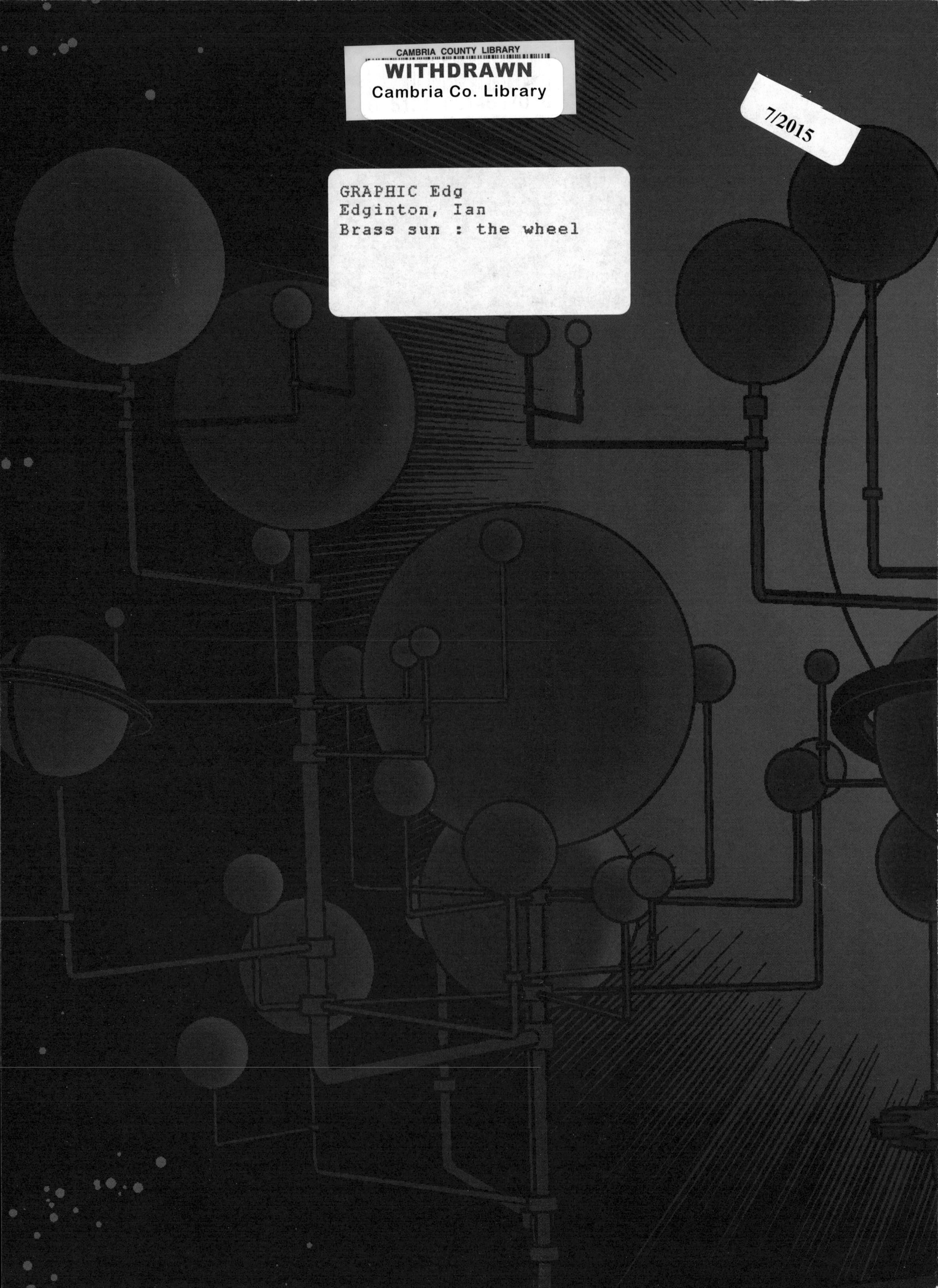